International Praise for the Authors

Erica Fuentes

"…weaves an interesting yarn that keeps you reading."
—*Elisa Robledo, El Financiero*

"…brings the reader into the inner-circle of power."
—*Maxim*

"Intrigue, conspiracy, corruption, danger, secrets
and the hidden face of power…"
—*El Porvenir*

Annemarie Stonewater

"A cornucopia of historical knowledge brought to life
in a way that captivates and enlightens…"
—*San Francisco Chronicle*

"…suspense, humor, adventure that engages,
entertains and is a must read…"
—*San Diego Evening Tribune*

Salve Regina, the Series

Salve Regina
(The adventure begins..)

During its one hundred year reign as one of the best Roman Catholic boarding schools in the country, Villa Vistamar was home to many young women —particularly politically vulnerable, but wealthy young women— from all parts of the world. Brought back by a class reunion, two former resident students haunted by the unexplained mysteries encountered in their youth, have set out to expose the secrets of the old Southwestern estate and the strange relationship between the Sisters of St. Thomas and their benefactor. Convinced that the key to the mysteries must be hidden away in the macabre old trunks that fill the basement of the old convent, a late-night escapade into the catacombs of the old abbey literally swallows them into —and past— the point of no return from their journey into Church history and intrigue. Several frightening encounters with Church Sentinels guarding the very secrets that the women have determined to unshroud, along with the death of an elderly nun and former Mother Superior of the order, leads the women to the discovery of a cache of priceless jewels that protect a far greater treasure; that which the Church has shielded from the world for nine decades of Eastern European history, under the ecclesiastical code name of Salve Regina.

Unholy Trinity
(The story continues..)

Unholy Trinity, loosely based on an intriguing true case, evolves from Marisa's pro bono defense of a purportedly innocent man accused of murder, into a frightening journey through a labyrinth of evil and deceit, the nucleus of which seems to point to an obscure parish church ministered by an enigmatic old priest with a special fondness for his young acolytes. Marisa involves her co-heroine, Erin, who brings in their unique clan of recurring support characters, including a semi-retired Jesuit monk licensed by the Vatican as an exorcist. This terrifying and spellbinding tale affirms the predominance of true power ever prevailing over the overt corruption and vying struggle between the powers of Church and State, but only after many unexpected twists and turns into realms that shake the characters' veritable core of truth and faith.

Sacred Secrets
(The story continues..)

The story begins when Marisa finds herself in a quandary after bringing a few pre-Columbian artifacts back from Mexico; their provenance questionable, at best. What begins as a prank evolves into a highly suspenseful escapade into the world of clandestine art trafficking that eventually leads the group to the unexpected discovery of the treasures amassed during the Jesuit missionary era in the Californias before their expulsion from New Spain in 1867. The historical provenance and international treaties inherent to the questionable ownership of such treasures throw both countries into a legal battle with each other and against the Jesuits, while the group of characters follow their own agenda. This novel is laced with the customary bantering among the cast of characters and humorous moments found throughout the series.

Other books by the Authors

Also by Erica Fuentes

Shakedown

Island Dreams

A Window to Paradise

Miguel's Cantina (First Love)

Hearts Ahoy!

Loving Deceit

Also by Annemarie Stonewater

Land of Gold

Kindred Spirits

Montana Brides

SALVE REGINA

Erica Fuentes
&
Annemarie Stonewater

SALVE REGINA

Casablanca 2010

SALVE REGINA
A Casablanca Book

Copyright © 2010, Erica Fuentes and Annemarie Stonewater
This edition Copyright © 2010 Editorial Casablanca
Barcelona · Los Angeles · Mexico · New York
www.editorialcasablanca.com   www.casablancapublishing.com

Cover design: Erica Fuentes

First Edition: December of 2010

ISBN: 978-607-8125-03-6

Printed in Mexico and/or the United States of America and/or Spain

Spanish version released simultaneously.

Also available in eBook format.

Prologue

September, 2004...

Salve Regina, mater misericordiae;
vita dulcendo et spes nostra, salve.
Ad te clamamus, exules, filii Evae.
Ad te suspiramus, gementes et flentes
in hac lacrimarum valle.
Eia ergo advocata nostra,
illos tuos misericordes oculos ad nos converte.
Et Iesum, benedictus fructus ventris tui,
nobis post hoc exsilium ostende.
O clemens, O pía, o dulcis Virgo María.

She stifled a giggle. Their voices didn't sound quite so sweet thirty-five years after graduation. She shot a sideways glance at her old friend, Erin, who grinned back.

Marisa smiled and rolled her eyes toward the open door that led to the terrace surrounding Saint Celeste Hall that had been their dining room while resident students so many years before; today the venue used by the sisters to welcome the alumnae back for their annual reunion and fund raiser.

Marisa hadn't been back to the convent in more than thirty years, but Erin had. She knew the fund-raising speeches would begin soon, and nodded in Marisa's direction

The women slowly edged their way to the door, breaking free by the time the last notes of the *Salve Regina* were intoned by the older alumnae gathered in their singing prayer of thanksgiving for their rather insipid luncheon of rubbery chicken and broccoli.

"Whew!" Erin exclaimed, then laughed. "Sister Phillipe must have left her recipes for the new generations of nuns to cook. Either that, or we just ate leftovers from the sixties!"

Marisa laughed, but her face saddened. "Sister Phillipe must be gone by now. She must have been in her seventies in the sixties," she said wistfully, "from what Sister Barbara said, a lot of our old teachers have passed on to nun-heaven."

"Yeah, considering that we're older now than most of the nuns were when they were teaching us," Erin said.

"Cheery thought." Marisa looked out toward the valley below the cliff on which Villa Vistamar had been perched for nearly a hundred years. She had thought of this exact view many times over the last thirty five years. It had become a private place in her mind's eye where she would go when the stress of daily life became unbearable; a place from which she had drawn strength and serenity during the difficult moments in her life. She felt strange, and somehow out of place, to be physically there again. She had never expected to be.

The women walked in silence down the path toward the statue of the Blessed Mother, just as they had so many times in their youth. Just as in the early years, Marisa had to quicken her pace to keep up with Erin, who, at her nearly six foot height, towered over Marisa's barely five feet.

Marisa glanced toward Erin, giggled involuntarily.

"What's so funny?" Erin asked.

"I was just remembering how we used to walk down here and how I always had to take two steps to your one. I was so envious of your height I was nearly green."

"And I would have killed to be your height! But hey, I'd say we've both aged rather well, at least compared to a lot of our classmates."

Erin had always held herself in a stately manner, and now as an older woman, she was strikingly attractive. She wore her silvery-blonde hair a little shorter now, in contrast to the long, curly blonde hair which had once framed her face, which was still gifted with the high cheek bones, deep blue eyes, and the dark, thick eyelashes of her youth. Her once almost skinny body had filled out with age, but her perfect posture carried the weight regally. Marisa, on the other hand, thought she showed every ounce of extra weight she had put on over the years. When she would wail in desperation over her imaginary middle aged body, her husband would often assure her that she was simply and pleasantly rounded, and that real women have curves. She would always retort that she would prefer being less of a real woman; she always felt fat, although she never weighed over 110 pounds. She still had the long hair of her youth, only now it took a bottle of hair dye to keep it the same light brown of her younger years. Although she usually wore it down, today she had decided a bun at the nape of her neck was far more distinguished and age-appropriate, for a convent reunion.

Marisa stopped suddenly, and pulled at Erin's arm.

"Hey, remember the... basement?" She grinned, her dark blue eyes sparkling with excitement.

Erin turned, her brow furrowing deeply. "Yes, but..."

"But nothing!" Marisa said. "Come on. So what are they going to do if we check it out? Campus us?" The absolutely off-limits, never-to-be-entered basement under the main convent had intrigued the boarders at the convent for generations, and Marisa was determined to satisfy her curiosity once and for all. "Besides," she said with an uncontrollable giggle, "all the nuns are milking our fellow alumnae for every penny they can get. They're certainly not going to leave all those potential donors to come looking for us."

Erin wavered, not entirely sure that she was still curious enough to risk the possible rage of the nuns if they were caught, but then she thought again. What rage? What nuns? There were only three religious on the faculty roster now; not the thirty three nuns that had lived there during the sixties. Why would they even care?

Her brow smoothed slowly, and she smiled. "Oh, hell. Why not?"

They turned and walked toward the side door of the main convent, then ducked under the breezeway to the dark steps below. They stopped before the foreboding black metal door and stared at each other.

Marisa stretched out her hand and turned the doorknob.

It was locked.

Erin heaved an uncontrollable sigh of relief. Marisa had always been the more audacious one of the two, and even thirty five years hadn't changed the dynamic between them. She felt the same emotional relief that she had felt so many times when she had been roped into one of Marisa's capers, only to have it fail for one reason or another... but her relief was short-lived.

"I'll bet you ten to one that the extra key is still hidden in the same place!"

Before Erin could protest, Marisa had climbed up the wrought iron trellis next to the door. She swung herself to the right and stretched her hand up to a small, barred window. On the sill above, from a tiny niche invisible to anyone who didn't know exactly where to look, she pulled out an old barrel key.

"*Et voilà!*" She held the key up like a trophy, giggling as she carefully climbed down the trellis.

With the key in her right hand, she hooked her left arm through Erin's, and pulled her back to the black door.

The lock opened easily, and this time the door swung open upon the slightest of turns of the knob. Marisa still had her left arm looped through Erin's, and pulled her as she stepped into the dark basement. Her free arm rested on what she was quite certain was a banister. Fearing there might be some steps to maneuver, she whispered, "Let our eyes adjust to the dark a minute."

She had barely uttered the words when she felt Erin's arm begin to tremble, then shake violently as her friend liberated herself, turned, and ran from the room.

Marisa's eyes finally began to adjust to the dark, and she squinted out toward the enormous basement.

There, in perfectly neat rows, were at least one hundred rectangular, coffin-sized trunks.

"What the..." she began to say aloud, but she suddenly was overwhelmed with waves of nausea, which was and always had been her reaction to blood-curdling fear.

She backed carefully out the door, closed it quietly and locked it with the barrel key. She stood there looking at the key for a long moment, as if wondering whether or not to return it. Shaking her head with disappointment in herself for even thinking such a thing, she carefully climbed back up the trellis and returned the old key to its proper place.

She jumped to the ground, looked around, and finally discovered Erin above her on the breezeway, grinning. Shrugging her shoulders, Marisa climbed back up the steps to continue their sentimental tour.

"Satisfied?" Erin asked.

"Not really, and I won't be until I know what, or who, is in those trunks."

"Somehow, I don't think I want to know."

From high above, on the top floor of the cloister, a face wrinkled with the markings of time peered at the women through the yellowed blinds. For a brief moment, the old nun's eyes sparkled in recognition, darkened in apprehension, then returned to the stare of a mind long since dulled by the cruelty of age.

Chapter One

Marisa linked arms with Erin. "There is no way I'm going to pass up an opportunity to solve a mystery that has haunted us for so many years. What happened back there was only a result of all the dire threats we heard when we were naive and impressionable. It's perfectly natural." She nudged her playfully in the side and smiled.

Erin knew that look all too well. She was like a bulldog when it came to solving a puzzle or finding out the truth. "You do realize we could face far worse than being campused. Does breaking and entering mean anything to you?"

"Don't go chicken on me, Erin." Her tone was cajoling. "What if I promise we could be in and out of there before anyone even suspected a thing?"

"Right," Erin shook her head. "How many times have you said that in the past, only to end up barely escaping by the skin of our teeth?"

"Ahh, but we escaped more often than we were ever caught." She waved a hand in the air. "Hmm, we'll need to go in at night, preferably after everyone's asleep."

"We?" Erin cocked a brow. "I hope you're referring to yourself and the mouse in your pocket. I haven't agreed to any of this."

She knew she would give in, she always did. Marisa had a way of minimizing the risks involved and glorifying the pay-off whenever she tried to convince her to go along with one of her hare-brained schemes. Erin could just see the headlines now: "*Eminent History Professor and Reporter Arrested for Breaking and Entering.*"

Ignoring her protest, Marisa steered them back towards the breezeway near the basement. "Cough, if you see anyone coming." She left Erin standing on the breezeway and hurriedly retrieved the barrel key from its hiding place.

"What are you doing?" Erin hissed as she nervously glanced around to make certain they were alone.

Marisa quickly returned and began walking briskly in the direction of the chapel.

"I need to make an impression of the key." She made it sound so reasonable and mundane that Erin knew there would be no stopping her now.

Entering the empty sacristy as though she had a right to be there, Erin recalled all the times she had gone along with her, as students, to steal some of the wine stored there for Mass.

Erin watched as Marisa went to where the altar candles were stored and removed one, plus a small section of the protective paper separating them. She then motioned for Erin to wait and went out to the altar. She genuflected, then moved to the side where one of the lighted tapers stood. She carefully replaced the lit candle with the one she had purloined, lighting it by touching the flame to the virgin wick. Upon her return to the sacristy, she blew out the flame and handed the candle to Erin.

"Hold this steady." Marisa pressed the barrel key into the softened wax until she was certain she had a good impression, and then peeled the wedge of wax free. "Bury the candle in the trash."

She carefully wrapped the protective paper around the impression she had made and slipped it into the pocket of her blazer.

Erin discarded the unused portion of candle and the two of them left the chapel.

"Seems like old times, doesn't it?" Marisa whispered as they rejoined their fellow alumnae as they spilled out onto the terrace next to St. Celeste's.

"Unfortunately, it does." Erin wondered when the next shoe would drop, as it always did when Marisa was around.

The first day of reunion events over, they had returned to Erin's townhouse after a stop at a local big chain hardware store so Marisa could have a copy of the key made. Erin had been nervous that using a wax impression to have a key made might raise some suspicion, but the teenage clerk had taken it all in stride as though it was an everyday occurrence and Marisa had had several keys copied to blur the clerk's memory of any specific key having been duplicated.

Erin pulled a bottle of wine from the refrigerator and glanced over at Marisa, who was setting out glasses and readying the corkscrew. Her expression resembled a kid's anticipating Christmas. It hit Erin how different they really were: even as an adult Marisa still thrived on taking chances and bucking the status quo, whereas Erin had spent years carefully building her career as a teacher taking thoroughly calculated risks only when she could bank on a positive result. It had served her well. She had risen through and above all the machinations and insider politics of Academia to reach tenure at her current position of Professor of Ecclesiastical History at a reputed Jesuit Seminary; an accomplishment unique for a woman, but especially someone of Native American ancestry. Yet here she was actively aiding and abetting a burglary. Marisa had that effect on her.

"Stop it!" Marisa shook her head as she accepted the bottle of wine from Erin and expertly removed the cork. "You're doing it again."

"Doing what?" Erin lifted her glass for Marisa to fill.

"Thinking too much!" Marisa laughed and poured wine into her own glass. "I can always tell by the tiny furrow that forms between your eyes." She followed Erin out onto a small terrace off the kitchen and took a seat across from her on one of the comfortable lounges.

Marisa set the open wine bottle on the small table between them and bit her lower lip in thought. She raised her glass. "What shall we drink to? How about: *and the truth shall set you free?*"

"Or get us locked up." Erin countered with a frown. There had to be some way to dissuade Marisa from going any further with her plan. Contrary to her friend's earlier assertion that they had been reacting to schoolgirl bogey men as they stood in the open doorway of the basement,

Erin had been overwhelmed with a sense of terrible darkness that had nothing to do with the interior lighting.

"Hardly," Marisa grinned. "Even in the highly unlikely event that we were to be caught, there would most likely not be any call to the police nor charges filed. It is far more likely that we would be threatened with charges being pressed, become *personae non grata* and summarily escorted from the property." She leaned over and refilled Erin's glass, then her own. "Would it bother you not being able to ever go back to the school again?"

"Not particularly." Erin shrugged. As far as she was concerned, never returning to the school was high on her list of desirable choices. "Why do you think our being barred from the school would be the worst case scenario?"

"Think about it," Marisa sipped at her wine. "The basement and its contents have been off-limits to generations of students and lay-faculty alike. Do you honestly think a police investigation or forensic team, not to mention the media, would be welcome? "

"You've been watching too much television." Erin scoffed. "It is far more likely that a patrolman would take a report, cuff us, take us downtown and book us. There wouldn't be any forensic team or investigation."

"Never happen." Marisa sat up and grinned from ear to ear. Fanning herself with her hand she nervously intoned, "But, Officer, the door was already open. And the basement is filled with coffins!"

"You wouldn't!" Erin giggled. She knew perfectly well that Marisa would, and carry it off like a pro. Before the nuns could blink, said patrolman would be checking out her claim and the proverbial would hit the fan.

Marisa raised her glass in salute. "We should leave here within the next hour or so, just as soon as it is completely dark and the nuns are in their quarters for the night."

"So soon?" Erin had assumed it would be closer to midnight before they returned to the school.

"We can't park too close to the school so wear comfortable shoes," Marisa paused, "and you'll have to change into dark clothing. That pink blouse will catch the light like a mirror. Do you have a flashlight and a folding kitchen ladder?" She poured the remaining wine into their glasses.

"I have flashlights, but what in the world do you need a folding ladder for?"

"Do you have one? Normally, I wouldn't ask, as it is a staple in most kitchens. But in your case I wasn't sure. If you don't, we'll have to stop at Wal-Mart on the way."

"What do you mean by *my case*?" Erin choked. "Just because I'm not height challenged like some people I know, it doesn't give you an excuse to be rude."

"Rude? Height challenged?" Marisa hooted with laughter. "Since when did you become so politically correct?" She hugged herself she was laughing so hard and gasped. "Does that make you height gifted? Oh girl, you've been locked in the classroom with all those fresh-faced seminarians too long!"

Erin felt her face turn pink with embarrassment. When had she become so politically correct? "It does sound rather silly and pretentious, doesn't it?"

"Yes it does!" Marisa agreed trying to catch her breath. "Do you or don't you have a folding ladder?"

"No." Erin burst out laughing.

Three hours later Erin found herself trailing after Marisa through the local Walmart Super Center. She still had no idea what the folding kitchen ladder was for or why they needed one. The store was surprisingly busy for that time of night, but it worked to their advantage. Now they were but two shoppers among many.

"Here try this one." Marisa opened a metal three-step ladder and set it on the floor of the Hardware Department aisle.

"You want me to do what with it?"

"Climb up on it. I need to see if it will be high enough." She motioned with her hands for Erin to ascend.

"High enough for what? You're the short one here. Shouldn't you be the one climbing it?"

"Just do it, Erin, you'll find out why soon enough."

Against her better judgment, Erin ascended the three steps and found she towered over the aisle shelving and had an almost unobstructed view across the store.

"Okay, you can come down. It's high enough. Now all we need are some plastic gloves. They should be around here somewhere. Maybe over by the paint department." She waited until Erin was back on the floor then folded the ladder and started walking.

"Plastic gloves?" Erin murmured to herself. Something told her that Marisa was no stranger to what they were going to be doing that night. And why did finding out soon enough have such an ominous ring to it?

The car loaded and back on the road, Erin turned in her seat and looked over at Marisa. "Tell me again, why we are using your car and not my truck?   I'm the local. Logic says I should be the one driving you around."

"I'm driving a rental." Marisa smiled. "If the car is noticed by anyone it can't be traced back to you, which if we had used your truck, could happen. Furthermore, I may not live here anymore, but I'm not exactly a stranger." Marisa smiled. "I do know where I'm going."

"My God!" Erin opened her eyes in amazement. "You **have** done this before, haven't you!" She closed her eyes tightly. "No! Don't answer that. I could end up being an accessory after the fact."

"Okay, I won't." Marisa struggled to keep a straight face. "If it makes you feel any better, just tell yourself that I do watch too much television."

Erin remained silent until Marisa pulled off the road about half a mile from the school and parked under some overhanging tree limbs. "I'm not getting out of this car until you tell me what that damn ladder is for!"

"You." Marisa shut off the interior lights before opening her door and climbing out of the car. She closed the door and leaned her crossed arms on the roof waiting for what she knew would come next.

Erin scrambled out of the car, bumping the top of her head on the frame in her haste. "Ow!" Her hand flew to her head as she whirled around and faced Marisa. "ME!" She hissed.

"We can talk about it on the way there." Marisa moved to the trunk and opened it. Reaching inside she pulled out the box of plastic gloves and tore it open. Removing two pairs she handed one pair to Erin. "Better put those on now."

Erin had to work the plastic over her sweaty palms before the gloves would fit correctly.

Marisa pulled the folding ladder from the trunk and set it against the bumper. "You take this, I'll get the flashlights." Pocketing extra plastic gloves, she grabbed the flashlights and closed the trunk. "Let's go."

Erin grabbed the ladder, hooking the curved top over her shoulder like the strap of a purse and followed Marisa. "This is ridiculous! What in hell do I need a ladder for?"

"To go over the wall."

"To go over what wall?" Erin stopped in her tracks and stared in disbelief at Marisa's back. "I'm not going over any wall!"

"The wall at the school." Marisa looked over her shoulder at Erin.

Erin caught up and grabbed Marisa by the arm. "And just why do I have to go over a wall at the school?"

"How else will you be able to open the gate from the inside? We don't exactly have a key for that." Marisa shrugged. She knew if she had told Erin anything about this ahead of time, she would never have left her townhouse. "It isn't that big of a deal, Erin. You're up, over and were in."

"It isn't that big of deal, Erin." Erin sarcastically mimicked Marisa. "It certainly is that big of a deal! In case you may have forgotten, we're not teenagers anymore. I could break my neck!"

"You're neck has become too stiff to break." Marisa snapped back at her. "Lighten up, will you? This isn't like you at all. You sound like a whiny old woman." She shook her arm free of Erin's grasp. "What's really bothering you, Erin? I know it's not the wall or getting caught. Something has you spooked. Now what is it?"

"I'm not sure we should even be doing this. When you opened the door and we stood in the doorway, I sensed a terrible darkness in that room. It isn't safe in there Marisa," Erin grudgingly admitted.

"You *felt* this darkness?" Marisa glanced in the direction of the school then back at Erin. "Could you tell if it was animate or inanimate?" Marisa knew enough about Erin's ability to sense and feel things others couldn't, to take what she told her seriously.

"I didn't hang around long enough to be able to tell for certain," Erin answered. "I just knew I had to get out of there. It took me totally by surprise."

"Understandably, but try to go over it in your mind now and see if you can get a better sense of what you felt." She didn't want to go back in there unprepared. Something inanimate she could deal with, but if it was someone rather then something, that was another story.

A swirl of light fog began to drift around them as the two women stood there while Erin recalled what she'd *felt*. "It's a combination of both, but the inanimate feels stronger."

"Did you actually feel like someone or something was in there?" Marisa pressed her to remember. If the answer were yes, they would be heading back to the car and getting out of there.

"Not really. It was just a feeling. I know I should have said something about it sooner. I tried to tell myself it was just nerves."

"No harm, no foul. We both know now. Do you want to finish what we've started?"

She knew she had to offer Erin the option of backing out. If she took it, Marisa would just come back another night on her own.

"If I break my neck going over that wall, I'm going to have to kill you." Erin's voice was shaky at best.

"Of course you will."

Marisa locked her arm through Erin's and they continued towards the school. The streets were empty in the older neighborhood.

By the time they reached the outside perimeter of the school the fog had thickened into a protective blanket. Erin and Marisa crept along the outside wall until they reached the gate they would be using to gain entry to the grounds. Erin slid the ladder off her shoulder and set it up close to the wall near the gate. She then grabbed the elastic waistband of her pants and pulled them up, then glanced over at Marisa before carefully ascending the ladder. Once at the top Erin said a quick, but sincere, prayer then hoisted herself up until she was sitting on the wall. She took a deep breath and tried to swing her legs to the far side of the wall, but her momentum was such that not only did her legs cross over, but her body followed in a less than graceful fashion.

Marisa cringed as she heard a muffled thump followed by a pained silence. It was a good two minutes before the gate quietly opened and a disheveled Erin appeared. Marisa quickly grabbed the ladder and went through the gate, which Erin closed behind her. Marisa hid the ladder in some bushes next to the gate.

"I can't kill you, but I do owe you a severe beating." Erin groaned in Marisa's ear. "I may not have broken my neck, but I came damn close."

"That's only fair." Marisa nodded. "Can you wait until were done here?" Erin did not immediately reply as though she had to think about it first.

"If I must," she finally said brushing small tufts of clinging grass off her clothes.

"Thank you. I'll be sure to remind you later, in case you forget." Marisa guessed Erin had probably knocked the wind out of her and would most likely have a few bruises, but was relieved to know the only real injury was to her pride or she would not have been able to threaten her.

"Don't **you** forget." Erin motioned with her hand for Marisa to lead the way.

Only the convent windows were dimly lit, signifying the occupants were in for the night. They made their way toward the side of the convent, pausing every twenty seconds or so to be sure it was clear ahead of them. Creeping down the stairs, they reached the basement door.

Marisa reached into her pocket and withdrew the extra plastic gloves she'd brought. "Slip these over the ones you already have on."

"You've got to be kidding! I had a hard enough time getting the first pair on."

"You may have small tears in them from your stunt work on the wall," Marisa shrugged. "but if you want to risk leaving DNA evidence, that's your choice."

Erin held her hands up in front of her eyes.

"What are you doing?"

"Checking to see if my gloves are damaged. Turn on one of the flashlights."

"I'll do no such thing! Someone could see us! Just slip on the second pair."

Erin complied, but wasn't happy about it.

"You did bring the key with you, I hope."

"Erin!" Marisa waved at her to be quiet.

"You don't have to get snippy. It was an honest question."

Marisa pulled the barrel key from her pocket and slipped it into the lock. The door smoothly opened revealing a stygian darkness beyond. "Tell me if you sense anything weird."

"The dampness from this fog is going to play havoc with my knees, but thank you for asking."

"Quit playing games, Erin. You know what I mean. Do you sense anything?"

"Only stuff, but it still feels wrong."

"Wrong, I can handle." Marisa grabbed one of Erin's hands and entered the basement closing the door behind them. They both jumped when the lock engaged with a loud click.

"Did you have to lock it? I hope you can unlock it again?"

Marisa reached behind her and turned the knob. The latch disengaged with a click. "Satisfied?"

"Is there a light switch?" Erin really didn't like the inky darkness that surrounded them.

Marisa snapped on her flashlight and handed the other one to Erin. The halo of light revealed they were at the top of three stairs with a handrail on either side of them that led down to the basement floor. "Watch your step."

Erin moved the beam of her flashlight in a slow arc across the basement floor: coffin-like trunks were arranged in rows as far as her eye could see. She adjusted the beam of her light for distance and pointed it to where she expected the basement wall to be. Instead of a wall, all she saw was more darkness that seemed to stretch on into infinity.

"It looks as though the basement might run the full length under the Convent. I never thought it would be so big. There must be hundreds of these whatever-they-ares!"

"At least." Marisa agreed. "Where do you want to start?" She moved closer to the nearest trunk.

"Start?" Erin stuttered. "You're not going to open one of them are you?"

"I didn't come this far just to admire the decor." Marisa trained her light along the side of the trunk. "There's some kind of brass plaque on this one."

Erin flashed her light on the next trunk in the row. "There's one on this one too. I think they all have them." She leaned a little closer. "Oh, my God! There's a name inscribed on this plaque: Sister Michael Thomas." Erin edged her way to the far end of the row. There were only five feet between it and the nearest wall.

"This one says Sister Paul Clement." Marisa read aloud. "Didn't we have her for Freshman English?"

"No. We had a lay-teacher for English, Sister Paul Clement was Religion."

"Oh, yeah. I always liked her. We were her first teaching assignment.

Remember how she would get so flustered her face would turn red with embarrassment?"

"She was so young and pretty." Erin shook her head. "I doubt she was much older than we were at the time. She was transferred our sophomore year, wasn't she?" Erin thought a minute. "If she was transferred, why would there be a trunk here with her name on it?"

"I'm more interested in why there are any names on these trunks. For that matter, why there are any trunks here at all?"

Erin continued along the row reading the names on the trunks she passed. None of them were familiar until she came to the last one in the row. "This one here says, Sister Joseph Vincent. Oh, my God! That was our Principal!" Erin gulped. "I don't like this, Marisa. You don't think there are bodies in these do you? I mean, wouldn't that violate Church Law?"

"Church Law, Public Health Regulations and at least another dozen or so state and federal laws." Marisa gauged the overall size of the trunk in front of her. "It is certainly big enough to hold a body. But the room would have to be temperature controlled, like a morgue."

"It's pretty cool in here." Erin shivered and looked around her. "Just how cold is a morgue anyway?"

"Cooler than this." Marisa ran her hand over the latches of the trunk. "I guess there is only one way to find out." She flipped open the latches and lifted the lid of the trunk.

"Marisa!" Erin closed her eyes and gasped.

"You can open your eyes, Erin. There isn't a body." Marisa panned her light across the opened trunk. "It isn't even very full. There are stacks of file folders, a small leather purse with drawstrings, and some clothes." She lifted the nearest folder and opened it. "There's a file in here listing all the classes she taught while at the school." She quickly scanned the few remaining pages in the folder. "It's all pretty mundane."

"That's all there is? How weird! I always thought whatever was in the basement had to be very important or there would not have been such severe rules and restrictions about even going near here."

"Well, she was just starting her teaching career." Marisa replaced the folder in the trunk and closed it. "There's bound to be more interesting things in some of these other trunks." She stood up and moved to where Erin was. "Sister Joseph Vincent, now she's bound to have more in her trunk. Let's check it out."

"Why not?" Erin's earlier nervousness was somewhat relieved now that she knew there weren't any hidden bodies to worry about. She helped Marisa open the trunk.

Once opened, they found that it was filled almost to the top with more folders, and the same small leather drawstring purse and clothes as had been stored in the other one. Rather than inspecting the top folder as she had before, Marisa reached further into the stack of folders and pulled one out. She checked out the contents of the folder and frowned. "There's even more documents in this one, but they are in Latin."

"Latin?" Erin bent closer to examine the folder.

"Here." Marisa handed her the folder and continued searching the trunk.

Erin scanned the top page. "These are her postulancy papers, but there are a bunch of other documents behind them. They look like legal papers, and they seem to be sealed. Some of them are in English, and the ones behind them are in German. Weird, huh?"

"Not really, since the old guy who endowed the nuns with the old estate was German," Marisa answered absently, as she dug through the other things in the trunk. "These clothes are something else. I've only seen styles like these in the movies and museums. I wonder why they were so important to merit being stored here?" Marisa gently moved the folded pile over so she could search deeper.

"That's what she wore when she joined the convent," Erin absently informed her. "They were kept so she would have something to wear if she ever left the order at a later date."

After reading the first page, she carefully moved to the second: "It says here, she was only sixteen when she became a Novice. Nowadays you have to be at least eighteen, and in some orders, twenty-one to even become a Postulant."

"That means she was only fourteen or fifteen when she entered the convent. She was still just a kid." Marisa's fingers brushed against the aged leather of what appeared to be a book of some kind. She grabbed it and pulled it from the trunk.

Erin's earlier fear and nervousness flooded over her as she stiffened and looked towards the door. "Someone's coming! What do we do?"

Marisa stuffed the book in the waistband of her pants and quickly retrieved the file from Erin.

"Get in the back where it's dark."

She replaced the clothes in their original positions. Just as she was about to tuck the folder back into its proper place, Erin grabbed it from her, and hurriedly closed the trunk.

Erin stuck the folder under her top, tucked into the waistband of her pants, then scurried into the dark at the back of the basement with Marisa right behind her. Brought up short as her body met the wall, Erin placed her back against it wishing she could melt into it. She almost squealed when Marisa's hand grabbed hers as she moved to stand next to her. Erin felt her heart racing a mile a minute and it was becoming difficult to catch her breath.

"Whatever happens, don't make a sound," Marisa softly ordered.

The sound of a key sliding into the outside lock was soon followed by a draft of damp air as the door swung inward. Erin jumped with fright as lights flashed on, leaving the women momentarily blinded; the short time it took for their eyes to readjust felt like an eternity. It was scant comfort to see they were concealed within the few shadows that remained in the room.

Terrified, Erin watched as a wizen figure dressed in black came down the stairs and into the basement. The elderly nun clutched a small parcel against her chest, wrapped in waxed brown paper and crisscrossed with twine, as she made her way down the rows of trunks. She paused at a trunk not thirty feet from their hiding place, opened it. She crouched down next to the open trunk and carefully placed the parcel inside. Rather than close the trunk, she then meticulously rearranged the clothes so that the parcel was hidden. She was so close to where they were hiding that Marisa and Erin could hear snatches of a hymn she was humming as she worked.

Suddenly the humming stopped and the nun's head snapped up; her eyes staring directly at them as though she could see them plain as day. She slowly closed the trunk and stood up, then began walking towards them. Marisa squeezed Erin's now trembling hand to remind her not to make a sound.

The nun stopped not eight feet away, still facing them, motionless for a good twenty seconds. Her face held a blank expression and her unblinking eyes looked almost glazed as though she might be listening to voices only she could hear. She blinked several times before she turned towards the trunk next to her and slowly opened it. She started to reach inside, but paused and gave a furtive look all around as if she could feel Marisa and Erin their eyes watching her.

Convinced they would be discovered at any moment, Erin pressed herself tightly against the wall, only to have it silently open and swallow them both.

Chapter Two

"Shhh!" Marisa whispered, hushing her friend. "Wait until she's gone!"

"Are you crazy?" Panic had taken over Erin's entire being. "She's our way out of here! Or do you, by any chance, have a key to open all the hidden passages in the convent, too? Or perhaps a map?" She gazed toward her friend in the nothingness of the oppressively dark place into which they had fallen, and shook her head.

"Don't you even try to tell me you're not scared, Marisa. I can sense your fear."

"Shhh!"

Erin knew it would be an exercise in futility to insist.

After a few minutes, Erin's breath began to come easily; she had stopped panting in fear; an uncontrollable habit that often resulted in hyperventilation. It had probably been three or four minutes since they had heard any sounds whatsoever coming from the other side of the wall.

Marisa finally turned toward Erin, who had been observing the subtle change in her friend's semblance as she calmed. She no longer showed fear.

"How do you always know what I am feeling?"

"I can read your aura."

Marisa laughed. She and Erin had shared a special empathy since their early youth in the convent, but Marisa had never truly believed in Erin's claim to her ability to read auras.

Erin was beginning to feel very claustrophobic. She reached her hand out until she touched Marisa's arm.

Marisa jumped, startled by her friends touch. "What's wrong?" she whispered.

"I don't think we need to whisper, I'm sure whoever was there is gone now," *and I only wish I had gone with her*, she thought to herself.

Marisa sat quietly for a moment, and then slowly raised herself from the floor to a kneeling position.

"Don't move, because I want to see how high the ceiling is before we try to get up. With your bad knees, I don't want you kneeling like I am."

"How considerate." Erin wondered if her friends concern was for her comfort or from fear of having to carry her out of their newly-found hell hole; a physical impossibility.

From her kneeling position, Marisa extended her hands toward the ceiling, stretching as far as she could. Only air touched the tops of her fingertips, so she slowly pulled her left knee forward, placing weight on her right knee as she placed her left foot on the floor. Resting her weight on that foot for a minute or so, she quickly pulled her other knee to a semi-standing position and pulled herself up.

She was standing freely in the space, but stretched her arms up as far as she could to calculate the space available for Erin's six-foot-tall body. Her fingertips touched only air, again.

She stretched out her hand toward Erin, and said, "Here! Let me help you up. There is plenty of room."

Erin moved her arms through the empty space above and in front of her until she made contact with Marisa's hands, gratefully allowed her friend to help pull her to her feet.

Once standing solidly, she couldn't help but laugh.

"I thought I felt like a kid again, until my knees buckled. The mind set may be right, but the older version of my body just isn't cooperating." She stretched, relieved. "So, now what?"

"I have no idea, but I suppose the best place to start is at the wall that swallowed us. Maybe there's a loose brick or something that will open it up again."

"It's worth a try, but something tells me that it was a one-way ticket to Hell."

Erin had stepped forward and was slowing moving her hands over the upper part of the wall, gently pushing on each brick, tapping the grout between the bricks. She was surprised to find the wall surface recently painted, as the paint wasn't patchy or peeling.

Marisa was moving her hands in a circular motion around the bricks on the lower part of the wall, kneeling again.

"The fresh paint on the wall is a good sign."

"Of what? That someone comes down here and paints every four or five years?" Erin was more than ready to go home, put her feet up and have a nice glass of wine, or perhaps something stronger.

Marisa stood up, scanned the adjacent wall. Nothing moved. The wall did not swing open. She was beginning to panic, but tried to calm herself before Erin realized how frightened she was.

She stood very still and closed her eyes: she put her mind in a blank state, concentrating all her efforts on creating her own special room that only existed in her mind's eye. As the image slowly appeared before her, she could feel her pulse slowing. The hues of blue and pink that decorated her room always calmed her; the view from the window was perhaps one of the more peaceful settings in the entire world. Her concentration sealed within, she consciously gazed out the window of her room to greet each part of the scenery as if saying hello to old friends.

Erin glanced over, comforted by the serenity her friend emanated.

"Have you found anything?"

Her words broke Marisa's meditation, but she was completely calmed now. Meditating in her own special room always worked, but only now did she realize that the view from her meditation room was actually from one of the windows of this very convent.

"I'm afraid not, but not to worry." She turned her back and leaned heavily against the wall. "Unless I am sorely mistaken, which is always a possibility, this tunnel will go under the chapel and over to St. Ursula's. As a matter of fact, I have a pretty good idea as to exactly where it will come out!"

"That's nice, Marisa, and if you are sorely mistaken?"

"Well, look at it this way: it's gotta go somewhere. I mean, what is the point of secret tunnels if they don't go anywhere? Tell you what... since your legs worry me the most, I will walk in front of you, to will feel the way for both of us. You, on the other hand, must use me like a walker."

Erin gasped. "I will do no such thing! I could use a real walker the way my knees feel, but you can't possibly carry my weight."

"I'm a lot stronger than I look, I could carry your weight if necessary, but it won't be unless there's something you're not telling me. The idea was to help you balance. With our flashlights on the other side of the wall, we are going to have to feel our way out of here."

"No, I'm not hiding anything, I promise I'm fine, except that my knees just won't take as much abuse as they used to. They haven't seen this much action since... well, since high school! I will gratefully accept your offer of balance."

Marisa stepped in front of Erin.

"Okay... my shoulders should be about the height of a high walker for you. I am directly in front of you."

Erin lightly rested her hands and forearms on Marisa's shoulders.

"Come on, Erin! It's not a problem! You can lean on me... honest!"

Erin leaned just enough to relieve the stress on her knees without admitting they had been hurting much more than she had said.

The women moved slowly down the passageway. Marisa guided them by the wall on their left, confident that the entrance to St. Ursula's Hall would follow. She tried to count the number of steps they took, but they were short steps and hard to calculate.

Suddenly her left arm touched an empty space. She had only counted what she thought were around two hundred steps, which would barely put them under the chapel.

She stopped.

"Erin, there is a blank space to my left that I need to explore, just to be sure that it is the continuation of the passageway we are in. You may want to lean against the wall for a minute while I check it out."

Erin silently pulled her hands from Marisa's shoulders and stepped to the left until she touched the wall. Strangely, she was comforted by its solidity.

Marisa stepped directly to her right until she touched the other side of the passageway. As she moved forward, her worst fears were confirmed: there was an empty space on the right side, coinciding exactly with the one on the left.

She turned and followed the wall for a few feet; her hand felt empty space again. A sense of panic was beginning to invade every pore of her being as she realized that this place felt like a maze, and she didn't have a mouse's instinct for choosing the right path. As she jerked her hand back, she hit it on what felt like a ledge, where she let it come to rest.

Lifting her hand slowly, it touched a brick above. Moving it slowly to each side, she discovered that her hand had inadvertently entered a cubbyhole.

"I may have found something here, Erin."

Erin didn't answer.

Placing her hand on what she calculated to be the mid-point of the cubbyhole floor, she moved it backward into the space, slowly.

"Aha! It's a candle!"

Touching the wooden holder, she traced her fingers upward until she found the base of the candle, found it to be thick. The candle and holder in her left hand, she continued feeling around the floor of the cubbyhole. Finally, she found what she had know would be there.

"And I found some matches, too." She shook the matchbox; found that it was nearly full. "If push comes to shove, we can probably find our way out with just the matches!"

She felt around the little plastic box, found a tiny drawer-pull on one end. "How Interesting! I think these are the Mexican wax matches. That's rather revealing, don't you think?"

"Just get the candle lit, Marisa. The darkness is beginning to close in on me."

Marisa struck one of the match heads against the long side of the box, and joyfully watched it flare. She immediately placed it against the wick of the candle and held it there until the flame sustained itself.

She could physically feel Erin's relief.

"Your wish is my command, Madame!"

Holding the candle high before her, she tried to get her bearings. Stepping back toward the passageway, she held the candle as high as she could.

Erin stepped forward, gently took the candle from Marisa's hands.

"Here. I can hold it higher."

As she did, a much larger area was illuminated. They could see the passageway from which they had come, and both laughed. They had only walked about fifty feet, so they could see the wall that had swallowed them.

As they turned, they both realized that they had entered a full basement just the size of the chapel.

"In all the years I lived here, I never knew the chapel had a basement!"

Marisa laughed nervously. "Neither did I, but we couldn't have. The little room where I found the candle is the size of the Sacristy but there isn't a door or stairs. For that matter, I don't remember seeing any steps in the chapel except to the balcony and pipe organ."

More confident now, they moved forward. Marisa clutched the matches in her hand, just in case the candle went out.

"Do you suppose the nun found our flashlights?"

Erin didn't answer. Frozen in her tracks, she stared at the longest wall of the basement, picturing the tennis court on the outside. She tried to recall the texture of the wall on the court-side. Was it rock? Was it brick or concrete? For the life of her, she couldn't remember. For some reason it bothered her.

Marisa stopped when Erin didn't follow. "What's wrong, Erin? Do you feel something bad?"

"Please, Marisa. I have felt nothing but bad things since we began this insanity. Do you remember what the other side of this wall is made of?"

Marisa didn't understand the importance of the question.

"I really don't remember, but that concerns me less than what is on this side," She walked up to the wall. "Bring the candle, will you? There is something really weird here, but I can't see what it is."

Erin approached the wall with the candle, and gasped. The entire wall was alive with tiny ant-like insects. When Marisa saw them she jumped back, bumping into Erin.

The women tumbled to the floor, the candle fell, the flame snuffed as the candle thumped on the ground with the wick down.

"God, Erin! I am so sorry! Are you okay?" Marisa felt around the floor for the matches that had flown from her hand. As she awaited a thorough and well-deserved diatribe from Erin, she found the candle, and soon thereafter, the matches.

The diatribe didn't come. In its place, Marisa heard a muffled chuckle, followed by others until the silent basement was alive with the most heartfelt laughter that she had ever heard. It was contagious. She had absolutely no idea why she was laughing, but it felt good.

She picked up the candle and turned it right side up, digging down in the wax to retrieve the wick. She burned herself painfully, but it made her laugh all the harder.

With the wick up, she placed the candle on the floor again, lit a match. The wax stuck to the wick spattered a bit. A halo of light soon filled the basement.

"Okay, can you explain what could possibly have us laughing hysterically? Personally, I should be panicking because I hate bugs!"

Erin tried to calm herself, but continued to laugh anyway. Marisa began to think that her friend was truly hysterical; it was beginning to worry her. She reached her hand out and touched Erin's forearm.

"Are you okay, girlfriend? You're scaring me."

Erin began holding her breath then slowly letting it out to control her laughter. Finally, between spurts of hilarity, she got a few words out:

"I'm sorry, it's just that if you had seen the look on your face when you saw the termites... it was priceless!" She giggled. "The intrepid Marisa, who hunts down criminals for sport, totally freaks out over a little swarm of termites, for God's sake!"

Marisa couldn't really see the humor in the situation.

"I have always been horrified by anything that creeps or crawls, and you know it, so it surprises you that I wouldn't like those swarthy little beasts on the wall?"

Erin finally stopped laughing. She slowly lifted herself to a kneeling position to rise to her feet.

Marisa jumped to her feet, held her hands out to Erin. "Here, let me help you."

Erin grabbed on to her friend and was pulled to her feet, surprised her knees didn't hurt.

"You know how they say that a good belly laugh will cure almost anything? Well, it must be true, because my knees don't hurt anymore."

Marisa smiled at her friend, suddenly feeling terribly guilty for getting her into this predicament. She leaned over to pick up the candle, handed it back to Erin.

"Let's go, Erin. I think it is high time we got out of here."

Guiding them by the light of the candle, Marisa was able to sense her way out of the chapel basement into another passageway.

Just as she had suspected, it had led to the former observatory, now being used as the school's music department.

When they finally came out into the basement of the rounded building, Marisa heaved a sigh of relief.

"We made it!"

"We made what? I don't know about you, but I don't see anything even remotely resembling a door or an exit from this room. I assume we are under St. Ursula's Hall because of the round walls, but do you see a way out?"

"No, but I know it's here. So do you. Don't you remember…"

"The elevator!" they said in unison.

No one had ever seen it, but everyone had heard the elevator at one time or another when living in the old convent. As the story had gone, when the old German had left the mansion to the nuns with an endowment hearty enough to basically support it forever, the nuns had sealed up the old elevator in this building. The elevator was old and rickety and they hadn't considered it worth repairing.

Generations of students, however, had heard the clanging of the metal cage doors and the slow rumbling of the elevator as it made its way up to the third floor from the bowels of the old music building.

It scared the hell out of most.

But now, it was all becoming very clear to Erin and Marisa.

Before them, in the center of the rounded basement room, was the old elevator.

"Erin, what do you feel? Friend or foe?"

"Hell, I don't need any extrasensory feelings to pick up on this one: I can smell fresh oil, and see a gleam on the copper walls of the old thing. The oil indicates a recent maintenance of the lift, and the shiny copper on the walls is a pretty good indication of some recent cleaning. I'd say we have definitely found our way out of this little hellhole."

Erin stepped forward and opened the wrought iron gate into the shiny elevator. She laughed.

"You know, we are summarily destroying each and every one of those wonderful legends of ghosts and spirits haunting the old place! Don't you remember how everyone always freaked over the elevator noises?"

"Yeah, and all the time it was just the nuns entering the catacombs through their own private elevator." She snorted. "And you know as well as I do that they knew about the ghost legends, and simply fed the tales. It seems wrong, somehow."

"Oh please, Marisa, let's not even visit the concept of wrong. I have a list of wrongs that's so long you wouldn't believe it."

Marisa didn't reply. She was intent on closing the gate properly before attempting to use the old-fashioned lever she hoped would lift the elevator. Once secure, she gently engaged it, the elevator made a clanking noise.

"Looks like we have found ourselves some transportation!" Marisa grabbed onto the brass railing that encircled the small enclosure. "Ready?"

Erin nodded nervously.

"Then here we go!" Marisa pushed the lever into the lift position.

By the markings on the lever, confirmed by the blank cement walls that didn't stop at any of the three floors between the basement and the observatory, there would be only one stop: the observatory room, where there had never been obvious signs of an elevator.

However, when the elevator stopped, there was only a small, dark passageway. Marisa pulled the matches from her pocket.

Marisa lit the candle and opened the gate.

They stepped from the cage into the dark passageway and found that it led only to a spiral staircase. They followed the stairs down about half a story, coming out into another straight corridor that appeared to lead them in the direction of the main classroom building. They followed it.

Erin stopped cold and turned toward Marisa, grinning:

"Remember in study hall at night when we used to hear steps on the roof? When Sister would always say it was one of the cats?"

"Cats, my foot! It was one of the nuns coming out of the catacombs, and I'll bet you anything this is going to end up at that other little staircase that leads right into Sister Superior's office!"

Sure enough, about one hundred steps further on, the corridor ended at the top of another small, spiral staircase. The women descended to a door, opened it, and entered the room beyond.

"Hmm..." Marisa said, "This was one of my fondest fantasies as a kid... and here we are, in Sister Superior's office. No one knows were here!"

"And we're not, either!" Erin insisted. "We are outta here, now. I mean it, Marisa. I am not staying in this place for one more minute!"

Marisa shrugged her shoulders and followed her friend out through the darkened halls of their alma mater, finally pushing through a fire exit to the street.

Several floors above the basement and two buildings over, the Sisters of St. Thomas were just sitting down to their evening snack before retiring. Sister Barbara, Sister Agnes and Sister Rose were in charge of administrating the school. Sister Thomas Marie was sitting at a small table under the dining room window looking out over the valley below. The oldest surviving member of the Congregation at one hundred years plus, she had chosen to live out her remaining days in the school where she had taught in her youth. The wanderings of her mind, which seemed to tune in and out like an old radio, were exacerbated by her failing health.

Sister Thomas Marie seemed agitated, murmuring from the time she had entered the dining room with the other Sisters.

Sister Barbara and Sister Agnes seemed unaffected by her murmurs, but Sister Rose glanced over at the old nun with a worried look on her face.

She rose from her chair, approached Sister Thomas Marie. She leaned close to the wrinkly old face. "Sister Thomas Marie, are you all right?"

The old nun didn't respond verbally at first, but smiled appreciatively in the younger nun's direction.

As her eyes shone in recognition, she sat up straighter than the other Sisters had seen her do in years.

"We have to campus those girls, Sister," she stated simply, but then her face contorted into wrinkly anger. "Erin and that Marisa girl were down in the basement again, and they have to be stopped! We have to stop this nonsense, Sisters, and now! It is far too dangerous a place for those girls, so we need to get them out of there, and make sure they don't go back!"

Sister Rose smiled sweetly, shook her head at the inquisitive stares of the other two Sisters.

"Yes, dear, we'll take care of everything, don't worry." She patted Sister Thomas Marie gently on the shoulder. "We'll campus the girls so they never think of going down there again. I promise"

"They have to respect our privacy!" The old nun was vehement. "They simply must!"

Satisfied, Sister Thomas Marie returned to her customary state of mind while the other Sisters returned to their evening snack.

Chapter Three

It was nearly midnight when the exhausted women arrived back at Erin's townhouse. The ride home had been a silent journey, each lost in thoughts of the night's events. They dragged themselves inside to their separate rooms to sleep, but once in bed, their minds raced repeatedly through the night's events. Neither of them fell asleep until nearly dawn.

It was mid afternoon before Erin shuffled into the kitchen with only two thoughts on her mind: gratitude to the inventor of programmable coffee makers and disbelief that they had survived. She poured a cup of coffee, settled at the kitchen table to identify her aches and pains. She was stiff and sore, but not as much as she'd expected, which was a pleasant surprise.

Half way through her second cup of coffee, there was still no sign of Marisa. Had she preset the coffee maker and gone back to bed? Erin sincerely hoped so. At that moment, the only thing Erin was willing to review was the amount of coffee remaining in the pot, not the previous night's events.

A second pot was brewing when Erin's peaceful communion with the patron deities of the wonderful elixir was shattered as the front door opened. Marisa breezed in carrying the ladder they had left behind in their haste to escape.

"I can't believe you went back there!" Erin shook her head. "Wasn't last night enough excitement for you?"

"One of us had to go back." Marisa set the ladder against the pantry door and moved to grab some coffee. "It is the last day of reunion events. Everyone sends their love and was sorry to hear you had a prior commitment." She took a seat across from Erin. "I wanted to retrieve the ladder before someone else found it and started asking questions."

"Oh, my God!" Erin rested her head in her hands. "What with every-thing else that's been going on I totally forgot about the reunion. Did I miss anything?"

"Not a thing! I didn't sense the slightest hint, even from the nuns, that anything out of the ordinary may have happened. How are you doing today?"

"Better than I thought I would," Erin admitted with a wry smile. "What about you? You couldn't have had much sleep, if you went back to the school."

"I managed a few hours. I am used to late nights and early morning responsibilities. Have you taken another look at that folder you brought back with you?"

"You've got to be kidding?" Erin sipped her coffee. "I'm still waiting for the caffeine to jump start my brain." She looked closer at Marisa. "It isn't fair."

"What isn't fair?" Marisa grinned. Erin had never been a morning per-son. She'd made this fact perfectly clear early in their friendship when they had to be up and at early Mass each morning before classes began: anything she said before nine in the morning could not be held against her in a court of law.

"You know as well as I do that your brain operating on only two cylin-ders, instead of its usual twelve, is capable of running circles around the majority of the populace."

Erin gave her **the look**. "At the moment, I would welcome two cylin-ders. It was dawn before either of us got to bed, yet here I am struggling to reconcile body and spirit with a massive intake of caffeine, while you have already been out, coherently interacting with others, managing to do so looking perky and refreshed." Her eyes narrowed. "You're just not hu-man, that's what it is."

Marisa laughed. "Just because I'm not using the furniture to hold me upright and I can reasonably articulate does not make me inhuman. I shudder to think what you have been teaching to all those unsuspecting seminarians in your morning classes for all these years."

Erin leaned back in her chair and grinned. "What morning classes? I no longer do morning classes. I have tenure. Heaven only knows what muddled information I may have spouted during those few years I was forced to endure a classroom filled with innocent minds before noon."

"It couldn't have been all that muddled. There haven't been any major schisms in the last twenty years; at least none that I'm aware of."

"You really don't want to know." Erin giggled. "I do recall a bit of a rumble the time I assigned a class to do a research paper relating the Prophecies of St. Malachy with the modern Church." She smiled to herself and went to refill her coffee cup.

Marisa leaned forward, intrigued.

"Oh no, you don't! Don't even think of leaving me hanging like that. Define rumble. And, why would such an assignment cause one?"

Erin rolled her eyes and leaned against the counter. "Let's just say that St. Malachy's Prophecies are controversial in some quarters of liturgical teaching, and leave it at that."

"Why Erin, you have a rebellious streak after all!"

"Of course, I do." Erin stretched to her full height and looked over at Marisa. "I just keep a tighter rein on it than you do. One of us had to." She returned to her seat. "I pick and choose when to push the limits."

"Only after I've bullied you onto something,"

"On the contrary." Erin shook her head. "Unlike you, who jumps in with both feet and rues the consequences later, I've chosen to be more subtle in my approach. Who was the one that managed to explain our way out of trouble when one of your ideas blew up in our faces and we were caught?"

"You've got a point there."

Erin had been the one to mollify the nun's anger more times than not to save them from punishments far worse than merely being campused.

Erin stirred her coffee.

"There were times I allowed you to think you had bullied me into something."

"You allowed? Hah! Most of the time I had to practically drag you, kicking and screaming."

She had often wondered why she even bothered enlisting Erin as her partner for all the fuss it caused.

"Exactly. I could always tell how important something was to you by how hard you pushed me to go along with it." She enjoyed the look of surprise on Marisa's face. "If you didn't argue and cajole strongly enough, I knew it was most likely a case of restless boredom on your part or a passing whim." She held up her hand to still the protest she knew would spring to Marisa's lips. "And, yes, there were those times when I asked myself how you managed to talk me into something I knew would end up with our being caught."

"We make a great team, don't we?" Marisa rested her hand on Erin's. "We balance each other."

"That we do."

They had always been there for each another and always would be. An only child, Marisa was the closest thing Erin had ever had to a sister.

"I suppose now is when you tell me that at some point we will have to go back to the school to reclaim our flashlights?"

"But, of course." Marisa laughed. "I'm just not sure when to do it."

"It is only a pair of flashlights. There's nothing about them that can connect them to us. Why go back for them?" It would take a very important reason to make her risk everything, a second time, by going back to that basement. This didn't qualify.

"Should the flashlights be found, they will know that intruders were in the basement."

"So what? They were old flashlights; they could have been left there anytime over the last ten years. I fail to see a problem." She rose from her seat and went into the kitchen. "Are you hungry? I haven't eaten anything since last night."

"I could eat." Marisa followed her into the kitchen. "Forget the flashlights for a moment. There could be a problem if they decide to do an inventory of the trunks to see if anything is missing." She paused. "We have that folder and book."

"Yes, but we are the only ones that know we have them." Erin set out the makings of a tossed salad. "Ranch or Italian?"

"Either one is fine. Do you have any of those Herb & Garlic Croutons?" Rinsing the red leaf and romaine lettuce, Marisa tore them apart for the salad.

"There are some in the pantry. I'll get them." Erin moved across the kitchen. "What it all boils down to is that reporter's sense of yours thinks there has to be something in either the folder or the book that warrants their being kept secret and hidden." She removed the box of croutons from the pantry, handed it to Marisa.

"Exactly." Marisa chopped some tomatoes to add to the bowl. "Ergo, the need to collect the flashlights before anyone else does."

"And, if you are wrong?" Erin added sliced mushrooms, shaved carrot and baby spinach to Marisa's contributions. "You're not infallible, you know."

"We won't know if I am or not until we take a good look at what's in that folder and book." Marisa grabbed salad tongs and began tossing everything together. "Are we doing seeds or bacon with this?"

"Seeds." Erin pulled two dinner plates from the cupboard and set them on the counter. "We used the last of the bacon yesterday."

Marisa sprinkled shelled sunflower seeds and croutons on top of the salad while Erin set out the pepper mill, dressing and forks. "Iced tea or lemonade?" Erin asked.

Almost an hour later, Erin was still translating the Ecclesiastical Latin used on the pages within the folder into English, while Marisa was reading what had turned out to be a journal kept by a succession of Mothers Superior at the school, beginning in the early part of the last century.

"How's it coming?" Marisa paused in her reading and looked over at Erin. "Are you cross-eyed yet?"

"Coming close." Erin sat back and rubbed her neck. "Some of this Latin is like Spanish and doesn't easily translate into English. I have to read an entire paragraph to get an idea of the content before going back and translating it."

"Take your time. You might miss something if you rush it. I've about had it with what I've been reading. Some of the older Mothers Superior were truly hardcore. The school was far stricter under their supervision than during our time there. They actually levied penance on the other nuns and even some of the resident students for nit-picking infractions. They kept a record of the infractions. Makes me glad we weren't resident students back then."

"For instance?"

Marisa marked her current place with a bookmark, flipped back several pages.

"The penance for a resident student speaking to a day student outside of class without permission was kitchen duty for a month."

"The resident students weren't allowed to speak to the day students? I can't even imagine why they had such a rule. What year was that?"

"Nineteen-nineteen."

"How many resident students were there?" Erin found it interesting that the date closely related to some of the dates she had found in the papers she was working on. She couldn't help but wonder if there might be a connection between them.

"Let me see," Marisa turned back a few pages more. "Fourteen in grades 2-12." She read a bit further. "That's strange."

"What's strange?"

"None of them were from English speaking countries. They all seem to be from Eastern Europe." Marisa chewed at her bottom lip. "There isn't a single American, Mexican, British, or Canadian student in the group."

"That is odd." Erin glanced back down at the pad on which she had been copying her translations. "Which countries in Eastern Europe?"

"It seems evenly split between Austria, Germany, Estonia and Latvia…

how weird is that! Is there something significant in this that I'm missing?"

"I think there may be, but I can't be sure." Erin rechecked her notes. "Damn! I knew I should have taken German."

"When could you have taken German? There wasn't enough time for you take another language. I think you did just fine with four years of Latin, Spanish, and English, plus all the other subjects we had to take. It was an intensive college prep curriculum."

"Had I taken German, I would be able to finish translating these papers and, possibly find some answers to our questions. As it is, I've gone as far as I can and all that's left is in German and maybe even Latvian or something... I really can't tell."

"Do you know anyone you can trust, who speaks German and can finish the translation for us?" Marisa fervently hoped that she did.

Erin was silent a moment, wondering if she should involve anyone else, especially a colleague who had been a good friend for more than twenty years. But then again, she knew herself too well, and although she was reluctant to admit it, once her curiosity was piqued, she knew she wouldn't rest until her questions were answered.

She nodded her head absently as she served a portion of salad on Marisa's plate and then on her own.

"Well, there is always Brother Ziggie."

Marisa giggled. "Brother Ziggie? You're going to have a Jesuit translate stolen Church papers?" Her giggle turned into a belly laugh. "And you accuse me of being intrepid?" She nearly choked on the crouton she had snatched off her plate as Erin was serving her.

Erin remained perfectly serious, but twisted her face into a sardonic smile. "Let's just say that he is a special Jesuit, who knows how to be discreet. I must add, he is one of the most brilliant linguists in Germanic tongues I have ever known, and more importantly, he is someone I know I can trust."

Marisa carefully chewed the offending crouton and swallowed it carefully. Her throat felt raspy where it had caught seconds earlier. She had dumped far too much Ranch dressing on her salad.

"Would he be there on a Sunday? Can we go visit him today?"

"Uh... he is a Jesuit who lives in a community, so I would assume he's home," Erin pushed a few of the unavoidable croutons to one side of her plate and sprinkled some Italian dressing on her salad. "I'll run down in a while and see what he can tell me."

"You mean WE," Marisa said as she reached toward Erin's plate with her fork. "Don't you want your croutons?"

"No, help yourself. I've been trying to follow the South Beach Diet, and with your visit, I have overdone the carbs." She picked up the serving tongs and gathered up all the croutons for Marisa, sprinkling them on her plate.

"Cool! More for me!" She patted herself on the stomach. "Carbohydrates are my second best friends," She flashed Erin a meaningful grin. "You're my first best."

"Flattery will not get you into the seminary with me." The hurt look on Marisa's face made Erin realize an explanation was needed. "It is nothing personal, dear; it's just that it took me more than fifteen years just to establish a decent rapport with the Jesuits. I have had two strikes against me from the day I began teaching there, and I have no intention of striking three."

"I am assuming I am the third strike, but what are the first two?"

"I am a woman, and not a nun. That's strike one and two, and yes, bringing a stranger into the hallowed halls of a Jesuit Seminary to expose one of the Brothers as somewhat larcenous, under pressure from a friend, would definitely qualify as strike three!"

Marisa knew that to insist would be an exercise in futility, so she concentrated on her salad.

Erin was relieved.

"Thanks for understanding."

Marisa smiled, chewed her last big piece of lettuce before enjoying the croutons softened by the dressing.

"Hey, I'm not a monster… just curious and impatient." She took a sip of her tea. "I would never do anything to jeopardize your position. I swear. You know I wouldn't."

Marisa stood to clear the table. Erin stood to help, but Marisa waved her away. "I'll clean up here, so you can take your shower and go down to the seminary before it gets too late."

While Erin readied herself, Marisa straightened the kitchen, and then carried a small briefcase to the breakfast nook. She placed it gently on the table, pulled the zipper open. Pulling out her laptop computer, she felt guilty for not having given her husband, Carlos, a second thought since her arrival. She had left a message on his cell phone voice mail before de-planing upon her arrival, but hadn't called nor emailed him since.

It was hard to believe that she had arrived less than forty-eight hours ago. She had seen so many people and had done so much since then that she felt as if she had been in town for at least a week.

As she booted the computer, she thought about what to write to her husband. His last words to her had been: "Stay out of trouble!"

She'd laughed, assuring him that there wasn't much one could do to get in trouble at a convent school reunion, for Heaven's sake!

She often remarked that Carlos was the most patient man in the world, that there wasn't another man on earth who would put up with her rest-lessness. Her restlessness had put Carlos in a number of precarious situa-tions, but he always seemed to emerge from his involvement in her ad-ventures with renewed love and respect for his wife.

Marisa, on the other hand, never tired of becoming involved in the lives and perils of others. She was the first to joke about being a court reporter and columnist for the smallest newspaper in the world, and yet she took her work and her writing very seriously because it afforded her the oppor-tunity to be involved in adventurous escapades.

Almost a year had passed since the last adventure that had nearly cost her life, and Carlos had still not fully recovered from the emotional or-deal. True to her essence, Marisa simply didn't get it. After all, she was fine, wasn't she?

She thought about what to tell her husband as she connected the modem to Erin's phone line, hit the "connect" icon on her email software. Carlos had configured her program to dial the local number for their Internet service provider.

Before long she heard the comforting hiss and ring of the computer establishing a proper link with the Internet.

She checked her email and three messages popped up from Carlos.

She read all three. They all said basically the same thing: she was loved and missed.

Clicking on the reply icon, she quickly assured him that she was fine, but very busy with her reunion. She made no mention of their adventures. Why worry him more?

As she clicked on the "send" icon, Erin emerged from the bedroom looking refreshed. She was dressed in a long, navy blue skirt, a white blouse and navy blue blazer.

Marisa giggled. "No wonder they treat you like one of the guys! Do you always dress like a nun when you go to work?"

Erin's face lost all expression, Marisa was immediately sorry for her unkind words. She jumped to her feet and hugged Erin.

"I am so sorry, Erin. That was thoughtless of me, and must have sounded really mean! I swear, I didn't mean it to come out that way!"

Erin laughed good-naturedly and stepped back, bowing ceremoniously.

"There is a definite reason I'm dressed this way. Since it's not a school day, Ziggie is probably in the library or in his cell working on one of his many research projects. Dressed like this, I can breeze in and out of any room in the seminary without drawing attention to myself. It's just not a place where you want to wear a red halter dress."

Marisa laughed.

"Well, you look perfect for the task at hand."

Erin grabbed her keys and purse from the kitchen counter, started toward the door.

"Wish me luck!" she said, and Marisa did.

As Erin pulled into the parking lot of the hilltop seminary, she planned her strategy with Ziggie. She trusted him, but she didn't want to involve him in her larceny by telling him too much; not because he would betray her, but rather because she wouldn't want him to feel he was participating in something illegal.

She had figured out how much to tell him by the time she was ascending the wide flight of steps that led to the main building.

She entered the main hallway of the university, engulfed by the very serenity that had sustained her soul for over twenty-five years. The university had been her home, church, social life, academic challenge, financial security and spiritual comfort throughout her adult life. Marriage had come and gone. Relationships had sizzled or frizzled her heart through the years. But the constant and dependable things that she could count on in life were the things she had found within these sacred walls.

She had decided to check her friend's office before searching for him elsewhere. She climbed the first wide staircase that led to the second-floor classrooms and lecture halls, finding the hallway to be darkened. Unalarmed, she knew the Brothers frugally lowered the hallway lights on Sundays in an ongoing attempt to keep the electric bills as low as possible. At the end of the hallway was a narrow staircase that led to the third floor where each professor had a small cubicle of an office for research or an occasional conference with a student.

The hallway was quite dark; Erin had to stop for a moment at the top of the steps to allow her eyes to adjust.

Halfway down the hall, she saw light coming from a cubicle, and smiled. She walked heavily down the hallway, singing out: "It's just Erin, Ziggie!"

"Erin! How lovely!" Ziggie called out in his learned British English with his slight German accent as he stuck his head out the door. "I was just thinking of you! You have been on my mind all morning. Is everything all right?"

Erin should have known that he would intuitively know something was up. All her resolve melted, she knew she would either have to tell him the absolute truth, or not involve him at all.

Her curiosity won.

"Yes, everything is fine, but you probably tuned into my thinking about you this morning!" She embraced her friend and lightly kissed the air next to each of his cheeks. "Do you have a few minutes for an old friend who needs a linguistic expert?"

Brother Ziggie smiled widely. "For you, I have all the time in the world!" He gestured toward the door of his cubicle with his long left arm. "Is my office all right? We could go down to the Student Union, if you prefer..." His long, slender face became gaunt, his expression worried. "I must assume this is something quite drastically important to bring you out on a Sunday... besides, wasn't this the weekend of your convent-school reunion?"

Erin walked into his office, sat in the only chair other than his. Brother Ziggie, dressed in his cassock, seemed even taller than his six feet, seven inches as he circled around the desk to fold his thin body into his chair.

Behind him was a bay window with a shelf of books and a coffeepot. Erin noticed that the steaming coffee pot was half full.

Before she could ask him for a cup, Brother Ziggie smiled. "I just brewed it. Want a cup?"

"I would love one," Erin watched as her friend served her. He handed it to her, she thanked him.

"I brought you something that I am very interested in, but the document is in German, and my German is about as good as my Chinese! Would you mind taking a look at it for me?"

"Of course not," Ziggie held out his hand for the file that Erin still clutched against her chest.

She hesitated before she handed him the file. It was only then she remembered that she hadn't removed the nun's postulancy papers from the top; a dead giveaway the papers were stolen.

"Ziggie, you'll surely notice that there are some documents in Latin on top of the German documents. I already translated them, naturally." She smiled and waited for his reaction.

He seemed to be glancing over the first papers, but suddenly stopped and grinned at her. "You must know that these are a nun's postulancy papers to enter a religious congregation, right?"

"Right."

"Okay…" he said hesitantly. "I won't ask."

Erin smiled. "Thank you."

But Ziggie didn't seem to hear her. He was deeply engrossed in the first of the German documents. Erin sat back to sip her coffee, determined not to ask questions until he'd had a chance to real the entire document.

After about five minutes, he placed the document face down on left-hand side of the file folder, on top of the postulancy papers.

He was concerned as he looked at Erin.

"Erin, where did you get these papers?"

Erin was suddenly embarrassed to admit what she had done, but she couldn't bring herself to invent some silly story that her friend wouldn't believe anyway.

She took a deep breath, spilled out the whole story of her adventure into the catacombs of the old convent with her childhood classmate.

Brother Ziggie listened intently, resting his sharp chin on the palm of his hand; his elbow placed protectively on top of the file on his desk. Erin noticed that his fingers had slowly crept toward his mouth as she finished her story. He was covering his mouth with closed fingers, containing his laughter. His eyes, however, were tearing from his stifled chuckles.

"… and that brings me to the here and now," she said in conclusion. "I could translate the Latin documents, but not the others. I knew you could, and so…"

"I'm sorry," he said between guffaws, "but this has got to be the most convoluted and crazy thing I have ever known you to do! It all just seems so out of character for you!"

Erin was embarrassed, but not ashamed. She saw a glint in her friend's eye that she hadn't seen in years, and strangely, a look of unmistakable admiration on his face. It felt good.

"Well, I guess it is slightly out of my current character, but certainly within the norms of a convent schoolgirl. You see, that convent basement had intrigued us for nearly forty years. Although we originally went in just to satisfy our curiosity, it only whetted our appetites for more. From the look on your face as you read the first document, we must have hit pay dirt, right?"

Ziggie laughed. "I don't really know if I would call it pay dirt, since that would depend on what you are looking for. That document seems to outline the endowment from the German scientist that left the estate to the Sisters. It's dated in 1918, and it seems pretty straight forward, except for a couple of rather strange conditions."

"Which are?"

"Well," Ziggie turned the first German document over onto the unread side of the file, "In the first place, the nuns can never sell the estate. Secondly, it must remain as a school, and third, it must remain as a girls' school. No man may ever live on the campus."

"That's weird," Erin said pensively. "But now that I think about it, even back when it was a boarding school, there was a custodian who took care of the gardens, plumbing, etc., but the school rented a place for him to live with his wife off campus. It always seemed strange that with all the cottages and living quarters on the grounds, that old man and his wife didn't live there."

"Well, now you know why," Ziggie began to read the next document in the file. He skimmed through the document then lifted his gaze toward Erin. "This one just talks about a yearly endowment through a trust account in Switzerland to maintain the grounds and buildings."

He turned that document face down on top of the others. When he looked at the following document, he laughed. "I appreciate your confidence in my linguistic abilities, but this one is in Russian!"

"What?" Erin stood, leaned across the desk to look at the following document. "I never noticed... I'm sorry!"

"I'm not... hey, it's a challenge. I understand spoken Russian to a certain extent, as my maternal great grandmother was Russian, but my reading abilities are rusty, at best. If you want to leave this here with me for a few days, I'll be happy to give it a try," he offered, as he skimmed through the long document. "At first glance, it may be the most interesting of all the papers."

"Oh?"

"Yes, I should say so! There is one surname that is repeated throughout the document."

"Is it a name I would recognize?" Erin tried to look at the document.

"Yes, as an historian, I would certainly hope so: the surname is *Romanov.*"

Chapter Four

"You'll never guess what I found out!" Erin shut the front door behind her. There was no answer. "Marisa?"

She went to the kitchen, took a glass from the cupboard. She opened the refrigerator, served herself some iced green tea and took a long, refreshing drink.

She lowered her glass and noticed a note scribbled on the chalkboard next to the refrigerator: *Erin... I'm down at the pool soaking in the hot tub. Join me!*

She glanced out the window and spotted Marisa in the hot tub, blithely reading the nun's journal while sipping from a wine goblet; wine was prohibited in the common areas of the townhouse community.

Erin hurried to the bedroom, undressing as she went. She quickly donned a two-piece bathing suit, a pareo over it. She took her green tea with her, along with the key she kept on a long chain near front door, placed it around her neck.

Marisa was so deeply engrossed in the nun's journal that she didn't notice Erin's arrival until she had removed her pareo, set her tea on the ledge next to the hot tub, and had sat next to her.

Marisa looked up and smiled.

"Boy! Am I glad to see you!"

"Anxious to know what I found out?" Erin's eyes involuntarily looked to the wine goblet.

Marisa laughed.

"Of course, but first things first. I locked myself out, and you have no idea how badly I have to pee!"

Erin chuckled and took the key and chain from her neck. She reached over and slipped it over Marisa's head. She was about to suggest that her friend take the offending goblet of wine with her, but Marisa beat her to it.

She pulled herself to the side of the hot tub, grabbed the goblet and set the journal a few feet away from the tub on top of a towel.

"I'll get myself another glass of grape juice, while I'm at it. Don't you want some?"

By the time Marisa was settled back in the hot tub, it was dusk. The cool air felt refreshing but made the warmth of the hot tub a welcome feeling.

"Okay," Marisa said, "now tell me what Brother Ziggie had to say."

"Well," Erin began, "first the German documents. They outline the terms and conditions of the endowment that went along with the estate when VonKrups left it to the nuns."

"Do the documents ever say why the old German guy left the estate to the nuns?" Marisa knew she was getting ahead of herself, but couldn't help it.

"Not directly, but his intentions were fairly clear. Remember, this was right after World War I, and the Russian Revolution."

"What does the Russian Revolution have to do with the price of tomatoes?" Marisa was confused.

Erin chortled. "Sorry, I jumped a ton of stuff. I'll get to that in a minute. But back to VonKrups: turns out that above and beyond the estate itself, he left the Sisters an endowment in the form of a trust account in Switzerland which gave them a stipend to support the school, no matter what, so long as they kept the terms and conditions of the endowment."

Marisa leaned forward, hugged her knees. Erin noticed she shivered involuntarily.

"Are you cold? We can go to the house, if you'd like..."

"Are you kidding? I'm not moving one inch until I hear the whole story! So what were the conditions?"

Erin leaned back.

"Well, everything seemed pretty straight forward at first, but then if you read between the lines, it is pretty weird. The estate must remain as a school for girls. It may never be coeducational and it must always be a boarding school. Furthermore, it must always accept politically vulnerable young women and always be run by the Sisters of St. Thomas."

"Oooookaaaay." Marisa was deep in thought. She turned to Erin.

"That is very weird, indeed, given that it hasn't been a boarding school since the mid seventies. Do you suppose that means they don't have any endowments to keep it running now?"

"Well, from what he could see in the paperwork, Ziggie said it wasn't a huge endowment, by any means. It would have been quite a bit in the 1920's and maybe up to say, World War II, but in this day and age, it would be a drop in the bucket compared to what that place actually costs to run."

"Why do you suppose they stopped boarding students here?" Marisa posed the question as much to herself as to Erin.

"Oh, that's easy: for the same reason that Sacred Heart closed down their dorms, along with most of the other Catholic boarding schools all over the country. By the early seventies and in part thanks to Pope John XXIII's Vatican II being implemented in the United States, religious vocations in women dropped by over 70 percent. The priesthood has suffered too, but religious orders for women have changed so drastically that no young woman in her right mind would want to be a nun anymore. The only way they could possibly run a boarding school like that was with thirty or forty nuns. Now they run it with three nuns, which means that there are at least twenty five or thirty salaries to pay just for the day school, and there is no way three nuns could take care of thirty or forty boarding students."

"How sadly true, but it makes sense. No nuns, no boarding school. But I can understand why no one would want to be a nun anymore. Why would anyone want to be out pounding the pavement to find a job and a place to live with no community life and no family?" She shook her head.

"Did you know I almost entered the convent?"

"I suspected as much, but you never shared."

"Well, it was hard to share something that at the time was so humiliating," Marisa giggled, "although in retrospect a hundred years later, it really was pretty funny!"

"Okay, spill it!"

"Well, when I finally mustered enough nerve, I walked into Sister Joseph Vincent's office, and announced that I wanted to enter the convent. I'll never forget it. Sister Leopold was standing on the other side of the room, ostensibly looking for a book on Sister Superior's bookshelf. Sister Joseph Vincent looked up at her, and they both broke up. Now, I'm not talking about a titter or a chuckle here, but belly laughs! Both of them! They were laughing so hard that Sister Leopold had to sit down before she fell down, and Sister Joseph Vincent was doubled over in her chair." Marisa stopped her story long enough to punch Erin in the arm in an attempt to make her stop belly laughing. "And now you're doing it! Thanks a lot, buddy of mine!"

Erin couldn't stop as she pictured the two most dignified women she had ever known, doubled over in laughter over her friends fervent and religious desire to be a nun. She straightened up, took a deep breath of air, and swiped at her tearing eyes.

"I'm sorry, but I'm getting this mental picture of the two of them, and you have to admit that it is pretty funny!"

Marisa giggled despite herself.

"Okay, I'll give you that much, and I know I would have made a lousy nun, but the point is that back then, they could pick and choose because so many of us really did want to enter the convent. Out of our class alone there were five or six, and who knows how many others like me who were, well... rejected?"

"Exactly. So now, the day school tuitions are nearly as much as boarding tuitions were back in the sixties, but with the lay salaries the nuns have to pay, the school barely breaks even. That's why all the fund raising drives."

"What about the other conditions? Won't the nuns lose the estate if it's not a boarding school?"

"No, all they lose is the endowment stipend. Apparently a bequest of this type cannot be conditional in California, so the real estate in itself isn't affected; only the endowment."

Marisa furrowed her brow in thought. "And what will become of the trust account if the nuns aren't receiving their yearly stipend?"

"I have absolutely no idea. The documents didn't address that issue, although I would imagine that the account would just grow. Back in the twenties, I don't imagine that it was even conceivable that things would change so much over the years. It would have been unthinkable!"

"I guess... but, then what else did the papers say?"

"I don't know yet; Ziggie needs a few days with them to figure that out."

"Didn't he give you an idea?"

Erin squinted.

"A pretty random one, because we didn't notice that the other documents were in Russian. Ziggie say his Russian is a bit rusty, so he'll need a few days to translate it for us."

Marisa stared at her with her mouth open.

"This is really weird, Erin. Look at my arm." The hairs on her arm were standing straight up. "The journal I'm reading is from the 1930's. From what I gather, most of the nuns' journals are buried with them as they die, except for the journals kept by the Sisters Superior. I suppose their journals form sort of a living history of the Order, so as the Superiors die, their journals are placed in the trunk of the Sister Superior who followed them. It's really quite fascinating. But here's the weird part: in this journal she mentions, two or three times, having to call Sister Thomas Marie to translate for a young Russian girl who is boarding at the school."

"Sister Thomas Marie? I am quite sure she was the Sister Superior of the whole Congregation way back in the early seventies, because I remember a trip to the Mother House that I made with the Sisters and I met her, but I don't remember her being Russian."

"She may not have been. I don't suppose being Russian is a prerequisite for speaking the language, but anyway, is that all he told you about the Russian documents?" Marisa's curiosity was getting the best of her.

"Just that there was one surname repeated throughout the lengthy document, and that was *Romanov*."

"Wow!" Marisa exclaimed. "Now that is indeed interesting!"

"Yes, I thought that might get your attention." As if on cue, Erin's stomach growled in hunger. "Aren't you hungry? My stomach is making starvation noises. That salad this morning is the only thing we've eaten."

As they pulled off Prospect Street in La Jolla toward The Cove, Marisa sighed deeply. "This just may be my favorite sight in the entire world."

"That's a lot coming from you, too. Is there anywhere in the world you haven't been?"

"Yeah, lots of places. But in all the places I have been or lived, there is simply no where in the world that gives me the same feeling."

"You may eat your words, my friend, because a lot has changed."

"What… have they added light shows to the La Jolla Caves, or diving boards at the end of The Point?" Marisa laughed, but her laughter stopped on a dime when she looked toward where her childhood summer home had once been. The quaint cluster of beach cottages had been re-placed by an art colony.

"Oh! My! God!" Marisa unlatched her seat belt and turned to stare at the elegantly upscale cluster of galleries that had replaced the beach cot-tages that her parents had owned in her youth. "If the rest of the Cove area has changed this much, then don't even bother to park the car. I don't think I can take it."

"Once we get down the grade, I think you'll like what you see. The res-taurant we're going to is in one of the little cottages across from the Cove. They managed to keep the charm of the old place while bringing it up to code as a restaurant. The food is fantastic."

"Don't we need a reservation?" Marisa was ravenously hungry, the idea of waiting for a table did not appeal to her.

"No, it shouldn't be a problem. The manager is a student of mine."

"A Jesuit seminarian working as a maitre'd?" Marisa giggled. "I mean, I hear the Church is into having the clergy mesh into society, but that's ridiculous!"

"Not all students in a Jesuit university are seminarians, Marisa. I knew you were living in a different country for thirty years, but I hadn't realized you were on a different planet. We have even had women students since 1980 when they closed the College for Women."

"Hey, I went to a Jesuit university, if you'll remember, but of course that was a hundred years ago. I just assumed there were no lay students because you always refer to the university as the seminary."

"Force of habit, I suppose. But no, we have all kinds of students, including some of those of the female gender who take great relish in flirting unabashedly with the seminarians. They run contests with a complicated scoring system that grades the response achieved in the seminarians."

"But of course! Ah, but if you can get one visibly hard you are an instant winner and your classmates have to take you out to dinner. It was great fun!"

Erin laughed despite her years of experience on the administrative side of the disciplinary coin, and shook her head again, smiling. She had to circle a couple of times before finding a space to park, but finally pulled into an empty spot right in front of the Ellen Browning Scripps Park, adjacent to the Cove and Boomer Beaches, where Marisa had played as a child. As she pulled herself out of the car she smiled widely and breathed in the salty sea air.

"This hasn't changed a bit! It even smells the same." Marisa took another deep breath and then turned toward the other side of the street. "Except that I smell something very, very good coming from that direction!" She pointed to the little cottage restaurant that Erin had described.

"Is that where we're going?"

Erin laughed. "Yes. Just follow your nose."

As they entered the quaint cottage overlooking the jutting cliffs, soft beige sands and shore break of The Cove, an extremely tall, deeply tanned young man with jet-black hair and huge blue eyes approached them.

"*Professor*," he greeted Erin. "How is my favorite mentor?" he leaned down to kiss Erin's cheek. "Let me find you the table with the best view.... would you like to dine inside or out on the terrace?"

Erin turned to Marisa, who was feeling like a midget next to them. "Where would you like to sit, Marisa?" Then as an afterthought, she introduced her student to Marisa. "Marisa, I'd like you to meet one of the most promising young theologians I have had the privilege to teach over the years, Pablo Santamaría."

Marisa held her hand out, and Pablo squeezed it. "It's very nice to meet you," she said, and Pablo returned the greeting. "I think it would be nice to sit outside, as long as there are no uninvited guests like gnats or ants?"

Pablo laughed. "I promise you that there are no such guests allowed on the premises, Madame."

"Marisa, please. You make me feel old. Madame sounds intriguingly interesting, but old."

Pablo laughed, led them out to a wide terrace furnished with glass and rattan tables and chairs, much as one would decorate a patio or terrace at home. There were potted plants strategically placed in such a way that each table was afforded the utmost of privacy.

He pulled out a chair for Erin, then circled the table to assist Marisa into her seat before she could sit on her own. He placed menus before them, offering them a drink.

"Should I bring a bottle of your favorite Chardonnay?" he asked Erin, and she nodded.

The young man disappeared into the restaurant.

Marisa let out a slow whistle. "Now that is one gorgeous specimen of the male gender. Are all your students like him?"

"Geesh, Marisa. He's a baby! He's younger than my son, for Chrissake!"

"That has absolutely nothing to do with anything. I only remarked that he is absolutely yummy."

Erin smiled. Her friend had never had children, so the concept was probably beyond her comprehension; she certainly was not going to make an issue of it.

"Yes, he is a nice looking kid, isn't he?"

"Oh, yes, indeed." Marisa's eyes opened widely as if she were seeing something only she could see. "Do you remember Arturo? You may have met him at our prom."

"Vaguely, but I think I only saw him a couple of times. Why?"

"Oh, nothing, except that your Pablo looks a lot like a slightly older Arturo. He was one hunk, but unfortunately, he turned out to be a jerk!"

Erin was not amused. "He is not *my* Pablo; he just used to be a student of mine. I'm currently his co-faculty mentor on this doctoral thesis."

Pablo returned with a tray holding a bottle of wine in a silver ice bucket, which he placed on a corner of the table.

"We'll let this breathe a few minutes, and then your waiter will serve it." He poured ice water into their water glasses and placed a bread basket in the middle of the table. "I took the liberty of bringing you a basket of freshly baked breads and a few spreads." He placed a small bowl of cream cheese and salmon pieces on the table, another vegetable and cheese spread, and yet another garlic and herb butter spread. "Your waiter will be over to take your orders shortly." He silently disappeared.

Marisa tried a bit of the vegetable cheese spread on a piece of rye bread, and sighed in pleasure. "Now this is good." She looked over the menu. "I know I want some sort of seafood, but I don't know what."

"The Moroccan Halibut is fabulous, and they serve it over a nice, crispy salad. That's what I usually order," Erin suggested.

"Sounds perfect."

After thoroughly enjoying the halibut, the women were chatting over a shared dessert of chocolate mousse with fresh berries, when Marisa suddenly shook, visibly.

"It's just so good you can't stand it?" Erin asked sarcastically, but her mocking turned serious when she saw the look on Marisa's face. "What is it? You look as if you'd seen a ghost."

"I did." Marisa was perfectly serious and seemed almost frightened. "The image of my brother just popped into my mind, smiling at me."

"Mauricio?" Erin stared at the empty railing. "Where is he now?"

Marisa smiled sadly, realizing that she hadn't told her old friend about her brother.

"I suppose he lives anywhere he wants, now." Her eyes glistened with tears. "He died five years ago, Erin. He only appears in my mind like that when something important is going on."

"Oh, my God! I didn't know, rest his soul." She leaned forward over the table. "Maybe he's glad you're home." Erin's voice was gentle. "I know I am."

"Yeah, me too. Sorry it took me so long."

"I have always believed that there is a reason for everything that happens to us in life," she said as she motioned to their waiter. He approached their table silently, with his order pad in hand. "I'd like a cordial, if you would... maybe a Kahlua?" She turned to Marisa. "Is that okay with you? Or do you prefer something else?"

"No, that would be nice."

The waiter disappeared and Erin continued. "You and I have been back in touch for over three years, but you were never able to make it out here before now, so now must be when you were supposed to be here. I would never have had the nerve to sneak into the convent basement and catacombs alone, but with you here, I could."

"Yes, but you have always said that I was just an adventure looking for a place to happen... nothing new there!"

"Sure there is, and I don't believe we just happened to stumble upon a mystery. I think that if we have found something, it is because it is something that needed to be found." Erin took a long drink of the Kahlua that the waiter had placed on their table, but not before clinking it against Marisa's glass. "It has nothing to do with chance or coincidence."

"Then, what?" Ever curious, Marisa always enjoyed the travels in her friends mind; she found them absolutely fascinating.

"Timing, Marisa, timing." Erin closed her eyes, then she opened them. "Haven't you ever noticed how every time a cataclysmic or calamitous event occurs in history, there are always sort of parallel discoveries and revelations surrounding the actual event?"

Marisa was only following half of the train of thought.

"Like a serendipitous, synchronous discovery of a new element or a new planet by many people?"

"Sort of," Erin said, "but not really. It's like many extraordinary discoveries have to be found first, but they only lead up to some incredible fact until then only a bizarre or supernatural theory being exposed as absolute truth. Something that has always been there, but never recognized or accepted as truth."

Marisa's eyes brightened. "Like the theory of tectonic plates that was never accepted as scientifically true until the mid eighties, when it was scientifically proven in seven countries at the same time?"

"Yes, something like that."

Marisa was intrigued. "So you think that the discoveries were making are sort of a prelude to an important historical discovery?"

"I am quite sure of it. Don't ask me why, but I am."

"Do you think Ziggie might have some more of the documents translated by now?" Marisa drank the last of her Kahlua, motioned toward the waiter to bring another round.

Erin smiled. "Be patient. Besides, I made quick photocopies of everything I left with him. So, how about our finishing up our drinks, and going back to the house to study the papers? I think I am buzzed enough after that bottle of wine and half bottle of Kahlua that I can probably read Chinese by now, and you're a few sheets to the wind yourself! You're always scathingly brilliant when you're slightly smashed, so what do you say?"

After splitting the rather pricey check and leaving a handsome tip, the women rose from their seats and headed for the small gate in the picket fence dividing the dining area from the outside bar.

Erin's student watched the women from inside the dining room door. He quickly removed his apron, and called out to one of the busboys:

"Here!" He tossed his car keys to the younger man. "I'm going to drive my professor home. Follow me in my car, will you?"

The young man nodded and ran toward the back door that would lead to the employee parking lot. It was readily apparent that he knew the drill.

Before the slightly weaving women could descend the first step, Pablo had placed himself solidly between them, hooking his arm through theirs. He breathed the salty ocean air deeply.

"Isn't it a glorious evening, ladies?"

Erin smiled, only too aware of the fact that her student was taking care of her. She wasn't very sure that she particularly wanted to be taken care of, but what the hell? She also wasn't particularly anxious to drive.

"I'm quite all right to drive, Pablo, but I am always appreciative of a nice young man's chivalrous attentions, aren't you, Marisa?"

Marisa grinned mischievously. "You have no idea!"

Marisa enjoyed the aroma of the freshly brewed coffee as she gazed through the breakfast nook window, observing Pablo as he boarded the taxi he'd called minutes earlier.

The sunrise had been a magnificent sight from their makeshift nest on the pool terrace next to the hot tub. As the first rays of the sun sending prisms of color through the wispy clouds of the dawning sky had awakened her, she'd nudged a peacefully sleeping Pablo to consciousness. They had watched the sunrise in silence before Pablo had silently dressed to walk Marisa to her friend's door before taking his leave.

Good Lord, Marisa, she thought, *you have finally lost the very last rem-*

nants of sanity you had! She chided herself severely.

She had no intention of allowing herself the luxury of any justification whatsoever, but at the same time she assured herself nothing truly compromising had really happened between them. She tried to convince herself that it was because she was morally above such a thing, while the truth of the matter was that if it hadn't been for the fact that they had been basically in plain sight of anyone who happened to be looking toward the pool area from an upper-story window, something most definitely would have happened.

She wasn't sure who inspired the deepest feelings of guilt in her: Carlos? After all, she loved her husband more than life itself. How could she spend an entire night opening her heart to another man? How could she share a painfully sweet, romantic interlude with someone a third her husband's age, and half her age? But then the memory of Carlos brief affair with one of his graduate students a few years earlier invaded her very being, and she realized that she needed no further justification. Her moment with Pablo had nothing to do with Carlos, just as Carlos had insisted that his brief affair had had nothing whatsoever to do with her. No, Carlos wasn't a problem.

Erin? She could feel herself heating in shame. The more she thought about her moment with Erin's student, the guiltier she felt. Erin's words at the dinner table were haunting her: *He's a baby! He's younger than my son, for Chrissake!*

No, she had far too much respect for Erin to share this latest event with her. Besides, Erin would feel somehow responsible for leaving a very tipsy friend with her irresistibly gorgeous student, and it certainly was not Erin's fault. She had simply fallen asleep in the car on the way home from the restaurant, so Marisa and Pablo had helped her up to her room where she cuddled down in her comforter and had slept for the rest of the night.

The overpowering attraction that Marisa had felt for Erin's young friend was also not Erin's fault.

It had seemed perfectly natural to invite Pablo for a nightcap after he had so attentively driven the women home; an invitation he had accepted almost gleefully. He'd excused himself briefly, only to return moments later to announce that he had sent his employee back to the restaurant to help with closing. He said he would take a cab later to pick up his car.

They had sat in Erin's living room talking about philosophy, religion, politics, and every other subject on the list of taboos in normal social situations. But Pablo was anything but intellectually boring. Marisa soon understood why Erin had referred to him in such glowing terms; something she very seldom did. He had a depth of understanding rare in people twice his age, and a knowledge base which would inspire envy in the most hallowed halls of academia.

His maturity in intellectual matters was exceeded only by his transparency in matters of the heart. Before long, he had recounted a painful separation from a live-in girlfriend of five years, wistfully insisting that they would still have been together if she'd only had the maturity of a woman like Marisa (he'd said as he'd gently run his finger up and down Marisa's arm).

She had found it rather endearing and cute at first, but two drinks later and by the time they had decided to adjourn to the hot tub to allow Erin to sleep in a silent house; Marisa was falling for the whole story. hook, line and sinker.

She could hear movement coming from Erin's room and immediately tried to hide her guilt lest Erin guess the truth. She put Pablo out of her mind and breathed deeply.

"Good morning." The hoarse and throaty voice coming from the hallway evinced a devastating hangover even before Erin's disheveled appearance graced the room. "I hope that is coffee I smell?"

Marisa quickly rose from her chair, served a piping hot mug of the life-reviving liquid and placed it on the table just as Erin was collapsing into the chair.

Placing her hands on her temples with her elbows to each side of the mug, Erin lowered her head toward the mug and breathed in the vapors emanating from the cup.

"Aaaah," she said. "Life resumes."

She lowered her left hand to her chin to rest her head while she lifted the mug to her lips with her right hand. She took a sip of the hot liquid, then lowered the mug to the table and closed her eyes, smiling. "There is nothing quite as good as coffee. It was brought to earth by the hangover gods. I am quite sure of this."

Marisa giggled, wondered why she wasn't hung over. She had consumed considerably more alcohol than her friend, and yet, she felt fine. On the other hand, she had probably only slept a matter of minutes before the rising sun had awakened her. She was quite likely still affected by the alcohol and would probably have the hangover of her life if she were to sleep for any length of time.

Marisa's thoughts returned to Pablo, and her earlier feelings of guilt invaded her entire being.

Even in her hung over state, Erin noticed.

"You look like the cat that ate the proverbial canary. Are you still gloating over our escapade into the convent, or is it something else?"

"Something else?" Marisa asked innocently. "Like what?" She looked down, and consciously feigned innocence. Her guilty feelings were beginning to make her mad.

"Oh, my!" Erin eyes opened widely now. "Don't get offended! I'm only kidding. After all, you were the one to start the kidding about Pablo being so yummy."

Marisa laughed, but out of relief. Erin didn't suspect anything at all.

"Sorry, but I was so wound up that I didn't get much sleep. I don't think I slept more than an hour. And as far as Pablo being yummy, I was just kidding. He is young enough to be my son!" she said sternly.

Erin's expression became serious.

"I barely remember you and Pablo tucking me in." She took another sip of her coffee, gently swished it around in her mouth before swallowing it. "You have no idea how embarrassed I am. I don't know if I can ever face

Pablo again."

"Don't be silly," Marisa assured her, thinking to herself that Erin had no concept of the true definition of embarrassment. She, however, most certainly did. "Pablo is a graduate student. Any self-respecting graduate student worth his weight in salt is highly experienced in the art of pouring a friend into bed."

"That's just the problem. I'm not his friend. I'm his professor."

And I'm the dirty old lady who allowed herself to be nearly ravished by your precocious young stud, uh, student! Marisa thought to herself while she cooed a kind platitude. "Hey, don't worry about it. He even stayed for a nightcap, while we discussed a myriad of subjects. He was not freaked out at all."

Erin looked up at Marisa. She arched an eyebrow, but Marisa didn't react.

Obviously, everything was all right in her world.

Marisa heaved an indiscernible sigh of relief.

Chapter Five

Erin could not help but feel a touch of compassion at the look of misery on Marisa's face as she slowly moved into the kitchen after her nap. "Ahh, Girlfriend! I know exactly how you feel. Trust me when I say it will pass."

Marisa found it hurt to even breathe. The slightest movement caused waves of nausea to wash over her. Her insides felt worse than when she'd had food poisoning. Her head was throbbing and, with each step, she prayed it would not explode. "Please remind me never to do this again. A delayed hangover is by far the worst."

"Certainly." Erin set some aspirin and a Vitamin B Complex on the table next to a glass of water. "These will help some, but it will still have to run its course."

"So how come you're not suffering?" Marisa squinted up at her. Even the light coming through the kitchen windows felt like a knife piercing her skull. "If I hadn't seen you this morning I would never know you had been hung over."

Erin poured herself a glass of iced tea and joined Marisa at the table. "Basic chemistry. We both drank the same amount, but I have more body mass than you do. This allows me to metabolize the alcohol faster. I'm not back to a hundred percent yet, but I feel much better than I did earlier. I took a hot shower after you went to bed."

Marisa winced. Erin didn't know that she'd had several more drinks with Pablo, after their return home. Heaven only knew how long it would take for her system to recover. She popped three aspirin and the vitamin into her mouth and drank half glass of water, praying they would stay down. "I owe several people an apology. I never had a hangover while I was in college and was less than sympathetic to those who did."

"Neither of us is as young as we were then." Erin sipped her ice tea and smiled ruefully.

"Apparently, we're not old enough to know better." Marisa rested her head in her hands. "Yuck! My mouth tastes like an army crept in, camped and crept out again. Do you have any mouthwash?"

"On the counter in the bathroom."

"Ooh, too far away. Maybe in a little while. I don't want to move right now. I'm still not too sure if the aspirin and vitamin are going to make things better or worse." She couldn't remember when she had ever felt like this. She was being punished, that's what it was: punishment for allowing her libido to override her better judgment.

"You need to eat something." Erin rose from the table and went to the refrigerator. "It will help settle your stomach."

"Don't bother. The last thing I want to do now is eat."

Erin was surprised that Marisa was suffering so. Chemistry aside, maybe Marisa was coming down with something over and above a hangover. She moved next to her friend and placed her hand on her forehead. "Hmm."

"Hmm, what?" Erin's cool touch felt wonderful.

"I'm checking to see if you might be feverish. You could be coming down with a bug. No fever." She paused thoughtfully. "I really think you should try eating something, it might help." Erin removed her hand and sat back down.

"Thank you for caring." Marisa sighed. "You might be right. I guess I could try some iced tea and maybe some toast." She knew she had to agree to eat something so Erin would not feel so compelled to mother her.

Forty-five minutes later, after eating two pieces of toast, drinking a full glass of iced tea with lemon and sugar, Marisa began to think she might live.

"You look much better." Erin nodded. "How are you feeling?"

"Well enough to take a hot shower and put on some clean clothes."

"That's odd." A puzzled look came over Erin's face as a whirring sound came from the back bedroom, where she had set up her office. "Someone is sending me a fax."

"And that's odd? You are a professor. Surely your students send things to you."

"Not during semester breaks or summer." Erin rose to go to her office.

"I'll let you handle it while I take that shower."

Marisa went to her room to gather her cleansers and lotions. She could remember a time when a bar of soap and a towel was all she needed. Those days were long past. She couldn't remember the last time she'd used a bar of soap to bathe.

When she was done and felt clean, refreshed, and almost human, Marisa returned to the kitchen to the sound of the phone ringing.

Erin answered it. "Ziggie? Yes. I have the fax right here. It came in a short while ago. Yes, I'm listening." She paused. "Ziggie, why are you whispering? Is something wrong?" A stricken look came over her face. "This isn't like you. Why are you being so mysterious?"

Marisa moved to stand at Erin's side. "Is there a problem?" She mouthed to Erin.

Erin held up her hand for Marisa to wait. "You want me to promise? Promise what?" Erin reached out and grabbed Marisa's hand and squeezed it. "Ziggie, calm down. Yes, I understand it is important. Okay, okay, I promise. Marisa promises as well."

She held the receiver out, a look of disbelief on her face. "He hung up."

"Tell me everything he said." Marisa led her to a chair at the table and made her sit down. "Don't leave out a thing."

"He said he had almost finished the Russian translations, and what he'd learned could put us all in danger. The fax he sent is a chronological list of the Mothers Superior at the school. It is paramount we find all their journals." Erin took a shaky breath. "He sounded frightened, Marisa."

"Did he say what it was that he'd learned? Or why it is so important we find the journals?"

"No." Erin shook her head. "Then he made me promise."

"What exactly did he make you promise?"

"That neither of us would tell anyone, and he stressed the word, any-one, under any circumstances that I was the source of the documents he'd been translating." Erin was pale and wringing her hands.

"Obviously he found something in those documents he felt presented a danger to us." Marisa thought out loud. "But what kind of danger? Damn! I wish he had been more specific! It would help to know where the danger is coming from. As it stands now we can't afford to trust any-one."

"Why did he hang up like that?" Erin was practically in tears. "He's never hung up on me before. He sounded so strange, not like my Ziggie at all."

"I don't know why he hung up on you, dear. Maybe someone came into his office and he couldn't talk any longer." Marisa tried not to frighten Erin any further and refrained from commenting about him be-ing "her" Ziggie. "Why don't we take a closer look at the fax he sent? Maybe it will give us some idea as to what he might have found."

"It is on the counter." Erin pointed to a small stack of papers near the sink.

Marisa gathered them together and brought them back to the table, where she sat down, scanning the top sheet. "This is a list of nuns' names and a series of dates following each name."

Erin had used the time to regain her composure though her voice was shaky. "Ziggie said it was a list of all the Mothers Superior."

Marisa flipped through the pages to the last sheet. "That's all there is. He didn't include any explanation or directions."

"We are supposed to locate their journals. He didn't say why, only that it was important that we did." She reached over and took the top sheet to read. "The earliest date on this page is nineteen-eighteen. What's the final date on the last page?"

Marisa glanced down to the last name. "Sister Barbara O'Shea nineteen-ninety-five to present. It still doesn't feel right to me when they use their birth names instead of religious names."

"I know what you mean." Erin nodded. "Another less than palatable result of Vatican II. What about the name above that one?"

"Sister Thomas Marie, nineteen-seventy-one to nineteen-ninety-four." Marisa felt the hairs on her arms stand up. "Didn't you say she was the Congregation's Mother Superior when you visited the Mother House? Why would she be at a school instead of at the Mother House? This doesn't make any sense."

Erin couldn't help but glance over at the phone, willing it to ring. "What were her dates again?"

"Nineteen-seventy-one to nineteen-ninety-four." Marisa leaned forward in her seat.

"Seventy-One? That was during the implementation of Vatican II." Erin frowned. "Remember, convent life was experiencing a radical transformation during the seventies and eighties. It does seem odd that she would be at a school, not overseeing the changes at the Mother House."

"Exactly!" Marisa nodded. "And why was she there so long? Twenty-three years seems unusually long. Isn't the usual posting six to ten years at the most?"

"Normally, it is. But with Vatican II everything was in transition. What was normal before, no longer applied. Once the new rules were implemented and community life was restricted to only a few congregations, vocations began to plummet." Erin paused. "Maybe she saw this coming and it was her bolt hole to avoid having to face some of the new realities of convent life."

"Being the head of the order, she had to know." Marisa frowned. It still didn't feel right to her. "I guess she could have overseen things from the school as well as the Mother House."

"You don't buy it, do you?" Erin could hear the doubt in Marisa's voice.

"Not entirely." Marisa shook her head. "Granted, the changes didn't happen overnight, but it certainly didn't take twenty-three years. And where is she now? Did she die? Is she alive and in retirement somewhere? I can't shake the feeling there is more to her than meets the eye."

"Let's face it." Erin chewed her lower lip. "This list by itself isn't enough. Without more information we are only guessing. We can't know anything with certainty other than who was Mother Superior. Ziggie is the only one who can give us more information." She reached over and picked up the phone. She pressed a button, which told Marisa that Ziggie was on Erin's speed dial.

"Hang up. Now." Marisa said sharply.

Erin reflexively ended the call. "Why did you make me do that?"

"I know you are worried about him, dear, but he had to have had a good reason for hanging up on you as he did. Give him the afternoon to get back in touch. If he hasn't called by early evening we'll go over there to check things out." Marisa tried to reason with her.

"I am over reacting, aren't I?" Erin laughed self-consciously. "His hanging up on me like that was so out of character." Erin nervously fingered the phone.

"But, of course it was." Marisa smiled. "None of us expect a friend to cut us off like that. Why don't we take a break, go sit out on the patio for a while?"

They had barely settled in the lounges with a fresh pitcher of ice tea on the table between them when the peaceful air was rent with the screeching harshness of Grunge Metal rock music blasting from the unit below Erin's.

Marisa jerked upward in her seat with her hands over her ears. "What the hell is that?" She had to practically scream at Erin to be heard. The only time she had ever heard anything as painfully loud had been during an assignment to a Heavy Metal Rock Concert in Mexico City. She had threatened to quit if her editor ever assigned her to anything like that again.

"It's my neighbor's hobby to torture me whenever possible." Erin shouted back at her. She rose from her seat and stormed back inside, returned a few moments later with a portable tape recorder and phone.

"You're going to record that noise?" Marisa was stunned. She sat in disbelief as Erin moved to the end of the patio and dangled the recorder by its strap over the iron railing. She let it hang there for close to a full minute; she punched a button on the phone and held it over the railing with her free hand.

The lounge chairs began vibrating and the iced tea nearly spilled out of the pitcher, the booming decibels filling the air. Marisa moved next to Erin and peered over the railing. Four speakers as large as the ones she remembered from Mexico City were positioned to point directly up toward Erin's unit. She glanced over at the units on either side of Erin's. The patio to the left was empty, but Marisa could see a woman with a screaming baby in her arms was at the patio door, a phone pressed to her ear. In the unit on the right an older man, his face red with anger, was glaring downward with a phone held over his railing.

As suddenly as it had started the music stopped. Its echoes could be heard throughout the complex, overlaid with the sound of raucous laughter from the unit below.

"How long has this been going on?" Marisa looked over at Erin.

"Three months now," Erin said through gritted teeth, "at all hours of the day and night."

"How'd you like that you old bitch!" A whisky roughened voice screamed up at them. "I know you're calling the Noise Police. Go ahead! It's before any of their damn curfews. There ain't a damn thing you can do about it."

"Oh my God!" Marisa gasped. "Has it been like this the entire time?"

Erin moved from the railing and sat back in her lounge chair. "He's only become verbally abusive since he was busted for marijuana and cocaine when someone called the police to report the unruliness of a party. Dan is convinced that I'm the one who called."

"Did you?"

"I wasn't even home that night." Erin took a sip of her ice tea.

"Why isn't he in jail? If he was busted for drugs, he should be."

"He has a high-price lawyer, and is out on bail until his trial. His trial date isn't for another six months."

"Six months! Why so long?"

"From what I've been told by other residents, his lawyer had him plead not-guilty in the arraignment. There's a backlog for jury trials on drug charges." Erin rolled her eyes. "The legal counsel for the complex's association has advised all of us not to confront him, but to document it whenever he does something like this. They've tried to censure him on more than one occasion for violation of association regulations, but his lawyer filed a court challenge against the association for infringement of his civil rights and harassment."

"What about the rights of the people he has harassed?" Marisa often wondered if the judicial system had become so overburdened with the letter of the law that it had lost touch with reality. Too often it favored the criminal.

"It is in the hands of the courts." Erin shrugged with a fatalistic attitude. "Our hands are tied: he can't be evicted because he is an owner. The charges against him are just shy of being serious enough to make the Feds use their zero tolerance policy to confiscate all his assets. So, we wait, endure, document his actions, and pray for the mercy of the court to send him away for a very long time."

"You'd mentioned you'd been having a few problems with a neighbor. I thought it was something minor, not anything like this. I've been here for a few days now, but this is first time anything like this has happened."

"He was most likely out-of-town checking on his tenants." Erin ran her hand through her hair. "Or he was here and passed out."

"Tenants? You mean he has tenants?"

"Oh yes. Believe it or not, he owns several apartment complexes up north. From what I hear he has no qualms about evicting anyone if there is the slightest hint of drug or alcohol abuse."

"I see! A classic case of do as I say, not as I do. Out of curiosity, who did you call?"

"The Noise Abatement Department."

"The ones he calls the Noise Police? Will they do anything?"

"Eventually." Erin leaned towards her and lowered her voice. "There have been so many complaints called in from the complex that the department finally gave us a special number to call. They are building a case against him for charges as a public nuisance and chronic disturbing the peace."

"Aren't those only misdemeanors?" Marisa matched her voice level to Erin's.

"On their own, yes. But, if coupled with the drug charges he's facing, it can't help but influence a jury,"

"I see." Marisa grinned. "Give him enough rope and he might just hang himself."

"One can only hope." Erin sighed.

Evening drew near without a call from Ziggie. Marisa knew they would be going to the Seminary. "Before we go, we need a plan."

"A plan? What's to plan? We go to his office to see if he's there." She had little patience for Marisa's plan.

"Erin, believe me, I understand how you feel, I really do. Yet we can't let our concern for him override the need for caution. Remember, we haven't a clue whom we can trust, so we can't trust anyone. You are a known associate of Ziggie's; a fact that alone will have the wrong people suspicious of you."

Erin knew Marisa was right, but that didn't mean she had to like it. "Why did you have to pick now to be logical?" She heaved a heavy sigh. "How am I supposed to check on him, if I'm already under suspicion?"

Marisa eyed Erin critically for a few seconds before shaking her head. "Wouldn't work."

"Don't do that!" Erin ran her hand through her hair in exasperation. "You'd better explain why you were eying me as though I'm a specimen on a slide and then saying something cryptic like that."

"I was just thinking that if we were men, we could dress in drag." Marisa grinned. "Then I considered our dressing like men, but it wouldn't work either way."

"Drag? Dressing like men?" Erin rolled her eyes in disgust. "If that's the best you can come up with, I say the hell with a plan and we leave now."

"Down girl!" Marisa reached over and laid her hand over one of Erin's. "It was a dumb idea. that's why I said what I did. Give me a minute to think before you jump in your car and rush headlong into the unknown."

"You have one minute." Erin tapped her fingers on the table. "And counting."

"We have to stay below the radar. So, we can't be obvious. We'll need to sneak up on what we need to find out, but do it in plain sight." Marisa held up her hand before Erin could interrupt her. "We pretend we are there for a totally different reason."

"Thirty seconds." Erin had yet to hear anything that sounded like a sensible plan to her.

"We pretend I'm a visiting friend to whom you are giving a tour of the campus. We stop and talk to a few students; you show me the main attractions and landmarks. This way, it will look perfectly innocent to anyone watching for someone, as well as take us up to Ziggie's area."

"Finally, something that might work! If we do this, we can only speak Spanish. It will keep things believable."

"We can't seem to be in a hurry and, should we be unable to find him, we have to show no more than casual regret he wasn't available because you had wanted him to meet your friend. Can you do that?"

"I'll do whatever I have to." Erin stood up and gave Marisa a critical eye. "You need to change. Shorts and a halter top are not the way to dress, if you don't want to be noticed."

Erin pulled into the faculty lot and parked in her usual spot. "Are you ready for this?" she asked Marisa in Spanish.

"*Sí.*" Marisa grinned as she got out of the car and randomly pointed at one of the ornate Spanish Colonial buildings nearby, asking Erin in Spanish what it was.

Erin replied in Spanish that it was the library. The anxiety level in her voice was so obvious that Marisa knew anyone they ran into would wonder what was wrong with her.

"Girlfriend!" Marisa softly hissed in Spanish. "Get a grip! You're broadcasting."

"Sorry."

"It's okay." Marisa encouraged her. She locked her arm with Erin's and let her lead them onto the sidewalk in front of the car. "Pretend we are having a good time. You're showing off the campus to your *turista* friend." They casually strolled passed the library. "What a lovely garden!" She said in Spanish, waving her free hand at the gardens up ahead.

They had spent an hour looking at all the buildings and gardens before they were approached by anyone. Marisa was taking a picture of Erin in front of the reflecting pond when she saw a young man and a priest coming toward them from the nearby building where Ziggie's office was located.

"Come here." She moved up to Erin when the two men reached them.

"Good afternoon, ladies." The priest's eyes widened in recognition of Erin. "Professor, I didn't realize it was you. What brings you to work on an evening like this?"

"Father Holtz," Erin smiled and nodded. "A dear friend of mine is in town visiting and badgered me into bringing her to see the campus. Otherwise, I would be at home sipping lemonade on my terrace."

"I take it, this is your friend?" Father Holtz waited for Marisa to say something.

"I'm sorry, Father." Erin stepped in. "Maria speaks only Spanish." She turned to Marisa and introduced the priest.

"*Mucho gusto.*" Marisa smiled shyly.

Father Holtz did not introduce the young man at his side, but began asking Erin questions about her plans for the coming term. Marisa knew he was stalling them, as though he didn't want them in the building.

Erin fielded a few questions before asking him to excuse them, as they still had things to see, and a dinner reservation in less than an hour.

"Oh, I'm so sorry. I didn't mean to hold you up." The priest turned towards Marisa. "It was a pleasure to meet you, Maria. I hope you enjoy you visit here in town."

Marisa smiled politely, looked towards Erin to translate what he had said, before replying, "*Gracias, Padre.*"

Erin linked her arm through Erin's to move them along toward the stairs leading to Ziggie's building. She didn't want to linger any longer than necessary. She instinctively did not trust Father Holtz.

Sticking to their roles of guide and tourist, Erin stopped them just outside the building to describe its architectural elements, snapping a picture of Marisa standing next to one of the statues at the entrance.

Marisa waved at the priest and young man, who had not moved, then followed Erin inside. "That man gave me the creeps!" she whispered to Erin as they walked slowly pretending to view the murals on the walls leading to the staircase and upper floors, "and, who was the kid?"

"Shh!" Erin shook her head slightly. She knew how sound carried in the vaulted room. "Do you want to see upstairs?" She asked Marisa in Spanish. Marisa nodded, followed her to the staircase.

They took their time exploring the upper floor. Erin peeked into several offices, greeting any of the brothers working there. It took them a good ten minutes before they stood before the closed door to Ziggie's office.

"I don't like this," Erin whispered to Marisa. "His door is never closed."

"Try the doorknob," Marisa whispered back as she casually glanced around to see if they were being watched.

Erin took a firm grip on the knob and turned it, only to find the door was locked. She couldn't suppress a gasp of shock. Marisa quickly faked a loud sneeze to cover the sound.

"We need to leave here now!" Marisa pulled Erin away from the door and practically forced her to move on to the next and last office on the floor. "Smile and walk slowly, but steadily, to the stairs."

Neither of them said a word until they were back in the car. Erin's hands trembled as she gripped the steering wheel and started the engine.

"It is very bad, Marisa."

"Yes, I know. Now get us out of here."

"No, you don't know." Erin lifted the hand that had gripped the door-knob and showed it to Marisa. It was streaked with blood.

Chapter Six

"Damn!" Erin slammed the phone down just as Marisa was coming out of the bathroom after a long shower.

"What's wrong?" Marisa stepped around Erin to enter her room, put her toiletries down in her bag. "Were you put on eternal hold, or what?"

"No, I was trying to call Ziggie, and he is still nowhere to be found."

Marisa furrowed her brow. "Be careful, Erin. He said not to let anyone even suspect that you had any knowledge of those documents. If you keep calling around, someone could get suspicious."

"Yeah, but this is too weird! Ziggie is one of those people that you can always locate. He seldom if ever goes out, and he always leaves an updated message on his answering machine in case a student needs him. Then, there was the blood..." Erin was very concerned and it was beginning to rub off on Marisa.

"Erin, I told you last night that the blood on the doorknob was enough to call the police, and you were the one to refuse. I mean, I understand that your job is involved here, Erin, but isn't friendship first?" Erin was staring into space, sadly shaking her head. Marisa stepped forward, her hair still wrapped in a towel, she picked up the phone. "At least let it be me who makes the next call. Give me the name of a student, and I'll call on behalf of that student."

Erin looked relieved. "Okay, try Judith. Judith Blainey. She's a graduate student, and your voices have the same general ring to them." Erin took the phone, dialed a number, then handed it back to Marisa.

It rang a number of times, but was finally answered by a deep voice. Marisa mustered the most cheerful of voices possible. "Good morning, is Brother Ziggie available?" She saw Erin wince, mouthed a silent "What?"

to her.

Erin was quickly writing on a note pad: "To students it's Brother Zigfried!"

The voice on the other end of the phone had not yet answered, so Marisa asked again. "Yes, excuse me, but is Brother Zigfried available? This is Judith Blainey calling."

The voice finally answered. "Yes, Judy. This is Father Gregory. May I help you with something? Brother Zigfried is not available right now."

This caught Marisa off guard, and she hesitated much too long before answering.

"No, Father Gregory, that's all right. It was nothing very important. It can wait until I see him, but thank you, anyway."

The monk's voice seemed rather severe, but he wished her a good day before hanging up.

"What did he say?"

Marisa returned the phone to its base, her brow deeply furrowed. "I am not sure he believed I was Judy."

"He called you Judy?" Erin's voice was trembling slightly.

"Yes. Why?"

"Because if he called you Judy and you answered to the name, then there is absolutely no doubt about it: he definitely knows that you were not Judith. You see, no one in the world calls her Judy. She only answers to Judith; the name 'Judy' offends her."

"Then I blew it, big time." Marisa walked to the living room and sank down into the couch, looked up questioningly at Erin. "Now what?"

Erin sat down in a lounge chair on the other side of the room, looked out toward the pool area. "Now we do exactly what Ziggie told me to do."

"As in finding the journals for all those sisters superior?" Marisa's eyes sparkled.

"Partly, but first, we have to play it very low key. Father Gregory may have suspected something already, so we can't take any chances. But yes, I think we had better start thinking about when and how to get into that basement again. We'll just take Ziggie's list and find each superior's journal." Erin was almost thinking out loud, speaking so quietly that Marisa had to strain to hear her.

Marisa realized that Erin was much too upset over Ziggie, which meant she would have to help a lot more than she had up to now. She stood up and walked over to the sliding glass door behind Erin's lounge. Gazing out the window, she put a comforting hand on Erin's shoulder.

"Look, we're probably getting all worked up over nothing. The man is probably getting his annual physical, or went to the dentist or something, and here we are thinking all sorts of terrible things."

Erin smiled unconvincingly.

"You're probably right, but I can't help it. I am just an old worrier."

Suddenly, she sprung to her feet and rushed to the phone again. She dialed a number and waited impatiently for an answer. Marisa was intrigued, but sat down again.

She was far more intrigued when she heard Erin asking for Pablo Santamaría. "Pablo?" she heard Erin say. "I'm fine, dear, thank you."

How very motherly she sounds, Marisa thought.

"Listen, Pablo, I need to talk to you about something, but not by phone. Mondays are usually pretty slow at the restaurant, aren't they?" There was a short pause. "If Marisa and I came over for brunch, would you have time to sit and talk for a while?" There was a longer pause, and Marisa saw Erin smile. "Good! Then we'll be over in a half hour or so. Thanks, Pablo."

She turned to Marisa. "If anybody can think of where Ziggie might be secluding himself, it would be Pablo. They have become very good friends since Ziggie took over as Pablo's primary mentor for his doctoral thesis."

Marisa rushed to the guest room to get ready. "I promise I won't be more than ten minutes, but I refuse to go anywhere with my bare face hanging out and wet hair!"

While Marisa dressed, Erin wandered into the kitchen to get herself a glass of water. Before she had finished tidying up the kitchen from their morning coffee, Marisa had reappeared, wearing a pair of very tight jeans and a white blouse made from an eyelet material.

"Ready?"

Marisa answered by grabbing her purse, throwing it over her shoulder.

During the fifteen minute drive to the restaurant, Marisa was able to control her nerves with very little effort, but as Erin parked the car, it was all she could do not to run across the beach park in the opposite direction. She was embarrassed to face Pablo, more fearful yet of Erin's picking up on any strange vibes between them. Erin was worried enough over the situation with Ziggie; she certainly did not need to be worrying about her married friend and young student!

Pablo was waiting for them at the door of the restaurant, his face showed concern. As he greeted them, Marisa studied his face carefully, but there was no sign of embarrassment.

She took a deep breath, maybe the whole interlude had been a drunken hallucination on her part.

He seated them at an outside table, and then excused himself to attend to a restaurant matter. Marisa felt completely at ease, but for the life of her, she didn't know why. She took a sip of ice water, cut a small piece of cheese from the plate of crackers, fruit and cheese Pablo had obviously placed on their table before their arrival.

"This is delicious. You should try it." She savored a small piece of Brie on a slice of apple.

"My stomach is churning," Erin said. "What I really need is a cup of hot coffee."

"By all means, drink more acid to settle a churning stomach."

Pablo rejoined them carrying a full carafe of the tempting liquid on a tray with three cups. He deftly served them all, and placed the tray on a dumbwaiter a few feet away. He sat at the table between the women.

"I took the liberty of ordering us some croissants and fruit spreads too, so that we could talk. I don't know how long I'll have before the place fills up."

Erin's face showed disappointment, Pablo picked up on it. He reached over and patted his professor's hand. "I also let my relief host know that he may have to come in, if you need me," he assured her. "So what is going on, and how can I help?"

Erin raised her hands, palms up, shrugged her shoulders. "The problem is that we don't know what is going on," She realized that she hadn't even given Pablo a prelude to an explanation. "It's Brother Zigfried, Pablo. He seems to have vanished into thin air."

Pablo seemed amused. "Ziggie? I can't imagine anyone in the world less likely…"

Erin interrupted him. "And it is entirely my fault, Pablo."

Now Pablo was more confused. "Why would it be your fault?" He visualized Erin and Ziggie together romantically; it took every bit of his will power not to laugh.

The women noticed his amusement: Marisa flashed a quick smile, but Erin remained deadly serious.

"Marisa and I came upon some documents that I took to Brother Ziggie for translation, it turns out that they may contain some…well, some compromising information."

"Compromising information? That's a little vague, Professor," Pablo's tone turned serious. "Intriguing, but vague."

Marisa realized that Erin was embarrassed over involving a Jesuit Brother in something that on the surface seemed as trivial as a high school prank. She wasn't embarrassed, but definitely felt pangs of guilt over the whole situation. She leaned forward with an air of secrecy, reached out to touch Pablo's arm. He turned toward her.

"Let me explain, Pablo. Erin and I went snooping around the catacombs of the old convent at Villa Vistamar and we came across some very sensitive papers."

"That you stole?" Pablo's amused expression returned.

"Well, let's just say that we borrowed them." She noted that Pablo's eyes were beginning to tear from contained laughter, and closed her index finger to her thumb where they were resting on his arm. The simple pinch brought a more serious semblance, so she resisted the temptation to twist the pinch.

"Anyway, there were papers in the package that we couldn't translate, because they were in German, so Erin took them up to Brother Ziggie. That's when they found that there were a bunch of documents in Russian behind the German papers."

Pablo softened his gaze as his eyes met Marisa's. She pretended not to notice, but she could feel the heat rising to her cheeks and immediately began working on her semblance for fear of Erin's noticing her reaction to Pablo.

It was too late. Erin had already noticed, just as she had duly noted her student's awareness. Ordinarily, she would have said something, but the business at hand was far too serious to minimize it with any sniping remarks. She pretended not to notice Marisa's relief when she realized that she hadn't said anything. Her friend was calming down.

Pablo shifted uncomfortably in his chair.

"This still doesn't tell me anything about why he supposedly vanished."

"I'm coming to that, Pablo. From the moment that Erin left him the papers, Ziggie mentioned some weird stuff that he had already found, then there was his phone call to Erin yesterday morning when he was definitely frightened. He told her that we could not tell anyone that we had been the source of the papers because it would place us in danger. Then he insisted that we find the journals for every nun on the list that he had faxed us."

"What nuns?" Pablo arched an eyebrow. The amusement was gone from his expression. "What list?"

Erin pulled the fax from her briefcase. "This list," She handed it to him.

Pablo looked it over. "Do you know who they are?"

"Yes," Marisa said. "It's a list of all the Sisters Superior of the Congregation of Saint Thomas from around 1918 to the present. He said it was of the utmost importance for us to make sure we had the journals that each one of the superiors kept."

"Why?" Pablo's curiosity was piqued, but as Marisa studied his expression, she realized that his curiosity came from a place of knowledge. Then she remembered how Erin had introduced him as possessing quite possibly the most brilliant young theological mind she had ever had the privilege of meeting. "What was the underlying gist of the papers?"

"Well," Erin found her voice again. "The German documents speak of the VonKrups bequest to the order; the terms and conditions of his will, and about the endowment he left them to care for the estate." She paused as if to emphasize the importance of what was to follow: "The other papers were in Russian, and their entire content is still a mystery to me, although there is a surname that is repeated through the twenty-some-odd pages."

Pablo leaned forward, his eyes sparkling in expectation. "I suppose I should ask, but I assume the surname is 'Romanov'?"

Both women gasped, and Erin hissed, "What? How?"

Pablo smiled. "It's no stretch, believe me. Everyone knows there is some weird connection between the seminary and the Russian Orthodox Church, and way back when, when I was a Seminarian,"

Marisa interrupted. "A what?" She couldn't contain her giggle. "You?"

"Yes, Marisa, I was a seminarian. I probably would be ordained today if it were not for the fact that I thought I could delve deeper into the investigative side of Theology as a lay theologian." He smiled at her. She thought to herself that the term *Lay Theologian* had taken on an entirely new meaning for her.

"I'm sorry for interrupting. Please go on."

"Anyway," he continued, "back in the days of Divine Celibacy, I remember the legends that were spread among the newbies about the older brothers. There were all sorts of stories, especially about the ones with mysterious accents from mysterious places. There were stories about one elderly priest who had supposedly been a religious brother to Grigori Rasputin around 1900, in the Verkhoturye Monastery in Siberia. This priest, like Rasputin, had been a student of the heretical Russian sects known as the Khlysty and the Skopsty; which were very interesting sects indeed: the Khlysty believed in masochistic beatings as a form of religious worship, and it was said that their wild rituals ended in sexual orgies because they believed that this was the only way to reach God. First one had to commit sin, to then confess it, in order to receive absolute forgiveness."

"Oh, my!" Marisa giggled. "What a wonderfully unique rationalization!"

"Exactly," Pablo said, "but if truth be known, there is really no evidence that Rasputin ever encountered that particular branch of the Khlysty sect. Of course, the presence or presumption of truth never stopped a rumor-turned-legend. The legend went on to say that before this priest's death, he had created an entire sect within the secrecy of the seminary that not only followed the rituals of old, but continued his mission... whatever that was."

Marisa and Erin were fascinated by Pablo's account. Erin was usually much less likely to jump to conclusions, but this was the exception. "Pablo, I just know this is all connected, somehow. Do you have any idea what the mission might have been?"

Pablo shrugged his shoulders. "I have absolutely no idea, but either we have the same feelings, or I am being persuaded by your conclusions. I, too, have a feeling that this is all connected somehow. I just don't know how."

"That makes three of us." Marisa took a bite of a croissant, winced; put it on her plate again. There was nothing worse than a cold croissant. "But none of this is putting us any closer to Ziggie."

"Maybe... or maybe not." Pablo tapped his fingers on the table. "You said that you had gone to his office? Tell me exactly what you found."

Erin explained every last detail or lack thereof while Marisa nodded in agreement or commented with a short interjection. "There was blood on the doorknob of his locked office." Erin could barely choke out the words.

Pablo finished his coffee in one gulp, and then called the waiter over.

"Jorge, please call Miguel, and tell him to come in immediately," he ordered the young man to have his relief manager come in, then he turned to the women. "If you came for my opinion and help, then there is only one path, as far as I am concerned: the only thread deals with the documents. The fact that they are nowhere to be found and Ziggie is missing is an obvious link. On the other hand, you have copies of the documents, so the next step is to examine them."

The young waiter nodded toward him from the doorway. Pablo rose to help Erin up, and then extended the same courtesy to Marisa.

"This is all fine and dandy, Pablo, but how is your German and better yet… how is your Russian?"

He laughed. "About as good as my Chinese, but that is not a problem with the new translation programs on the net. They may not be entirely accurate and the grammar and sentence structure are usually pretty crazy, but even a bad translation is better than none."

He guided the women toward the stairs, he suddenly stopped. "Erin, do you have a scanner? I'm sure your computer keyboard doesn't have the Cyrillic alphabet even if any of us could type in Russian."

Erin thought a minute. "I have an old one in my office closet that I haven't used in years, but I imagine it still works."

Pablo wasn't convinced. "You two go on ahead, because I need to take my own car anyway. I don't quite trust your old scanner, but I have my laptop with a hand-held scanner in the restaurant. I'll bring it along, just in case."

As they entered the townhouse community, there seemed to be an inordinate amount of activity: residents were walking around looking worried; the street that led to Erin's townhouse was blocked by a patrol car.

Marisa reached over and patted her friend's arm. "Don't worry, Erin, it's probably just a water leak somewhere."

Erin had stopped her car and rolled the window down. "What's wrong, officer?" she asked the uniformed man who approached her car. "I live in unit 14."

The officer visibly winced. "There has been some trouble up there, Ma'am. I'm not supposed to let anyone through, but if it's your home, you may be able to help." He lifted the barrier to let her car pass.

As she pulled forward, she leaned out the window. "My son is following us. His name is Pablo Santamaría, and I need you to let him through."

The officer waved his hand in an informal salute in recognition of Erin's request. When they pulled up to her unit, they both breathed a sigh of relief. The townhouses were divided in two, and it was the downstairs unit that was cordoned off with open doors. There was smoke and water damage inside.

Other than some smoke stains on her front door and around the common entrance patio, her apartment seemed fine.

"It's terrible for me to say this, but thank God it wasn't mine! I hope Dan is okay."

Marisa had to stifle a nervous giggle. After experiencing his music assault firsthand, she had little doubt he was the type of person that would complain about everything and anything, as if making life difficult for other people were his only entertainment in life.

They saw a stretcher being wheeled through the front door of the unit. There was a black bag on it.

"Oh, dear Lord!" Erin said. "Dan!"

Marisa's general cynicism reared its ugly little head, she spoke without thinking. "Hey, what goes around comes around. He probably just really pissed some of your other neighbors off, so they offed him!"

The horrified expression that slowly crossed, then planted itself solidly on Erin's face made Marisa realize that she had gone much too far with her off-handed quips.

"Erin, I am really sorry, I am really ashamed of myself. I guess it's just the lawyer-turned-journalist in me. Sometimes I say very insensitive things."

But suddenly, Erin's entire posture changed: first there was a hint of a smile, then her eyes started tearing. She covered her face with her shaking hands, sobbed silently into them.

"It'll be okay, Erin. Hey, he was a jerk. It's not as if your best friend died," Marisa stroked the back of Erin's neck.

Erin lifted her head, threw it back to laugh even harder, working words in between guffaws. "This is just the icing on a really shitty cake!" She laughed again, opened the door just as Pablo pulled up beside them. "Hey, Pablo... want to help us check my unit for damages? It looks like my jerk of a neighbor spontaneously combusted or something, and we'd better be sure there's none of him in my place."

The three pushed their way through the crowds of neighbors, firemen, police and rescue workers to reach the common entrance patio that led to the semi-circular cluster of four units. It was there they were stopped by a uniformed officer.

"Sorry, folks, but the fire department hasn't released the units yet. You can't come in."

"Uh, but mine is the upstairs unit from the one where the problem was," Erin explained. "I see no one has opened it, so I would appreciate your letting us in for the fire department to check for possible hot spots or danger areas... I mean, if Mr. Baxter's ceiling burned, I may not have a floor!"

The officer nodded, called a fireman over to explain quickly who they were. The fireman nodded, motioned them to come in.

With no formalities or introductions, the fireman immediately began to explain: "There really shouldn't be any damage in your place, folks, but we'll check it out anyway. Do you have the key?"

Erin turned over her key gladly and the three of them sat on a small wrought iron garden bench to wait. Erin was visibly trembling. Pablo put his arm around her.

They watched in nervous suspense while the fireman opened the front door. Surprisingly, the stairwell light came on, everything looked all right. As the three men ascended the stairway, Erin suddenly focused on a small object that seemed to be running upstairs in front of the men.

"What the..."

Marisa had seen it, too. "Since when did you get a cat?"

Erin shrugged. "Don't have one."

Pablo turned, smiling. "A Siamese cat, at that. They're very magical, you know."

"But I don't have a cat."

"Apparently, you do, now." Pablo was openly amused.

It suddenly dawned on Marisa that the cat might very well have belonged to Erin's neighbor. "Do you suppose the cat was Dan's?"

Erin nodded absentmindedly. "Now that you mention it, it may be the howling that I have heard coming from downstairs. I thought was emanating from some of Dan's rather skanky and boisterous lady friends."

All three of them broke up.

After a couple of minutes, the three firemen emerged from the unit with no cat. The same one that had taken the key minutes earlier approached them, held the key out. "Everything seems fine, Ma'am, other than a little smoke on the sliding glass doors that go out to your patio, and a little smoke stain on the carpet in front of the open doors."

Which is how the cat got in, Erin thought to herself as she took the key from the man's hand. "Thank you, so much. What actually happened in Mr. Baxter's place?"

"That's something the police will have to figure out, Ma'am, but it's a real mess in there. It looks like a home invasion gone sour, if you ask me."

"A home invasion?" Pablo and Marisa turned to look at Erin, their eyes reflecting the very feeling that was creeping into her voice. "Why do you think so?"

"Everything is topsy-turvy: there are drawers dumped everywhere, the sofa is upside down. It looks like someone was searching for something. Plus, the fire was contained to the drapes around the patio doors, and it looks like the owner started it himself."

"I don't get it," Erin said almost to herself.

"There was a chef's torch next to his body, or at least pieces of a chef's torch. It looks like he was using it as a defensive weapon when the drapes caught fire. They probably knocked him out from behind and then the gas cylinder exploded. The autopsy will confirm it, but it looks like it was a piece of the metal cylinder puncturing the carotid artery that killed him." The fireman looked furtively behind him as he saw a police officer approaching. "But you didn't hear that from me!" He stepped to one side as the police officer stepped forward.

"Good evening folks. Which of you is the neighbor?"

Erin said, "I am."

"I see you were out when this all took place, but can you recall anything out of the ordinary happening this morning? Any strange people around? Anything at all that might help us to understand what happened here?"

Erin and Marisa shook their heads. Marisa cleared her throat: "We went out to brunch a few hours ago, but everything seemed perfectly normal around here when we left."

Erin nodded in agreement. "If you would give us your card, we'll certainly give you a call if we remember anything that might be helpful, but unless you need us for anything else, I think we'll go in. This has been kind of a shock, and I really just want to see my place and make sure everything is okay."

"Everything seems fine, Ma'am, other than the fact that your cat is very upset." The officer handed each of them a card. "That is one very loud cat. I have heard of one-man orchestras, but you have a one-cat orchestra. That is not a happy Siamese!"

"Thank you," Erin said weakly. "I'll take care of..."

"Mozart," Pablo said, fully realizing that he had just named the noisy little fellow while he stood to help Erin and Marisa up from the bench.

"I know it's only four o'clock in the afternoon, but I am fast fading." Erin yawned for the seventeenth time while Pablo was scanning the first couple of pages of Russian documents into his computer. Her scanner, as he had feared, had not worked. "I guess the wine didn't help, either," She sipped from her goblet and set it on the coffee table.

They were seated on the floor with Pablo's laptop computer and the scanner on the table. The documents were spread out over the table in three piles; away from the fans they had pointing out the open sliding door to clear the stench of smoke from the air. The English and Latin documents in one pile, the German documents in another, and the Russian in the third pile, from which Pablo was taking them one at a time to carefully scan them.

"Sure it did," Pablo assured her. "It calmed you down. You were a wreck when we got here, and you have mellowed nicely. However, Marisa mellowed even better!"

Marisa was sound asleep on the couch behind them. He had removed the wine goblet from her hand before she spilled it on the couch as she'd cuddled down into the pillows. It was just as well, because she had been urging him to try to translate each page before scanning in another. His mind didn't work that way. He wanted all ten documents scanned in before translating any of it.

What had happened in the neighbor's house had given him renewed resolve to have a backup copy of each and every piece of paper involved in this ever-deepening mystery.

As Erin yawned again, he turned to her. "Listen, it honestly won't bother me one bit if you take a nap. This isn't a fast process. It is going to take a while, and I am perfectly alert to do it. I promise you that I will wake you as soon as I can make any sense out of anything I manage to get translated."

Erin was grateful for the suggestion. She was embarrassed to be such a lousy hostess, but his offer seemed sincere.

She lifted herself to her feet using the coffee table as leverage, and then stepped to her lounge chair to sit down with a thud. She pulled the wooden lever on the right side of the chair, stretched it out as flat as it would go. She fell into a deep sleep within minutes, lulled by the whirring of the hand-held scanner as Pablo traced it down and across each page.

Once the documents were scanned in, Pablo pulled out a telephone cord, unplugging the telephone that was on the table next to Erin's chair to replace it for the telephone line. After connecting it to his computer's modem, he pulled up his Internet browser and set up the main scan file in a format that would be easily accessible to the browser.

Finally, he established a solid connection to the Internet, and googled "online translator Russian." A number of sites came up, but he soon realized that the sites that advertised free translation were just come-ons for expensive services.

Between Brother Ziggie's disappearance and the coincidental home invasion downstairs, he was positive he couldn't trust the content of the documents to any human being on the planet. After pondering the problem a few minutes, he googled "software, translation, Russian." He finally found a site where he could download a limited edition of a popular translation software for a free 30-day trial.

With the dial-up connection, the software took what seemed like an eternity to download. When Pablo leaned back against the sofa, a small bundle of fawn-colored fur crawled from its spot next to Marisa directly onto Pablo's shoulder, where he sat straight; his pointy, dark brown ears twitching slightly.

"Hey, there, Mozart... how're ya doing, buddy?" Pablo greeted the cat, who squeezed his eyes closed in response before touching his nose to Pablo's right ear. Pablo jumped in surprise when he felt the cat's icy-cold nose on his ear, and laughed.

The cat remained seated on Pablo's shoulder, as if he simply belonged there.

Pablo glanced over at the computer screen, and realized that the download was finished. As he leaned forward, Mozart simply shifted his weight, with apparently no intention of moving. He was obviously quite comfortable there. They had set out a bowl of water for him and Erin had sacrificed a can of her best tuna as a feline treat, evidenced by a tiny burp of very fishy breath let out in Pablo's general direction.

"That's okay, Mozart. You've had a hard day, haven't you?" Mozart squeezed his eyes closed, but began to purr very softly, as if he knew he had to be very quiet so as not to awaken the women.

With the cat watching closely, Pablo began the slow process of learning to use the translation software. Once he felt sure he had mastered the rather laborious process of digital recognition —the process of "teaching" the software to recognize the characters from the written pages— he pulled up the first scanned document in Russian from the computer file.

After loading it into the software, he checked twice to make sure it was loaded properly, then pushed the button for the electronic translation. He sat back.

"What do you think, Mozart? Do you think we'll be able to figure out what it says by this machine translation?"

As if answering the question, Mozart leaped gracefully from Pablo's shoulder to the coffee table. Pablo started to grab the cat, but then immediately realized that the lithe feline had landed on one of the few spots on the table not covered by papers or electronic equipment.

"What is it, Mozart?"

The cat immediately began watching the computer screen as if he were just as curious as Pablo to see what would appear.

Finally, the computer bleeped, the screen was filled with English words.

Pablo read the entire page without making one bit of sense out of it. The sentences were disjointed; they read like the English instructions translated from Chinese for the simple assembly of a child's toy.

Even Mozart had a confused look in his turquoise blue eyes, but gazed at Pablo intently as if saying that he had complete confidence in his ability to do this. He then leaped to the arm of Erin's chair, moved his head from one side to the other, picked a comfortable spot, and turned three times before cuddling down on Erin for a nap.

Pablo checked every option available on the translation software, and finally found an option that worked like a Thesaurus by changing the key words of each sentence into the second synonym available in the Thesaurus.

He figured that nothing could be worse than what he had in front of him, so he used the option.

After another few minutes the computer bleeped again. The new page was on the screen with a different name, and although not all of it made sense, there were a few sentences, here and there, that did.

He ran each page he had scanned until there were a few intelligible sentences on each page, then cut and pasted each sentence into a separate document. By the fourth document, he was smiling.

As the machine was doing the second Thesaurus translation of the tenth document, he found he could no longer contain his excitement.

"Ladies, I believe we have a winner!"

Marisa was the first to lift her head and stare in his direction. It took a moment for his words to register in her brain, but they finally did. Erin was still snoring very quietly.

"Don't tell me you have it all translated?"

"I wish!"

"What's that, then?" She looked at the screen.

"Well, I was able to pull up a few sentences in each document that sort of made sense, and I cut and pasted them into a separate document." Erin was stirring now, sat up to listen.

"Welcome back, Professor," he said, and then he continued. "Anyway, we have about thirty sentences that sort of make sense, in the order by which we got the documents."

Erin was excited. "Let's see them… can you enlarge the font so we can study them all? Or have you figured it all out already?"

"Not even close." He laughed. "I am beginning to realize why Ziggie said they were so sensitive. I believe I can even understand why people might break in to what they thought was your house to find any possible copies. I suggest that we get anything sensitive out of your house, in a very overt way, to insure your safety. Do you have a safe deposit box in a bank somewhere?"

Erin nodded. "Yes, of course."

"Then we should make a very open deposit of a bunch of journals and all these papers, tomorrow. If someone wants them, they'll have to figure out a way into a bank vault."

"And of course, the documents will be here." Erin understood perfectly. "Very good, Professor. Very good. Now, let's study the sentences."

Chapter Seven

"I'm still a bit sleep fogged," Marisa said as Pablo enlarged the font on his laptop screen so that they could study the first two sentences. "Could you please read the first few aloud?"

Pablo couldn't avoid smiling as he read the words: "*Assassination Ferdinand Sarajevo and Rasputin bring to war. Rasputin friend with Germany is spy with German Empress Alexandra.*"

"You woke us up for this?" Erin groused.

Pablo winced at her tone, decided not to let Erin's querulous attitude deter him.   He quickly scanned ahead. "The important thing here is probably the signature of Grand Duke Nicholas Nicholaevich, a grandson of Tsar Nicholas I, who was the Commander-in Chief of the Russian army in the first battle of World War One." Pablo's voice was low and he spoke slowly, as if recalling a piece of history for a college exam. "The date is also important, because it closely coincides with the date of the assassination of Franz Ferdinand of Austria. I'll have to check for the exact date."

Marisa nodded. "Many see that as the start of World War One." She was beginning to realize the importance of the document. "

"Yes, and no," Erin chimed in regretting her earlier outburst. "The war was inevitable at that point."

Pablo didn't entirely agree. "Yes, that is part of the accepted history, but if this machine translation is even vaguely close to what the document actually says, it may affirm what many have always believed: that the Grand Duke Nicholas Nicholaevich, or Nicolasha as they called him, was the intellectual author of the master assassination plot. This report, signed by him, seems to describe Rasputin as dead, when in fact, he had survived. It also seems to allude to both Rasputin and Alexandra as German spies."

"That's a long stretch, if you ask me..." Erin laughed.

"Maybe not," Pablo said. "Alexandra was German born, and as European bloodlines go, she would consider her children as both German and Russian. It would have had to be painful for her to see her two countries at war. I wouldn't go so far as to say that she would consciously spy for Germany or harm Russia in any way, but her sentimental leanings must have wavered occasionally. Then you have Rasputin, whom most people considered a threat to the very survival of Russia because of his influence over the royal family."

"But only because he was a scoundrel, an alcoholic, a womanizer and a heretic!" Erin added.

"What I don't get," Marisa said, "is that if he was there only to exploit the Tsar's family, why is it that by all accounts I have read he actually did keep the Tsarvich alive?"

Erin's expression was almost wistful. "Oh, there was never any doubt about his natural healing powers, and it has even been admitted or accepted in many historical circles that he was truly very fond of the Tsar and his family. But it was undeniable that he was —shall we say— distracted? From the otherwise esoteric and religious life of a monk by the finer things in a man's life: like alcohol, women and debauchery." She laughed. "He was also one of the most enigmatic men in history, and it seems as if every historian has uncovered but another facet to the many faces of his personality. He is a fascinating character."

Marisa had stood and was pacing around the townhouse. Erin glanced over at her friend. "Sit down somewhere, will you? You're making me nervous."

Marisa sat down and gazed at the screen as Pablo scrolled down the sentences. She realized that most of the machine translations were going to take a lot more analysis than what any of them had the strength to do that evening. "You know, we're not going to be able to decipher everything tonight anyway, and it occurs to me that we're not seeing the forest for the trees. Think about it: there has to be a reason why all these documents are together. That's the part I think we're missing."

Erin and Pablo turned to stare at her, waiting for an explanation. Marisa was staring out in space, but laughed when she realized that they were expecting some sort of wisdom or intelligence on her part.

"Oh, don't expect much more than that out of me tonight, because the only thing that comes to mind is that there must be a connection between VonKrups and the Tsar's family."

"I suppose that's possible," Pablo mused, "but it sounds like a stretch, to me."

"I know, but what I do feel very strongly about is that the only way we're going to find out is to get back into the basement at the convent to get all the journals from the superiors' trunks. I just don't know where else we can start."

Erin was unsure, but Pablo nodded. "I agree. From what little I could get translated from the documents, it would seem to be the most important thing to do, and when you consider the fact that Ziggie said to do precisely that, after having translated at least a thousand times what I could translate with the computer, then yes: I think this is the only way to go."

Marisa nodded. She yawned, glanced at her watch. "Oh, my God! It's three-thirty in the morning!"

She stood, noticed Pablo quickly picking up all the papers strewn on the coffee table, putting his laptop away.

"We're not kicking you out, Pablo, but I think Erin and I are definitely going to hit that basement again tonight. That means we need some sleep. We need you alert and ready on the outside to come and rescue us if needed, which means you need sleep, too."

He looked up at her with a wide grin, and she smiled.

"What time do you have to work tomorrow?" she asked.

"Wednesday is my day off, but I may switch with my sub and work it so that Thursday we can get together to see what you two have found.

Wednesdays and Thursdays are the slower days of the week, so it really doesn't matter which one I take off."

Erin was observing from her lounge chair, her brow furrowed a little more with each exchange of words between Marisa and Pablo. They were so engrossed in their conversation that Marisa had momentarily forgotten they had an audience.

Marisa glanced over at her, realized immediately that she had been caught. There was no point in hiding her attraction toward Pablo from Erin any longer. She smiled at Erin and shrugged her shoulders, knowing that this would not suffice.

Pablo stood and hoisted the laptop case's strap over his shoulder. He took a few steps to Erin's chair, leaned down to kiss her cheek. "Don't get up, Professor, I know the way out."

Marisa followed him to the door, painfully aware of Erin's staring at them. She opened it for Pablo. The minute he started to pass through to the outside, she skirted out behind him, almost closing the door behind her. "I'll walk you to your car," she said loudly enough for Erin to hear through the crack.

The two walked down the dark stairs in silence, Marisa could feel Pablo's presence burning the very core of her being.

She stepped forward to open the tricky lock on the street door, brushing up against Pablo's back with her chest. That momentary physical contact with him sent shivers through her body, and Pablo noticed.

"Are you cold?" He slipped an arm around her shoulder. She started to answer, but then realized by the grin on his face that he knew perfectly well that she was not cold.

"No." She side-stepped to wiggle from his grasp while she glanced up toward Erin's front windows. The living room was dark, and that relieved her.

Pablo instinctively understood, lowering his arm.

Marisa walked a few paces ahead until they reached his car. It was a black, late model pickup truck with a short bed and a back seat. Pablo unlocked the truck a few feet away, opened the back door. He placed the briefcase with his laptop on the floor.

As he turned toward the driver's door, Marisa was standing between it and the back door he had just closed. He reached past her with his left hand, opened the driver's door, gently circling his right arm around her waist.

She gasped, but let herself be gently guided toward the floorboard next to the driver's seat. She felt herself being gently lifted to the floorboard in a sitting position, as Pablo pressed his body against hers.

Shielded from anyone's view by the truck door, she melted into his kiss, relishing in the sensations that his body was provoking in hers as he gently moved against her. She would have given anything to have been wearing a skirt at that moment, not those damned tight jeans. Those jeans would ruin the very spontaneity of what otherwise could have been a moment of impromptu bliss.

Her momentary lapse into insanity was interrupted by an ever-nagging sense of scruples, but it still took every bit of willpower to break their embrace.

Pablo stepped back slightly; she lowered herself to the ground. He turned around, looked up toward Erin's living room. It was dark, but he could see the figure of a woman in the darkened room next to it.

"Does Erin have the front bedroom?"

"Yes," Marisa turned toward the townhouse. She, too, saw the figure and immediately felt painful pangs of guilt. "This is really disrespectful to my friendship with Erin, and I have absolutely no excuse for myself."

Pablo smiled and put his arm up against the truck so that Marisa couldn't wiggle out from the open door. "And what does Erin have to do with anything? The last time I looked, she wasn't my mother, nor is she yours."

"No, but she is my friend, and you are her student." Marisa really did feel like a heel.

"Correction. She was my professor about five years ago, and she is currently a dear friend and a secondary mentor for my doctoral thesis. That does not make me her student, any more than it makes me her son." He glanced back at the townhouse and found that Erin was no longer standing at the window. "I am hardly a child, and neither are you."

"And neither is my husband." There! She had finally said it.

Pablo grinned. "Ah, so the truth comes to light!" He stepped back an inch or so, but didn't remove his arm that blocked any possible escape by Marisa.

Marisa didn't know exactly what he meant, but she felt somehow threatened. "I never hid the fact that I'm married," she said defensively.

"No, of course not, but you have been blaming Erin for your hesitation, when the truth of the matter is that it's your husband who is holding you back."

"Hesitation? Holding back? You're not sure of yourself or anything, are you?" She laughed despite herself as he lifted her back onto the floorboard of the truck.

This time Pablo positioned himself more intimately as he pushed gently against her body, she was left breathless. This time it was Pablo who broke the moment.

He stepped back slightly, smiled tenderly. "I would love nothing more than to throw you into the car and kidnap you to my place for the sleep that we both acutely need." He moved closer and gently pulled her to her feet. "But I'm quite sure it would take us about three to four days before we would get any sleep at all." He leaned down and kissed her sweetly. "And Ziggie obviously needs us, now."

As Marisa walked toward the house, she dared not turn to look at Pablo lest she throw all discretionary caution to the wind and jump into that sexy, black truck.

Having left the street door propped open with a rock, she was able to enter the house silently, pulling the door and locking it behind her. She crept up the steps, opened the apartment door. Erin was waiting for her with the cordless telephone in her hand.

"Carlos called," she said dryly. "I said you were in the shower, and he was impressed by your getting up so early." Her sad expression was slowly turning to anger as she observed the guileless expression of relief taking over Marisa's face. "Marisa, I don't like lying, and I will not do it again. I don't particularly care what is going on between you and Pablo, but I most definitely will not cover for you with Carlos."

That said, she turned and walked into the kitchen where she served herself a glass of water. When she returned to the living room, she found Marisa sitting on the couch; embarrassment and guilt written all over her.

Erin sat on the edge of her lounge chair and placed a hand gently on Marisa's forearm. "Listen, Marisa, I am not judging you, because I am the last person in the world to judge anyone. I left a wonderful husband who loved me more than life itself for an adventure that was short-lived, not to mention emotionally devastating. And it destroyed Marcos, who was a kind and gentle man."

"I thought Shawn was the love of your life." Marisa's gaze softened.

"Oh, I never said I didn't love him. Believe me, this was not a boring relationship, but it was an emotional roller-coaster from which I have never quite recovered." Her face turned ashen. "It cost me the love and respect of my only child."

"I thought you and Christopher were great friends now."

"*Now* we are, or sort of, but he didn't speak to me for nearly five years after his father and I broke up. He insists, to this day, that I would have left him behind with his father if he hadn't already been away at college, and that I would never have given either one of them a second thought."

"Is that true?" Marisa didn't believe it for a minute.

"I don't know, Marisa. I really don't, because that's not how it happened. I hate it when people second guess themselves. I say we can never predict our reactions or anyone else's for that matter until we actually live the circumstances." She sighed. "But I already made my mistakes and I have paid the price, dearly. I would hate to see you have to pay an exorbitant amount for the tryst you're about to have."

Marisa was silent for a few moments, as if weighing each one of Erin's words. Erin knew her well, but she didn't know how miserably unhappy she had been since Carlos' affair with his graduate student. Was she getting even?

She finally put the phone down on the table and faced Erin. "I don't know if I'm about to have an affair, or not, Erin. Hey, Pablo is delightful. He is attractive, smart and charming. But I still love Carlos, and I wouldn't leave him for a man half my age." She forced herself to laugh, although she would have loved to allow herself to cry. "I was just sitting here trying to analyze myself."

"Are you confused about your feelings? I don't know if I can help, but I can certainly listen."

Marisa picked up Erin's glass of water from the coffee table. "Do you mind?" She took a long sip of water, put the glass down. "Did I ever tell you about Carlos' affair four years ago?" Once Erin shook her head, Marisa elaborated about Carlos' graduate student and the wild affair they'd had, and how Carlos did not consider his tryst as having anything whatsoever to do with Marisa or his marriage. "So in conclusion," she ended the narrative, "I guess Carlos wouldn't really care, anyway."

Erin furrowed her brow. "I doubt that very seriously, but I must admit that you have just come up with one of the better rationalizations I have heard in my life."

Marisa smiled in spite of herself. "Yeah, I guess that's all it is. That's what I was thinking about, in part. That, and wondering if I was using Pablo to get even with Carlos."

Erin stood, crossed over to the window and opened the curtains. The sun was barely up, but the hues of blues and pinks streaking the sky were spectacular. She turned to Marisa. "Only you know the answer to that, Marisa, but I can tell you this without the slightest doubt in my mind, and it has nothing to do with your marriage nor does it have anything to do with Pablo: we have stumbled upon something important here, and we all know it. I truly believe that destiny tends to throw us a lot of curve balls just as we are about to do something important. Or maybe we throw them at ourselves. But the point is that something always comes up to sabotage the best of plans."

"And you think what is going on with Pablo is sabotaging our mission to find the truth and rescue Ziggie?" Marisa was getting testy. "I don't really think that's fair, Erin. Pablo worked like a Trojan on that translation, and is there for us, 100%."

"For us or for you?"

"For us and for Ziggie. Hey Erin, he is the one who cooled his heels and pulled away. He said that it was all very tempting, but that Ziggie needed us, now."

Erin smiled. "Wow. I misjudged him. It won't happen again." She crossed over to her chair and sat down. "Now, what are you going to do about Carlos?"

Marisa glanced at her watch. "It's too late to call him back now. He's probably left for the university. "That's a good thing because it'll give me a chance to take a nap and then think about what I want to say to him, or not."

As she stood, the phone rang.

Erin quickly rose to her feet, checked the caller ID, waved toward Marisa as she walked toward her room; ostensibly to give her some privacy, but more honestly to get some sleep. It had been a long day, and sharing the most painful moments in her life with her friend had left her emotionally drained. She was in need of some deep sleep.

Marisa answered the phone almost defensively, then immediately relented. It wasn't Carlos' fault that she had been entertaining the idea of another man in her life. Her voice softened. "I didn't mean to answer so bluntly, it's just that I had just fallen back to sleep after my bath."

Carlos laughed. "That's exactly what you're supposed to be doing, resting! I was just missing you, so I thought I'd call. We've hardly talked since you left for the coast."

She could hear concern in his voice, wondered how she could possibly have thought she could deceive him. They were far too connected. She was sure he knew what was going on, at least on an intuitive level. She cleared her throat.

"Carlos, I'm glad you called, because we need to talk."

"Yes, I know," he said gently. "You know you can tell me anything. Absolutely anything," The tone of his voice conveyed his sincerity.

Marisa took a deep breath and told her husband not only all about the mystery that she and Erin were trying to solve, but Ziggie's disappearance, too. Finally, she told him about Pablo, and didn't minimize the strong attraction she felt for the young man.

"I am telling you about all this because, above and beyond the fact that you are my husband and I adore you, you are also my best friend. I don't know why this is happening because I don't fit into any of the excuses women use to have affairs. I am happy in my marriage. Our physical relationship is good, and it always has been. You fulfill me in every way... so why do I feel this ridiculous, teenage crush for a man half my age?"

Marisa's candid admission of her feelings for Pablo had inspired a myriad of feelings in Carlos, but the strongest feeling he had was tenderness because of her honesty.

"I think the question, as posed, contains the answer." He was kind. "Not because of the clichés you hear about middle-aged people falling for younger mates. I think it goes deeper than that. I think the attraction is a mixture of physical, intellectual and emotional factors. These people are very much into everything we stopped following years ago, technologically speaking, and have a different way of looking at life than we do. We may have looked at life the same way at their age, and have simply forgotten how. I don't know, nor do I really remember."

"That makes sense, I suppose, and I thank you for not minimizing things or dishing me platitudes about a young man inflating an old woman's ego. I don't think I could have taken that, no matter how deserved."

"You are not an old woman, and I wouldn't know how to dish out a platitude. It's not in me."

"I know, Carlos, and that is one of the reasons I love you so much. That, and the fact that you are probably the best lay I have ever had." She giggled, waited for her husband's reaction. She had never said anything like that before, but his words and understanding had somehow empowered her.

"I would be flattered was it not for the fact that to my knowledge, that would be the only lay, which leaves very little margin for comparison, my darling." Carlos was amused, but was also growing more jealous with every remark from Marisa. He controlled himself knowing instinctively that any anger on his part would permanently close the door of communication with his wife.

Marisa picked up on his tone. "That didn't come out right. I don't even remember what I was trying to say, but it definitely wasn't that!" She was too exhausted to correct his misconception about her chastity before marriage. It would have to wait for a later conversation.

"It's okay, Marisa, and on the contrary, I shouldn't have answered ironically."

"Actually, it's time for us to lighten up, anyway, don't you think?" Marisa felt relieved, but at the same time drained of all energy after confessing her deepest feelings for another man to her husband.

"Well, I would love to, but I am walking out the door as we speak because I'm late for class. Why don't you just have a nice day, and stop beating yourself up... hey, you're entitled!"

Marisa was in a state of shock. She had always known that Carlos was an exceptional man, but she knew this conversation had been an acid test of tolerance for him. He had stood to the challenge and had not only surpassed her expectations, but her wildest dreams.

"I love you so much. You are my hero, Carlos."

"Love you more," The phone went dead.

Marisa shuffled off to bed with renewed self-acceptance and serenity.

Now she would sleep. Minutes later and comforted by the yellow and pink ribbons of late morning sunlight streaming through the white chiffon curtains of the bedroom, Marisa fell into a deep sleep. The lingering stench of smoke no longer disturbed her or her friend in the next room.

In a convent across the valley, Sister Thomas Marie had retired early. She tired so easily lately. The rest of the nuns were convinced that it was because she slept so fitfully at night, that neither her body nor her mind rested enough. As usual, she was tossing and turning in her bed, haunted by ghosts of a past she couldn't remember.

"You'll be safe with these men," the beautiful woman said, as tears welled in her eyes. "I promise you that. Now promise mother that you will not be afraid."

"But momma," the small boy clung to his mother, "I don't want to go!"

She stepped up, gently pulled the child from his mother's arms.

Turning, she gazed imploringly at a bearded, black-robed man standing in the background. The man stepped forward, held out his arms to the small child, who took a crying refuge within the embrace.

"Go, my child, be well," the man whispered.

She held out her hand and waited for the boy to grasp it.

He turned and took her hand, then walked stoically by her side, holding his head high and turning his head regally from left to right as he had been taught to do when passing through the hallways of his home, usually lined with servants who would halt their daily activities to offer their best wishes to the youngster as he walked by.

There was no one in sight as the two followed the robed man and the man in the uniform that spoke their mother's language strangely.

Someone was calling her. Why couldn't she be left alone to sleep?

"Erin!" Marisa called out for the third time. "Come on! It's almost nine o'clock, and if we don't get up now, we won't have time for showers or to stop for something to eat!"

Erin turned sleepily and stared at Marisa, her mind only partially aware of her surroundings. The hallway wall behind Marisa was gilded in gold, giving off a light of its own.

She sat up suddenly, opened her eyes widely as she focused on the wall. The gold was gone.

"I'm glad you woke me! I was having a very strange dream that made no sense at all. All these people seemed to be sending me away with a little boy, and neither one of us wanted to go." She furrowed her brow. "And there were priests and soldiers around."

Marisa shrugged her shoulders. "You probably just fixated on something from what we've been talking about for the last few days. The priest thing is obvious because you're worried about Ziggie, don't you think?"

"You're probably right, but it kind of freaked me out." She stretched, and Mozart rose lazily from his spot next to her leg. He yawned and yowled softly, then squeezed his eyes in her direction. Erin reached over to pet his head; the cat seemed pleased as he purred softly. Erin looked up at Marisa. "Could you fix Mozart something to eat? Just something to tide him over until we come back would be good, and we mustn't forget to get some cat food while we're out."

"Oh, I don't know, he seems to be quite happy with the can of tuna, jar of caviar and tin of smoked oysters he has downed since he moved in."

Marisa had found the cat's obvious taste for the better things in life hilarious. When offered such mundane fare as a scrambled egg or a bit of bologna, he had quite literally raised his nose into the air before stomping off in a huff. Marisa had remarked that one had never seen a true huff until one saw a "Siamese Cat Huff".

"Okay, Mozart: front and center!" She called to the cat, who amazingly obeyed by jumping off the bed and rubbing against her legs. "Yeah, yeah, lotsa love, huh, Mozart?" she cooed at the cat. "But we both know you just want food! At least it's nice to know that your appetite wasn't affected by the trauma of losing your friend!"

Erin grinned at her as she sat on the side of the bed gathering strength to make a dash for the shower. "I thought you didn't care for cats?"

"Mozart isn't a cat, Mozart is a Siamese. That's different."

Erin was beginning to believe it.

Chapter Eight

"There's nothing in here!" Marisa whispered in a hiss.

"Not in here, either." There was no surprise in Erin's tone.

The women had arrived at the convent just after eleven P.M., and had easily slipped over the wall with the help of the stepladder that Marisa had rescued during Sunday's reunion activities. This time, Marisa had gone first, but twisted her ankle slightly after jumping to the ground. It still ached, but she didn't complain.

"So now, what?" Marisa sat down on the cement floor in front of Sister Joseph Vincent's trunk. Her legs out of Erin's direct line of vision, she began to massage her twisted ankle because it was swollen.

"We can always look into a couple surrounding trunks, but I can almost guarantee you that anything of interest has been removed. Besides, we should probably call it a night and get you home where you can put an ice pack on that ankle."

Marisa released her ankle. "Not on your life!" She crawled to the trunk next to Sister Vincent Joseph's.

She opened the trunk, quickly pulled out a journal. She opened it, and then lowered it to the level of the fluorescent lantern next to her. Finding that page devoid of anything that even remotely interested her, she flipped through other pages. They all appeared to contain the nun's deepest reflections on the purification of her soul for eternal life.

She threw the journal into the trunk and dug around to see if there was anything else there. "Nothing here.." she said, discouraged.

Erin was closing another trunk. "Nothing here, either."

After three or four more trunks, the women gave up. There was no doubt that the old nun had reported them; the nuns had summarily removed anything of possible historical interest from the trunks stored there.

Erin closed the fifth trunk quietly and sat down on top of it. "I guess that's it. We're not finding anything that gives us a clue on Ziggie, that's for sure." She stood, lifted her lantern from the floor. "Shall we? Are you ready?"

Marisa wasn't convinced. "Not quite, Erin." She stood, walked back to the wall that had swallowed them during their previous visit. She placed the lantern on the closest trunk, began pushing against the lower bricks in the wall to calculate approximately where the weight of their bodies had caused the wall to open up.

Nothing happened.

Erin crossed over to help.

"I remember distinctly that we were right here, behind these trunks," She pushed and tapped every brick.

Discouraged, they sat on the nearest trunks.

"So now what?" Marisa wondered aloud: she knew she would have to be the one to figure out a new plan, because Erin was an emotional wreck at this point. Her worry for Ziggie's wellbeing was causing her to turn inward, just as she had always done in their childhood. Marisa knew the signs. "Erin, don't close down on me. I need you here!"

Erin looked up. "Yes, and so does Ziggie. And what a fucking great help I have been to you both!"

Marisa smiled despite herself. It was probably only the second or third time in her life that she had heard Erin use that word. She didn't answer the question, she was too preoccupied thinking about the night they had fallen through the wall.

"Listen, if the journals and other papers aren't here, where would they be?" Erin knew her friend's mental process only too well, realized that she was thinking out loud: she didn't respond.

Now Marisa was pacing, Erin sat down quietly to wait for her to come up with something ingenious.

Suddenly she turned. "I've got it! Do you remember the old safe in Sister Superior's office? I bet the stuff is in there!"

"Which is out of our reach, unless you happen to have a key to the main building?"

"We'll just have to go in the way we did that first night. That's all there is to it!" Marisa pushed at the wall again.

Erin walked over to Marisa. She placed her hand on Marisa's wrist.

"What? Do you have a better idea?"

"Maybe," Erin said. "Let's retrace everything we did that night."

She sat down against the wall just as they had sat that night. Marisa sat down beside her, exactly as she had.

Nothing happened.

"That was fun, but it didn't help much, did it?" Marisa stood up, began to pace back and forth. Erin was still seated on the floor, her back against the wall.

Suddenly, Erin's face lit up like a Christmas tree, sat forward without touching the wall behind her. "Marisa! Go stand where the nun was that night!"

Marisa obeyed, circled around the trunks to the exact spot where the nun had been standing that night.

"What do you see?"

Marisa looked around her. "Nothing."

"There has to be something! Look more carefully. Use my lantern and really search."

Marisa crossed over to where they had been sitting earlier and picked up Erin's lantern. She turned it on, returned to the spot again. She looked around, but was still unable to see anything out of the ordinary.

"Nothing?" Erin was losing her patience.

"Nothing."

"Wait a minute! Don't you remember? She kneeled down and opened the trunk. Then she looked directly at us, stood up again, and closed the trunk. She was still staring at us when the wall devoured us." Erin scooted forward a bit, placed herself further from the wall. "Do what she did. Exactly."

Marisa kneeled down and opened the trunk, then stood and let the lid fall.

The wall opened behind Erin, but this time, she didn't fall through. As if she had never had a problem with her knees, she veritably jumped to her feet; but just before she could step forward through the opening, it closed.

She turned to Marisa ready to ream her out, when Marisa shrugged her shoulders.

"I didn't touch a thing... I swear!"

Erin approached Marisa; put her lantern on the floor. "There has to be something down here, or in the trunk, that triggers the mechanism that opens and shuts the doors in the wall."

Marisa dropped to her knees, pushed the heavy trunk a few inches back. "Aha! There it is!"

Right where the front of the trunk had been was a small block of cement elevated from the rest of the floor. She pushed it and the wall opened. She pushed it again and it shut.

"Now it begins to make sense! When the trunk lid fell, it was just enough pressure to activate the wall doors. Then you put your lantern on top of the trunk, it was enough pressure to make them close again." Erin was excited.

"Do you suppose that means that the nun knew that she was activating the doors? And then she closed them again?" Marisa didn't like the sound of that... not a bit. "A murderous nun is a concept that I am not quite ready to digest."

"Somehow, I don't believe it either. I imagine the lid falling made the doors open, which is when we fell in. Then she probably put her hand on top of the trunk to steady herself, and that's when they closed. Maybe she had no idea that she'd made the wall open."

"Poor old thing!" Marisa giggled. "She probably thinks she was hallucinating!"

"Or maybe not." Erin was pensive again. "Look... we saw too many things in the tunnels and in the music hall's elevator not to realize that the nuns have been using these tunnels for generations. No, I have a feeling that she knew. I don't know why she did it, but I have a very uneasy feeling about it." She turned to Marisa. "I think we've done quite enough for the day. Let's get out of here!"

Marisa wasn't ready to give up, even though she was uneasy about the old nun. "I'm not sure, Erin. I still think we need to pay a visit to Sister Superior's safe. Besides, from there it's an easy exit through the Junior Court to the gate where we left our stepladder. What's the difference?"

"My question is: What's the point?" Erin was anxious to get out of the place. "Not only am I feeling very dark things in here, but supposing we can get to Sister Superior's office, unless one of your hidden talents is safe-cracking, I don't see where it serves us to any purpose whatsoever!"

Marisa grinned. "Actually, back in my days in Protocol, I was given an office with a very old safe; much like the one in Sister's office, only much bigger. It was locked and I had to call in a government locksmith who had been a safecracker in his naughty youth. I was fascinated by the whole process and he showed me a few tricks."

"And after a ten minute lesson twenty years ago, you are now going to crack Sister Superior's safe?"

"I'm a quick learner. You know that..." Marisa pushed the cement block on the floor, and the doors opened. "After you, Girlfriend..."

Erin gave up, knowing her arguments would fall upon deaf ears. Her natural instincts for survival were screaming at her to walk out of the basement through the breezeway door and leave Marisa to her own devices, but she couldn't do it. Marisa's own devices could be involuntarily suicidal, she couldn't allow that. She walked slowly toward the doors, her lantern in hand. "I hope you can figure out how to close the wall again."

"There has to be another cement block on the other side," Marisa followed Erin through the gap in the wall.

Once on the inside of the tunnel, she held her lantern low, searched the surface of the floor. "We just didn't know where to look that first time." She moved her lantern back and forth across the floor. "Aha! Here it is!"

She stomped directly on the small square of cement protruding from the otherwise smooth floor, the doors closed.

"You know, now that we have sufficient light, the catacombs don't feel quite so ominous." Erin raised her lantern.

"The nuns have been using them for years. It's not as if they were abandoned or dangerous." Marisa was already thinking about how to crack the safe in the Superior's office. "You know, we may have to drop by the nurse's office."

"Are you sick? Or do you just have a nostalgic whim to go visit the place where you played sick all those years?" Erin laughed.

"Nope... perfectly healthy, thank you, but a stethoscope will make the safe-cracking go a lot faster."

Erin moaned. "I just pray we get through the night without landing in jail."

Marisa pulled the iron gate of the elevator open, pushed her inside.

The old cage creaked and groaned as it rose slowly to the attic level. The women climbed the stairs, walked over the study hall roof and down the spiral staircase that led into Sister Superior's office.

"There it is!" Marisa pointed her lantern toward the old box safe. "I knew I remembered that old thing!"

She went straight to the office door, opened it carefully. She peered into the hallway.

"I can assure you that no living soul is walking the hallways of the classroom building at two in the morning." Erin assured her.

"Probably not. Did you say two o'clock? How can it be two A.M.?"

"Oh, time goes by really fast when you're having fun!"

Marisa ignored the comment, entered the hallway. She turned off the fluorescent part of her lantern, switched on the normal flashlight at the end of the tube lest she be seen from the street.

She quickly walked down the main corridor until she saw the familiar little infirmary where she had indeed faked a number of ailments while a student. She found the door unlocked, so she entered. She searched every shelf and drawer, but there was no sign of a stethoscope.

She let herself out closing the door behind her, and cautiously retraced her steps back to the office.

"It may take me longer than we thought," she said as she opened the door, "because I couldn't find a..." She gasped, then jumped up and down giggling. "How did you do that?" She covered her own mouth before Erin could hush her.

Erin was seated on the floor in front of the open safe, carefully going through its contents. "Oh, it's not so hard," she said with a sly smile, "especially when you have the combination!"

"How the..." Marisa stammered.

"I remembered that my grandmother had a safe much like this one in her office. She also had the combination in a very special place, because she could never remember it." She continued to shuffle through the papers.

"And?" Marisa sat on the floor on the other side of the open safe door, held out her hands for some papers.

"And, it occurred to me that most cagey old ladies tend to think alike, so I pulled out the middle drawer of her desk, and taped to the underside of the desktop was what I was looking for: the combination!"

"I love it! Here I am, taxing my brain to remember how to crack a safe, and you simply figure out where to find the combination. You always were rather brilliant, come to think of it."

"Flattery will get you nowhere, except to a copier. I imagine they still have a Xerox machine over in the administration office." She handed Marisa a pile of papers. "See if you can make some copies of these."

Marisa hesitated, and then shook her head. "I think not. The administration office's windows open directly to the street. I'm sure the police patrol fairly often, given that it is a convent and all, and the last thing we need is a curious cop noticing a green copier light, or movement in the administration office."

"I don't see that we have any choice, because it'll take us until noon to get through all this stuff to know what is important or not," Erin insisted.

Marisa stared at the papers for a moment, then shrugged her shoulders. "At this point, what possible difference can it make?" She saw the confused look on Erin's face as she stared up at her. "No... seriously. What difference could it possibly make at this point if we put the papers back or if we just steal them?"

"Uh, the difference between freedom and hard time?" Erin wasn't laughing.

"Look. Breaking and entering and document theft pales by comparison to what we suspect is going on here, so who is going to accuse who?"

"Whom."

"Exactly. I don't think we are risking anything at all. By the time we break this case open, our activities will seem heroic compared to everything that these people will be going down for."

"No, Marisa. I said 'whom' in a grammatical sense, not because I agree with you." She realized by the blank expression on Marisa's face, that she hadn't even understood the grammatical correction. "But get a grip, Marisa. What case? What people?"

Marisa reflected a moment, recognized the truth in Erin's words.

"I'm sorry. You're right. We really don't know what is going on, and the only ones that we know for sure are breaking the law right now are you and I." She shrugged her shoulders, reached up to a hook at the top of a small chalkboard next to the door, and lifted the strap of a book bag that hung there. "So since we're breaking the law anyway, I suggest we make proper use of this nice little book bag."

She neatly placed the pile of papers that Erin had given her at the bottom of the bag. "Come on! Hand me the rest!" she ordered her friend, and Erin began passing her piles of papers.

"I know I'm going to be very, very sorry for this." Erin continued to hand Marisa papers.

Once the documents were tucked at the bottom of the bag, Marisa reached over and took the pile of journals. "Now *these* are going to be yummy!"

"I wish you would find a new word, Marisa. *Yummy* is for food. Not men, even delectable ones, and certainly not a bunch of journals written by a bunch of dead nuns."

Tucking the last journal into the stuffed book bag, Marisa laughed. "Anything you say, Professor, Now let's get the hell out of Dodge, shall we?"

By the time they reached Marisa's rental car, the first ribbons of color began to appear on the Eastern horizon.

"We made it just in time." Marisa started the engine. Erin slid into the seat after stowing the stepladder in the trunk of the small compact car. The book bag was on the floor of the back seat with Marisa's sweater thrown over it. "I can't believe we were in there for almost six hours!"

She reached down into her purse, pulled out her cell phone. She handed it to Erin. "Just select 'phone book' and you'll see Pablo's number in the third or fourth position. Push 'select' and it will dial him."

"You plan to call him at five-thirty in the morning? You've got to be kidding!" Erin handed the phone back to Marisa. "I will have no part in that."

"Okay, but since we did promise to call him the minute we got out of there, the poor guy probably thinks that something has happened to us. The last thing we need is for Pablo to storm the gates of the convent with half the city's police force looking for us!"

Erin shook her head. "I suppose you're right, but if I call him and he is sound asleep, I am going to kill you."

"Of course you will, and I will help you." Marisa was slap-happy at this point, so she would have agreed to almost anything.

Erin followed Marisa's instructions and dialed Pablo. He answered on the second ring and did not sound sleepy at all.

"Hello?" he answered. "Marisa?"

"It's Erin, Pablo. Did we wake you?"

"I wish!" Pablo laughed. "But no, I have been waiting for your call. Is everything all right? I've been worried."

"We ran into a few obstacles, but everything is fine, Pablo." Marisa was mouthing something at her, but Erin didn't understand. "Hold on a minute, Pablo. Marisa is trying to tell me something." She turned to Marisa and said, "WHAT!"

"I don't want to take the documents to your house. Get his address and tell him to make some very strong coffee. We'll stop by a bakery or something and take breakfast."

Erin nodded and put the phone to her ear again. "Marisa doesn't feel like going to my house right now. She says to get your address, and for you to make some hot coffee. We will bring breakfast."

"Good idea, but give the phone to Marisa so she'll know how to get here." Erin handed the phone to Marisa, who pulled over before telling Pablo to go ahead.

Once she was ready, he explained. "Okay, I live on Country Club Knoll, in La Jolla. If you go up.."

Marisa interrupted. "I know where it is. Are you on Cabrillo or Rhoda?"

"Rhoda. It's the last house on the left."

"Isn't that the old Segovia place?"

"Yes." Pablo was silent a moment. "Why?"

"I take it your maternal surname is Santamaría, right? and your paternal surname is.."

"Segovia." He laughed. "Is that a problem?"

"No, of course not. We'll see you in just a bit, Pablo. I know exactly where you are."

She hung up the phone, handed it to Erin. Her hand was shaking visibly.

"What's wrong?"

"Oh, nothing." Marisa pulled onto the highway that would take them from the valley in the eastern end of San Diego directly to La Jolla.

She turned on the radio, tried to hum to every familiar song that she could find. Erin realized that something was bothering her, but she thought better of asking, for Marisa obviously needed time to think.

By the time they reached La Jolla Shores, most of the markets were open. Marisa picked a market and bakery in a small village-like center, parked the car. "Come on! This place probably makes great coffee, and even better croissants. I think we both need a cup of coffee before we go up the hill."

Erin climbed out of the car, carefully checking to see that Marisa had taken the keys from the ignition before locking the car doors. She followed Marisa into the bakery.

Marisa grabbed a complimentary newspaper, ordered two double espressos before sitting at a small bistro table in the corner. Erin sat across from her, staring her down until Marisa lifted her gaze.

"Are you going to tell me what has you so freaked out?" Erin had no intention of moving until she found out what was going on.

Marisa smiled. "Really, Erin, it's nothing important. It's just that I can't figure out what Pablo is doing living in one of the most expensive homes in La Jolla, if not the world."

"Maybe he is the house-sitter or the live-in gardener?"

"I doubt it. I seriously doubt it. In fact, I am now quite sure why I have been so utterly and completely attracted to him from the day I met him."

Now, Erin was intrigued. "Okay, I'll bite. Why?"

"Because he is identical to his father. That's to say, his father twenty-five years ago, when.."

"When he took you to the Senior Prom." Erin finished her sentence. "Oh, my God!" she yelled and the few other customers turned in her direction. "You think he's Arturo's son? That means he is the Segovia's.."

"Yes. He would have to be their grandson. That would make Pablo a very rich boy, indeed; heir to the Segovia Airlines fortune."

"Also Arturo's son. I mean, Arturo was an only child, wasn't he?" Erin spoke softly.

"That's right." Marisa lowered her head to the table, hitting it against the metal as if to punish herself. She only lifted her head when she saw the waiter's shoes through the lattice work of the bistro table.

Once he had placed their coffee in front of them, Marisa smiled. "Could you toast a half a dozen croissants with butter, to go, with a selection of jams and jellies, please? We'll be ready to go as soon as they are," She drank from the demitasse placed before her until the waiter retreated.

"He is living in Arturo's grandparent's home, where Arturo lived when I met him." She fished her cellular phone from her purse, turned it on again. "I have to cancel, or have him meet us somewhere. If I walk into that house and find his father there, I will die. You will never have another chance to threaten me with death. I will be dead."

Erin reached out, took the phone from Marisa's hand before she could complete the call. "You're not going to call anyone. I happen to know that Pablo lives alone, because he has mentioned it a number of times, and because Ziggie has been to his house many times. Ziggie says it's a beautiful home, but he never mentioned it was the old Segovia place."

"He probably didn't know, and wouldn't have cared if he had known." Marisa smiled. "I mean, why would he care? He wasn't the one who, well, who.."

"Went to the prom with Pablo's father?"

"I'm afraid I went a lot further than the prom with his father, and you know it. So now what? Do I tell him I 'know' his *Daddy*? Or do I hide it and wait until his *Daddy* shows up?"

"You flatter yourself, my dear. Who is to say that *Daddy* would even recognize you? It has been thirty-five years, after all."

"Ouch! Now, that one really hurt!" Marisa's expression saddened. "But you are absolutely right. He probably wouldn't recognize me, and I probably wouldn't recognize him. He's probably fat and bald and.."

"If he was anything like Pablo as a young man, he couldn't possibly be too bad now!"

"Oh, but I am? Gee, thanks a lot!"

"You know what I mean. You have to laugh, Marisa... come on! It's funny. It is so bizarrely improbable that you have to find the humor in it!"

"Of course I do." Marisa's tone was flat. "Hahahaha." She pronounced every syllable, dryly. "I can't stop laughing, really I can't." Her face went from serious to grave. "But you know what? It doesn't make sense. Why would the heir to one of the larger fortunes on this continent be working as a maitre'd in a restaurant? I don't get it."

"I'm sure there's probably a reason, or maybe he just enjoys it." Erin didn't find this particularly important: many of her wealthiest students had insignificant jobs because their families found it important for them to learn the value of money. She said so, but Marisa wasn't convinced.

As soon as the waiter brought the box with their croissants, Marisa left a twenty dollar bill on the table, and they left.

"That was a pretty big tip for an eight dollar check," Erin said.

"I have developed a recent interest and fondness for restaurant employees," Marisa grinned.

The clanging of the metal door as it opened woke him, he sat up.

Artificial light beamed in from the hallway. He looked around the small room quickly before lifting himself to a sitting position on the edge of the uncomfortable cot on which he had been sleeping for three nights now.

He had come to anxiously await his only contact with the outside world.

"Good morning, Sister Agnes," he greeted the nun who crossed the small room with a tray in her hands.

"Good morning, Brother Zigfried." The nun placed the tray on his bed, then turned to leave. There was a plate of scrambled eggs, hash browned potatoes with toast, and a cup of hot coffee on the tray.

"Please, Sister, please don't leave. It is so unpleasant to try to eat in the dark! Won't you sit with me, leaving the hall door open for light, while I eat? You cannot imagine how much I would appreciate it."

The nun was hesitant, but finally sat on a small chair next to the bed. "I suppose I could do that."

"Tell me, Sister, why am I here?

"Because you need your rest, Brother."

Ziggie realized she knew no more than he did; it was pointless to interrogate her.

"So I do, Sister, so I do. At the moment, though, I need this wonderful coffee, and a bit of sustenance."

He sipped his coffee. He clearly remembered Father Gregory entering his office, and quickly hanging up on Erin. The next thing he knew, he was here, but he did not know why.

The only thing he knew with any certainty was that Erin would be looking for him.

Would she think to look here?

Chapter Nine

Marisa pulled up, glancing over at the house: the trees were taller but as graceful as ever, partially shading the winding slate walkway with its ivy covered boulder and rock border. Through the lush greenery at the base of the trees, she could see the v-shaped entryway leading up to the massive double doors of wood and glass.

Erin grabbed the book bag, waiting patiently for Marisa to shut off the engine. She finally reached over and turned the key in the ignition and the engine died. "In your own words, Marisa: get a grip. We don't have time for you to wallow in the past, or in the peccadilloes of your present love life. The croissants are getting cold. Set the parking brake, unlock your seat belt and move your ass."

Erin climbed out of the car, book bag in hand, and leaned back in to look at Marisa still motionless behind the steering wheel. "Damn it! Now!"

Marisa jumped in her seat at the tone of exasperation in Erin's voice. She'd rather face the wall of termites in the tunnels than go inside, but Erin was being so adamant Marisa half expected her to bodily drag her from the car and inside if she didn't go on her own.

If it boiled down to a choice of walking upright or being dragged, she opted for upright.

Pablo was waiting for them at the open double doors. He bent down and greeted Erin with a kiss on her cheek. "Is there a problem?" He frowned seeing the look of consternation on her face.

Erin glanced back at the car before answering. "Nothing important." She entered the house and stood at Pablo's side as Marisa joined them.

Pablo leaned down to greet her in the same way, but Marisa ducked under his arm and hurriedly stood by Erin. She nearly dumped the box of croissants in her haste. "I hope the coffee's ready." She smiled tightly.

"In the kitchen." Pablo closed the doors. Marisa started toward the kitchen, but stopped herself. She wasn't supposed to know where it was.

Erin took pity on her. "Here hold this." She handed Pablo the book bag. "I'll take the croissants." She grabbed the box from Marisa's hands before she dropped it. "You unpack the book bag, while Pablo and I take care of these and bring the coffee."

Marisa held out her hand to a now confused Pablo, who gave her the bag.

"And where is the kitchen?" Erin took charge, preventing Pablo from being left alone with Marisa.

"It's this way." He waved his hand to the left as Marisa hurriedly moved towards the living room.

"What's wrong, Professor?" He watched her set the box on the counter. He reached around her and pulled cups from the cupboard. "Please don't insult me by saying it is nothing."

Erin couldn't tell him of Marisa's self-indulgent guilt trip, but she refused to lie. This did not, however, prevent her from giving him an honest answer; just not to the question he'd asked.

"I wouldn't think of it. But, it is as close to nothing as one can get. Unfortunately, my dear, you have two sleep deprived middle-aged women who are in desperate need of caffeine and calories barging into your beautiful home, with the loot from their latest burglary in tow. I fear we owe you a most sincere apology."

Pablo could not help but smile at her colorful self-description. "No apology is necessary. *Mi casa es su casa.*"

Erin flashed him a tired smile of gratitude and set out the croissants on waiting plates while he poured the coffee. She silently prayed that Marisa had used this time to refocus herself to the true task ahead of them.

Marisa stood frozen in the living room, clutching the book bag as though it was a life preserver. From the moment she had walked through the front door it had been like walking through a time portal: she was that innocent and infatuated girl again. It mattered little that the interior decor was more contemporary, or the arrangement of the tables and lamps not the same. The house *felt* exactly the same as it had the night Arturo had broken her heart.

She glanced down. The sight of her white knuckled fingers made her cringe. It was too much. Erin was right. *"I need to get a grip."* She sternly scolded herself. Erin needed the Marisa of now, not a ghost from the past.

She deliberately released her death grip on the book bag, one finger at a time, and walked over to the wide coffee table where Pablo had set up his laptop and scanner. Marisa opened the book bag and blindly began to unload the contents. All the papers ended up in a haphazard pile that threatened to topple to the floor.

She was about to set the last journal on the table when she jerked at the sound of Pablo's voice, as he and Erin made their way from the kitchen. Her knee hit the table edge sending the precarious pile of papers cascading to the floor.

"Shit!" She hissed softly, quickly dropped to her knees to gather them up before Erin and Pablo arrived.

Erin turned the corner into the living room to the sight of Marisa on the floor surrounded by scattered papers her hands filled with still more papers and a look of frustration on her face.

"Marisa? I asked you to unload the book bag, not dump it."

"I didn't dump it!" Marisa replied through clenched teeth. "They slid off the table while I was unloading the journals."

Pablo set the coffee tray on a nearby side table. "Ladies!" He spoke with quiet firmness in his voice.

Erin stopped in her tracks, a stunned expression on her face. She had never heard Pablo sound this way before. The look on Marisa's face dared him to say the wrong thing.

Pablo didn't flinch. He moved to Erin and relieved her of the tray she carried.

"You have done enough. Sit. You are both very tired and understandably on edge." He eyed the two of them steadily. "You will drink your coffee and enjoy several of these delicious croissants, while I deal with what you have brought us." His tone wasn't harsh or loud, but Erin and Marisa knew he was not merely making a suggestion.

Marisa set the journal on the table and dropped the papers she had in her hand. She then stepped over the mess on the floor around her and sat down in the nearest armchair, all the while feeling like a chastised child. Erin followed suit, embarrassed that Pablo had been witness to their sniping at one another. Neither said a word, with the exception of a thank you to Pablo as he served them their coffee and croissants.

Pablo quietly and efficiently gathered the scattered papers into two manageable stacks, which he set to one side near his scanner. The tension-laden scene that had played out between the women was not unfamiliar to him; he had played both referee and peacemaker numerous times while growing up with and around his many aunts and female cousins.

He waited until they had all eaten and were on their second cup of coffee before he lifted a paper from the top of the nearest stack. It was a copy of an inventory of textbooks and computer supplies on order for the coming term at the school. The next was a classroom assignment sheet; the one after that was a missive from the Mother House. Fifteen minutes later, Pablo had finished sorting the paperwork. He sat back and eyed the results.

The earlier tension between Erin and Marisa had disappeared as the piles in front of Pablo grew.

"More coffee?" Marisa cleared away the used dishes.

"Yes, please." Pablo reached for the first of the three Journals, opened it to the first page. At the top it was dated several years in the past, but not far enough to help them in their search. He rifled through the journal, stopping only to scan the dates on various pages as he went. Nearing the end, he paused to read the entry for the day Erin and Marisa had made their first foray into the basement at the school:

The Class Reunion for the class of 1970 concluded today. We were fortunate to secure   promises of several large donations towards the Scholarship Fund. Sister Thomas Marie has been unusually agitated during the course of the Reunion, even complained about certain students trespassing in forbidden areas of the campus. Given her advanced age and deteriorating faculties, I would ascribe this to the return of the numerous Alumnae. Should her agitation increase or continue I will consult with our Physician.

Pablo whistled softly.

Erin entered the room with fresh coffee. "What? Did you find something?"

"He found something?" Marisa came in on the tail end of Erin's question.

Pablo glanced up at them and shook his head. "You have no idea how lucky the two of you are."

"Whatever are you talking about?" Erin set a cup of fresh coffee within Pablo's reach.

"Someone saw the two of you the night you went into the basement." Pablo glanced back down at the journal and read them the entry for that night. He hoped it would dissuade them from any further risk taking.

"Sister Thomas Marie!" They exclaimed almost in unison.

"She's still alive? She has to be in her late nineties, at least." Marisa gasped at Erin. "It never occurred to me she might still be at the school."

"She saw us?" Erin's hand went to her mouth. "That must have been the nun that came into the basement while we there."

"Oh my god! You're right. Thank goodness nobody believed her when she told them."

"Hold on a sec." Pablo broke in. "Who is Sister Thomas Marie?"

"Her name is on the list of Mothers Superior." Erin replied. "We thought it unusual that the dates after her name indicated she had been Superior there for a lengthy period of time."

"By lengthy, are you saying eight years, ten years?" To hear that the nun's name was on the list of Mothers Superior that Ziggie had faxed to

Erin piqued his curiosity.

"Not even close." Marisa shook her head. "Try twenty-three years."

Pablo sat upright. "It isn't a typo? Maybe it should read thirteen years?" This was an unprecedented amount of time for a Religious posting.

"There is no gap in time between the end of her term and the start of the next Superior's term." Erin told him. "We have felt from the start that this had to be significant in some way."

"I agree it is a puzzle, but significant?" Pablo was skeptical. "What are the dates in question?"

Marisa gave him the dates. "She was also the head of the Congregation during her stay at the school."

"Now that is significant." Pablo mused aloud. "Okay, that was during the time of the Vatican II implementation."

"We already discussed that." Erin shook her head. "It could be a contributing cause, but not the primary reason. The head of the Congregation has always been at the Mother House."

"Maybe one of these older books might tell us something." Marisa picked up the oldest looking journal on the table, opened it. A folded paper, yellowed with age, slipped out and onto the carpet. "What could this be?" Marisa reached down to pick it up.

"Don't touch it." Erin stopped her. "I've seen paper like that before. It is very old and very fragile. Pablo, do you have any white cotton gloves?"

"No, but there might be some thin plastic gloves in the bathroom. My cousin Angelica stays here at times and she bleaches her hair."

"Please be a dear and go look." Erin bent down, looked closer at the folded sheet. "And some tweezers, if possible." She called after Pablo.

Marisa bent down next to Erin. "What do think you think it might be?"

"I'm almost afraid to touch it. From the look of it, it is very old. We need to be very careful in how we handle it."

"It must have had some importance to the Mother Superior whose journal it was in." Marisa stared at the sheet as if by wishing she could see what was written on the hidden side.

Erin took a deep breath to steady herself. "Clear a space on the table where we can lay it out."

Pablo returned with tweezers, but no gloves. "These are all I could find." He handed them to Erin.

"Wait!" Marisa straightened. "There's still that box of plastic gloves in the trunk of the car." She started toward the front door. "Don't do anything until I get back." She returned in less than two minutes with enough gloves for each of them.

Gloved, Erin carefully lifted the sheet onto the clear section of the coffee table. Using the tweezers, she slowly and carefully unfolded the fragile sheet. She lightly flattened it on the table with her fingertips.

"Please let there be something there," Marisa prayed aloud, "and, in English." She remembered the pages in German and Russian that had initiated the mystery they were trying to unravel.

"Yes, there is something written here," Erin said, "and, it's in English."

"Thank you, God." Marisa glanced quickly towards the ceiling before looking back down. "Can you read it?"

"I think so. The ink is faded in places, but I should be able to decipher what it says."

Erin took a quieting breath and began to read:

I write and leave behind me this letter at St. Petersburg. I feel that I shall leave life before January 1st. I wish to make known to the Russian people, to Papa, to the Russian Mother and her children, to the land of Russia, what they must understand. If I am killed by common assassins, and especially by my brothers the Russian peasants, you, Tsar of Russia have nothing to fear, remain on your throne and govern, and you, Russian Tsar, will have nothing to fear for your children, they will reign for hundreds of years in Russia. But, if I am murdered by Boyars, Noblers, and, if they shed my blood, their hands will remain soiled with my blood, for twenty-five years they will not wash their hands from my blood. They will leave Russia. Brothers will kill brothers, and they will hate each other, and for twenty-five years there will be no No-

blers in the country. *Tsar of the land of Russia, if you hear the sound of the bell which will tell you that Grigori has been killed, you must know this: if it was your relations who have wrought my death then no one of your family, that is to say, none of your children or relations will remain alive for more than two years.*

They will be killed by the Russian people...I shall be killed. I am no longer among the living. Pray, pray, be strong, think of your blessed family.

Stunned silence filled the room as Erin finished reading.

"I recognize that," Marisa said. "We studied it in Political Science, when I was in college. that's the letter that Rasputin wrote to Alexandra before he was killed. What is it doing in an old nun's journal?"

"It is also known as Rasputin's Prophecy," Pablo added. "We studied it as well at the University."

"There are those in certain circles of Academia who feel it is indeed a Prophecy," Erin said. "Twenty-three days after Rasputin wrote it, he was murdered by two relatives of Tsar Nicholas II. And nineteen months after his death, the Tsar and his family were murdered."

"That still doesn't answer my question of why it was hidden in the private journal of a nun." Marisa chewed at her lower lip. "I don't think I like where this might be leading."

"What do you mean?" Erin frowned. "Just where do you think that may be?"

"I haven't any idea; just that this coupled with the frequent mention of the Romanovs in those papers Ziggie was translating for us, makes me wonder."

"While this is extremely intriguing," Erin said, looking from Marisa to Pablo, "I fail to see how it will bring us any closer to locating Ziggie."

"On the contrary, Professor" Pablo disagreed. "It may do exactly that."

"How?" Erin demanded.

"You really think so?" Marisa asked. "So what now? We only have two threads, and fairly thin ones at that. How do we make a tapestry out of them?" They all looked at one another, each waiting for someone to come up with an idea or a plan.

"Come on now! None of us are exactly geniuses here, with the exception of Erin, of course, but neither are we dullards. Think, people!"

"You seem so anxious for us to do something." Erin looked at her. "What would you do if it was just you and you were investigating leads towards a story?"

"See!" Marisa smiled. "I said she was a genius. Of course!" She grabbed a pad and pen and quickly drew two lines down the page making three columns. At the top of the first column she wrote, *Romanov.* At the top of the other, she wrote, *Rasputin.* And, at the top of the last column, she wrote, *C. of St. Thomas.*

"Okay, now we list what we know about each of the names at the head of the column, then compare columns looking for common denominators."

"I think we will need more than one page to list everything." Pablo smiled. "How do you keep everything straight and avoid repetition?"

"I usually do this on my laptop," Marisa said. "But, before I had a laptop, I used the old cut and paste method where you tape the sheets of paper together into one long continuous page."

"Effective, I suppose." Pablo thought it time consuming and awkward. "But, we do have a laptop here. Why can't I put everything on a spreadsheet format? It will make cross referencing that much easier."

"What are you waiting for?" Marisa waved at his laptop.

"This will take forever! There have been volumes written about the Romanovs and Rasputin alone. How will we be able to find any commonalties with so many irrelevant facts?" Erin was worried they might be wasting time; time that could be spent in constructively locating Ziggie.

"You're right, if we were to try to list their entire lives." Marisa laughed. "We'll just focus on the pertinent time frame."

"Which would be?" Erin was still dubious, but willing to give Marisa's way a chance. She had a gift for connecting people, or events, that by themselves were innocuous, but when put together, very revealing. It was what made her such an excellent investigative reporter.

"How about six months prior to when Rasputin wrote the letter to Alexandra?" Marisa suggested.

"Too short." Erin shook her head.

"How long would you suggest, *Professor*?" Pablo quickly accessed a spreadsheet program and formatted a page.

"We are dealing with an Imperial Dynasty with its internal and external politics. A man viewed by some as an Evil, by others as a Saint, which brings in Religious differences and conflicts. Then trying to somehow tie them with a Religious Congregation in America, I think we should expand our search to one to two years." Erin explained in a professorial tone. "He wrote that letter in December of 1916.

"That would be 1913 or 1914 then?"

"Make it 1914. That's two years."

"Two years it is then." Pablo set the parameters on the screen.

Three hours later and the page in front of Pablo was filled with dates, names of known associates, religious preferences, affiliations, court politics, familial relationships and virtues/vices for both the Romanovs and Rasputin. In the column for the Congregation, Pablo had entered all they knew with regards to its establishment, role in the United States, the names of the appropriate mothers superior during their time frame, and any political interaction on the international and national fronts.

Used dishes from a quick lunch were scattered around the room. Pablo stretched out his hands and fingers to prevent their cramping from all the typing he had done. Erin searched her extensive memory for anything else she could find to add to their database, while Marisa read the entries in the Mother Superior's journal for each period.

Pablo looked up. "Can anyone think of anything else to enter?"

Erin looked over at Marisa, who shrugged.

"Let's see how far we get with what we have," Marisa suggested.

An hour later, they had almost as many commonalties between the

Romanov Dynasty and Rasputin as they had entries.

"This isn't getting us anywhere," Erin said. "It has all been a waste of time."

"Not necessarily," Marisa disagreed. "We've established multiple connections with two of the suspects on our list. What we need to do now is dig for a commonality with the Congregation."

"Suspects?" Pablo looked askance.

"Sorry, I'm used to working with law enforcement this way. It just slipped out."

"A fortuitous slip perhaps." Erin moved over to look at the printout of their spreadsheet. "Why not treat them as suspects? Would it not widen our possibilities?"

"Suspected of what?" Pablo knitted his brows.

"Murder," Marisa interjected with fresh enthusiasm. "We have two sets of murders here, separated by a nineteen month time lapse. We take each one and approach it from the perspective of motive and opportunity."

"Motive and opportunity." Pablo nodded. "We are certain to find many with a motive to kill Rasputin. Where will that leave us?"

"Then we look at who had the strongest motive, with the most to gain." Marisa explained as she closely studied the spreadsheet; then referred to the journal she'd been reading, and traced her finger back and forth between the columns of the spreadsheet.

"But it is well documented that a group of conspirators, primarily involving Prince Felix Youssopov, were the ones responsible for Rasputin's death," Erin interjected. "He and his wife Irina fled to Paris and lived in greatly reduced circumstances after the Russian Revolution. What did he gain from it?"

"Exactly!" Marisa pounced. "I have always suspected that he may have been the pawn of someone who hoped to gain a great deal from Rasputin's death."

"I notice, you said, hoped to gain rather than stood to gain, why?" Pablo asked. In the last several hours he had come to be amazed by the depth and breadth of knowledge these two women held. He had always known Erin was impressively intelligent. Yet, Marisa, for whatever reasons she might have, tried to play down or keep hidden her own equally impressive mind.

Listening to them toss little known facts and events around as though they were common knowledge had caused him, at times, to lose track of what he was typing.

"Yes, why?" Erin echoed his question.

"I don't think it was someone in Russia who was behind Rasputin's death."

"What!" Erin shook her head. "Certainly you can't think it was Franz Joseph? He was Alexandra's cousin, for goodness sake. He would never do something that would hurt her like that."

"And his declaring war on Russia wouldn't hurt her?" Marisa shot back at her. "As in: *Sorry, Cuz, nothing personal?*"

"Joseph was her cousin?" Pablo was shocked. This was complete news to him.

The women ignored him, lost in their debate:

"He had no choice but to declare war." Erin retorted.

"You're right, which is exactly why I don't think he was the one behind Rasputin's death," Marisa told her. "He had no choice. I'm after the one who left him no choice."

"And, just who might that be? And please don't bring up your ridiculous Black Pope Conspiracy."

"Black Pope? Conspiracy?" Pablo felt like a spectator at a tennis match watching two top seated players go at one another. "Time!" he called out. Erin and Marisa looked over at him with surprise on their faces.

"Time?" Erin looked confused.

"I think he means, time out, as in a ball game." Marisa explained. "I think we may have lost him there somewhere."

"You didn't lose me," Pablo corrected. "I've heard some of the Jesuit Generals referred to as the Black Popes, but to seriously suggest a Jesuit

General was the one behind Rasputin's death is stretching things, don't you think?"

Erin smiled pleased to see she had an ally in her defense of the Jesuits.

"Oh, I've only begun to suggest what a Jesuit General was behind." Marisa looked each of them straight in the eye. "You think I'm stretching it to say a Black Pope was the one to ultimately gain the most by Rasputin's death? Try this on for size: this same Black Pope was also responsible for the start of World War I."

"Dear Lord, save us!" Erin's hand flew to her chest. "Now you have truly overstepped the bounds of decency! That's libelous calumny, and you should be ashamed of yourself."

"What she said." Pablo moved to stand at Erin's side.

"It is not libel, or calumny if it is the truth," Marisa calmly answered, "but judging from your reaction, it is clear to me that neither of you have any objectivity where your precious Jesuit Generals are concerned. I doubt if you would accept the truth, if you heard it."

"Try us," Pablo challenged.

"Don't give her a forum, dear." Erin placed her hand on his arm. "Ever since Marisa did a term paper in college on the historical and political influences of the Jesuit Generals, she has been on a crusade to discredit them."

"Not all of them," Marisa corrected Erin. "Only the ones that deserve to be shown for what they truly were. The vast majority were as advertised in history: men of vision, courage, integrity and honor."

"See?" Erin nodded. "She even admits it."

"And there was a time when your honored Professor and my dearest friend, whom I love dearly, conceded that not all of the Jesuit Generals were the paragons, martyrs, and saints they've been made out to be." Marisa informed Pablo. "Sadly, I've witnessed a change over the years as Erin became dependent on the Jesuits for her security in life. Now, she blindly refuses to hear a word against them, even if it is truth."

"Marisa!" Pablo gasped. "How can you say such a thing about someone you profess to love and call a dear friend?"

"It's all right, my dear." Erin smiled softly. "We have never held back from each another. Marisa is right in reminding me that I should not condemn and deny something before I have heard what it is."

"Are you willing, better yet, able to listen with an open mind?"

"I will listen, and try to keep an open mind," Erin replied. "In turn, I would ask that you not rely merely on conjecture. The charges you have levied are as serious as can be. I would expect and demand solid proof of what you allege."

"I'll explain the best I can." Marisa acknowledged. "Solid, incontrovertible proof as in a smoking gun may take me a while longer, though considering the time gap between then and now, I may end up being lucky to find only the gun."

"I will be amazed if there is even a gun to find." Pablo shook his head. "But, in deference to my mentor, and yourself, I do will try to maintain an open mind."

"While you're at it, try to be a tad more condescending next time," Marisa said sarcastically.

"Was I being condescending?" Pablo asked Erin with obvious disbelief in his voice.

"Most definitely. But, then, you can't really help it. I've learned over the years that it is an automatic pride thing with most men when they are faced with a situation where a woman may know more about something than they do. I chose to ignore it, whereas, Marisa has never had a problem pointing it out."

"I truly thought I was being polite."

"But you were, dear, quite condescendingly polite." Erin moved to a comfortable armchair and motioned for Pablo to find a seat as well.

"Please feel free to ask questions as I go along. First, can we all agree that the Jesuit Order is almost equal in power to the Papacy, and that the Jesuit Father Generals have always been highly influential in World affairs?"

"Historically this is true." Erin agreed. "The appellation Black Pope began as a way to differentiate between the Pope in Rome, who always wears white, and the Jesuit Father General, who wears the black robes of his order."

"Professor? You agree that the Father General is as powerful as the Pope?"

"Some suggest he is more powerful because he does not have the bureaucracy-laden Curia with which the Pope must contend, with the exception of when he is speaking *Excathedra*," Marisa answered for her.

"Professor?"

"I must agree with Marisa on that. I know that when Marisa and I went to Rome, it was harder to gain an audience with the Jesuit Father General than it was to gain an audience with the Pope." Erin was forced to concede. "Now tell us, which of the Father Generals is under your indictment?"

"There are two actually. The twenty-fifth Jesuit General Franz Xavier Wernz, who was the Black Pope from 1906 until 1914. And, his successor, Wlodimir Ledochowski, who was in charge from 1915 until 1942."

"You know all this off the top of your head?" Pablo was skeptical. Marisa's recitation of the names and dates seemed too glib to him. For all he knew she could have been making it up as she went along.

"As Erin can attest, I have total recall." Marisa felt a bit testy with everything she said being questioned by Pablo or Erin, but she had given them permission to ask. "A double Masters degree in Political Science and World History, and my Master's Thesis was entitled, Theocratic Influences in the Political Spectrum of Europe and Orient from 1760 to 1960. Do you require any other credentials or may I continue?"

"That's more than enough," Pablo wanted to ask her why she was wasting herself as an investigative and court reporter, but refrained, not wanting to antagonize her any further. He was in enough trouble from his earlier faux pas as it was.

"Wernz was obsessed with the destruction of the Orthodox Churches, in particular the Russian Orthodox Church. He was intent on consolidating the Catholic Faith under one Pontificate. As spiritual advisor to the Kaiser Franz Ferdinand, Wernz was aware of the enmity existing between Tzarist Russia and the German State. He saw this as his opportunity to use the Kaiser to destroy the Russian Orthodox Church by telling him he was doing God's will in destroying heretics, declaring war and invading Russia."

"A theory that's been bandied among Theologians with much debate for decades." Erin pointed out.

"Yes, it has. Do you concede that until it is ultimately decided, that its viability is still valid?"

"Out of fairness, one would have to."

"Wernz was yet another cousin to Empress Alexandra, on his mother's side." She held up her hand in Pablo's direction anticipating his doubt. "European Royalty was prolific by nature and with Royals only able to intermarry with other Royals, practically all the Royal Houses were interrelated in one manner or another. Wernz maintained a correspondence with his Imperial Cousin, and knew of her religious fervor, which he thought to nurture to his own advantage."

"Said advantage being what?" Erin questioned.

"Wernz hoped to eventually convince Alexandra of the heretical nature of the Orthodox Church in Russia, and use her influence with her husband, the Tsar, to have it banned by Imperial Decree. This would leave open the breach needed for him to send in his Jesuits to tend to the Russian people and himself as Counsel to the Imperial Family."

"Conjecture or fact?" Erin pressed.

"The Mothers Superior of St. Thomas were not the only religious to keep journals." Marisa tried to keep her calm. At the rate this was going it would be the middle of next week before she would be able to lay out her theory in full. "Wernz kept journals of his own, as well as copies of the correspondence between Alexandra and himself."

"Why would he incriminate himself by writing this out in his journals?" Pablo shook his head. "Mind you, I'm not disputing that he had journals. All the Fathers General kept them to be used by their successors as a guide, and for the History of the Order."

"You just answered your own question." Marisa laughed. "That is precisely why he wrote it all down. But, I'll get back to this in a bit."

"Wernz was dismayed at Alexandra's growing soon to become blind reliance on Rasputin. Even though there was no love lost between Rasputin and the Russian Orthodox Church, this relationship still greatly endangered his own agenda. The Russian Orthodox Church was the first to officially investigate Rasputin. He was a monk, but adhered to few Church laws indulging his many vices where and whenever possible. At times, convincing upstanding Church-going women that by having sex with him, they were not sinning, but being purified."

"And they believed him!" Pablo was dismayed.

"He was very charismatic and highly persuasive. You must remember women were not as liberated as they are today."

"I can see where you might take all this as proof that Father General Wernz would have the most to gain at Rasputin's death." Erin broke in. "Yet, I think you may have a motive alone, but not opportunity. You've said yourself that he died in 1914. How close was this to the start of World War I?"

"He died three weeks after it started." Marisa knew where Erin was headed.

"I will agree you have valid reasoning to imply this Father General may have been an influencing factor in the Kaiser's decision to declare war on Russia." Erin frowned and then shook her head. "However, I cannot agree with the allegation that he was responsible for the death of Rasputin, when Rasputin's death wasn't until two years later?"

"That's where Wernzs successor, Ledochowski comes in," Marisa was quick to say, "and Wernz's journals."

"Even if you could establish probable cause because of these journals, you have lost your prime motive. What could Ledochowski hope to gain?

He was not related to Alexandra, and thus could not exercise any influence with her to cause the Tsar's banning of the Orthodox Church. I fear, dear girl, that your theory collapses at the death of the Father General Wernz."

"No, it doesn't," Marisa insisted. "Ledochowski was able to follow through on his predecessor's orders."

"And even if he was, what could he gain by doing so? I fear this may be when you take one of your flights of conjecture." Erin slowly stood up. "Unless you can give solid proof that this is so, I'm far too tired to pursue this anymore." She turned towards Pablo. "Could I impose on you to give me a ride home? Knowing my sweet Marisa, she will be glued to your computer until it becomes abundantly clear to her that there is no way to prove her wild theory. It is, as I had feared from the start: we have wasted a full day on a wild goose chase, which could have been better spent trying to locate Ziggie."

"Erin!" Marisa gasped. "This isn't a wild goose chase! Believe me! It will lead us to Ziggie."

"I so wish I could believe you, Marisa. But the facts say otherwise."

"But of course, I will see you home." Pablo shot a look of disappointment at Marisa.

"I wouldn't act so high and mighty, Pablo." Marisa challenged him. "At the start of this you were in full agreement that it could lead us to Ziggie."

"That was then. Now I have serious doubts that it will lead us anywhere near him."

"Oh Ye of little faith." Marisa quoted the Scripture to him, as he escorted Erin towards the garage and his car.

Chapter Ten

Marisa vaguely heard the door when Pablo returned, but didn't lift her gaze from the computer screen. She had opened another small file that she had tiled on the screen; she was taking notes to remind her of names, dates and places that could be of importance.

"Have you finished your cross reference?" Pablo asked, breaking her line of concentration.

"Not unless you can figure out the Dimitri or Petrovich connection…" She lifted her gaze toward Pablo.

"Perhaps I can. There was the Grand Duke Dimitri Pavlovitch Romanov, said to be Felix Youssopov's lover, which may or may not be true, but which does not detract from his more notorious distinction as being the co-assassin of Grigori Rasputin in Youssopov's Moika Palace in December of 1916." He observed Marisa's face to catch a glimpse of admiration, but her expression was blank. "Or perhaps you are referring to Prince Dimitri, son of the Grand Duchess Xenia?" This time he was pleased to see a glint of expression in Marisa's gaze.

"I'm not sure. I imagine that the Grand Duke Dimitri is at least six feet under by now. Did he have any children?"

"I seem to recall that he was exiled to the Persian Frontier for his part in Rasputin's murder, and no, I don't believe he had any children. It was said that he and Youssopov were lovers, but no one knows for certain."

"Wasn't Youssopov married to Irina?"

"Yes, but that has nothing to do with anything: he was also a bisexual and a transvestite."

"How about the other Dimitri or the Petrovich guy?"

Pablo closed his eyes, digging into his memory. "The other Dimitri could be the son of the Grand Duchess Xenia, and I believe he had one female issue."

"A female issue?" Marisa huffed. "Nice term, Pablo. Really nice term."

"Sorry, I was recalling the succession pages as I read them, and that's how they refer to daughters." He saw that Marisa was grinning at him, and realized she had been joking. Somehow this put him more at ease.

Through Pablo's description of practically reading a page he had seen once, Marisa had just realized that she was not only dealing with a brilliant mind, but that she was dealing with a brilliant mind that possessed a photographic memory, much like her own, although she didn't actually see the pages of things she once read in her mind's eye, like he obviously did.

"What do you remember about Petrovich?" She was grinning widely by now, thoroughly enjoying the memory "light show."

"That would be Prince Roman Petrovich, son of the Grand Duke Peter Nikolayevich. His son, Prince Nicholai Romanovich is the undisputed successor to the crown, if there were still an Imperial Crown. As a matter of fact, the other Dimitri you asked about could also be Prince Dimitri Romanovich, his brother."

"Interesting, but I'm not sure it is quite what I'm looking for."

Pablo laughed. "Maybe it would help if you were to tell me what you're looking for?"

Marisa thought about it for a moment, but she didn't know quite how to explain it, even to herself. "I wish I knew." The expression on Pablo's face made her laugh. "I know, I know… it makes no sense. It's something that has happened to me since forever. I have a vague, inexplicable idea of what I'm looking for, but I won't know exactly what it is until I find it."

"Okay, I get it…" Pablo didn't get it at all, but he was willing to concede the validity of her mental process, because his process would probably seem just as strange to her as hers was to him. "Can I help?" he asked, stifling a yawn.

"Not really." She glanced at her watch, and realized that it was after eleven. Embarrassed, she stood up. "I am so sorry, Pablo. I didn't realize it was so late!" she stammered, afraid she had overstayed her welcome. "I have monopolized your home since breakfast!"

Pablo realized his involuntary yawn had made her feel uncomfortable and felt badly about it.

"Marisa, it's really no problem. You should know better than that by now. I only asked because if I can't help, I may just go to my room and watch some television for a while. Hey... I may even take a nap, but please, just work as long as you want, and make yourself at home! I am as interested as you and Erin in finding Ziggie, but I'm afraid I just don't have your stamina. My mind doesn't function very well when I'm over-tired."

Marisa hesitated, but then acquiesced. "If it really doesn't bother you for me to be invading your home like this, then I'll take you up on it. Thanks," she said. "If you're asleep when I'm done, then I'll just let my-self out, and lock the door behind me."

"Okay, but you'll have to set the alarm. Just punch in 052070 and it will give you sixty seconds to exit and shut the door."

Marisa recognized the numbers as a very significant date as she wrote them down on a note pad next to the computer, but ascribed it to coinci-dence.

"Thanks, Pablo. I really do appreciate it."

"No problem... and hey, if you get sleepy or lonely, I'm down the hall. It's the second door to the right, and I'll leave the door open."

Marisa laughed. "I thought we had settled that little issue."

"We did. It was a purely platonic invitation."

"Good night, Pablo." She had to physically force herself to look at the computer screen. One more look at his face, and her research would have to become a far more personal and intimate team effort. "Sleep well."

"Good night," he said as he wandered down his hall to bed. "If you get hungry, help yourself to anything you want in the kitchen... there's some great pasta in the fridge that I brought home from the restaurant."

"Thank you, Pablo," she answered, and continued to read through the files on the screen.

Marisa extended her search for the connection she knew she was missing, but each lead she thought she had found led her to a dead end.

At midnight, she gave herself a limit until two in the morning, promising that she would give up and be back at Erin's by two-thirty. Tomorrow was always another day.

It was nearly 1 A.M. when she finally found what she had been looking for, but the information was sketchy, at best.

She was quite sure that Pablo would probably know more of this part of history than any link she might find on the Internet, but she vacillated over waking him.

She rose to her feet and stretched. Her muscles were stiff from sitting in one position too long, and it felt good to stretch them out. She considered her options: the kinder option was to take her leave, plug her senior prom date into the alarm pad and let herself out.

But on the other hand, she wasn't feeling quite that kind of heart because Pablo and Erin were supposedly the two people on earth most concerned about Ziggie's wellbeing, and they were both asleep.

She straightened her blouse and made her decision.

She could hear the television as she neared Pablo's room, heaved a sigh of relief. She wouldn't have to awaken him, after all.

"Pablo?" she called out softly as she stuck her head in the doorway.

Pablo had apparently fallen asleep watching the television, for he didn't stir.

"Pablo?" she called out a little louder, but there was no answer.

Finally, she stepped into the room "Pablo?"

Pablo literally jumped from the bed, startled. "What's wrong!" he stammered.

"I'm sorry. I didn't realize you were asleep."

He rubbed his eyes, but smiled. "I must have dozed off for a few minutes. Is everything all right?"

"Yes, perfectly," she said. "I just came up with some stuff I thought you might be able to help me with... but it can certainly wait until tomorrow." Her voice oozed sympathy. "I'll just let myself out, and call you tomorrow."

She turned and started to walk out, but Pablo caught up with her. "I won't hear of it!" he said. "I only came back here to get out of your way, but the truth of the matter is that I would love to feel useful."

It wasn't until that very moment that Marisa realized that Pablo was wearing his jockey shorts. She turned to resist the temptation to look down.

"How about if I go make some coffee while you throw some clothes on?" She didn't wait for a response and stepped through the open doorway. "I'll see you in the living room in a few minutes."

Pablo donned the jeans he'd left on top of the quilt trunk at the foot of his bed, then crossed over to his bathroom. He turned the cold water faucet on, quickly splashing his face. After patting his face dry, he quickly brushed his teeth while he opened his closet. With his free hand he grabbed a black shirt and pulled it from its hanger.

He was still buttoning his shirt when he entered the kitchen. Marisa was filling the water tank of the coffee pot, having filled the filter with the finely ground coffee that Pablo usually kept on hand for Espresso or Cappuccino.

"Good idea," he said. "The find grind will make a stronger coffee, which we both need if we're going to work much longer tonight." He sat down on a bar stool next to the breakfast bar.

Marisa faced him after starting the coffee pot.

"What do you know about a Father Iliodor?" she asked with no preamble.

Pablo laughed. "Nothing like getting right to the point, but let me think a minute." He was toying with Marisa and enjoying it thoroughly. He closed his eyes briefly, and then opened them again, laughing. "I'm teasing you." He straightened himself on the stool to tell her what he knew about the priest known as Iliodor.

"Well, here goes… Sergei Michailovich Trufanoff, or Iliodor, was one of Bishop Theophane's students who befriended Rasputin. Over a period of about twenty five years, Iliodor vacillated between being a good friend and a veiled enemy of Rasputin's, depending on his own influences at the time. At one point he went to warn Rasputin about an investigation being launched by the Bishop into Rasputin's notorious sexual adventures and his rumored links with the Khlysty sect, but then turned on him a few years later when he was informed of Rasputin's attempted seduction and rape of a nun." Pablo noticed that the coffee was perked, and crossed over to the cupboard to bring out two mugs. As he served them both a mug of the steaming liquid, he continued. "Anyway, Iliodor was not terribly trustworthy, nor truthful, for that matter. Anything he said or wrote about Rasputin was improbable bordering on preposterous. Eventually, he became a Baptist, married and had seven children. What else do you need to know?"

"Thanks," Marisa accepted the. "I needed this." She took a welcome sip of the coffee. "So basically, Iliodor isn't an important link? Was he ever involved, say, with Youssopov? Or Dimitri?"

Pablo had to think about that for a moment, but then slowly nodded his head. "Yes, now that you mention it, there could be a link there. Iliodor was around during the period when Youssopov and Dimitri would have plotted Rasputin's murder. Iliodor, as I said earlier, was easily influenced by others. He was said to be Youssopov's confessor, and had been Rasputin's for many years. If in fact he was Youssopov's confessor, he must have at least known about the plot to kill Rasputin. I wouldn't be at all surprised if he had somehow manipulated it."

"I thought they were friends."

"They were, at times, and then they weren't." Suddenly, he grinned wickedly. "I think I know where you're going with all this, Marisa."

"Do you, now…?" She grinned innocently.

"You're transparent! You obviously think Iliodor was following the Jesuit General's directives, that he manipulated Youssopov into killing Rasputin. You think he may give you proof of your theory."

"Uh, yeah... I believe I declared my mission in rather outspoken terms, the likes of which sent Erin screaming for you to rescue her and take her home. Brilliant deduction, my dear friend, brilliant!"

"Then why not just ask me directly!" It wasn't a question. "Come on. Let's get comfortable in the den." He picked up the half-full coffee carafe. "We can share all we know about dates, places and times in the Society's presence in Russia. After all, I didn't sleep through Jesuit History 101 in the Seminary."

Marisa followed him from the kitchen. "I hope we can clear it up between us, because right about now I am beginning to think that all the knowledge I have gathered is useless."

"No knowledge is useless." He placed the coffee on the table and plopped on the floor. Marisa settled down on the other side of the table, placed her cup next to his computer.

She opened up a new file, then looked up. "You don't mind if I take pertinent notes?"

Pablo laughed. "I don't know how pertinent they'll be, but here goes, anyway... the Society of Jesus was founded in 1540, but they only got established in Russia in 1772, when Poland was divided for the first time and White Russia became part of the Empire. But their stronghold in Russia became, and as far as I know still is, in Novosibirsk, Siberia, then under the auspices of Bishop Joseph Wertz. By the end of the next century, there were around twenty five thousand Jesuits. It has only grown from there."

"Not to interrupt, but wasn't the next century when Pope Clement XIV issued a document suppressing and condemning the Order?" Marisa stretched her fingers.

"Yes, but he never actually made any judgment. He did not actually condemn the Society, but rather listed the charges against it. Jesuit schools and colleges were seized all over the place by local authorities. Even Lorenzo Ricci, the Superior General, was imprisoned in Castel Sant'Angelo, and died two years later."

"And that is when the friction between the Pope and the Society reached its peak." Marisa stood up, started to pace.

"Yes, and from 1773 to 1814 when Pope Pius VII restored the Society, Russia was the only place in the world where the Jesuits maintained their corporate identity. Apparently, Empress Catherine had her own political agenda, and disallowed the papal decree. The Jesuits were actually able to accept novices all over the world, including in the United States, thanks to a corporate affiliation with the Society of Jesus in Russia."

"Exactly!" Marisa exclaimed. "What could they have done in six short years from 1814 to 1820 to so royally piss off Tsar Alexander the First, after having been the Jesuits only support for 38 years? I mean, they remained officially expelled from Russian territory from 1820 until 1992!"

Pablo laughed. "It's very simple: they were teachers. They built more schools than the Imperial Court. However, their teachings came from a Roman Catholic point of view. Alexander the First felt they were a threat to very survival of the Russian Orthodox Church, so he had them officially expelled. But a good number of Jesuits remained to work clandestinely in Russia, even during the Soviet regime; some of them from prison cells."

"Even in Siberia?" Marisa's eyes opened wide.

"Mostly in Siberia. Why?"

"Because that is where Rasputin is from; Iliodor and Youssopov too." She could see Pablo shaking his head. "Don't shake your head, because it's true. From the way you describe Iliodor, I am more certain every minute that he was probably looking to join the Society of Jesus, and manipulated Rasputin's death as some sort of initiation to get in."

Pablo let out a hoot that would have awakened a dead Jesuit. "Come on, now! That is really a stretch. The Society is not an East L.A. gang, for God's sake! They don't have initiations!"

"Not officially, but bear with me a minute... if Iliodor eventually converted to the Baptist faith, why is it such a stretch for him to want to be Roman Catholic?"

"No, I suppose it isn't." Pablo yawned. "But I still don't see where this brings us any closer to finding Ziggie. Or have you found a magic link?"

"Nothing magic about it, I can assure you. The fact that I can establish even with a slight stretch a feud between the Jesuits and the Russians that endured for a number of centuries has to make you agree that not only the documents, but the fact that Ziggie is of Germanic Russian heritage could be the reason for his disappearance.

"That was quite a mouthful, but I'll concede the possibility." He rested his chin on his folded hands on top of the table.

The bags under Pablo's eyes were beginning to make him look a bit like a raccoon, Marisa felt guilty for keeping him up all night.

"I think that is as far as we're going to get with any certainty tonight. Perhaps with rested minds, we can figure out where they have taken him. The why is obvious." She ignored Pablo's unconvinced expression. "And to find out the where, I think the first stop is to see Father Gregory up at the seminary."

"What if he is involved?" Pablo felt danger, although he couldn't pinpoint why.

"I don't doubt it for a minute. He acted guilty as sin, and suspicious when I called as Judith." Pablo yawned again. "Will you take me there tomorrow? I'd go alone, but I think I'd have better luck if you took me. We can say I'm your mother; that you want to introduce me to Brother Ziggie."

"He probably knows that my mother is deceased." Pablo said, and waved Marisa's embarrassed expression off. "Hey, I'm over it. Mom died when I was seven. I owe Father Gregory no explanation as to who you are. You are with me and I am looking for Ziggie. Period."

"Thanks, Pablo. You're a good guy."

She rose to her feet and waited as Pablo did the same. Turning toward the door, she lifted her purse and tossed the strap over her shoulder. Stepping around the table, she leaned over to kiss him on the cheek.

"And now I am going home, so that you can get some sleep!"

Pablo took her by the arm and pulled her toward the hallway, instead of the front door.

"Uh, I don't think so, as tempting as it might be," she said, laughing.

"This is not seduction," His tone was serious. "It is practicality."

He released her arm and walked ahead of her, past his room, to an open door at the end of the hallway.

"Here!" he said, smiling sincerely. "This is the master bedroom, with its own bath, and the door has a lock, in case you don't trust me," His expression turned serious. "It is absolutely ridiculous for you to go driving around the Muirlands at 3:00 A.M. by yourself, even more ridiculous for you to wake Erin. She wasn't in a very cheerful mood when I took her home."

"She's going to be in an even less cheerful mood if she wakes up in the morning and thinks I have spent the night with you. You can trust me on that one."

"Which is entirely her problem, not ours."

"But I need clothes to wear up to the seminary tomorrow morning," she insisted weakly.

"Also not a problem. My cousin Angelica keeps a couple changes of clothes here, and I'm sure something of hers will work just fine. If not, we can throw your stuff into the washer and dryer. Anything else?" His expression was challenging.

Marisa could see the, but still wasn't convinced. "Is there a lock on the outside of the door for you to lock me in?" She laughed. "Just in case you don't trust me, either?"

"Enough! I won't take 'no' for an answer!" Pablo gently pushed her into the enormous room, gently closed the door behind her. "Good night."

"Good night." She immediately realized that she was in the very room where she had spent her Prom night with Arturo.

Marisa had avidly avoided this end of the hallway much less the bed-room but now that she was behind its closed door, she began to feel an unexpected sensation of well being that she didn't understand.

She crossed the room and entered the enormous bathroom. It was the same as that night; but the garden jacuzzi that had seemed quite an odd-ity in the seventies, seemed commonplace now.

There were fresh towels laid out, and a large bottle of bubble bath on the vanity. She picked up the bottle and gazed at it in amazement: it was Plumeria scented, her favorite.

Did Pablo plan this? she wondered, but then even if he had planned to invite her or Erin or both to spend the night, how could he possibly know that she loved Plumeria bubble baths?

That's ridiculous! she decided, eying the bottle from the throne a few feet away.

Oh, what the hell! she thought as she flushed.

Five minutes later and her clothes heaped in a corner, she was languish-ing, with bubbles up to her chin, on the padded lounge-shaped bottom of the tub after filling it with warm water and a few capfuls of the scented liquid. The warm jets massaged her tired back: she felt as if she'd died and gone to heaven.

The water was nearly cold when she awoke. Startled, she spit out a mouthful of water, coughing.

Idiot! she chided herself. *Nothing like drowning in your ex-boyfriend's bathtub with his almost-your-lover son in the next room.* After quickly rins-ing her hair, she clicked open the drain, lifted herself from the tub. She laughed as she grabbed the terry cloth robe hanging from a hook next to the tub.

She put the robe on, and realized it, too, had to be Arturo's, as it hung nearly to the floor on her.

Oh, well, it's not the first time I've worn his clothes, she thought to herself. She pulled a towel from the vanity and towel-dried her hair.

Once her hair was just barely damp, she hung up the towel on the hook where the robe had been, switched off the light before entering the bedroom again. Sleepy again, she crossed over to the king size bed, and pulled the covers down. It was freshly changed, and she wondered again if Pablo had somehow planned for her to stay over.

No, she thought, *he probably has a maid come in to clean and change sheets and towels every few weeks.*

She had already climbed into the bed and cuddled down before realizing that the lamp on the chest of drawers near the door was still on.

She pulled herself up with a groan, sat on the side of the bed, and then slowly pulled herself to her feet. Half asleep, she crossed the room to turn off the offending light, when her gaze suddenly fell on a framed photograph placed next to the lamp.

It was her Prom portrait!

The young couple stood in the foyer of the convent: Arturo in his tuxedo, he looked much like a younger Pablo now, and next to him was Marisa, her hand resting on his lifted forearm, very properly.

At first, she just gazed at the ankle-length gold brocade dress with the bolero jacket: she remembered how Sister Robert had helped her cut the material just a little bit higher in the bodice than what was marked on the pattern, just to be sure she didn't show any cleavage. She laughed, thinking how wonderful it would have been to actually have some cleavage to hide!

Slowly her wistful gaze grew serious, and deep furrows began to form between her eyebrows.

"Wait a freaking minute!" She picked up the photograph.

She looked at it carefully, and reality's Boeing 747 slowly began its approach to the runway. She looked at her face in the photograph, and then her face in the mirror: yes, she had aged, but her features were the same; her hair was the same color, in almost the same cut.

By the time the reality plane touched down, Marisa was out the door, stomping down the hallway. Pablo's door was open. She moved her hand around the inside wall until she found the light switch and snapped it on.

Reality screeched to a halt with its flaps down and brakes smoking at the foot of Pablo's bed.

Pablo opened his eyes, saw Marisa fuming, photograph in hand. He sat up.

"Good morning! Is it time to go already? I feel like I just went to bed."

She was so angry that her hands shook as she silently threw the photograph in the middle of his double bed.

Pablo didn't have to look at the photograph to know what it was.

He smiled. "I see you found the photo. So, in view of the fact that we both know exactly who you are and who I am, do you suppose we can both stop playing this stupid little cat and mouse game?" His face showed practically no expression, and that disarmed Marisa.

This was the last reaction Marisa had expected. She felt her anger toward him dissipating as she stood there glaring at him.

Suddenly the whole situation struck her very funny, she started to laugh.

Pablo's face softened into a smile. He patted the bed beside him. "Come on, Marisa, this is funny. You have to admit, this is funny."

"Either it really is very funny, or we both have a very, very sick sense of humor." She sat down on the foot of the bed. "So, now what?"

Pablo controlled his laughter. "We continue the same way we've been, but now I don't have to hide the fact that I know who you are, and you don't have to hide the fact that you once dated my father. It's really very simple, don't you think?"

Marisa sat and stared at him for a long minute before replying, trying to find a valid argument, but couldn't. "You're right, of course, but I need to know something."

"What?"

"When did you figure it out?"

"I suspected from the day Erin introduced us, just from your name, but I wasn't absolutely sure until I told you where I lived yesterday."

"Why from my name?"

"For the love of God!" he said as he leaned over to muss her hair. "My father has talked about the convent school Marisa as long as I can remember."

This was too much for her. "Oh, please. Seriously, how did you know?"

Pablo wasn't laughing. "Exactly how I told you: through my father's stories. I know that he was a playboy until he met Marisa from the convent school. He fell head over heels for you." He saw that Marisa finally believed him. "But after your Prom and graduation from the convent, you disappeared. You didn't show up for a date, and the next thing he knew you had left for Mexico City without so much as a goodbye."

"So that's the version you got?" She laughed.

"Is there another one?" His question was straight forward.

"You're kidding, right?"

"No, not at all." Pablo was intrigued.

"Okay, Kiddo... would you like to know why I left for Mexico City?"

"Yes, I would, and I imagine my father might have liked to know, too."

"It's not like he left me any choice. I showed up for our date, all right... my parents had come to town; we were supposed to have dinner with them. That was the night that I was going to ask... no, beg them to let me stay in the States at Erin's home for the summer, then begin my university studies at Sacred Heart College for Women." She looked down with a sad expression.

"So what happened?"

"I was staying at the Valencia with my parents, who had walked down to the Cove. They had lent me their rental car, so I decided to come up here to surprise your dad. Your grandparents had been in Europe that entire last semester, so Arturo had given me a key to the house. I let myself in, and went bounding down the hallway. Turns out I was the one surprised!"

"I won't even ask." Pablo was shaking his head, sadly. "What a jerk."

"My exact sentiments. Anyway, I let myself out and returned to the hotel. I told my parents that I had already run by to say goodbye to my friend, that I really preferred having dinner at the Top O' The Cove instead of the hotel. I never said another word. We left on the plane to Mexico City at eleven that night. I never saw your father again."

"Didn't he ever try to reach you? Didn't you ever call him? If only to tell him to go to hell?"

"No, what possible good would that have done? I was a dumb kid, but at least I was a dumb kid with a little dignity. To contact him would have also robbed me of what little dignity I had left."

"In whose eyes, yours or his?"

"Either. It would have served no purpose."

Pablo couldn't help but admire her. He wasn't blind to Arturo's faults, but after all, he was his father.

"What can I tell you? I was so young when Mom died, that I really can't say what their marriage was like, or if my father was faithful as a husband."

"How did your mother die?"

"Breast cancer," he replied with very little emotion. "Anyway, since my mother died, I can conservatively say that my father has probably dated at least ten percent of the single women in New York City, Paris and Mexico City. He is a womanizer. I would be hard-pressed to believe that he was faithful to my mother."

"Listen, your father had a lot of really good qualities, too. He was kind and he was attentive and..."

"And that describes the perfect womanizer. How else could they seduce so many women?" Pablo laughed, but his heart wasn't in it.

"Are you going to tell him that you've met me?"

"I already have," he said, then quickly clarified when he saw the horrified look on her face. "I didn't tell him your name or anything, but rather that I had made a wonderful new friend that I couldn't wait for him to meet."

Marisa leaned back on the bed, doubled over in laughter. "Oh, my

Lord! Can you imagine his face if he were to walk in here this minute? He'd have a stroke!"

Pablo grinned. "There's not much chance of that. He is going to be in Europe until at least November. He lives there most of the time now. Mexico City has become a very dangerous place to live, especially if you have a rather high profile like my father. He loves New York City, but I think there's someone in Paris that may have wormed her way into his heart. Who knows?"

"It doesn't seem to bother you whether or not you see him."

"For God's sake, Marisa, I'm twenty six years old. I have been on my own since my grandparents died when I was sixteen. It's not like I ever lived with him after my mother's death."

"Oh, I didn't know that. Sorry..." Marisa felt like she was only opening her mouth to change feet, so decided not to comment any further. Listening was an art.

"Nothing to be sorry about. It's just the way it was, and is." He sat up in bed and took a drink of water from the glass on his night stand, offered some to Marisa, who gratefully accepted. "I have had everything anyone could need or want. I have this house with a nice stipend to keep it up, and I have never really wanted for anything."

"If it's not a financial thing, may I ask why you work as a Maitre'd?" This made no sense to Marisa.

"I actually enjoy it. I guess making my own money and seldom touching my father's account or credit cards is my way of showing him that I am quite capable of making it on my own."

Marisa smiled. "I doubt very seriously that he would ever doubt that. On the contrary, I will bet you anything that he as proud as any man could be of his son." She had been creeping up the other side of the bed. Her head now rested on his extra pillow. As she spoke, her eyes began to close involuntarily.

Pablo soon joined her.

He sat up long enough to pull the feather quilt over her, then turned the light off from the switch behind his night stand.

They both fell into a deep sleep, free of secrets.

Chapter Eleven

Marisa awoke disoriented, she slowly rolled over. Where Pablo had been there was only an indentation in the pillow. She could hear the shower running and quickly decided it was the better part of valor to leave while she could. She threw back the covers and made a break for the Master bedroom.

Marisa closed the Master bedroom door behind her, leaned against it shaking her head. She could envision Erin asking her if she had slept with Pablo. Erin would never believe that nothing had happened between them. *That's Erin's problem, not ours.* Pablo's words echoed in her head. He was right; they had done nothing for which to be embarrassed or ashamed. It was Erin's problem if she chose to believe otherwise.

A knock on the door behind her made her jump.

"Coward!" Pablo's warm laughter sounded from the hall. "I hope you slept well. I know I did."

"Yes, I did." She turned and opened the door. Pablo was leaning back against the wall with his arms crossed, a wide grin on his face. His hair was still damp from his shower. He was dressed in tight jeans and a black tee shirt.

"Good morning." He stood and faced her. "Did you still want to see Father Gregory today?"

"Most definitely." She remembered her clothes were wrinkled, and she had tossed them in a pile the night before. "I can't go in this robe. I don't suppose you have an iron and ironing board around here?"

"I wouldn't know where to look for one, even if there was. Obviously, you don't remember my telling you that my cousin may have left a few things in the guest room. She's a bit taller than you are but there might be something you could wear. I'll whip us up something to eat, while you get dressed." Pablo stood aside to allow her to pass. "We can never say we haven't slept together."

"It's probably more accurate to say we passed out together." Marisa grinned and walked towards the guest room.

"That we did." Pablo followed her down the hallway and turned towards the main part of the house.

Pablo's cousin had indeed left a few things in the closet, but she had only one real option: a long skirt and peasant blouse. The blouse fit well. The skirt was a little long, but she could still walk in it. She would have to be careful not to trip on the hem when climbing stairs.

She ran a brush through her hair, which had gone wild with curls, took a last look in the mirror. Curls framed her face and onto her shoulders making her look almost exotic. The sky blue blouse with its scoop neckline showing a hint of cleavage and the flowing black skirt with no slip added to the image. She definitely looked far different than she had when she had gone to the University with Erin, which was probably a good thing.

"You make me sorry I passed out." Pablo whistled a teasing glint in his eyes, as she entered the kitchen. "You're bound to make several seminarians reconsider their vocation in that outfit."

"You think so?" Marisa laughed and sat down at the table, where Pablo had set out plates of scrambled eggs, bacon, and toast for them. "It was either this or next to nothing."

"Have you given any thought to what you are going to say to Father Gregory, if he should ask why you need to see Ziggie?"

"I hadn't until you gave me an idea." Marisa took a bite of toast.

"I gave you an idea?"

"Yes, when you mentioned the seminarians rethinking their vocation. I'll say I was interviewing you on why you had left the Seminary and you had suggested I speak with Brother Zigfried because he could give me a more complete overview of why so many young men decide to leave and pursue a different path. I'll say I had spoken with Brother Zigfried on the phone, we had set up an interview for today."

"Sounds plausible enough. Ziggie has given other interviews in the past. Father Gregory might buy it. Just make sure you say you scheduled the interview several weeks ago."

"Okay," Marisa agreed. "Other than that, I think we're going to have to wing it as we go." She took a last bite, surprised that she had cleared her plate so. She glanced over; saw Pablo had finished his as well. "Let me brush my teeth and we can leave."

"Your vehicle or mine?" Pablo rinsed the plates before loading them into the dishwasher.

Marisa paused in the doorway, on her way to the bathroom. "We'd better take yours. I'm not supposed to be familiar with the University. "

Pablo weaved expertly through the surface street traffic, had them on the freeway in a matter of minutes. Traffic was in the short gap between morning rush hour and lunchtime crunch.

Pablo flipped on his blinker as they neared their exit.

He turned onto the road that led them up the hill and to the student parking area. He pulled into the lot, which was over half full, even though classes were not scheduled to start for another week. Rather than park in an open section of spaces, he pulled into an empty one with a Jeep on one side of them and a lifted pick-up on the other. He turned off the engine and climbed out.

"How far is it from here to Ziggie's office?"

"It is on the other side of the campus." Pablo led the way towards the sidewalk at the far end of the parking lot.

"Are you sure, you want to do this?" Pablo asked her. "Father Gregory can be an irascible old man on a good day. He's not known for his people skills."

"Neither am I." Marisa smiled coldly. "Does he speak Russian?"

"Fluently" Pablo frowned. "Do think he somehow got a look at the documents Erin left with Ziggie?"

"He not only got a good look at them, but translated them for himself," Marisa replied. "There is something in those documents that caused Ziggie to disappear." She glanced up at the imposing building behind them. "My gut tells me that Father Gregory knows exactly what that something is, and where Ziggie is as well."

"Whoa!" Pablo held up his hands. "You do realize you are accusing a senior member of the faculty of conspiracy and kidnapping?"

"I haven't accused anyone of anything," She smiled, "yet." She started towards the stairs.

Pablo hurried to follow her, convinced that she may have bitten off more than she could chew where Father Gregory was concerned.

To Marisa's happy surprise they were nearing the building where Ziggie's office was located without running into anyone like Father Holtz. They'd been slightly delayed a few times when a few former classmates of Pablo's had stopped them on the pretext of speaking to him, though it was almost embarrassingly obvious they really wanted to have a better look at her.

After the last group had left, Pablo looked over at her and chuckled, "Fifty points, easy."

"Fifty points?" A look of realization came over her face. "Erin told me about the scoring system. We had a similar one when I was in college." She couldn't help but smile. "I wasn't aware the males on campus knew about it as well."

"Trust me, it is part of the unofficial Freshman Orientation for the guys." Pablo laughed. "We even have a scoring system of our own."

"But of course you do." Marisa lowered her voice as they entered the building. "Most men do." They started up the interior staircase that would lead them to the upper floors and Ziggie's office. She had experience knowing where to look for surveillance cameras or plainclothes security, but saw neither. They reached Ziggie's office to find the door was still closed. Marisa leaned down to take a closer look at the doorknob in the dim light. "It has been wiped clean," she whispered to Pablo.

"What do you think you are doing?" A deep male voice asked from behind them.

Marisa slowly stood erect, turned to see a square built, heavy-set figure of medium height with sparse white hair, wearing the robes of a Jesuit. His face looked as though it had been carved from stone; his lips were drawn tight with disapproval. She'd recognized his voice the moment she heard it: So this was Father Gregory!

"Could you tell me what the date is today?" She ignored his hostile attitude, pleasantly smiled.

"I can assure you that you won't find this out by prying at locked doors. If you need to know the date that badly, I suggest you buy a calendar." He tried to intimidate them with his voice.

"What a marvelous sense of humor, you have." Marisa giggled and held out her hand. "I'm Paulina Sanchez from The Holy Name newspaper in Mazatlan, Mexico."

Father Gregory rudely ignored her outstretched hand looking at her up as if she were a lower life form. "You should purchase a map along with the calendar. It will expedite your return home."

Marisa playfully nudged a tense Pablo in the arm and laughed. "You never mentioned what wicked senses of humor could be found in the Seminary."

Father Gregory's scowl deepened and he glared at the two of them. "Miss Sanchez, I did not intend my comments to be amusing. This is a restricted area. Unless you have a valid reason for being here, you," He sneered in Pablo's direction, "and your companion will vacate the premises at once or I shall be forced to call Security and have you forcibly removed."

Marisa hadn't liked the man the moment she set eyes on him. He was cold, arrogant, dictatorial, condescending, and filled with his own self-importance. She fought back the words she would really like to say to him, and smiled brightly. "Oh, there's no need to call anyone. I'm sure Brother Zigfried will be arriving at anytime now for our interview."

His brow lifted slightly, which made him look even harsher in the dimly light corridor. He snorted derisively. "I highly doubt that Brother Zigfried will be arriving at all. He is away, and not available for any interviews, neither now nor in the future."

Marisa feigned a confused look. "How very odd. Brother Zigfried said he would meet us here at his office on the fourteenth." She glanced down at her watch. "At eleven thirty in the morning. It is eleven twenty-five now." She looked over at Pablo for confirmation.

Pablo merely nodded, keeping an eye on Father Gregory, who looked as though he might throttle Marisa at any moment.

"There will be no interview!" Father Gregory stridently insisted.

"Forgive me for disagreeing with you, Padre, but our interview was scheduled several weeks in advance. Brother Zigfried was most adamant it be done before the start of the new term."

Father Gregory's hands clenched into fists at his sides, he looked down the corridor and loudly called out: "Security!"

He turned back to face them, anger and frustration clearly etched on his face. "There is no such appointment, Miss Sanchez, if that is indeed your real name. Perhaps you would prefer, Judy Blainey?"

Pablo reached over to cup Marisa's elbow with his hand in preparation for getting them both out of there before things truly got out of hand. She startled him when she clapped her hands together as though pleased to hear what Father Gregory had just said.

"You must be the nice gentleman I spoke with when I called to reconfirm my appointment with Brother Zigfried!"

Pablo almost choked. He had heard Father Gregory called many things by distraught students, but nice gentleman wasn't one of them. He glanced over and saw the priest's body was vibrating with barely suppressed rage at Marisa refusal to leave as he had ordered.

Undaunted, Marisa didn't give Father Gregory the opportunity to get a word in edgewise. "I should apologize for using a fake name when I called. I knew Brother Zigfried wanted to keep our meeting confidential.

As for the name I gave you, I just picked it at random from a list of students my editor gave me. And, I can assure you, I am who I say I am." She fished around in her purse and confidently pulled out a Press I. D. Card with the name Paulina Sanchez, and her affiliation with The Holy Name, imprinted beneath her photo.

This same ID, had served her well many times over the years, especially when working an undercover investigation. It could even be verified by a phone call to the Offices of The Holy Name. The newspaper was owned and run by a most helpful and supportive cousin.

Pablo had to stare at the floor to conceal the smile that sprang to his face. The longer he was around her, the more he discovered. He couldn't help but wonder what other surprises her handbag might hold.

"When do you expect Brother Zigfried to return?" Marisa persisted.

Father Gregory's jaw clenched, he almost spit his reply at her. "That is not known at present. He is on an extended retreat."

"Isn't it rather unusual for a faculty member to go on an extended retreat so close to the start of a new term? Surely he will have returned before classes begin?" She could tell she was beginning to wear the tough old man down. Small beads of sweat were starting to form on his forehead.

"Brother Zigfried is consulting on some newly discovered text. A substitute instructor has been assigned to take over his classes." The priest pulled a handkerchief from a pocket in his robes and wiped his brow, he glanced back down the corridor in search of the Security he had called for.

"Really? I'm sorry. I must have misunderstood you earlier. I thought you said he was on an extended retreat? Now you say he consulting on some newly discovered text. How fascinating! I assume this new text must be in a foreign language as I know Brother Zigfried is a Linguist." Marisa paused only a second, to catch her breath before asking, "He does specialize in Eastern European languages, does he not? I'm certain his fluency in German and Russian will be most helpful in the translation of the documents found at the convent."

Pablo's head snapped up, he looked at her as if meeting a stranger for the first time: it was Russian coming out of her mouth.

The sounds of running footsteps echoed at the far end of the corridor as Security approached. Father Gregory looked in their direction, relief evident on his face. He answered her question without thinking, waving his hand towards the approaching guards.

"Da! Da!"

Marisa startled him by grabbing his hand and shaking it enthusiastically. "Thank you ever so much. You've been most helpful. I'll check back in a few weeks time to reschedule with Brother Zigfried." She released his hand, stepping around him as she did so with Pablo close behind. They walked as quickly as they could away from the priest and the arrival of the guards towards the back staircase that led back down to the main entrance.

They were at the top of the stairs, starting downward, when Marisa took one last look back at the Priest. He was shaking both his hands in the air and pointing in their direction as one of the guards was speaking into a radio.

Once outside, Marisa gathered her skirt up almost to her knees and began running towards the parking lot at the far end of the campus. Pablo stayed slightly behind her to protect their backs. A group of students, their arms loaded down with newly purchased textbooks parted before them like the Red Sea at hearing Marisa's shouted:

"Make a path! We have an emergency!"

Breathless, they made it back to the truck in record time. Pablo unlocked the doors and they clambered inside with Marisa curling up on the floorboard out of sight. She was gasping for air, but managed to urge Pablo. "Get us out of here now! But, don't attract any unnecessary attention."

Pablo pulled straight through the empty space in front of them and fought the need to floor the accelerator and use the high performance engine under the hood. He maintained the posted speed limit as they re-traced the route they'd used to get there. They were waiting at the stop light at the bottom of the hill when two San Diego Police cars, red lights flashing, turned the corner and raced up the hill towards the University. He had little doubt that they had been called because of them.

"We're back on the freeway. You can stop hiding now," he told Marisa a few minutes later.

Marisa uncoiled from her cramped position on the floor and settled into her seat, making sure to fasten her seat belt. She glanced over at Pablo. "Fasten your seat belt! The last thing we need now is to be stopped for a traffic ticket."

Pablo kept one hand on the steering wheel and reached up with the other to pull the belt down and across his chest, while Marisa reached over and grabbed the end to lock it into place.

"You're a crazy woman!" Pablo exclaimed. "You know that don't you?"

"So I've been told." High on the adrenaline of running and eluding the authorities, Marisa couldn't stop grinning. "At one point, I thought the old man was going to have a stroke, he was so mad!"

"I thought I might have a stroke when you started spouting Russian out of nowhere!" Pablo glanced over at her, his face wreathed in a smile. "How come you never said you could speak Russian?"

"I can't." Marisa laughed. "You heard just about all of it back there. Between doing research for my Masters, and various newspaper assign-ments over the years, I've been able to pick up a word or two of it, but that's all."

"You sounded damn fluent to me!" Pablo shook his head in disbelief. "Did you hear him? He was so rattled that he actually admitted he knew about the documents that Ziggie was translating for Erin."

"Thus confirming my gut feeling about him. You have no idea how badly I wanted to grab him by the throat and shake him until he told us where Ziggie is."

"I think the feeling was mutual, but in his case, I think he just wanted to shut you up. I've never seen the man so mad! His temper is legendary on Campus."

Marisa looked out the window at the passing landscape. "Are we heading back to your place?"

"I couldn't think of anywhere else to go." Pablo changed lanes to avoid slowing traffic ahead of them. "We need to call Erin ASAP. She could be in danger. It won't take long for Father Gregory to put two and two together. He knows Erin is a friend of Ziggie's, he knows that she was my teacher, and about Ziggie's being my Thesis Mentor."

"You're right. We could all be in danger. Park at the Country Club. We'll cut across the golf course on foot to your place."

Pablo pulled into the Country Club parking lot. He had to circle around twice before he came upon a car backing out. He pulled into the newly vacated space and glanced over to his left. "Isn't that Erin's truck over there?"

"Where?" Marisa rose up in her seat to get a better look at where he was pointing. "She only parks here when she's playing a round of golf. I can't imagine she would be doing something like that now. It's probably one that just looks like hers."

Father Gregory moved to the phone on the desk in his office. Lifting the receiver, he quickly punched in an International Area Code followed by a ten-digit number. When the phone was answered at the receiving end, he merely said, "Salve Regina has been compromised."

Chapter Twelve

While Pablo and Marisa had been enjoying breakfast at Pablo's, Ziggie had barely touched his, but he'd felt very sleepy afterwards.

As he'd dozed off to sleep after Sister Agnes had left with his tray, he realized that he'd been dozing off after breakfast for days. Of course, he could only surmise the time of day from the type of food on the trays he was served. He had been assuming it was morning when his breakfast foods were served to him.

He had a small lamp on a tiny desk across from his bed, and other than the dimly lit bathroom with only a sink and a toilet, that had been the only light he had seen in several days. He had been provided with a Bible, and a notebook and pen had been set upon the desk.

The cell was similar to any monk or nun's cell anywhere in the world, except for the fact that this particular cell was locked from the outside whenever he was left alone there.

Other than Sister Agnes' voice and the voice he had heard the day before, these were the first voices he had heard since someone had crept up behind him in his office while he had been talking on the phone with Erin; that someone had placed the gauze over his nose.

The voices seemed to be coming closer, and he immediately recognized them. It was Father Gregory and Father Holtz; of that he had no doubt.

He started to call out to them, but a sixth sense stopped him. In this case, it was a sense of inexplicable danger.

He could begin to understand their words.

Father Gregory had a deep, throaty voice that somehow seemed to match his rather heavy-set, square body. Father Holtz had a more mellifluous, radio announcer type of voice that had served him well over the years to keep his students' attention.

"Shhh! Zigfried's behind that door!"

"It doesn't matter," Father Gregory said. "He's out like a light. The sisters gave him some extra Seconal in his oatmeal."

Ziggie was glad he hadn't called out to them. He lay down again, and closed his eyes, just in case they entered the room.

"Check the notebook," Father Gregory said, "just in case he has written something there that might help."

He heard the key in the lock, the door opened. He could hear Holtz flipping through the empty pages of the notebook, and wondered just how long it might take two men that he had always considered to be quite intelligent to figure out that a man of his height, regardless how thin, could not possibly fold himself onto that tiny chair in any way that would make it possible for him to fit his legs under that miniature desk and write.

He almost laughed, but contained his mirth in the hope that he might be able to eavesdrop on some further conversation that would clear up a few doubts he still had regarding the strange behavior of his two Brothers in the Society of Jesus; ever grateful that he hadn't been hungry enough to eat the insipid Seconal-laced oatmeal earlier that morning.

He heard the door lock click again and their voices.

"Nothing?" Father Gregory asked with a disappointed tone to his voice.

"Nothing, but you were right. Zigfried is dead to the world. I was tempted to wake him and give him a little physical convincing, but he's probably so drugged that he'd be no good to us, anyway." Ziggie thought Father Holtz was talking like a mafia hit man from a bad gangster movie, and had to stifle a giggle. It seemed very out of character.

"I don't think he knows, anyway," Gregory said. "I heard Sister Agnes' confession at six this morning before Holy Mass, and I am quite sure she would have confessed to keeping a secret from her superior if he had told her anything. They seem to have developed a nice rapport."

"It's probably just out of desperation," Holtz said. "He is probably going crazy with no one to talk to. I suppose that is the entire reason for keeping him here, right? To keep him from talking to Erin or her little friend?"

"There's that..." Gregory said, and Ziggie did not like the sound of his voice. It was very threatening. "What concerns me now is the element of time. Things are about to come to a head, and we need to be in control again. Those people may have just set the alarm clock."

"You're just being paranoid over that grad student and Erin's friend's visit this morning. We are still in control."

"The General doesn't agree. There is just too much at stake to take any chances, or to chock things up to coincidence. Between the documents Ziggie had, the nosy Mexican reporter hooked up with an ex-seminarian turned waiter, the new missing documents from Sister Superior's office... it all adds up to some information being out there that we don't know about. The old lady isn't talking, either. I had hoped she would say something in Confession, but she never has, and today was no exception."

"What if she dies without telling you where she hid them?"

"Then we tear the place apart until we find them."

"And if we don't?"

"Then we'll have to make very good and sure that her cousin doesn't, either."

"And what about Brother Zigfried and his friends?" Father Holtz's voice was as deep as Gregory's, but he no longer sounded like a gangster.

"I suppose they'll all have to join Cousin Nicky, but we're getting ahead of ourselves." Father Gregory's voice became stronger as he said, "Right now, I need to keep a watchful vigil on Sister Thomas Marie. It's only a matter of hours, now. She might relent and tell me something before death."

Ziggie would have given anything to know, for sure, what day or time it was. If he had only been unconscious for minutes or hours when he had been abducted, then this would be Friday. If he had been unconscious for days, then only the Lord knew.

The old nun was dying. She had to be the one connected to the documents that Erin had brought to him for translation. Of this he was sure.

He made a mental list of the facts as he knew them. Without a doubt, he was in danger and he was in good company. So was Erin, her friend, Pablo and some cousin of the old nun's by the name of Nicky. He was beginning to suspect who the mysterious Nicky might be, but he had no time to ponder on that at the moment.

He would have to escape, and that was all there was to it.

He knew he was probably in the catacombs that Erin had described to him. He had suspected as much from the time he recognized Sister Agnes from the many times he had ministered to the Sisters and students at the convent, but being a cautious man, had waited to confirm his suspicions before acting.

His mind was racing. He knew that Sister Agnes would be there soon with his lunch; that her visit would be his only chance to get out.

He had to protect Erin. He immediately chided himself for thinking only of Erin when other lives were at stake also, but he couldn't help himself: her friendship was very precious to him. Erin was very precious to him. It was a fact that he seldom admitted even to himself. He was a Jesuit. He had taken vows of Poverty, Chastity and Obedience. There could be nothing more between them than the wonderful friendship they had shared for so many years.

He tried to recall Erin's account of everything she and her friend had done and found in these catacombs, he remembered there was an elevator in the Music department basement that would take him to stairs that would get him into the Principal's office. From there, all the halls in the classroom building would have emergency exit doors.

Where could he go? It wasn't like a Jesuit in full robes could simply walk around without being noticed. It wouldn't take Sister Agnes very long to get out of his cell and give the alarm that he had escaped.

By the time he heard the key turn in the lock, and Sister Agnes' voice calling out to him cheerfully, he had figured out exactly where he would go, and how he would get there.

He quickly rose from his bed and hid in the bathroom, but did not turn the light on.

Sister Agnes entered the room, he groaned weakly, "Sister! Help me! I can't get up!"

He hid in the corner next to the small sink and in front of the toilet as she dropped the tray onto the desktop. As he had hoped, he heard the metallic sound of her keys being dropped on the tray.

He counted her steps to the bathroom door. He grabbed her out-stretched hand just as she was about to lift the light switch. He pulled her in gently, felt no resistance.

She cried out as he picked her up by the waist and switched places with her.

"I'm not going to hurt you, Sister. I just must leave now. God bless you," he said as he twisted out of the small space into the cell beyond. Unlike most bathroom doors, this one swung out into the room, which served his purpose perfectly. He closed the door, grabbed the desk chair before she could react, and tipped the back of the chair until it fit perfectly under the door knob.

"Someone will come looking for you soon, Sister." He assured her before taking her keys from the lunch tray to let himself out. The cavernous hallway was dimly lit in both directions as far as he could see. He could hear her pushing at the chair holding the bathroom door closed as he tried key after key in the old lock.

One finally worked, it turned the lock.

He placed the keys a few feet from the door, called out gently to her, "I have left the keys by the door so the Sisters can let you out, dear. They'll be here soon. I promise you that."

Then he ran toward the Music Department.

Following Erin's description to the letter, he found the elevator in the basement of the Music Department, used it exactly as Erin had described her friend's using the old-fashioned lift device. He soon found himself in

Sister Superior's office.

From there it was an easy escape to the nature paths leading around the point of the school and into the dry brush that covered the cliffs that would hide him from any vantage point at the Villa until he could cross the valley below and then climb up another cliff that would lead him to a cloistered convent where the Jesuit priests offered Holy Mass many times to the silent Sisters.

The part of the Cloister that perched on the cliff was a round structure that looked like the tower of a medieval castle. Ziggie had been worried that it was a spot where anyone might see him if looking in that direction from the convent, but he was pleased to find a narrow footpath at the bottom, he managed to slip behind it quickly, placing him out of view.

On the other side of the tower, the footpath led up another trail to the high walls that circled around the beautiful convent.

Once at the foot of the high walls, he was forced to make a decision. He had thought his height would make it a fairly simple scale up the wall and over, but he now found the wall much higher than he had remembered it. With his long robes, he could easily find his feet entangled at any point while climbing, and the fall down wouldn't be only to the footpath, but he could find himself projected beyond the cliffs into the valley below, which was far more of a fall than any human body could possibly withstand.

His only other option would be to find his way to the street and enter the Cloister through the front door. If Father Gregory were looking for him, he might follow the same exact logic as his. He might be waiting at the Cloister door.

Ziggie gazed up at the wall, decided he would just have to err on the side of caution. He would have to observe every car and every inch of neighboring bushes and trees to be sure Gregory wasn't there before approaching that door.

When he reached the street, he was well hidden by a row of bushes before he would have to walk in the open on the deserted street. He carefully checked every inch of space in sight of the coveted door, tried to see between the leaves on bushes in case anyone was crouched behind them.

Feeling safe, he made a run for the door. He opened it, darted into the dark foyer. Before closing the door behind him, he gazed out through a crack, heaving a sigh of relief. The street was deserted.

He stood a moment to allow his eyes to become accustomed to the dim. He moved across the room to a round barrel that protruded from an otherwise blank wall. As soon as he reached the barrel, it swung around. In front of him was a shelf in a half-circle, with a screened window above it. He could see a dark-habited nun behind the screen, but not well enough to recognize her as one of the few Sisters with whom he had become acquainted over the years.

"Good afternoon, Brother," she said softly. "Is Mother Superior expecting you?"

"Good afternoon, Sister. No, Mother Superior doesn't know I'm here, but I would appreciate your announcing me to her, please. I'm Brother Zigfried." His mind was racing a mile a minute. He needed a reason to be there, and literally for the life of him, he couldn't think of one. He was hoping that the nun would simply go to announce him to her superior, so that he would have time to make up a good story.

"Yes, Brother, I'll be glad to announce you." The barrel turned around again, the screen was closed.

By the time Mother Superior had come out, he had a story.

Expecting the younger nun to return, he was still standing at the barrel when a door in the paneled wall opened.

"Brother Zigfried," Mother Superior greeted him. "How nice to see you! Please, come in!"

Ziggie held his hand out, she placed hers gently on it. He glanced down and realized his hands were filthy. This embarrassed him, but it actually worked well for his cover story.

"I'm sorry I am such a mess, Mother Superior. Please forgive me," he said as he entered the receiving area. He was pleased that the tiny woman clad in black with a transparent black veil over her face, had closed the door behind them. "It seems that my car has broken down just a couple of blocks from here, so I have come to intrude on your serenity and impose on your hospitality for a brief moment in the hope that I might use your telephone to call the university for help."

Mother Superior smiled kindly, opened the inner door that led to the parlor where priests were normally received.

"Of course, Brother, I assure you that it is no imposition whatsoever: we always enjoy a visit from our Brothers in Christ." She motioned toward the inviting parlor where he had been many times.

"Thank you, Mother Superior." He was relieved to see a telephone on a side table next to the sofa. He hadn't remembered there being one, but had assumed that even the most cloistered of cloisters would need a telephone for emergencies. He was pleased to see that his assumption had been correct.

"May I bring you something cool to drink, Brother? I believe Sister Mary has some fresh lemonade in the kitchen, and perhaps something to snack on while you're waiting for someone to come for you?"

His mouth watered merely at the thought. "That would be lovely, Mother Superior. It truly would!" If she went to fetch the lemonade, he would have a moment of privacy to phone Erin or Pablo.

As soon as she had disappeared into back of the convent, he picked up the phone and dialed Erin's number. Thankfully, she answered on the first ring.

"Hello?"

"Erin?"

"Ziggie! Where are you! I've been worried to death!" Erin's voice was shaking with emotion.

"Erin, don't speak, just listen. I'll tell you all about it when I see you. I need you to come for me. Do you remember the Cloistered convent near Villa Vistamar?" He didn't wait for a response. "Just come there quickly. Go in and tell the nun behind the barrel that someone has come from the university to pick me up."

"Ziggie, what is going on?" Erin couldn't just drop it.

"Erin, please, in the name of our friendship, please do as I told you, and don't tell anyone where you are going." Mother Superior was returning with a tray, and he sat up straight. "That's okay, Harry, just bring your sister along. That way you don't even have to get out of the car. Just tell her to inform the Sister behind the barrel that you've come for me." He nodded his head, although Erin had already hung up the phone. "Thanks, Harry. I appreciate the help."

He hung up the phone and rose to his feet.

"No, no, Brother. Please stay seated," Mother Superior insisted. "I'll just leave the lemonade and homemade cookies here for you, then I must take my leave, as the afternoon prayer vigil is starting; I must be there to lead it. But please, Brother, make yourself at home. Sister Rose will tell you just as soon as someone arrives. I may see you before you leave, but if not, I'll surely see you soon."

That said, she turned and withdrew from the room.

Ziggie sat back with a cookie in one hand and the lemonade in the other, enjoyed both, not entirely sure which tasted better... the snack or the freedom.

He was barely on his third cookie when the door from the reception area opened. Sister Rose peeked in. "Brother, someone from the university is here, a Brother Harry?"

Ziggie had never been so glad to hear a fictitious name in his life.

Erin was on the freeway far below the convents before she spoke. The fear and urgency in her friend's expression was more than enough to make her realize that this was very serious business; that she needed to get him out of there quickly.

"Where do you want to go, Ziggie?" she asked gently. "I don't imagine you want to go up to the university..."

"Heavens, no!" Ziggie said, "and actually, what I probably need the most is a pair of jeans and a tee shirt. As if my height weren't enough, the robe is sort of a dead giveaway, and I say "dead" very literally. Do you know a store where they might outfit someone my height?"

"Hey, you're talking to your female counterpart, here! Of course I know of a place." She immediately took the first off-ramp toward Fashion Valley, where her favorite specialty store for the tall happened to be located. "My favorite store is just a stone's throw away."

"I'm afraid I'm not carrying any money," Ziggie said sheepishly.

"I have some, and a credit card if I don't have enough. Not to worry." She pulled into mall parking lot, and pulled up close to one of the doors. "Now, I don't think it's a very good idea for you to be seen in your robes in public," she admonished him, "so you should sit behind the wheel with the engine running while I'm in there." She set the hand brake, opened her door, and jumped to the ground. "Scoot over!" She demanded, and Ziggie did.

"Now, I promise I won't be long. What do you wear... like a 34 waist with a 38 inner seam in pants, and about a 16 neck 38 inch sleeve?"

Ziggie was shocked that another human being, and a female one at that, could actually imagine his exact sizes. He nodded, dumbfounded.

"I'll be right back! If anyone suspicious approaches you, just take off, and go to..." Her mind raced, trying to think of a place. Her house would be too obvious. Then it occurred to her. "To Pablo's! That's the perfect place!" She turned and disappeared into the mall.

He sat behind the wheel of Erin's truck for what seemed like half an eternity, observing every car that drove by and every person who walked out of the mall, fearful that any one of them could be Gregory or Holtz.

Finally, Erin walked through the mall doors, large bags in hand. She jumped into the passenger seat. "Just pull up to the men's room door over at that gas station." She pointed toward a discount gas station at the far end of the parking lot after placing the bags on the console between them. "Take these into the bathroom and change while I get some gas in the truck. Put your robes into the bags in case you need them later." She realized she had just spoken as if Ziggie was leaving the Brotherhood, and was ashamed of herself. "Of course you'll need them later... I just meant that.."

Ziggie smiled at her. "I know what you meant, Erin. Thank you, dear friend. You are saving my life."

He drove to the gas station, pulled up outside of the men's room door. Thankfully it was open, so he wouldn't have to fetch a key from the attendant. He put the truck in "park" and opened the door, grabbing the bag handles as he did. He slid to the ground and ducked into the men's room, turning to smile thankfully at Erin as he closed the door behind him. She was already sliding over to the driver's seat.

As he turned the light on, he could hear the truck pulling away to one of the pumps.

With the light on, he looked into the mirror, and was shocked at his own bedraggled appearance, for the days of Seconal and lack of appetite had taken their toll.

His normally gaunt face looked worse than many of the cadavers he had seen at funeral masses, but far dirtier thanks to his trek through the underbrush between the two convents. He hadn't been given a razor at Villa Vistamar, so his four-day growth of beard only made matters worse. He could only imagine what the poor Mother Superior must have thought when she'd opened the door to her pristine Cloister to the likes of him.

He shook his head, carefully removed his outer robes, folding them neatly before placing them on the sink board. He opened the bags that Erin had brought: the medium-sized bag had a cowboy shirt and jeans, with packages of undershorts and undershirts on top. The largest bag had two items that had to make him laugh, as they were so out of character for him: a pair of cowboy boots, and a cowboy hat!

There was one last bag, and in it was a travel-size tube of deodorant, a nice triple-bladed razor, a can of shaving lather, a toothbrush with a tube of toothpaste, and a bar of soap.

Once Erin had filled the tank of her truck, she pulled it to the front of the small convenience store and parked it. She walked casually into the store. After picking up a few snacks for her obviously starving friend, she paid for the gas and her purchases in cash so as not to leave a paper trail.

The only thing she had paid for with a credit card had been the boots and hat, but she had made a point of telling the sales clerk in the Country Western store that they were for her because she was going to a rodeo out in the desert. She had remembered that Ziggie had once teased her because she wore the same size shoe as he did, so the fitting of the boots hadn't been a problem.

The outfit had been her contribution to the transformation of Ziggie from a mild-mannered Jesuit into a cowboy; the idea had made her almost giddy. She hoped Ziggie had found the humor in the disguise.

As she left the store with the snacks in hand, Ziggie was coming out of the men's room, and she gasped.

"You look incredible!" she said admiringly as he approached the truck. "Now, you need to drive, because it would be suspicious for a highfalutin' macho cowboy to be riding along with his cowlady, doncha' think?"

Ziggie hated to admit it even to himself, but he had liked the image looking back at him from the mirror when he had finished shaving, washing and dressing. Not only did he not look like himself, but he looked like the heroes he had watched on television as a child.

"Whatever you say, Ma'am," he said with as much of a Western twang as his British education would permit.

Once on the freeway again, he asked, "So, do you really think Pablo's house is the safest place for us to go?"

"Yes, but do you know how to get there from the golf course? I think the Country Club parking lot would be the safest place to leave the truck, don't you?"

"Probably. And I'm sure we can get from there to Pablo's over the golf course. But how do we get into the club? Membership at the La Jolla

Country and Golf Club is not one of the privileges of the Society of Jesus... at least not at my level."

"Also not a problem. You happen to be talking about the only sport I practice, and I have kept up the golf membership my grandparents left me when they died." Ziggie looked at her with even deeper admiration, if that was possible, and she blushed at his gaze. "I always carry my clubs in the truck."

"I had always wondered why you had a locked cover over the bed of your truck. Now I know."

"Okay, now that we know where we're going, and you are decked out like John Wayne, would you care to tell me what happened, and why you sent me that list of Sisters Superior... and where you've been?" Erin couldn't wait any longer. "Now come on!"

Ziggie smiled, shaking his head. "Erin, it is all so weird, and so complex, that I'm not sure I understand it all yet. But I can tell you what I know, which isn't much."

"At this point, anything is more than I know." She pointed toward the next exit. "Look, if you take Ardath to Via Capri, you can go over the back way to the Club, just in case anyone is watching the streets around Pablo's house."

"Good thought. Well, to put it all some sort of order, I suppose I should start with what I found in the documents you gave me." He looked down at the seat and saw the bag of snacks. "If you would open that bag of cheese puffs, I would be forever in your debt! Sorry, but I digress. I am starving."

Between mouthfuls of cheese puffs and sips of soda, Ziggie explained:

"The last thing I remember is talking with you on the phone, when someone came up behind me and put a piece of gauze over my nose. I assume it was chloroform, because the next thing I knew, I woke up in a tiny cell with no windows, behind a locked door."

"Who took you?" Erin asked. "When we got to the seminary later that day, your office was locked, and there was blood on the doorknob."

"I'm not surprised. I had quite a cut on the back of my head when I came to." Ziggie pulled onto Via Capri, and followed the twisty road as Erin had indicated. "By the way, is this Friday?"

"Yes… Good Lord, Ziggie! How long were you knocked out?"

"Apparently, not long, if this is Friday. Anyway, for the last three days until I escaped this morning, the only other human being I have seen is Sister Agnes, who has brought me meals three times a day. Other than that, I might as well have been in a grave."

"That would be Sister Agnes at Villa Vistamar?" Erin's anger was beginning to flare. "Who'd 'a thunk!"

"I figured as much, but then I didn't know where in the convent, and it isn't exactly a tiny place, nor did I know why I would be there, of all places." He took another long drink of his soda, popped a few more cheese puffs into his mouth.

"If we'd only known! Marisa and I were there night before last trying to find the journals, but they had all been removed from the trunks in the basement."

"Now, that is bad news. There is some specific information we need to get from them to confirm my suspicions." Ziggie shook his head.

"Oh, we got them, all right… They were in Sister Superior's safe, in her office."

"You two *cracked a safe!*? Holy Mother of God! What does one take a prisoner on visits when she doesn't smoke?" Ziggie couldn't help but laugh. The mental picture he was getting of Erin and her friend cracking a safe was just too much for him to bear. "Where are they now?"

"At Pablo's house. Actually, I found the combination." She laughed, too, picturing the image running through her friend's mind. "Sorry to ruin the image. So then, what happened?"

"Well, this morning I heard voices. Gregory and Holtz were down there searching for something. I have no idea what, but the journals should give us an idea."

"That's interesting, because the day we went to look for you at the

Seminary, it was Father Holtz that literally tried to keep us from going to your office. I was pretending that Marisa was a friend visiting from Mexico, that I was giving her a tour. I said I wanted to take her to meet you."

"And that's when you found the blood on the doorknob, right?"

"Right. What else did you hear from them?"

"Well, first of all, that the nuns had put Seconal in my oatmeal, and that if it weren't for the fact that I hadn't been hungry when Sister Agnes brought me my tray, I would still have been asleep. At one point, Holtz came in to see if I had used the notebook they had left for me on the desk."

"And you hadn't?"

"No, I couldn't even sit at the desk. I think it was left over from the days when Villa Vistamar had a primary school." He laughed as he pulled into the parking lot at the La Jolla Country Club. "Should I park the truck in any special place?"

"Hmm... maybe over there under those trees, so we can dart into the bushes there and follow along the fairway, close to the edge, until we can make a dash for Pablo's house."

Ziggie parked the truck where she indicated, and put it in "park."

"Anyway, the rest of what I heard isn't pleasant. There is an old nun dying at the school, and Gregory is trying to find out where she has hidden whatever it is. On the other hand, they spoke of her cousin coming... someone by the name of Nicky, and that if they didn't find whatever it was, then the General had ordered that he be eliminated." Erin was about to speak, but he placed a finger over her mouth. "I know, I know, but don't even say it, until we can get into those journals. Until then, it is only conjecture." He had opened the truck door, and was pulling the bags with him. "Oh," he said almost absentmindedly, "all of us are on their little hit list too, if they don't get their hands on whatever it is they want."

"That goes without saying," Erin said nonchalantly. "I would have expected nothing less." She was eying the bag, but just shrugged her shoulders.

"What?" Ziggie noticed her hesitation.

"I was just thinking whether you needed to carry those bags or not, but it probably doesn't matter."

"Aren't you taking the golf clubs? I thought we'd push the bags into your bag."

Erin had completely forgotten about the golf bag, and laughed. "I'd forgotten. It's amazing how quickly one forgets about these mundane matters when thinking about one's own mortality, isn't it?"

She opened the lid to the truck bed, lifted out her golf bag. Once on the ground, she opened up a zippered compartment on the side, hollowing it out. Ziggie's bags fit perfectly there.

She hooked her arm through his, pulled the bag behind, right up to the edge of the bushes that separated the golf course from the parking lot.

She stopped, looked around them casually, there was no one in sight.

"Come on!" she ordered Ziggie, ducked into the bushes.

Ziggie followed suit.

Once on the other side, they walked arm in arm along the edge of the fairway, just like so many of the club's retired couples. No one objected as long as people didn't walk directly on, or across the fairways.

"If we weren't running for our lives, this would be very pleasant," he said. "I almost feel as if we were an old, married couple enjoying our afternoon constitutional."

"If you think about it, Ziggie," she said almost wistfully, "we have been together longer than a lot of married couples we know."

Ziggie just sighed. "I wonder sometimes."

"About what?"

"If I had met you before entering the Seminary, and we had developed a relationship and had eventually married, would we still be together?"

Erin felt like she was going to cry, but she controlled herself.

"Who knows, Ziggie. Personally, I am just grateful that we have what we have."

"And what, precisely is what we have?" Ziggie said the words spontaneously, without thinking about what he was implying. He wanted to fix it, but he realized he couldn't. "I mean, when I heard them talking about you being eliminated, you cannot imagine how I felt. I can't help but question my own feelings."

Erin smiled. "I understand completely, because I know how I felt when I thought you might be dead."

Pablo's house was directly in front of them.

"Before we go in," Ziggie said, "are these feelings something we need to deal with?"

Erin smiled, squelching the desire to throw herself into his arms. She hoped it was just the flood of emotions that was making her react that way, and imagined that the same emotions were affecting.

"Not today, Ziggie. We have enough to deal with, without muddying things with our own feelings." She smiled at him, fought off the desire to hug him again. "Do you know the code for the alarm system? I know I don't."

"Yes," and I also know where the key is."

"Pablo must really trust you."

"That's a common mistake a lot of people make!" He laughed, but Erin didn't react. He punched her lightly in the arm. "Hey, lighten up, girly friend. That was funny!"

Chapter Thirteen

"I never thought I would appreciate the family keeping up our membership here," Pablo smiled. "At least, I know I don't have to worry about my truck being towed." He helped Marisa out of the passenger side, then activated the alarm from his remote.

"I take it golf isn't your game?"

"Shhh!" Pablo pretended to look around for eavesdroppers. "If anyone heard you say that, my truck might be safer if it was towed." He grabbed Marisa's hand and led her through the bushes at the far side of the parking lot. "Stay off the fairway," he warned, but his expression softened. "You know, I didn't take you or Erin seriously enough when you first came to me at the restaurant."

"And now?" Marisa shielded her eyes from the sun with her hand as she looked up at him.

"I think the two of you have unwittingly opened a Pandora's Box. Things are way past serious. Ziggie's disappearance, the botched home invasion and fire at Erin's Complex and Father Gregory's overreaction to you wanting to see and interview Ziggie, all tell me that you have definitely ticked off the wrong people. I will be calling work to let them know I'm taking some personal time off. There's no way I'm going to let you and Erin deal with this on your own."

"We more than appreciate the help. It could get ugly."

They reached the rear entrance at Pablo's, moved through a side door into the house. "While you change, I'll call Erin to warn her." Pablo said as they walked into the kitchen.

"Warn me about what?" A voice sounded from the dining room.

Pablo and Marisa stood in the doorway leading to the dining room shocked to see Erin and a tall man sitting at the table drinking coffee. Pablo had to do a double take before he recognized the man was Ziggie, but Ziggie as he had never seen him before. He looked like a model for a Rodeo poster right down to the cowboy hat hanging off the back of his chair.

He couldn't miss the look of affection that passed between Ziggie and Erin as she withdrew her hand from his outstretched palm, calmly picking up her coffee cup. What the hell was that all about? Were his two favorite people in the world involved? Did Ziggie's disappearance have more to do with his leaving the Jesuit community to be with Erin, than it did with the missing documents?

Marisa rushed to embrace Erin. "I was so worried about you." She leaned back and looked at Erin's face, only to lean down again and whisper in her ear. "Yes, I did end up spending the night, but all we did was sleep. Is there anything you want to tell me about the two of you?"

"It's not what you are thinking," Erin whispered back.

"Brother Ziggie, it's too good to see you."

"Not as good as it is to see you, my boy." Ziggie stood up, enveloped Pablo in a giant bear hug. "There were times over the last few days when I wondered if I ever would again." He looked over at Marisa. "You must be Marisa. Erin has spoken so much about you that I feel as though I already know you. I wish we were meeting under better circumstances. I am Brother Zigfried."

"Erin has spoken as much about you." Marisa smiled. "So, to me you are Ziggie, if that's okay with you?"

"Perfectly."

"What's with the new look?"

"Do you like his disguise?" Erin asked as Marisa stepped back and stood next to her.

"Disguise?" Pablo and Marisa asked in unison.

"I'll let Ziggie tell you, while I make a fresh pot of coffee for us." Erin stood up.

"I'll be right back to help you. My clothes looked like I had slept in them for days", so I borrowed these from Pablo's cousin to wear before going up to see Father Gregory.

"Why would you go to see Father Gregory?" Ziggie frowned.

"Yes, why?" Erin echoed.

"Let's everyone do whatever they need to, then we can all sit down and share our stories," Pablo suggested.

"Sounds like a plan to me, I can hardly wait to get out of these clothes." Marisa started to move towards the bedroom side of the house.

"You do that." Erin nodded. "I'll make the coffee and see if there's anything we can scrounge up to eat."

"I should probably launder my robes, that is, if it is not an imposition?" Ziggie said.

"Efficiency counts here, people." Marisa broke in. "We all have a great deal to talk over. The sooner everything is taken care of, the better. Pablo, it is your kitchen. You make the coffee and find something for all of us to eat. Erin, you help Ziggie do his laundry. I have yet to meet a man who knows how to do it right. And, I will make every effort to make myself more comfortable and presentable." The others stared at her in surprise. "Snap to it! Time's a wasting."

"I could use some help with my robes." Ziggie admitted.

"I don't hear anyone moving!" Marisa called from the back of the house.

"Looks like we all have our assignments," Pablo headed into the kitchen.

Forty-five minutes later, they all had their post meal beverages in hand, and took their places at the dining room table.

"So, who wants to start?" Pablo asked looking around the table.

"Personally, I'm dying to hear where Ziggie has been these last few days and what brought about his transformation into a post-millennial Gary Cooper," Marisa piped up with a grin.

"Gary Cooper?" Ziggie looked down at himself and frowned. "I thought it was more like John Wayne."

"Gary Cooper, John Wayne, who cares! What happened?" Marisa found herself liking him more and more with each passing minute. He was a gem. She could understand why Erin harbored such feelings for him; they fit well together.

"My story can wait." Ziggie's face took on a serious expression. "I think it may be more important for you to tell us why you went to see Father Gregory?"

"Let me tell them." Pablo looked over at Marisa, who nodded her assent. "You both know how intimidating Father Gregory is. Well, today he met his match in our Marisa."

Ziggie and Erin listened intently as Pablo gave his view of what had taken place. "Finally, she had him so rattled that he was not only sweating bullets, but had yelled for Security."

"Security!" Erin gasped. "Why do you always push the limits like that?"

"Because I can," Marisa grinned.

"What topped it all off, is out of nowhere, Marisa starts speaking to him in Russian, of all things. He was so intent on hurrying the Security guards, that he answered her in Russian."

"Before anyone asks, the only Russian I know is what I've picked up from doing research on my Masters and a few assignments in Moscow. It cannot be said that I speak Russian." Marisa interjected.

"What did you say to him?" Ziggie leaned forward in his chair.

"I said that your fluency in German and Russian would certainly be helpful in translating the documents found at the convent."

"And, he answered, yes!" Erin exclaimed in surprise, exchanged a quick look with Ziggie.

"If Da, means yes, he did." Pablo told them.

"But, if the guards were almost there, however did you avoid them?" Ziggie asked.

Marisa hid her face as Pablo went on at length about their sprint across campus, barely missing the arrival of the SDPD cars, and their decision to park at the Country Club.

"You were the one who lectured me on our needing to stay below the radar, and then you go and do something like this!" Erin looked to the heavens for help.

"It got us here safely," Marisa countered.

Ziggie startled them all by letting out a booming laugh. "Ah, Erin you did tell me that at times, your friend lacks a certain amount of subtlety. But this was not a time where subtlety was called for. She bearded the lion in his den and escaped to tell the tale." He sobered. "We should be most thankful that she and Pablo are here with us now. Brother Gregory is a very dangerous man."

"And you are going to tell us why," Pablo insisted. Too much had happened in a short time to allow him any more room to be surprised. It was enough for him that Ziggie said Father Gregory was dangerous.

"Yes, it is time that I did." Ziggie went on to tell them of his capture, imprisonment in the catacombs of Villa Vistamar, and the conversation he had overheard between Gregory and Holtz. He followed this with how he had managed to escape, Erin's rescue, and finally, his disguise.

"This is a Pandora's Box." Marisa looked over at Pablo. "What I can't put together is what Sister Thomas Marie could possibly have that would drive the Jesuit General to go so far as to order an Assassination? She is just an old nun. You know: Poverty, Chastity, and Obedience. It doesn't make any sense. And just who in the hell is this Nicky they were talking about?"

"Occam's Razor," Ziggie said. "The simplest answer is that Sister Thomas Marie is more than just a nun. We figure out what this is, it will lead us to who Nicky is."

"How do we go about doing that?" Marisa rubbed the back of her neck with her hand.

"Where are the Mothers Superior's journals?" Ziggie answered her question with another.

"In the living room, by the laptop," Marisa replied. "I went through them all and couldn't find anything that would help us figure out who

Sister Thomas Marie is, if indeed, she is more than just a nun as you suggest." Marisa was still trying to wrap her brain around the fact the Black Pope wanted someone killed. It was all the proof she needed to validate her conspiracy theory.

"You've gone through all of them?" Ziggie frowned. He doubted Marisa had missed anything. He knew from what Erin had told him about her, that Marisa was a very thorough researcher.

"All but the first one," Marisa looked over at Erin, "which is still at your place."

"I need to go through it," Ziggie told them. The answer he was looking for had to be in that journal. "What about the documents you brought me? Please tell me you made copies."

"Pablo scanned them into his laptop." Erin explained. "He ran them through a translation program."

"And all he got out of it was Gobbledygook and fragmented sentences." Ziggie shook his head.

"Why, yes. How did you know that?" Pablo asked.

"I never use them. Foreign languages depend heavily on context as to what a particular word or phrase means. Programs like these have no way of discerning context. Translation is also a visual endeavor. All languages evolve through time. Spelling, syntax and usage all vary depending on when something was written." Ziggie explained. "This is why, whenever possible, I prefer using the original documents or good hard copies."

"Pablo used the copies I'd made to do his scanning," Erin told him.

"I should take a look at these as well." Ziggie was relieved to hear there were hard copies. Together with the last remaining journal, he was fairly confident he would be able to find out what they needed.

"You mean, leave here?" Pablo didn't like the idea. "Nobody can get to us here. The Security System is state-of-the art. We'd be sitting ducks at Erin's."

"You want us to sit here in relative safety, while someone else has a death sentence hanging over their head? We may be the only chance this

Nicky has to survive." Ziggie was blunt. "Make no mistake, we are dealing with extremely dedicated and dangerous men; men who will stop at nothing to complete the task that has been given to them by their Father General. And, yes, they would have no compunction about killing anyone, including us, if it means their mission will be accomplished."

"When you put it that way, I would rather be a sitting duck, than be responsible for another man's death." Pablo said gravely.

"We would be far from sitting ducks at my place," Erin said. "There is Security all over, including a guard who seems to be permanently stationed in front of Dan's. Only residents and their guests are allowed entry. I suggest we gather whatever is here that we may need, then leave as soon as we can."

"I quite agree with Erin," Ziggie seconded her suggestion. "Pablo, you may want to bring appropriate clothing for a funeral. I overheard Gregory telling Holtz that it was only a matter of hours before Sister Thomas Marie passed on. We may have a funeral to attend."

"I'll grab my clothes, notes and Pablo's laptop." Marisa stood up. "Pablo, pack what you'll need."

"I'll stuff Ziggie's robes into a trash bag. We can dry them at my place." Erin said. She glanced down at the table. "I'll take care of these cups and glasses."

"Ziggie, if you could disconnect my scanner and printer, we may need them. There should be a box in the utility room they'll fit into. If they don't fit with us all in one vehicle, then we can sneak back later for them."

"Will we all fit in Erin's truck?" Marisa frowned. "She's the one with the resident parking sticker."

"We should. We can toss the clothes and stuff in the back, and squeeze in the cab." Erin looked over at Marisa. "You'll probably end up sitting on Pablo's lap, but we can do it."

"Let's get to it." Ziggie urged everyone to action. He regretted they had not shared their stories earlier. Now he feared they might have wasted precious time; time that the mysterious Nicky might not have left to him.

Anyone who might have seen them as they silently made their way along the periphery of the Country Club's Golf Course, would have been justified in thinking they were a gang of highly unusual cat burglars, booty in hand: tall, lean, Cowboy Ziggie carried a box comparable in size to a medium-sized Microwave Oven, Erin carried a large trash bag over her left shoulder, and Pablo tried to maintain his balance with a duffel bag in one hand, a zippered weekender bag in the other. Marisa followed, hugging an unidentifiable bundle close to her chest.

They made it to Erin's truck without incident. Erin opened the locked cover on the bed, and each divested themselves of their burdens.

Erin's earlier prediction that Marisa would end up sitting on Pablo's lap turned out to be true, but as soon as she sat down, he yelped. "What the hell do you have in your back pocket? Something just stuck me in the leg!"

"Hold on a minute," She jumped from the truck, carefully pulled a plastic bag from her pocket out of the line of vision of her companions. She placed it in the front pocket of her sweatshirt in such a way that it wouldn't be bent or broken, then climbed back into the cab.

"Sorry 'bout that," she said. "I had taken my earrings off earlier and put them in my pocket. I guess they stuck you, so I put them back on." She grinned and pulled her hair up to show that she had her diamond studs on, hoped no one noticed that she had never had them off.

The ride through town was silent as Erin concentrated on obeying all of the traffic laws, while the others kept a steady watch for any lurking police patrol cars or vehicles that might be following them.

Once at Erin's they lost no time in unloading the truck. "Pablo, you can hang that garment bag in the coat closet to your left. Ziggie, set up the laptop and scanner."

"The journal you want is on the desk there." Marisa pointed it out to Ziggie. "The copies of the documents should be right next to it."

"So exactly how are we going to approach this conundrum of ours?" Pablo asked the group.

"We are better off viewing both Sister Thomas Marie and her hidden items as equally important. This way we eliminate the risk of overlooking anything that may be vital to our investigation." Ziggie spoke up first.

"Well said." Marisa smiled. "For a moment there, you sounded exactly like a police detective." She held up her hand. "But, if you will excuse me. I must heed the call of Nature. Don't get too deep while I'm gone."

Marisa entered Erin's bathroom, immediately turned on the ceiling fan. From the pocket in her sweatshirt, she pulled out a plastic bag with a cigarette, the long hat pin that had stabbed Pablo, and a lighter that she had fetched from the car when she'd retrieved her jeans. She had never been a smoker, but this was a special blend of tobacco mixed with just a touch of marijuana buds that she knew would take the edge off her nerves and help her to focus on what was important.

After making herself comfortable on the throne, she carefully removed the cigarette from the bag, then took the hat pin and tamped the tobacco mixture down into the cigarette. Replacing the hat pin in the bag, she absently picked up the Entertainment section of last Sunday's newspaper from the magazine rack next to the throne, lit her cigarette, and began reading about upcoming events in San Diego as she inhaled deeply. The smoke burned the back of her throat, but she suppressed the desire to cough, holding the smoke as deep in her lungs as long as she could.

A headline on the second page made her exhale not only the smoke in a heaving cough, but also what felt like half of her lungs.

TRADITIONS IN TRANSITION RUSSIAN ICONS FROM THE AGE OF THE ROMANOVS

Exhibition showcases icons produced during Romanov Period (1613-1918) and includes examples made from precious metals and stones, filigree enamels, pearls, diamonds and emeralds.

The exhibition was to be inaugurated by none other than Nicholas Romanov, the rightful heir to the Imperial Crown of Russia. The inauguration was to take place at 2 P.M. on Saturday.

Marisa didn't even bother to snuff the cigarette carefully to save the expensive little ground marijuana buds, like she normally did. She took another drag inhaling it deeply, threw the rest of the cigarette into the toilet, and flushed.

She washed her hands and then brushed her teeth, squirted a little perfume around the bathroom, misting her hair in the process, to rid the room of the smell of burning hemp.

She returned to the living room, newspaper in hand, but paused. She needed to make what could be an important phone call.

"I think I may have just discovered what the Jesuits are after!"

Pablo, Erin and Ziggie all stared at one another with dumbfounded expressions, but Pablo was the one to get up from the table. "I'll go see what she's talking about."

As Pablo approached, he could her Marisa's side of the conversation.

"Geesh, I cannot believe it is actually you, Alex, after all these years! And that I would happen to find you in San Diego, too? This is just too unbelievable!" She turned as Pablo entered the room. "Hold on a minute, would you Alex?"

She covered the phone with her hand, handed the newspaper to Pablo. "Look at the second page and you'll start to understand what is going on," she said, then put the phone to her ear. "Listen, Alex, you must remember from our days in Protocol, that I am not an alarmist. Right?" She listened for the reply as she mouthed the words *Russian Consulate* to Pablo, who was standing with his mouth open, pointing to the article about the Romanov Exhibit at the Timkin.

"Okay, then please, Alex, listen to me very carefully. Prince Nikolai Romanovich is in grave danger: there is an assassination plot against him." She waited a few seconds. "I know it sounds far-fetched, and that Prince Nikolai is not a high security risk, but you need to listen here, Alex. This is a rivalry that has gone on since the early eighteen hundreds, and it has to do with age-long struggles between the Roman and the Russian Churches." She paused again. "Yes, I know that an elderly cousin of the Prince's has died, so..." Her eyes opened wide. "Yes, that's right." Her eyes got even bigger. "So he will be attending? Is that for sure? Hold on another second, Alex."

She turned to Pablo with a look of triumph on her face. "His Highness Prince Nikolai Romanovich will be attending a funeral tomorrow, which obviously means that Sister Thomas Marie has, in fact, died." She loved the look on Pablo's face. "I do believe we will be there too, don't you think?"

When Pablo nodded, she directed her attention toward her telephone conversation again. Something seemed just a bit off balance in her physical movements. Pablo hoped she wasn't feeling ill.

"I am attending that funeral also, Alex, because the nun was a former principal of mine at the convent school where I lived as a child." She spoke lightly, as if talking to an old girlfriend or planning a tea party. "I do hope you'll be there, I would love to see you again!" There was another pause and Marisa grinned. "Of course, Alex. One way or another, we'll get together before I return to New York, but promise me, old friend, that you will not let His Highness go anywhere without security, will you?" She silently pumped her fist, thanked Alex profusely.

She hung up the phone, turned quickly. What Pablo saw was a very slow turn. She stood there, stared at him with the huge glassy eyes and dilated pupils he had seen looking back at him from the mirror so many times during his undergraduate years; but less often since he had begun graduate school.

"New York?" he asked. "Are you going to New York for any particular reason?"

Marisa gazed at him a long moment before answering. "No, New York just sounds better than Boondocks, Virginia." She gave him a silly look and paused much too long before continuing. "Anyway, His Highness will be well guarded from the time he steps off the airplane." She sighed. "It is nice to have old friends in very strange places."

"This Alex from the Consulate is an old friend?"

She nodded at him before answering. "Well, not a friend-friend, just an acquaintance friend, if you know what I mean."

Pablo nodded. Marisa studied his nod for quite some time.

"Alex used to work in the Russian Consulate in Washington, DC, we met a couple of times when I was advancing our Mexican President's official visits to Moscow if the President was stopping in Washington." She paused, thinking. "If it weren't for the fact that he recognized me from former presidential advance work, he probably would have thought my call was just a prank, and might not have ordered any security."

Pablo smiled. "Marisa, where the hell did you get the pot you've been smoking?"

Her eyes opened widely with feigned innocence, but Pablo wasn't buying it. "Marisa, you are talking to the all-time former pot head champion of University High School. Come on!"

She started to giggle. "I swear, I only took two hits, then I flushed it when I saw this article." She tried, but couldn't stop giggling. "I guess those buds I got from one of my convent reunion buddies were a lot stronger than the mild stuff we get back East!" She stared at him again. "But know what? I am really, but, really hungry. Would you care to join me in a refrigerator raid?"

"Hell, why not? We can figure things out as we eat. Erin and Ziggie have been going over what happened to all the Romanovs, but this information should make it a lot easier," He waved the newspaper.

They returned to the living room, Pablo put the newspaper on the table in front of Ziggie.

"I do believe we now know who the famous 'Nicky' is: he is none other than Nicholas Romanov, also known as His Highness Crown Prince Nikolai Romanovich, the rightful heir to the Imperial Crown of Russia, if there were still such a thing." Pablo watched Marisa make a beeline for the kitchen, calmly ignored her rummaging through the refrigerator. "Marisa just called the Russian Consulate, and believe it or not, found someone she has worked with before. This Alex person has promised to get a full security detail on His Highness from the moment he arrives at the airport."

"Was she able to find out how His Highness is related to Sister Thomas Marie?" Ziggie was more than intrigued, but was watching Marisa through the open door. "And while you're at it, can you possibly enlighten us as to what Marisa is doing? She seems a little, well..."

"Spacey?" Erin said. "If I didn't know her better, I would think she was..."

"Exactly. She is stoned."

Erin barely cracked a smile, but Ziggie broke up. "I thought I saw that vaguely glassed-over, dilated pupil so fashionable among undergraduates," he said, "but Marisa? I don't get it."

"I do," Erin rose from the table. "Marisa, may I see you in the bedroom a minute?"

Marisa skipped behind Erin to the bedroom, stuck her head out the door to make a silly face at the men before closing it.

Erin wasn't amused.

"Marisa, as worried as you were about talking to Carlos the other night, now you not only spend the night with Pablo, but you are getting stoned? What are you going to tell him the next time you speak to him?"

"I'll simply tell him what I did when we spoke the other night: the absolute truth!"

"Have you lost the last vestiges of sanity you were saving for a rainy day?"

Now that was an Erin reaction! Marisa grinned. "No, I regained it. You see, Carlos was my best friend before he was my lover, which was way before he became my husband. We always said that we could count on each other in all three forms: as a lover, as a spouse, or as a friend. Our marriage vows spelled it out, so anytime one of us needs the other as a friend, we say so... and that means that nothing we can say as friends can be used against us in the love or espousal relationship."

"Oh, I see... you married someone just as insane as you are?"

"Something like that, and hey, it's worked. We have been together for over twenty years. Maybe it wouldn't work for most people, but it has worked for us. Anyway, I told him about the feelings that I was having toward Pablo, and he understood. He even helped me try to analyze why I was so attracted to him."

"His eyes, physique and sexy mouth may have a little something to do with it," Erin suggested.

"Of course, but what that it were so simple, but it's not. It really does go a lot deeper than that."

"I'm sure it does, but I can't really comment on that because I have never gotten that deep." Erin was on a roll.

"Neither have I," Marisa said seriously, but then understood how rationalizing her words seemed, and she laughed. "Oh, but would I love to!"

"I hope that's not how you left the conversation with Carlos..."

"No, of course not. But at least there are no secrets, no hard feelings and if he is harboring any feelings of insecurity or jealousy, he certainly is hiding it well."

"Or he is so busy with another graduate student that he is really quite happy that you have found yourself a little toy for your own entertainment!"

"Ouch!" Marisa had never thought of that, the thought was acutely painful. "I'll need to chew on that one for a while," she said. "Come to think of it, I am starving!"

The subject was closed as far as Marisa was concerned.

Marisa spun on her heel and left with a stunned Erin in her wake. Passing the men, Marisa waved as she entered the kitchen.

"My God, Marisa! What is it with you?"

"What's with my what?" Marisa spread some peanut butter on a cracker.

"First you spend the night with a kid half your age, and now..." She stopped. "What in God's name is that?"

"Cream Cheese."

"On top of the peanut butter?"

"Of course," Marisa said, "but this, my dear," she lifted the bottle of raspberry preserves with chipotle peppers, "is the *piece de resistance!*" She poured a dollop on top of the cream cheese and took a bite, obviously relishing her invention. "Now this is good!" She took another bite. "And now, what?" she asked Erin.

"Whatever..." Erin said.

Marisa pushed the rest of the cracker in her mouth and slowly chewed it while she stared at Erin. "No, I mean you said that first I had spent the night with a kid half my age, and now... So I am asking about that now, not my now." Erin had a blank look on her face, so Marisa repeated the question. "So now... WHAT?"

"Oh, that. I was going to say that now you were getting stoned, that's all." Erin looked at her old friend with a loving expression. "I mean, are you okay, Marisa? You're just not acting like yourself, and you haven't been for days. Is everything all right?"

Marisa prepared another two crackers, handed one of them to Erin. "Yes, Erin, I'm fine. I just have a major case of the munchies, that's all. One of our buddies from school gave me a few buds, another buddy gave me a half-full pack of Marlboros, so I fixed the Marlboros just like we used to when we went down to "meditate" at our Shrine to the Virgin of Guadalupe down off the point. Remember?"

"Remember!" Erin took a bite of the cracker concoction, had found it surprisingly good. "That shrine is where I harbor some of my very fondest of memories!"

"Anyway, I took two little hits to calm my nerves and to help me focus, but that is some mighty powerful shit! I guess I'm not as young as I used to be, after all."

"Geesh! Were we ever really that young?"

"Oh yeah," Marisa pushed the last bit of cracker into her mouth, "and we're getting younger every day!"

Erin picked up the box of crackers and returned it to the top shelf; then picked up the bar stool Marisa had obviously used to boost herself up to the crackers, replaced it back at the breakfast bar. "But know what? I think we need to get back to our detective work in the other room. Are you feeling better now?"

"Yes, I think so, but I know where everything is in case I get the munchies again."

When they returned to the living room, both Ziggie and Pablo looked up and grinned at Marisa. "Feeling better?" Ziggie had a definite sparkle in his eye.

Marisa turned to Pablo. "Did you tell on me?"

"Nope, didn't have to. Erin and Ziggie are both college professors. Like they really weren't going to notice?"

Marisa sat down at the table, across from Pablo. Erin sat across from Ziggie.

Marisa gazed at them all for a long moment, but not as long as she had been gazing before speaking to him in the den. He was pleased to see the food had helped. Finally, she spoke. "Did I hear you two trying to remember what had happened to all the Imperial Family since 1918? Were you trying to figure out who Sister Thomas Marie might be?"

They all nodded, surprised.

Marisa laughed. "Hey, I'm stoned, not deaf and dumb." Pablo started to apologize, but Marisa waved him off. "Hey, no harm, no foul, Pablo." Her face became more serious. "But don't bother, because I am quite sure who Thomas Marie was, before she became a nun."

Their intense gazes fixed on her eyes, she laughed. "Hey, lighten up, guys. It's really very simple: if she was a cousin to Nikolai Romanovich, then she must be at least a princess. If you go down through the offspring, you will find that it is mentioned a number of times that two of the Princesses became nuns: one was Grand Duchess Elizabeth, who was the Abbess of the Convent of Sisters of Mercy of Martha and Mary, which she founded in 1910. The Order was reestablished by her niece, Princess Alice of Greece, the mother of Prince Philip, Duke of Edinburgh, in 1949. So this covers one Imperial Princess." She glanced around to see if she had lost any of them. "Everyone still with me on this?"

They all nodded.

"Okay then. The only other Imperial Princess that is untraceable would be the Crown-Princess Cecelie of Germany, daughter of Grand Duchess Marie Mikhailovna. I know very little about her, because very little was ever written, but her age would be about right. Her mother was one of the Romanovs that escaped on the H.M.S. Nelson from the Villa Harax, near Sevastopol."

"Wasn't that the Marlborough?" Something didn't ring true to Erin.

"No, the Marlborough carried the Dowager Empress and the other Romanovs that had been freed by the Germans in Yalta in 1918, then moved near Sevastopol. George V of England sent the two ships for them."

"Yes, now that you mention it, I do remember that, and part of the Royal Family was singled out to go on the other ship," Erin recalled.

"That was to assure the Dowager Empress' safety. They separated her from the Nicholaevich, or the Montenegrin Grand Duchesses. They were called "black perils" because of their meanderings into to the occult, and had been the ones that introduced the Empress Alexandra to Rasputin. Anyway, they were a security risk for the Dowager Empress, so they were sent on the Nelson."

Marisa became pensive for a minute, and then jumped up from her chair. "Listen, all that isn't important, but saving this man's life is!" The excitement was building in her voice. "Give me a moment here. I have a seed of an idea germinating."

They warily exchanged glances with one another as Marisa began talking to herself. "Okay now, if we ...then we could... Yes!" She smiled triumphantly. "I think I may have just thought of a way to save Prince Nikolai's life."

"I'll bite," Pablo said, amused. "But I thought you'd just taken care of that with your call to the Consulate."

"I did, and I didn't," she said. "I did warn them and they did say they'd put a security team on His Highness. But all they are going to tell him is that there has been a threat made, and that he will have to put up with some body guards."

"That sounds like more than sufficient information to me..." Pablo said.

"But it's not!" Marisa insisted. "Don't you see? We need to explain everything we know, including the Jesuit General's connection and the Black Popes overall plan. That is his only chance at thwarting the Jesuits once and for all!"

"My God, Marisa," Erin shook her head. "I swear that sounds like a very bad plot in a really low budget movie. Nicholai isn't going to buy that for one minute. Hell, for that matter, I can't even buy that one, myself!"

Marisa kicked at an imaginary ball on the floor. "I know, it sounds crazy, and believe me, Ziggie will know how to explain it all in such a way that the Prince will take him seriously."

"Ziggie?" Erin and Pablo's voices cried out in unison.

"I what?"

Marisa found this intensely funny. She also desperately needed something else to eat. "Hold that thought!" she cried out as she ran to the kitchen. This time she found a box of "push ups" in the freezer and gleefully ripped the wrapper off one of them.

She returned to the dining room sucking on the ice cream treat, but pulled it from her mouth long enough to speak. "Back in the good old days, there was a closet directly across from the back staircase of the convent. In that closet, there were all kinds of religious items and relics, including... guess what? No, don't. There are some beautiful priest's vestments in that closet, but there is one box that stands out in my memory: the Russian Orthodox robes!"

Ziggie was intrigued. "Russian Orthodox vestments in a Roman Catholic convent? What on earth for?"

"That is the question we need to answer," Marisa replied, "but if we are going to get you close enough to Prince Nikolai to talk to him, then I suggest that Pablo and I make a run to the convent to get those boxes."

Ziggie was still mulling over the enigma of the Russian Orthodox priest's robes. "Now I know why I have to see that journal you two kept here. The answer has to be there."

Erin shook her head. "I have been over every page of that journal. There is plenty that makes no sense, but nothing that would explain what we're looking for right now."

Ziggie wasn't convinced. He rose to his feet and walked into Erin's den. He immediately spotted the journal on her desk, crossed over to pick it up.

He returned to the living room paging through the journal.

"While you are doing that," she said, "Pablo and I can take off and get the robes. That way, Ziggie, you can become an Orthodox priest sent by the Orthodox Bishop to accompany Nikolai. From what I have read, he is a religious and deeply feeling man, so he will appreciate the gesture by the Bishop, no doubt."

"And then?" Ziggie was still somewhat confused.

"And then you stay right by his side until you are alone with him and can explain his situation and everything you know."

"I think you're missing something here, Marisa. My Russian is only family oriented and barely conversational. I don't think I can say all that in Russian."

Marisa was pleased to see that Ziggie was arguing the details, not the concept, and she smiled widely. "You don't have to, Ziggie. Prince Nikolai speaks five or six languages, including Spanish, German, English and Italian. I assume you can handle things in one of those languages?"

"Of course, but won't it look a little strange for a Russian priest to be talking to a Russian Royalist in English?"

"Not really, because Nikolai has lived abroad all his life."

"No, I suppose not."

Marisa was thrilled to see Ziggie convinced, and before he could change his mind, she turned to Pablo. "Come on, Pablo, I think we had better do this now."

Pablo didn't budge. "Marisa, the only vehicle here is Erin's, and I don't believe we have even asked her if we may borrow it."

Erin laughed. "Of course you may borrow the truck."

As Pablo and Marisa walked toward the door, Marisa called over her shoulder. "We will be back with the vestments. Trust me on that one!"

Once they heard the truck pull out of the parking spot, Erin turned to Ziggie. "There is something I wanted to talk to you about without Marisa and Pablo around."

"Shoot!" he said. "I'm all ears."

Erin filled her coffee cup from the carafe they had left on the table. "Would you like some more?"

"No, I don't need any more caffeine tonight."

"Good, but to get back to what I wanted to talk to you about." She sipped her coffee, but it burnt her tongue, so she put it back on the table. "Are you familiar with Saint Malachy's Prophecies?"

"Yes, of course. According to his prophecy, Pope Benedict XVI is either the last, or the next to last Pope. Why?"

"Because I believe we are witnessing an attempt to change the course of the history of the Roman Catholic Church."

Ziggie started to smile, but stopped. "Tell me why you think so, Erin. I promise I will listen with an open mind."

That's all Erin needed. "This is something that has been bothering me for a very long time, and I know some of it is conjecture, but logical conjecture. In St. Malachy's prophecies, the list of Popes contained the Anti-Popes, also. Right?"

Ziggie nodded. "But there are supposed to be four Popes after Pope Paul VI. If I remember, St. Malachy referred to Pope John Paul I as *de medietate lunae*, or of the middle of the moon. He was elected to the papacy on August 26, 1978, and died 33 days later, on September 28, directly in the middle of the lunar month marked by the full moon."

Erin picked up from there. "Then there was Pope John Paul II, referred to as *de labore solis* or 'from the toil of the sun.' I have never been very clear on the meaning of this."

"No one is, so you're in good company, but you must count in the fact that the prophecies of St. Malachy were given to the Holy See in around 1139, or twenty five years before Galileo's birth. So, the sentence '*de Labore Solis*' could refer to Pope John Paul II's travels around the world, since it was thought at that time that the sun orbited the earth," he added. "Then there are the last two, *de gloria olivae* or 'glory of the olive' or tradition, and *Petrus Romanus* or 'Peter of Rome.'"

"Exactly, and everybody is looking toward Pope Benedict XVI as the penultimate Pope. I think he is the last."

"Why?" Ziggie had promised to listen with an open mind, and would.

"Because the Anti-Popes were also numbered in the list." Erin tried to explain her reasoning. "About the same time as Pope John Paul II was elected, there was a break off from the Church of Monsignor Marcel Lefebvre, who chose to follow the older tradition of the Church. This, if I am not mistaken, is the definition *par excellence* of an Anti-Pope, is it not?" Erin sat back and waited for Ziggie to react.

Ziggie thought long and hard about Erin's statement. A slow smile began to form on his lips, and he stood up, stretching. He picked up his coffee cup and the carafe of coffee and walked to the kitchen. He poured himself a cup of the now cold liquid, placed his cup in to the microwave oven. He tapped in one minute, and pressed the button for the machine to start.

As he waited for his coffee to heat, he absently nodded his head a couple of times, as if arguing with himself.

Erin was familiar with her friend's debates with himself, so she remained silent, pleased that he had taken her seriously enough to think things over before replying.

Finally, he returned to the dining room with his hot coffee, sat down. "I started another pot. I have a feeling we may need it, after all." He smiled at her. "Your statement is very interesting, but my immediate reaction was to belittle it. However, then I remembered that the very mission of the Society of Jesus, to which I adhere, is the investigation and research into all matters of Church, faith and knowledge."

"Thank you for not just blowing me off."

"I would never do that to a friend. In fact I would never do that to anyone, but here you go: Yes, you are correct in your views of Malachy's prophecies, as they are written. And I will even concede your view of Lefebvre, to a certain extent."

"He was excommunicated from the Roman Church because of his refusal to celebrate the new Mass, just as every Anti-Pope in History has been excommunicated." Erin had dared not hope for such a concession from Ziggie, but was thrilled to get it.

"That's where you are slightly off base, Erin. He was not excommunicated from the Church for refusing to celebrate the new Mass. He was excommunicated for ordaining four priests, and this didn't happen until 1988, which would indicate to me that Pope John Paul II was quite tolerant for a long time before axing him." Ziggie laughed. "But here is a tidbit you may or may not know: did you know that Cardinal Ratzinger, better known as our beloved Holy Father Benedict XVI, was on the commission of eight curiae Cardinals that decided the fate of Monsignor Lefebvre?"

"I had never thought about it, but it does make sense, since the Holy Father was in charge of the Office of the Holy Inquisition during Pope John Paul II's papacy."

"Exactly!" Ziggie stood and began to pace. "So let's just say that Lefebvre was an Anti-Pope, for the sake of argument." Erin nodded. "That would mean that Pope Benedict XVI is the last Pope, according to Saint Malachy and not the penultimate Pope. Right?"

"Right."

"Now let's go to another prophecy, that of Our Lady of Fatima." Ziggie paced faster, now.

"What does Fatima have to do with Lefebvre? I don't find the common link."

Ziggie did. "That's because you probably don't know that our Holy Father was involved in this matter." He stood behind his chair. "Again, Cardinal Ratzinger was the one that put the whole spin on the story about Pope John Paul II's demanding to be sent the fabled Third Mystery of Our Lady of Fatima."

"Yes, I remember that, but didn't it speak of the Holy Father being slain by bullets on the top of a mountain as he prayed at the foot of a cross?" Erin asked. "I could never figure out why the Vatican never released it before Pope John Paul II's assassination attempt."

"Nor could anyone else," Ziggie agreed. "Many scholars of the Church have secretly felt that the Third Secret or Mystery of Fatima was something entirely different, and that Cardinal Ratzinger gave it the spin he did to protect the Church from its own demise."

"Its own demise?" Erin's eyes opened wide. "Do you mean the Third Secret of Fatima could be that Lefebvre was, in fact, an Anti-Pope, and therefore Pope Benedict XVI is actually the last Pope?"

"Exactly. So just on supposition, again, let's say that Cardinal Ratzinger gave the Third Mystery a different, meaningless spin. He even went so far as to say that the Third Secret had never been published by the Church because it was nebulous and confusing. But if the Third Secret was about

Lefebvre and his break from the Church, making him the Anti-Pope, then everything else does fall into place. Don't you agree?"

Erin thought about it a minute, then tried to review it all in her mind. Almost thinking aloud, she said, "So Cardinal Ratzinger is, as the Holy Inquisitor, the one who had the original Secrets of Our Lady of Fatima, including the Third Secret, which tells of the last Anti-Pope and the last Pope, marking the end of the Holy See. He takes it upon himself to change the destiny of the Church, by first sending a forged Third Secret to Pope John Paul II after the assassination attempt. Then in 1988, he excommunicates Lefebvre and his four new priests. Then he becomes Pope, upon the death of John Paul II," she concluded. "Have I got it right?"

"More or less, yes. It is also thought in many Church circles that he took the name Benedict XVI because it was thought that this Pope would come from the Order of St. Benedict, also known as the Olivetans, adhering to Malachy's list, and *de gloria olivae*. Since he was not of the Benedictine Order, he adopted the name."

"In other words, he is going to great lengths to appear to be the penultimate Pope, when in fact, he knows he is the last Pope?" Erin had goose bumps.

"Exactly."

"So what does this have to do with the Romanov situation? Or with the old nun?"

"Well, to begin with, do you suppose it is simple coincidence that Pope Benedict XV, his namesake, was Pope during World War I and the Russian Revolution?"

"No, but now that you mention it, it's a pretty sobering thought, at that." Erin was becoming more pensive by the minute.

"Now, Erin, what I am going to tell you is something only the Jesuit General knows in its entirety, but that many Jesuits know bits and pieces of."

"Okay, and what would that be?" Erin was more intrigued than ever.

"The Jesuits are the sentinels of the faith in the Roman Catholic Church, which means complete loyalty to the Church."

"Of course. That is the duty of all Roman Catholics, isn't it?"

"I didn't say complete loyalty to the Holy Father. I said completely loyal to the Church. There is a difference, and it lays precisely in the question of the Anti-Popes."

"Okay, that makes sense, but I can hardly accept the concept of the Jesuit General running around knocking off people like Lefebvre or..."

"Or anyone who could be a threat to the survival of the Church? Why not? The Muslims are not the only ones who have a history of wars for religious fanaticism; we Catholics have our own place in history."

"But why Nikolai Romanovich? What threat could he possibly hold?"

"The rest of what I am going to say is pure conjecture, but think about it: the Russian Orthodox Church has always contended that they are the true Church. Since the fall of the Imperial Family and during the Soviet regime, the Orthodox Church has lost a great deal of its power."

"Well, yes, since the Soviets were quite against religion."

"Exactly, but now that Russia has emerged politically, the Orthodox Church has become rather strong again, which is why the Jesuits have returned in force to form a true stronghold in Siberia, and in other areas as well, including a Roman Catholic Diocese in Moscow."

"Okay... and?" Erin wasn't getting the connection.

"What would happen if the Monarchy were reinstated?" Ziggie smiled at Erin, waited for her to figure it out for herself.

"The Russian Orthodox Church would be even more powerful," Erin conceded, "but it would never have the financial resources that the Roman Church has, unless..." She rose from her chair, with her eyes as big as saucers. "Unless the Monarchy were reinstated with the entire Romanov fortune, which could even rival the Vatican's wealth."

"Which is why the Society of Jesus will stop at nothing to prevent it."

Chapter Fourteen

Pablo pulled up to the corner near the school. The normally empty parking slots in front of the school were full, with other cars disgorging passengers down the street near the Convent entrance. "What's going on?"

Marisa watched as another car stopped and several women exited then headed towards the Convent. "Damn! I should have thought of this. They are having the Rosary tonight. Nuns are coming from all over to pay their respects and say the Rosary for Sister Thomas Marie."

"There's no way you can go in there with all those people around. It's far too risky." Pablo warned her. "We'll just have to come up with some other way for Ziggie to get close to Nicky."

"There is no other way. I'm still going in. I'll just have to go about it differently, that's all. Just take us back to the main drag and find an open florist shop." Marisa quickly improvised.

"A florist?" Pablo shook his head and looked over at her. "You aren't seriously thinking what I think you're thinking?"

"That all depends on what you're thinking," Marisa smiled. "I'm planning on getting into the convent, retrieving the vestments and taking them back to Ziggie. Do you have something else in mind?"

"For a start, my driving us back to Erin's. Then for all of us to sit down, where it's safe, and figure out some other way for Ziggie to warn Nicky."

"I've already told you, there is no other way. We need those vestments, period." She watched as Pablo drove down the main thoroughfare closest to the school with the obvious intention of taking them back onto the freeway and to Erin's. "Slow down!" She ordered him. "There's a Florist up there on the corner. Pull in."

"Marisa," Pablo voiced his disapproval.

"Just do it!" Marisa ordered him a second time. She smiled when Pablo heaved a giant sigh of resignation and pulled into the parking lot next to the Flower shop.

"You are certifiable, you know that." He parked the truck and looked over at her. "What good is it going to do any of us or Nicky, for that matter, if you get caught?"

"None." Marisa beamed. "I just won't get caught." She climbed out of the truck and headed into the florist.

A pretty young black woman was assisting a young man at the counter. "Be right with you, folks. Feel free to look around."

"Thanks." Marisa waved in acknowledgement, and moved towards the wall of coolers at the side of the shop. She peered into the first one, but saw only daisies and gladiola and moved on to the next one.

Pablo joined her. "How about the white chrysanthemums, or lilies?" He pointed to a pair of obvious funeral arrangements in the cooler in front of them.

"No." Marisa moved on to the next cooler. She knew exactly what she was looking for and hoped she would find it.

Pablo caught up with her a confused look on his face. "No? You are looking for a funeral arrangement, aren't you?"

"In a manner of speaking." Marisa didn't see what she was looking for in that cooler, either. There was only one cooler left. She said a silent prayer that what she needed would be there.

"What is that supposed to mean?" Pablo demanded in a low voice.

"Did you find anything you like?" The clerk asked as she joined them.

Pablo started to say, no, only to be overridden by Marisa's, "Yes, we'll take those roses there." She pointed at a grouping of golden yellow roses at the back of the cooler.

"Roses?" Pablo felt Marisa's elbow in his gut.

"How many would you like?" The clerk asked in a hesitant voice having witnessed Marisa's action.

"How many do you have?" Marisa smiled as if nothing had happened.

The clerk opened the cooler, pulled out the holding container and began to count the roses. Marisa leaned closer to Pablo. "I hope you have a credit card with you. I don't have anything with me."

"That's four dozen." The clerk looked up expectantly.

"Fine." Marisa nodded. "Well take all of them.

Pablo glanced down at the price marker that read eight-five dollars per dozen and gasped. He barely managed to side step Marisa's elbow as she tried to nail him a second time.

"Is there some type of problem?" The clerk paused unsure of what to do next.

"Not really," Marisa laughed. "My son-in-law here forgot my daughter's and his second anniversary and needs something to dig his way out of the dog house and back into her good graces. He just wasn't ready for how far he is going to have to dig."

"Second anniversary!" There was an instant sympathy bond between the young woman and Pablo's fictitious wife. She looked over at Pablo, censure in her eyes. "Honey, you better hope she really loves you. If you'd forgotten our second anniversary, it would take more than a few dozen roses to get you out of trouble with me. You should be thankful your momma-in-law is willing to help you out. My momma would let you just twist in the wind, and then tell me she'd told me so."

"What type of vase would you like these in?" the young woman asked Marisa. "May I suggest one of these cut crystal vases?" She pointed at a large etched crystal vase that would easily accommodate the four dozen roses.

"I think that will do quite nicely, thank you." Marisa glanced at Pablo daring him to react to the hundred and fifty-dollar price on the vase.

"Let me arrange these for you. I'll even throw in some fern and baby's breath at no extra charge." She moved to an adjacent counter and began putting the arrangement together.

Marisa strolled around the store glancing at what other offerings might be for sale. She paused when she saw a rack of baseball caps with adjustable backs. Looking through them she saw one with the shop's name on it, pulled it from the rack and set on the counter near the cash register.

The clerk finished the arrangement and rang up their purchases. "With tax, the total comes to five hundred and forty-six dollars and forty-seven cents. Will that be cash or charge?"

Pablo rolled his eyes as he withdrew his wallet, pulled out a Platinum Visa Card and handed it to the clerk. "Maybe this will teach you to remember next year." Marisa had a hard time keeping a straight face.

"I have no doubt it will." Pablo gathered the receipt and stuffed it and the card back into his wallet. He moved over and lifted the box the clerk had set the finished arrangement in to keep it steady in transport.

"Thank you for all your help." Marisa smiled, picked up the bag holding the baseball cap and exchanged winks with the young woman before following Pablo out to the truck.

Pablo set the box on the floor of the passenger's seat and waited for Marisa. "I think you were enjoying yourself a bit too much in there."

"What was I supposed to say?" Marisa defended herself. "We need some flowers so I can break into a convent and steal some priest's vestments? Besides, you're a rich boy. You can afford it."

"Oh, it won't be costing me a cent." Pablo said as Marisa climbed into the truck and sat on her legs to avoid crushing the roses at her feet. He closed her door and went to his side and climbed in.

"Are you saying you expect me to pay you back?" Marisa was appalled. True, she had unfairly trapped him into paying for the flowers, but it was for a very good cause.

"It never crossed my mind." Pablo smiled, started the engine and backed out and onto the street and into the turn lane that would take them back to the school.

"Then what? I don't understand.

"I used the Visa good old Dad gave me for emergencies." Pablo grinned at her and began laughing.

"You what?" Marisa exclaimed. "It's your father's Visa card!"

"Yep. He gave it to me when I started graduate school, saying one never knew when an emergency might arise. I've never used it until now. Somehow I think there's some poetic justice in this somewhere. Hell, he might not even notice it isn't his signature when he gets the bill. After all, it is for flowers."

"This is too rich!" Marisa crowed with laughter. "Do you think he'd ever ask you about it if he did notice?"

"I could only wish that he would," Pablo laughed even harder. "Then I would be able to tell him that they were for a beautiful older woman I'd met, named Marisa."

"Oh my God! You would, wouldn't you!"

"In a heart beat! Just out of curiosity, why the roses and not the usual funeral flowers?"

"Golden Yellow roses are prized in Russia as a sign of love." Marisa explained. "I felt it was the least I could do for Sister Thomas Marie. We've pretty well established she is of noble birth, what with Nicky being her cousin. Besides, Father Gregory will recognize the significance right off, and with there being no card attached, it may give him something else to think about."

"You mean worry about, don't you?"

They neared the school, Marisa told Pablo to let her off near the convent entrance. She reached inside the bag, pulled the baseball cap out and yanked the price tag off before adjusting it to its largest size. She smoothed her hair away from her face, rolled all of it up into a knot on the top of head before putting the cap on.

"You want me to let you off? I thought I would be the one to deliver the flowers," Pablo protested.

"I appreciate the thought, but you can't. You haven't a clue where the closet is. Even if you did, you don't know what the box holding the vestments looks like or how to get out using the catacombs. I do." Marisa patted his arm. "How do I look?"

"Like a crazy woman about to try the impossible."

"Works for me." Marisa grinned unrepentantly. "After you let me out, wait in front of the school entrance. Keep the engine running. If anyone comes your way, leave."

"What if I'm not out there when you come out?" Pablo didn't like the idea of leaving her alone.

"If you do have to leave, just park a few blocks to the west. I'll find you."

Pablo stopped just beyond the gates that led to the Convent entrance. Marisa opened her door, carefully climbed out wincing at the pins and needles that washed through her legs as she stood next to the open door of the truck. She reached back inside and removed the vase from its protective box. She wasn't completely ready for the weight of it all, but managed not to drop it.

"Are you sure you can handle that?" Pablo called over to her. "It's fairly heavy."

"Now you tell me!" Marisa grimaced. "You could have warned me."

Pablo started to get out of the truck. "No!" She hissed. "Stick to our plan. I can handle these. Now close my door and wait for me." She paused. "If I'm not back in an hour, call in the Calvary."

"Marisa?" Pablo didn't want to think of what may have happened if she wasn't back in an hour's time.

"No fear, Pablo. Trust me. I've made it through worse situations than this one. And, thanks for caring, it means a lot." She turned and started towards the entrance to the Convent.

By the time she reached the double front doors, she thought her arms were going to fall off. The heavy crystal vase, plus four dozen roses and water felt like it weighed a ton. It took her a few seconds to figure out how to ring the bell without dropping the vase, but she finally settled in using her elbow.

The door opened almost immediately, and she heard a woman's voice. "Yes, may I help you?"

"Florist delivery, Ma'am. They're for the Chapel tomorrow." Marisa tried to keep her voice bored and neutral.

"Oh! Do come in. You can put them on the sideboard right over there. Someone will make sure that they are set in the Chapel in the morning." The visiting nun escorted Marisa straight ahead into what she remembered as the small parlor. Marisa set the vase on the sideboard, took a small step back happy to relieve the strain on her arms and shoulders.

"Do I need to sign anything?" The helpful woman asked as she admired the roses.

"No Ma'am. Everything has been taken care of," Marisa politely replied. "Ah, Ma'am," she lowered her voice. "I hate to ask this, but I've been making deliveries for the last three hours and I would greatly appreciate it if I might use your restroom?"

"Oh, you poor dear. Certainly, it's right this way." The nun led Marisa to the left of the small parlor past the staircase with the half-sized closet door beneath it, which was Marisa's ultimate goal, and through a narrow hallway. She stopped and pointed to a door that said Faculty on it. "It's right in there, dear."

"Thank you, I'm most grateful, Ma'am." Marisa pushed the door open and went inside. It was almost like walking through a time portal. The room was exactly the same as it had been years ago, when Marisa used to sneak away from phone duty in the tiny office next door, to duck into the bathroom and have a cigarette. There was the window on the far wall where she had stood blowing the smoke from her cigarette outside. The solitary toilet was there with the old fashioned sink next to it. She certainly had never dreamed she would be here again, especially for the reason she was there now. She glanced back at the door, wondering if the nun was waiting for her to finish. She shrugged. She might as well make use of it while she was here.

Finished, she went to the door and cracked it open to see if anyone was lurking in the hallway beyond. The hallway was empty. She quickly exited the bathroom and hurried back towards the closet. She was nearly at her destination when fear froze her in mid-step at the sound Father Gregory's deep voice asking one of the nuns who had delivered the yellow roses. Move! She silently screamed at her body.

"They were delivered a short while ago, Father. In fact, the delivery girl asked if she might use the restroom."

Marisa thought she would die of a heart attack, right on the spot. Suddenly a surge of adrenaline rushed through her and she crossed the remaining distance to the closet door in a flash. She knew from experience the door was never locked. She grabbed the handle and pushed against it. Nothing happened.

"Which way are the restrooms?" Father Gregory asked.

"Through there, half way down the hallway beyond, Father."

"Thank you, Sister. Would you please gather the other Sisters into the Parlor? We'll be starting the Rosary Service shortly."

"Certainly, Father."

Marisa tried pushing against the door harder this time. It still didn't budge. She could hear heavy footsteps heading in her direction. A memory flashed of the last time she had been in the closet with Sister Patricia Marie. The same thing had happened back then. Sister had said something about it being old and prone to sticking. Now what had she done to make it open?

Marisa could swear that any second she would feel the heavy hand of Father Gregory on the back of her neck. Push up! A voice yelled in her head. She lifted the handle, raised the door ever so slightly and then pushed against it. It smoothly and silently opened in front of her.

She immediately entered, closed it behind her, praying that she'd done so in time. The heavy footsteps stopped right outside. Marisa was certain by now he could hear the sound of her ragged breathing and pounding heart right through the thick wood she was hiding behind.

"Sister? Was there anyone else back there?" She heard Father Gregory ask.

"No, Father. I didn't see anyone. Are you looking for anyone in particular?"

"I was told a delivery girl had asked to use the restroom." Father Gregory replied.

"Yes, but I'm sure she left a while back." Marisa could have kissed her unknown benefactor.

"Father? The Sisters are all together as you requested." The first nun informed him.

Father Gregory roughly cleared his throat. "Thank you, Sister. Shall we all go in?"

The sounds of multiple footsteps leading away from the door were like music to Marisa's ears, as was the sound of multiple voices responding in prayer a short time later.

Marisa murmured a short prayer of thanks, reached for the light switch and flipped it on. The closet was little changed since she'd last seen it. There were a few more religious statues and religious artifacts that had been donated to the school over the years. She ignored these and went straight to where she remembered they had stored the priestly vestments in the past. It took some searching, but she finally located the box she was after, wedged in the back corner behind the newer hanging vestments. Pulling it free, she set it on the floor and rearranged the remaining vestments to erase any signs they had been disturbed.

She picked up the box and flipped off the light, allowing her eyes to readjust before opening the closet door. She involuntarily flinched as the heavy tones of Father Gregory's voice calling out the next decade of the Rosary hit her like a wave. Exiting the closet, she closed the door behind her then moved to the full size door to its right that led downstairs to the basement. She didn't pause to take another breath before opening the door to hide behind its re-closed length.

Marisa paused briefly on the top step, taking slow deep breaths to calm her racing heart. That had been way to close for comfort. She positioned the box in her arms to make it easier to descend the narrow stairway to its end. Once there she unerringly made her way to the wall panel at the far side of the basement, clicked it open with her foot, then closed it again once she was safely inside the catacombs. A sudden laugh bubbled from her throat at the thought there might as well be a sign saying enter here, she had used the entrance so many times.

She steered her way through the darkened passageways to the elevator. It was rising to the upper levels when she glanced down at the box in her arms and unaccountably thought of Sister Thomas Marie making a similar journey of her own bearing a parcel wrapped in waxed brown paper, crisscrossed with heavy twine. But where would she be taking it? Obviously not into the Music Conservatory, too many students were in and out of there for lessons and practice sessions. The same rationale applied to the level above that. This left only the roof.

Marisa hurried from the Mother Superior's office to the front doors of the school. She opened one of them, sighing in relief at seeing Erin's truck parked in front. She leaned out and waved for Pablo to come to her.

He turned off the engine and hurried to the doorway. "What? Is there a problem?"

"No, no problems. I've got the vestments." She handed him the box. "Put this in the truck and wait. I'll be back in a little while. There is something I must check out."

"I don't think so." Pablo shook his head. "There's no way I'm letting you go back in there alone."

"Fine, then. Lock the box in the truck and come with me. Just hurry." Marisa stunned him by readily agreeing. Pablo did exactly that and quickly returned to the door. Marisa let him closing the door behind him.

"What exactly is so important that you have to check it out now?" Pablo asked as he followed her through the hallways back to the Mother Superiors office.

"I'll tell you when we get there." Marisa led the way up the spiral staircase.

By the time they'd reached the elevator, Pablo was dumbstruck at the intricacies of the hidden areas of the estate. Marisa motioned him into the elevator and followed after him. "Where are we going in this relic?"

"The roof." Marisa answered as she set the elevator in motion.

"The roof!" Pablo exclaimed. "You're risking everything to check out a roof?"

Marisa explained to him about Sister Thomas Marie and her parcel, adding that the only logical place she could have been taking it was the roof.

Once on the roof Marisa began to look around for anything out of the ordinary. She cursed the fact they were without any lights, but other than the old and ever present dovecote that stretched across the full length of the roof, there was nothing else to see.

"Damn!" she muttered. "It doesn't make any sense. Why carry a parcel with her in the elevator if she wasn't planning on leaving it somewhere?"

"Maybe she did leave it, but somewhere else?" Pablo glanced down at the illuminated dial of his watch. "In any case, there will be no more searching tonight. We have to get those vestments back to Erin's"

"You're right." Marisa reluctantly agreed. "I could swear she left it up here somewhere."

"Marisa," Pablo took her by the arm and began leading her back to the elevator. "It's dark, maybe in the daylight something will jump out at you. Now let's get out of here. I don't like the way we're pushing our luck."

They made it all the way back through the Mother Superiors office and were heading to their exit, when Marisa suddenly halted in her tracks. "Geesh! Can't forget that!" She changed her direction, moved toward the new theater that had once been the old auditorium years before.

"Marisa!" Pablo hissed after her, then hurried to catch up. "What are you doing now? There isn't time for us to go off on another one of your hunches."

She ignored him and made her way into the theater through an unlocked side door. Taking a swift inventory of her surroundings, she headed for the stage, and from there to the back hidden storage areas beneath the stage where all the costumes and props were held.

Pablo had to rush to keep her in sight as she hurried through the tight maze of corridors. He was out of breath when he found her kneeling before a large box. "What in hell are you doing?"

She'd ripped open the box and was searching through it with the single mindedness of a cat digging for a gopher. "Aha!" she exclaimed, withdrew a salt and pepper colored handful of something unrecognizable to Pablo.

Pablo had reached the end of his patience. He grabbed Marisa by the shoulders and lifted her bodily to her feet. "Enough!" He sternly informed her. "Are you totally out of your mind, woman? There are very dangerous people not a stone's throw away who would like nothing more than to do us bodily harm or worse, and you suddenly decide to go on a scavenger hunt!"

"We need this!" Marisa held up the clump of whatever it was and practically shook it in his face. "Now we need some adhesive." She bent back down, oblivious to Pablo's growing anger. She leaned into the open gap with only her legs hanging out searching for only heaven knew what.

This was the last straw for Pablo. He bent down and grabbed her by the waist, dragged her out. "Got it!" Marisa cheered as her upper torso and head reappeared.

Clutched in her right hand was the handle of an oblong box the size of a giant box of facial tissue. Scrambling to her feet she set it, and the clump in her other hand, down away from the opened cavern to stuff the boxes back inside. "Don't just stand there gaping! Help me do this. We have to get out of here."

Pablo began shoving boxes with her, muttering, "I understand now why Erin is always threatening to kill you."

They finally made it back to the truck. Marisa was inside, Pablo began to climb in, when a voice called out to them from farther down the sidewalk. "Hey, you in the truck. That is a No Parking Zone. What are you doing there?"

Marisa glanced in the side mirror outside her window and saw the young man who'd been with Father Holtz at the University, walking towards them. She immediately slid to the floorboard and curled up, hissing at Pablo, "He's Father Holtz's stooge. Get us out of here."

Pablo started the engine and lost no time in pulling away from the school.

Marisa started to get up, but Pablo shook his head. "Better he think there's only one person in here. I'll let you know when you can get up.

He drove several miles, Marisa crouched on the floorboard.

"Is it safe yet?"

"Yes. You can come up now."

"No problem." Marisa levered her way back into her seat and glanced behind her to be certain the box of vestments was still there.

"Tell me exactly what it was you needed so badly back there." Pablo insisted. "I thought I was going to have toss you over my shoulder and carry you back to the truck."

Marisa lifted the salt and pepper colored clump and shook it out, then held it up to her face.

Pablo glanced over at her and almost choked. There was Marisa with a salt and pepper beard covering the lower half of her face and reaching down almost to her chest. "That's what that is! A fake beard! You risked our being caught over a theater prop!"

"It isn't for me!" Marisa lowered the fake hair and carefully folded it. "All Russian Orthodox priests have beards."

It was late by the time they made it back to Erin's. Ziggie and Erin looked quite relieved to see them walk in. Marisa took the box of vestments from Pablo and walked over to Ziggie. "I promised you I'd come back with the vestments. Here they are. Now go try them on so we can see if they fit you."

"Did you have any trouble?" Erin caught Pablo's vigorous nod behind Marisa.

"Nothing we couldn't handle." Marisa understated the truth. "I'll fill you in when Ziggie comes back. Is there any wine left? I could use a drink."

Ziggie laid the box on the bed and carefully opened it. Inside were the traditional Russian Orthodox funeral vestments. "Why funeral vestments?" He wondered aloud.

He respectfully removed them from the box and laid them out on the bed, then lifted the box to move it out of the way. He frowned. The box felt unusually weighty for being empty. He returned it to the bed and ran his hand across and around the empty interior. "Hmm, what is this now?" He paused as his fingers detected a slight indentation at the top inside corner. He traced the indentation to its terminus and nodded. He had seen such a mechanism before: the box had a false bottom.

He gently pressed the center of the indentation and a small panel slid open. Inside was a thick envelope sealed with wax. He pulled it free and took a closer look at the insignia imprinted on the wax. It was the Imperial Seal of the Romanovs.

"Dear God!"

His hand shaking, he gently laid the thick envelope next to the vestments on the bed. He returned his attention to the box and carefully searched the hidden compartment. He felt his fingers slide over something smooth and metallic and withdrew a small portfolio that gleamed in the light. It was made of gold! He slowly opened the portfolio, which revealed an ornately inscribed verse. He recognized it as the Russian Orthodox Prayer of Absolution. He closed the portfolio and laid it alongside the envelope.

Looking back down at the box he was almost afraid to check it again. He forced himself to repeat his earlier inspection. A soft groan escaped him as his fingers encountered what oddly felt like a mounted jewel.

"Saints preserve us!" He withdrew a small and magnificent vial covered with diamonds and rubies. Looking at it closely he recognized the intricate trademark craftsmanship of Fabergé.

He held the vial up to the light and was almost blinded by the prismatic reflections from its jewels. He looked back down at the golden portfolio and realized the vial must hold the holy oils with which the deceased must be anointed according to Orthodox tradition.

A certainty began to grow within him that was too immeasurable to believe. He reverently gathered his newly discovered treasures and returned to the studio where the others were gathered.

"Ziggie?" Marisa was the first to see him. "You're not wearing the vestments?"

Erin saw the shock in his eyes and the slight tremor in his hands that held strange and unexpected items. The energy being sent out from them made her gasp.

"Hush, Marisa!" Erin jumped to her feet and helped a shaken Ziggie to a chair. "What is it, my dear?" She asked him softly. Ziggie ever so gently laid the treasures before him on the table.

More concerned with the paleness of Ziggie's face and the glazed sheen in his eyes, Erin ignored them, until Marisa whispered a breathless, "Oh my God!"

Erin glanced over at her and saw she had crawled from where she was sitting on the floor to kneel next to the table, her eyes riveted to what lay there. Erin followed her gaze and the true importance of what she was seeing took her breath. Her hands tightened on the back of Ziggie's chair as she fought the overwhelming need to faint dead away.

Pablo rose from his seat across the room puzzled by the sudden inexplicable behavior of his friends. He stood by the still immobile Marisa and glanced from her to Erin and Ziggie. All were transfixed on the table before them. He glanced downward and the instant recognition of the items lying there spurred him to action.

"Right! Nobody panic. Erin, I really think you should sit down before you fall down." Pablo began taking charge. "Marisa. Marisa!" He had to say her name sharply a second time before she looked over at him. "Go into the kitchen and bring water and brandy for everyone."

She frowned and blinked her eyes slowly as if coming out of a trance. "What?"

"Brandy. Water." Pablo calmly pointed towards the kitchen. Marisa slowly rose to her feet and went to the kitchen. He reached over, gently took Erin by the arm and led her to sit in a chair next to Ziggie.

Marisa returned with a tray bearing a decanter of Brandy, a pitcher of water and four glasses. She stood near the table uncertain what to do next.

Pablo relieved her of the tray and set it on a nearby sideboard telling her softly, "You need to sit down as well."

Marisa took a seat across from Erin and Ziggie. None of them spoke. Pablo poured Brandy from the decanter into each of the glasses. He added a touch of water to the women's glasses and an additional splash of Brandy to his own. He set the glasses within reach of the others, careful not to endanger the precious items.

He grabbed his own glass, sat in the remaining seat next to Marisa. He raised his glass and his voice, ordering them all to drink, which they did. The paralyzing shock that had held them enthralled began to lessen with each small sip. The utter significance of what Ziggie had discovered played through each of their minds.

Erin was the first to speak. "Ziggie, please open the envelope and read us what is inside."

Ziggie took a deep breath and straightened his shoulders. "Are you certain this is what we should do? Would it not be best to wait and turn it over to the proper authorities?"

"Because you were the one to find this, you are the one meant to reveal its contents," Erin said with quiet certainty.

"Yes, Ziggie. Erin is right." Marisa added her support. "Nothing happens without a reason." She looked over at Pablo for his view.

"It is clear we all share the same understanding of what Ziggie has brought to us and that we will treat these priceless artifacts with the care and respect required." Pablo looked at each of them in turn. "I agree with Erin and Marisa, in that nothing happens without a reason. I would take this one step further: I believe that with all that has happened over these last days there is a higher synchronicity here. For reasons we may never know or understand in our lifetimes, the four of us were meant to be where we are now and to hear whatever might be written on the pages contained in that envelope," Pablo quietly stated.

Marisa smiled at the sense of rightness she heard in Pablo's words. "One moment, I beg you." She rose and went back into the kitchen. When she returned she laid a pair of plastic gloves on the table next to the envelope.

Ziggie nodded and donned the gloves, pleasantly surprised that they comfortably fit over his large hands. "Is there a sharp implement available?"

Pablo reached into his pocket and retrieved a folding knife, which he opened and handed to Ziggie hilt first. "Be careful. It's sharp."

Ziggie accepted the knife and painstakingly worked the blade beneath the wax seal that held it closed hoping to preserve as much of the seal itself as possible. Everyone held their breath until the wax suddenly released its grip, the flap of the envelope suddenly was freed; the wax seal still intact.

Ziggie closed and handed the knife back to Pablo before gently removing the sheaf of paper inside. The envelope now empty, he carefully set it aside. The paper was surprisingly modern in composition being what appeared to be a twenty or thirty pound cotton bond. Ziggie unfolded the pages and looked down at the first page and began to read aloud.

June 14, 1997
Villa Vistamar
San Diego, CA
United States of America

To You, be you of God or Family, be it known that you have Been Chosen By the Good Lord to witness my Truth.

I write this in the language of my adopted Homeland, which has given me sanctuary and security for a vast portion of my life. Today I celebrate my ninety-seventh year. For the last eighty-two years, I have been known to the world, and to my fellow Sisters of the Order of Saint Thomas, as Sister Thomas Marie.

I was born at Peterhof in my true homeland, Mother Russia, on June 14, 1899.

I am Maria Nikolaevna Romanov, daughter of By the Grace of God, His Imperial Majesty, Nicholas II, Tsar, Emperor and All-Russian Autocrat and Her Imperial Majesty, Alexandra Fyodorovna, Tsarina of all the Russias.

I have fervently prayed these many years for the Dear Lord to dim my faculties and take from me the sad and painful memories that have so haunted me. He, in His Wisdom has deigned not to answer my prayers. It has been revealed to me in my meditations that my prayers will not be answered until I chronicle for posterity an account of those most terrible and painful times of my life. In doing so, I hold close the hope that at long last my prayers might be answered.

Being of Imperial birth, my life was preplanned by tradition and protocol before I ever took my first breath, as were the lives of my most loved sisters. This was especially true for our cherished Sunshine.

It was not until I had reached a greater maturity and perspective did I come to realize we were, as well, at the mercy of the ever-shifting tides of political disquietude and necessity.

I was most painfully made aware of the harshest and most cruel aspects of these tides when confronted with the horrific news of my Family's tragic and most vicious murders. That this terrible news did not come until three months after the fact in no way lessened its impact or the sudden and complete isolation that enveloped me. I was now alone in a strange and beautiful, but quiet alien land mourning the loss of our Sunshine but two weeks earlier. The Tsarvich Alsey Nicholaevich Romanov died in my arms on July 5, 1918 in the Territory of the United States of America called Hawaii.

I unexpectedly received great sympathy and understanding from some of the Native people of this land, referred to as Restorationists, who themselves had felt the recent loss of their Beloved Queen Liliuokalani, who had died the previous year from complications of a stroke. The Restorationists offered to give the Tsarvich a Royal burial such as they would accord one of their Royal Line. I humbly and most gratefully accepted this offer in the hope that someday he might be returned to Mother Russia and interred where he truly belonged: among his family.

And just how did this come to be that the heir to the Imperial Crown of Russia should die with only a sister with him in a land so far from his home? I can speak only of that which I know. History has and will deal rightly or wrongly with all else.

My mother sent Alsey and I to Sevastopol in March of 1918, with two children that greatly resembled us left behind in our stead. Once in Sevastopol, we were put aboard an ocean going ship of the Russian American Fur Company, which was owned by members of the family and serviced the highly lucrative fur trade in Alaska and the northern continental United States. It was decided, by whom I have never known, that the usual Polar Route was too harsh and dangerous for myself and Sunshine to risk. We embarked from Sevastopol on March 18, 1918 sailing the Pacific Route to the United States of America.

We anchored in Hawaii to replenish stores and provisions six weeks later. It was while we were here that the cumulative effects of our sudden and hasty departure from Tobolsk, the rigors of traveling to Sevastopol and the subsequent ocean voyage took their toll on Sunshine's sensitive health. I nursed him myself when he became seriously ill. I told him funny stories and joked with him to try to keep his mind off the pain, much as I had always done for him. Weeks passed, but he slowly overcame this illness, though left too weak to travel. The ship's doctor judged that Alsey should be strong enough to continue our voyage in another two weeks. We were a week from departing, when Alsey suffered a relapse from which he never recovered. My heart died with him that day.

I was allowed a further two weeks to recover from the loss of our Sunshine, and the news of my Family's murders at which time I was informed we would be departing for the United States of America. I did not want to go. I could not bear to leave my Sunshine behind, and saw nothing for me in the United States. I pleaded with the Captain to allow me to stay in Hawaii. Relatives of the late Queen had offered sanctuary and a place for me to reside for as long as I wanted, but the Captain coldly insisted that his orders came directly from the Tzarina; that I was to be taken to the United States, where arrangements for my safety and well being were already in place.

I was unable to convince him that my family would want me to stay with the Tsarvich in Hawaii, and powerless to force him to do so. I fell into a deep depression and spent the entire voyage in my cabin unable to eat or sleep. I could only cry.

This was a terribly dark and bitter time for me. I am not proud to admit that I shouted to my Mother in heaven asking her why she had abandoned us so, and to my Father for not being there when I so desperately needed him. I lay sobbing in my bed demanding of God how He could be so cruel and unfeeling a Deity to take my family away from me as He had. It is a time in my life for which I have done much penance to repair.

We made land fall in Bodega Bay, located in the northern area of California. I was taken by carriage to Fort Ross, an outpost for the Russian American Fur Company and the oldest established Seat of the Russian Orthodox Church in America. The Patriarch, who blessed me, and said the Prayer of Absolution for the Tsarvich, and my Family in Mother Russia, greeted me there.

I did not remain there long, and was soon transported with my meager belongings overland to the southern regions of the State. We stopped in Los Angeles while on the way farther south to the small city of San Diego. It was there that I was approached by a Brother of the Society of Jesus, who was introduced to me as a Representative of the Father General in Rome. He handed me a letter from my mother explaining that out of respect for their late Father General Franz Wernz, her cousin, the Order had agreed to escort me to my final destination in San Diego and watch over me in her stead.

I waited until the Jesuit had departed before opening my Mothers letter. It was in this letter that I learned of my coming to Villa Vistamar and of the

Dowry that had been sent ahead to safeguard me in life.

The welcome knowledge that this is being read tells me that I have at long last been called home to God and the waiting embraces of my Family. I would charge you dear Reader, to vow to make certain that the current legitimate heir to the Imperial Throne be entrusted with my legacy to my Family and for Mother Russia.

When the last of the twenty-one bells has sounded, you will know what it is you must do.

May Almighty God in His Infinite Wisdom and Mercy bless us all.

Ziggie took a quiet breath before continuing. "It is signed, *Sister Thomas Marie SST*, and beneath that it is signed once again, *Grand Duchess Maria Nikolaevna Romanov*."

Chapter Fifteen

Erin, Pablo and Marisa sat halfway down the right hand side of the Chapel, in the last three seats of the pew. Marisa had chosen their places, as after taking an approximate head count of the diplomatic guests, she knew the guests would have to be seated behind His Highness and Ziggie. She, Erin and Pablo would be about two pews behind them, but on the side aisle, just in case they had to beat a hasty exit.

The only positive thing that had come from their attendance, so far, was the fact that Fathers Gregory and Holtz seemed so bothered by their presence and the large bouquet of golden yellow roses at the side of the altar they hadn't given a second glance to the tall, gangly Russian Orthodox Bishop that had immediately greeted Prince Nikolai upon his arrival at the convent. They also hadn't noticed that rather than having entered the grounds first to introduce himself to the Sisters, he had remained outside the gate until His Highness' limousine had arrived.

"So far, so good," Pablo whispered to her. He was seated between Erin and Marisa; Marisa was on the aisle.

"From your mouth to God's ears," she replied, "but all Hell may be about to let loose. Look!"

Ziggie and the prince were speaking in low voices outside the chapel, and Father Gregory was approaching them with a firm step. All three observers sat perfectly still, hoping to hear what the Jesuit was about to say.

"Your Serene Highness," he greeted Prince Nikolai, extending his hand. "It is an honor to make your acquaintance. I am Father Gregory, and I will be celebrating the Holy Funeral Mass this morning."

Marisa, Erin and Pablo all tensed, holding their breath to see if Father Gregory would recognize Ziggie. If he did, then God only knew what might happen. He might not react at all, or he might be pushed into trying to kill the Crown Prince right then and there. It had been a risk that they had all discussed, but they'd decided that anything they did would have a certain risk involved, and that this was the lesser of the two or other possibilities they had managed to think up.

Prince Nikolai shook his hand and smiled warmly, although Marisa was sure there was something slightly off-handed about his smile. She hoped it was because Ziggie had already been able to tell him the source of the danger lurking just behind the formalities of his aunt's funeral.

"Likewise, Father. May I introduce His Grace, Bishop Sergei from our Parish in Fort Ross, California?"

Ziggie extended his hand and Father Gregory shook it, with no outward sign of recognition. Ziggie gazed down at the ground, never met Father Gregory's eyes directly.

Father Gregory released his hand and addressed Ziggie, although he was looking directly at Prince Nikolai. "It is a pleasure, Father," he said, and then continued in Russian to Prince Nikolai. "I thought perhaps Bishop Sergei might care to concelebrate the Holy Mass with me, in honor of and with the highest respect to the Grand Duchess' birthright." He bowed ceremoniously. "Would this please His Highness?"

Prince Nikolai hesitated a moment before replying, but there was a sparkle in his eyes that hadn't been there before. He glanced at the three observers, who could hear the entire conversation.

Marisa leaned toward her companions. "It's not too often that one enjoys the privilege and honor of sharing a bit of private humor with a Prince, is it?" She had never met him, yet she already liked him. He was a regal figure of a man, and showed no frailty whatsoever, despite his eighty-plus years. His hair was a salt-and-pepper gray, he was tall with an athletic body, and he sported a tan that a La Jolla surfer would have killed for.

The Prince straightened, withdrew his hand. "My aunt was a Roman Catholic for about eighty years, Father Gregory," he said in perfect English, "so I would expect her soul to be fully comforted by the Roman

Catholic Funeral Mass." He smiled widely. "Besides, most of the guests would be confused by the Russian Orthodox reading of five Gospel passages." He laughed softly. "The only request that I would make for the sake of the Orthodox rituals of a Holy Royal burial, and for which I have asked His Grace to attend today, is that a pause in the Roman ceremony be made just prior to the Consecration. This would be to allow time for His Grace to place the Holy Absolution Prayer in her casket. I would ask that another pause be made for him to anoint her with the Holy Oils directly after Communion." He flashed another wide smile. "Oh, yes, and at the end of the service, as the guests leave, the bells in the tower must be rung 21 times, in honor of her station in life. Everything else may proceed per the instructions my Consulate brought to the convent on my behalf."

Father Gregory seemed surprised, but immediately acquiesced. "Of course, your Serene Highness. Your request is my command."

Then he actually bowed and backed away. Marisa had to bite the inside of her mouth to keep herself from laughing out loud. As he backed away, Prince Nikolai motioned toward him. "Oh, Father Gregory, I may not have mentioned it, but His Grace will be remaining with the casket until I have attended to another matter with my entourage, at which time, we will return for the funeral procession to proceed to the airport. We will be departing to St. Petersburg this evening." Father Gregory nodded, then turned and entered the Sacristy to don the Funeral vestments.

Marisa turned discreetly to Pablo and smiled. "Did you hear that?" she asked, and Pablo just stared at her. "I mean, the part about Ziggie staying with the casket?" This time Pablo nodded. "That means that he won't be going to the gallery with the Prince, and that means."

"That I will be there before anyone else arrives, and will stay close until the Prince is back here again."

Marisa frowned. She didn't like the change in plans, it frightened her. She looked over at Erin and could see she didn't care for it either.

"I don't like this. I don't like it one bit."

Pablo smiled at her lovingly. "It'll be okay, Marisa. I promise you, it will."

The Prince sat in the first place on the middle aisle, Ziggie beside him. The rest of the guests filed in; the diplomats and official Russian dignitaries sitting in the pews behind Prince Nikolai, as Marisa had predicted.

The rest of the chapel slowly filled with the Sisters of the Congregation of Saint Thomas, many of whom Marisa and Erin were quite sure they remembered from many years before when they were students.

Behind them, the religious from many other orders began to file in, quietly taking their seats until the entire left section of the chapel was full.

A small group of sisters filed upstairs to the choir loft at the back of the chapel, and one of them began to lightly play the pipe organ. Marisa glanced back, smiled fondly at the Sister standing in the middle of the small choir. The nun had been their classmate, had entered the convent directly upon graduation. Her friend smiled back cheerfully, and Marisa thought about how little she had changed since high school.

There was a pause in the music, before the familiar five-noted scale of the *Ave Maria* began. Precisely on the twelfth note the nun's perfect soprano pitch began a sweetly clear rendition of the *Ave Maria*, while eight muscular Brothers from the Order of Saint Augustine, dressed in their black robes, slowly carried a gold-gilded and jeweled casket befitting of an Imperial Russian Grand Duchess down the middle aisle of the chapel.

As the last notes of the hymn brought it to an end, the monks deposited the casket on a mahogany platform in front of the altar, and the Mass began.

Ziggie was a little nervous about the placement of the Prayer of Absolution and the Anointment with the Holy Oils, but he had seen the rituals done a number of times in the past. He went over them in his mind many times in preparation for the rituals.

After the reading of the Gospel, Father Gregory stepped to the pulpit and cleared his throat. All the guests were silent, waiting for his Eulogy.

"I find myself humbled before you today." he began his sermon. "We honor the life of a magnificent woman who dedicated her life to the service of God. Her devotion to her Congregation of Sisters is legendary; her many years of service to the religious and academic education of thousands of young women is laudable, and every one of those young women have grown into exemplary Catholic women who are a blessing to their communities throughout the world." He paused a moment and smiled at the guests. "Every one of our lives was touched by her kindness and dedication, and her memory will live on, long after her return to her homeland." He stepped away from the pulpit and descended the three steps from the altar to the Royal casket before continuing. "For any of you who don't understand the presence of our Russian Orthodox friends, or the magnificence of the Royal casket in which Sister Thomas Marie has been placed, I must suppose, at this point, that Sister Thomas Marie won't mind her former identity being revealed." He stepped forward and held out his arm toward Prince Nikolai. "It is my honor and privilege to introduce His Serene Highness Prince Nikolai Romanovich Romanov, son of the late Prince Roman Petrovich and Grandson of the Grand Duke Peter Nikolaievich, who is also the chairman of the Romanov Family Association to which all members of the Imperial Family of Russia belong."

Prince Nikolai rose to his feet, bowed ceremoniously toward Father Gregory before stepping up to the pulpit. He looked out at the congregation and smiled. "Good morning. It is with a heavy heart that I address you, my departed Aunt's friends, on this beautiful day. This Mass is not only a celebration of the life of a holy woman, but of a woman who had to hide her true identity as the last living member of the Imperial family murdered in Ekaterinburg, Russia, in July of 1918. Just nineteen years old at the time, she was sent with her baby brother, Tsarvich Alexei, to safety, months before the rest of her family was murdered. Sadly, she had to watch her baby brother die en route to her new home in California." Gasps could be heard throughout the chapel as people speculated whether or not he could be talking about Anastasia. "Yes," he said, "the magnificent woman laying at rest in the Royal Casket is the Grand Duchess

Maria Nikolaevna Romanov." He smiled and waited for the exclamations and whispers to end before he concluded his eulogy. "My heart is heavy because I am here to celebrate the life of a brave woman whom I never knew in life. It would have been too dangerous for her and for my family for her whereabouts to be revealed to me, and it was by her request that I only be notified of her existence upon her death. I welcome your views and memories of my Aunt Maria, or Sister Thomas Marie, as it is through you that I will know my Aunt. I will cherish your memories as if they were my own." He paused a moment, then thanked all the guests for attending before stepping down to his pew.

Father Gregory stood in silence for a long moment, apparently dumbfounded by the Prince's words. From the onset all communiqués received from Rome had referred to Sister Thomas Marie as only the Grand Duchess. He had always assumed that she was the famous, missing Anastasia. He turned slowly and climbed the steps back to the altar, where he continued the Mass.

Just before the Consecration, he paused, announced to the congregation that according to the Russian Orthodox Rite, the Ritual of Absolution would be performed.

Ziggie stood, walked to the casket. Facing away from the altar, he ceremoniously placed the Prayer of Absolution into the casket, then prayed over the Grand Duchess' body as the choir, led by Marisa and Erin's old friend, began to sing the *Kathismas*. Surprised to hear the Roman Catholic Sisters singing the Psalms of David in Russian, Ziggie raised his gaze toward the choir loft, and his eyes met with none other than Sister Agnes. Her smiling face and sparkling eyes were unmistakable to him, even though today she was wearing a full habit that covered part of her face.

He was recognized by his former jailer. He lowered his gaze, felt a slow wave of panic begin to engulf him. Almost involuntarily he lifted his gaze again, and found the little nun smiling brightly at him as she sang the last psalm with the choir. He could have sworn that she had winked at him, but he decided it was just his mind playing tricks.

He slowly strode to his place next to the Prince again and sat during the Consecration and Holy Communion. He thought about it long and hard, wondering if he should receive Holy Communion or not. In the case of a dire emergency and when no Roman Church was available, a Roman Catholic was allowed to receive the Sacraments in Orthodox Churches, but he had no idea if the same thing was true for Orthodox Catholics in a Roman Church.

He decided to err on the side of caution, not standing for Communion. He gratefully noticed that Prince Nikolai did not, either, and as far as he could tell, none of the other Orthodox Catholics did.

After Holy Communion, Father Gregory paused again. Ziggie rose from his seat with the vial of Holy Oils in his hand. As he circled the casket to the open side, he glanced up at the choir loft, as if imploring Sister Agnes' help. She stood; the other Sisters followed her lead. A Capella, she began to sing the *Salve Regina*, but the other Sisters quickly joined her, as did the organist.

Father Gregory's face twisted in anger, and he looked up at the choir, only to realize that they couldn't possibly know that his heretofore failed mission was named the *Salve Regina*, so the nuns couldn't possibly be mocking him in his moment of failure.

Sister Agnes duly noted his change of expression, wondered what was wrong with him. The whole situation was confusing her more and more. First, Brother Zigfried was brought to the convent, ostensibly because he was having a nervous breakdown and needed some time to himself. She had been told just to take him his meals, but to pay absolutely no attention to anything he might say, because he had been hallucinating of late and just needed rest.

However, through the days that she had been taking his meals to him, she had found him to be anything but delirious. Sad, yes. Frightened, certainly. But certainly not crazy.

Then he had locked her in the bathroom of the cell. If there was a way for one to lock someone up nicely, he had certainly found it. She had not felt threatened in any way, and had been quite accepting of her incarceration. After all, she had been locking him in that tiny cell for days. *Tit for Tat*, she had thought at the time.

But now, the same Jesuit was officiating as a Russian Orthodox Bishop in a former Mother Superior's funeral, only to find that the Mother Superior was the legendary Grand Duchess Maria of Russia.

It was all just too weird for her to fathom, so Sister Agnes just sang her heart out in the hope that in some small way, she might be helping her Brother in Christ whom she had befriended in his cell.

Ziggie was going through the motions of the Anointing, saying the Roman prayers of *Extreme unction* in a low whisper as he did so. He hoped this would suffice for the Orthodox requirement, as the last thing in the world he wanted to do at this point was to disrespect their rite in any way.

As Sister Agnes and her choir finished the *Salve Regina*, he looked up at her with a grateful smile. This time there was no doubt about it: she definitely smiled back, and then definitely winked.

Feeling somehow much more secure, he returned to his seat, sat comfortably until the Mass was over.

Prince Nikolai leaned over to him. "Would you do me the honor of accompanying me in the reception line at the door? It is customary for one's priest to be with the next of kin in royal circles."

"Of course, your Serene Highness."

They both stood, went to the large double doors to the right of the altar. Ziggie opened them, they both stood outside the doors waiting for the guests to exit.

After the diplomatic corps and Russian dignitaries in the pews in front of them, Marisa, Erin and Pablo filed out. They stopped to extend their condolences to Prince Nikolai, his demeanor indicated clearly that Ziggie had filled him in completely. He squeezed each of their hands, thanking them profusely for coming.

When it was Pablo's turn, he was especially gracious. "It is an honor to know a young person of such fervent beliefs and standards."

Pablo felt humbled, thanked the Prince before telling him briefly that he would be at the exhibition to be certain that proper security measures were taken. He then moved out to the lawn where others were saying their farewells before boarding the limousines and other chauffeured vehicles lined in the circular driveway behind the Prince's limousine.

As the last guest left the chapel, the bells in the bell tower began to toll. One loud peal after another, their chimes filled the air with the glory that was this incredible old woman's life. Marisa looked up at the bell tower that she had watched from childhood, but this time it was different. It was literally glowing as the birds flew from the dovecote behind it.

Glowing? Marisa had to squint to focus on the tower. The old iron bells were definitely not glowing, but something was. She squinted and suddenly it all became clear: the bells were tolling for about the eighteenth or nineteenth time, and there were practically no birds frantically escaping the noise now; their refuge in the dovecote having been disturbed by the noise.

Marisa grinned. She knew exactly where the old nun had hidden her treasures.

She turned to tell Pablo about her discovery, but saw him take off in a flash through the smaller gate, obviously en route to the Timkin Gallery.

Once only the Sisters were left, Marisa and Erin approached Ziggie, who was seated in the Chapel.

They excitedly told him of Marisa's discovery. "Ziggie, the lost Romanov treasure is in the dovecote!" Erin said with a trembling voice.

Ziggie smiled. "That makes sense, in some strange way. To her it was probably the closest place to heaven she could put it, the poor dear."

"But now, we have to figure out how to get it down, and where to put it." Erin said, being the ever practical one of the group.

Ziggie looked toward the gardens. "We are going to need help, and I think I know exactly where to get it."

He stood, walked into the court yard where a group of sisters were gathered; among them, Sister Agnes.

"Sister Agnes, could we talk to you for a minute?"

She walked over to where Marisa and Erin were still standing, hugged them both. Ziggie looked confused. "I was going to introduce you to my friends, Sister, but I see that isn't necessary!"

Sister Agnes flashed them all her same wonderful smile that Erin and Marisa remembered so fondly from their days in the convent. "Brother Zigfried, Erin, Marisa and I have been friends for forty years! There is no need for introductions. In fact, if I had known you were their friend, you wouldn't have had to lock me in that cell. All you would have needed to do was ask me to release you, and in the name of my friendship with these two wonderful ladies, I wouldn't have thought twice about it!"

"Well, then you are definitely the right person for us to talk to," Ziggie said. "You see, we seem to be in a very awkward position here."

Between the three of them, they quickly told Sister Agnes all about the entire situation, Fathers Gregory and Holtz' orders from the Jesuit General, how Nikolai was in danger, and how they felt responsible for making sure that the Crown Prince was given the treasure that the old nun had been safekeeping for eighty plus years.

Sister Agnes never stopped smiling. She only nodded her head and said an occasional *I see* or *I understand.*

Once they had related their entire story, she smiled even more brightly.

"Listen, I think I have the only solution, given the shortness of time that we have." She looped her arms through Marisa's and Erin's and called out to Ziggie. "Come on Brother... we need to see Sister Superior."

Within fifteen minutes, a short talk with an already informed and completely knowledgeable Sister Superior, a human chain had been formed from the chapel, past the music hall and bell tower, through the study hall, into Sister Superior's office, up the stairs to the roof and into the dovecote. The only thing that they had not discussed with Sister Superior was the Jesuit mission to assassinate the Prince. By this point in time, it seemed unreal to them all, and they were beginning to think they had all been the victims of some very powerful paranoia.

The human chain was formed by the Sisters from the Congregation of Saint Thomas who had come to bid a loving farewell to their former Mother Superior, and other nuns representing most of the congregations in Southern California.

Each small package, wrapped in waxed butcher's paper and wrapped in twine, was passed from hand to loving hand down the human chain clear to the Chapel. Sister Superior had sent another group of Sisters to bring Sister Thomas Marie's two dowry chests to the chapel.

"The trunks!" Marisa and Erin exclaimed in unison.

Sister Superior looked at them accusingly, but then smiled, rolling her eyes toward the sky. "You must know, of course, that we humored poor Sister Thomas Marie when she said that you two had been snooping down in the basement?"

Erin was embarrassed.

Marisa became defensive, and started to make up an excuse, but she was too tired to squirm. "Yes, Sister. Guilty as charged." She admitted their responsibility. "But if this is a valid defense, we weren't in it for any personal gain. It was just a matter of curiosity that simply got somewhat out of hand."

"Out of hand?" Erin whispered. "Try larceny, breaking and entering, trespassing and safe-breaking for starters. Watch out, because she could have us thrown in jail for the next thirty years for what we've done!"

Marisa smiled sweetly and looked over at Sister Superior, who apparently hadn't heard Erin's remarks. "Sister Superior, you aren't planning to have us thrown in jail for our snooping, are you? Erin is worried about that."

Sister Agnes was a few feet away, she broke up. "Sister Superior, I think at least a year in Brother Zigfried's cell downstairs would be nice for starters, don't you?" She laughed. "Personally, I would love to keep them around for a very long time, and they are welcome to serve out their sentences in my rooms, if the cells downstairs are full of Jesuits..." Then she laughed harder, which broke Sister Superior up.

Marisa wandered over to the first trunk, which was full. "Is there some way we can seal the trunks?"

Agnes filled the second trunk with the small packages so that there was no room for them to bump each other or break open. "Yes, actually, we have rolls of that shrink-wrap stuff that shrinks with a hair dryer. We use it for the communion wafers we make every year. Sealing the boxes keeps the wafers fresh." She turned to Sister Superior, sheepishly. "May we use a bit of it, Sister Barbara?"

"Certainly." Sister Superior stood up. "As a matter of fact, I need to stretch my legs, so I'll go over and find it in the kitchen." She started to walk to the chapel door, but then turned back. "Erin, why don't you walk with me? It will give us a minute to chat."

Erin stood, followed the nun out to the gardens they would cross to reach the dining rooms on the edge of the cliff overlooking the valley. She was still upset and angry over Ziggie's being locked up in the convent, welcomed the chance to discuss the matter with Sister Superior.

Deliberately calming herself before speaking, she walked in silence next to Sister Superior.

Sister Superior broke the uncomfortable silence by remarking, "Erin, you seem troubled. Is there anything you would like to talk about?"

Erin welcomed the opportunity. "Yes, Sister, as a matter of fact, there is something troubling me deeply. Perhaps you can help me clear it up?"

"I would be happy to try," the Sister replied.

"Well, I must admit that I am troubled by the fact that you allowed these hallowed grounds to be used as a prison by Fathers Gregory and Holtz, or that you would allow Brother Zigfried to be locked up like a common criminal and drugged for nearly a week." She took a deep breath. "This is something that most definitely troubles me," she added with a sarcastic tone she could no longer conceal.

Sister Superior put her hand on Erin's shoulder to stop her from walking ahead. "Here, Erin, why don't we sit here a moment and talk?" She took a few steps back toward a garden bench.

Erin followed her and sat with her. She stared at the nun, waited for an explanation.

Sister Superior smiled and tried to explain. "Erin, in the first place, I was not asked nor did I give my authorization for Brother Zigfried to be locked in one of those cells, or glorified closets, to be more exact."

"Do the Jesuits have full access to everything on this campus, then?" Erin wasn't buying the explanation.

"Not exactly, but I can assure you that I was told, after the fact, that Brother Zigfried had suffered a mild breakdown, that his physician had ordered him to a few days of sedated rest. Fathers Gregory and Holtz asked only that one of the Sisters that I trusted the most be the one to take him meals. I suggested Sister Agnes, and they explained things to her."

Erin still wasn't buying the whole story, and huffed slightly.

Sister Superior continued. "Look, I don't expect you to understand, nor am I using this as an excuse, but you must realize that Sister Thomas Marie was very near and dear to me, and I was more concerned about my dear friend dying, than about your friend's nervous breakdown. I suppose I wasn't paying a great deal of attention to anything else that was going on around me."

Erin finally smiled at Sister Barbara. "Let's just put it in the past and deal with what we must, shall we?"

They both stood, continued their walk to the dining halls and kitchen behind.

As they entered the kitchen, Erin could smell chicken cooking, and suddenly felt transported back to her days as a student sneaking into the kitchen to grab a cookie or two for study hall.

A small nun was stirring a pot as they walked in, and for a second, Erin almost thought it was Sister Phillipe, the cook so many years before.

Sister Barbara greeted the nun cheerfully, and Erin smiled at her as they were introduced.

"Sorry to barge in on you," she said apologetically to the nun, who just smiled back at both of them.

As they walked into the pantry, Erin remarked, "She's a cheerful one, isn't she?"

Sister Barbara laughed. "I would hope so. You may not have noticed that she didn't understand a word we said?"

"Uh, why?"

"Because she has just come from Japan, and still doesn't speak a word of English, and of course my Japanese is about as good as my Russian!"

"Which is about as good as my Farsi?" Erin laughed.

"Exactly."

They found the shrink wrap in the kitchen pantry, a hair dryer next to it.

"Here we are." Sister Barbara turned to leave, Erin on her heels.

They waved good-bye to the little Sister in the kitchen, and walked back to the Chapel. By the time they reached the open doors, Erin was over her anger, and the two women were talking as friends.

The Sisters had finished packing the trunks, so Agnes was ready for the shrink wrap. Between them, Marisa and Agnes managed to wrap the trunks and seal the wrap to them with the hair dryer.

Then they stood in front of the casket observing the opening, the shrink wrap and the hair dryer.

As if both their minds had thought of it at the same time, they stepped forward and carefully closed Sister Thomas Marie's casket. They enclosed the entire circumference.

Marisa held the ends together while Agnes ran the hair dryer across the shrink wrap, managing to seal the casket tightly.

Erin and Sister Superior observed the women at their task, with curious expressions. Erin finally asked, "Why are you sealing the casket?"

Marisa and Agnes both grinned, but Agnes explained.

"It's a very long trip to St. Petersburg. I don't imagine there is an extremely large refrigerator aboard the Crown Prince's jet?"

Even Ziggie turned toward them from where he was standing at the door of the Chapel, looking out toward the street. He wondered when the motorcade would be returning.

They all exchanged disgusted looks at the thought of a warm cabin and a warm cadaver, and said nothing more about the women's labors to seal the casket.

Sister Barbara suddenly pulled a phone from her pocket. "Yes?" she said. "Yes, Brother?" there was a long pause. "Oh, dear God!" She gasped. "Yes, Brother. Of course."

She hung up the phone and sank down on the front pew. All the nuns, Erin, Ziggie and Marisa gathered around.

Her eyes were filled with shock. "There has been an attempt on the Crown Prince's life!"

"Is he all right?" A number of voices asked.

"Yes, the Prince is fine. But a young man has been killed. Apparently there was a priest involved."

Ziggie was nodding. "Yes, Sister, that is what we had suspected all along. Fathers Gregory and Holtz."

"No, that was Father Gregory on the phone, and Father Holtz was with him. He said that the priest had been killed by the guards after he'd killed the young man who threw himself in front of the Prince to save him." She crossed herself. "May God protect their souls in His Heavenly Glory!"

"Did they say who the young man was?" Ziggie's heart filled with dread.

"He asked for Marisa before he died."

Marisa swayed as the room began to spin around her. "Pablo!"

Erin turned to Ziggie, who instinctively gathered the two weeping women protectively in his arms. Tears streamed unabashedly down his face as they stood locked together in their anguish and grief.

Erica Fuentes & Annemarie Stonewater

Chapter Sixteen

"We share your pain and loss, my dear friends." Sister Barbara spoke softly. "I fear this is far from over. We must set our grief aside for now, for there is still a great deal left to do."

Ziggie nodded in understanding as Erin and Marisa slowly pulled themselves together. Sister Agnes moved next to her friends, held out a box of tissues.

"Sister Mary, please ask the Brothers of St. Augustine to load Sister Thomas Marie's casket and trunks into the hearse." Sister Barbara took charge. "Knowing the manipulative and devious minds of the Society of Jesus, present company excepted," She smiled at Ziggie, "they have most likely managed to shift the blame away from them, and onto someone else. And my first guess would be to you, Brother Zigfried."

"How could they do that? Ziggie is one of their own." Erin gasped, her voice rough with tears.

"Easy," Marisa looked up at her friend. "Gregory or Holtz just tell the authorities that Ziggie has betrayed the Community, and was acting out some quasi-political agenda because of his German-Russian heritage." It was clear to Marisa that even after all that had happened, poor Erin still held onto a few lingering illusions regarding her oh-so-holy Jesuits.

"Sister Agnes," Sister Barbara paused a moment before continuing. "I want you to take Brother Zigfried back to the cell in the catacombs."

"Sister?" Agnes looked over at Ziggie in dismay.

"It is the only safe place he can hide. Please inform all the Sisters that we are granting Brother Ziggie Right of Sanctuary according to our congregation laws. After you've done this, please wait for me by the hearse."

Ziggie had no strong desire to return to his former prison. The Sister Superior's use of his nickname told him that congregation law was her way of justifying her actions. This had become personal to her.

"Brother, if you would please go with Sister Agnes. I suspect the authorities may be arriving at anytime now."

"But, of course. Thank you." Ziggie stood, looked over at Erin and Marisa. "It is for your safety that I am most concerned."

"Don't worry about us." Marisa smiled weakly. "Remember, were the ones who have been looking all over for you this last week. How would we know where you might be?"

"Go. Be safe." Erin urged him. "Marisa and I will be fine."

Ziggie left with Sister Agnes wishing that Erin and Marisa would request sanctuary for themselves as well. He had no doubt it would be granted, if they did.

Marisa rose and walked to the steps that led to the altar. She kneeled on the bottom step, overcome with a mixture of profound grief and seething anger. She began beating her fists on the marble step until they hurt so badly that she cried out in pain. With tears running down her face, she looked up at the crucifix above the altar. "Why, dear Jesus? Why Pablo?"

Erin knelt beside her, took Marisa's bruised hand in hers to pray.

"O God, in your great mercy, we humbly beseech you for the soul of your servant Pablo, whom you have commanded to depart from this world today; that in your wisdom you not deliver him into the hands of the enemy, nor forget him in his hour of need, but command him to be received by the holy Angels, and led into Paradise, his true country; as in you he has hoped and believed, may he not suffer the pains of hell, but take possession of eternal joys. Through Christ Our Lord... Amen"

"Amen." They heard Sister Barbara's voice from the pew behind them.

Marisa turned and put her head on Erin's shoulder. "Why Pablo, Erin? Why him? I feel like it's all my fault."

Erin struggled for control of her own emotions. "It's not your fault, Marisa. If there is any blame, it's all mine. I'm the one who got him involved in this whole mess."

"You didn't know it would end up like this," Marisa stiffened. "Arturo!

He has to be notified!"

Erin frowned. "Don't even go there. It's not your place, and besides, I would imagine the Jesuits took care of that. Just leave it alone, Marisa, there is nothing we can do about it right now. We'll sort it all out later. For the moment, we just need to follow Sister Barbara's lead. She will know what to do."

Marisa nodded, wiped the tears from her eyes. She stood and helped Erin up.

Sister Barbara rose from the pew. She reached into the depths of her formal habit and pulled out the cell phone that Prince Nicholas had given her to use if she needed to speak with him confidentially, which she then speed dialed. "Your highness? Can you speak freely? It is not safe for you to return to the convent. Go directly to the airport and board your jet. It is highly imperative that you leave as quickly as possible. The Grand Duchess' casket and trunks will have already been loaded. Sister Agnes will be there with an envelope containing all the documentation and provenance proving you the legal and rightful owner of the Romanov jewels and artifacts. These have been under dowry deposit protection since Sister Thomas Marie entered the Congregation as a safeguard for the day she would leave. They have never been the property of the Congregation, or of any American citizen." She paused and listened. "You're most welcome, your Highness. Might I suggest that once your plane is air borne you high-tail it as quickly as possible for International Air Space." She listened. "I will, your Highness. May God go with you." She ended the call.

"What now?" Erin asked softly.

"Now you come with me. I have some papers to retrieve for Sister Agnes." She led them back to the convent. "I realize that this may be of little comfort to you now, but know that the young man who died made the highest of sacrifices. He gave up his life trying to save another's and is most certainly a hero, now with the Lord."

"Thank you for those sentiments, Sister." Erin replied. "But they do little to ease the pain of losing him. He was a brilliant young man with his whole life ahead of him; a dear friend to me, to Marisa and to Brother Ziggie. Perhaps in time your words will be the comfort you intend, but his loss is one that will be with us forever."

"I more than understand, my dear." Sister Barbara embraced her. "Now we must look to the living and do what must be done." She took them through the convent to the large parlor, where the Rosary had been said for Sister Thomas Marie. She moved to one of the large oil paintings on a far wall and ran her hand along the lower half of the frame. An audible snick was heard. She then pulled the edge of the painting towards her, which caused it to swing open like a cabinet door, revealing a state-of-the-art safe in the wall behind it.

"Ohh!" Marisa exclaimed softly and nudged Erin. "This is one secret on campus we never knew about."

"It's refreshing to hear we have managed to hide something from the two most inquisitive students we've ever had here at Villa Vistamar." Sister Superior smiled as she dialed the last number in the combination, unlocked the safe. She opened it and withdrew a large legal-sized envelope. "I would advise you erase this secret from your minds. Prior to now, only the Sisters Superior have ever been privy to it."

"What secret?" Marisa deadpanned. She knew that she would have to push her sorrow deep and call upon her hidden reserves of strength to get through whatever might come at them next. Though she had tried to reassure both Ziggie and Erin, she had worked with law enforcement officials often enough to know things could become pretty ugly, pretty fast. They weren't totally out of the woods yet. Ziggie was a prime suspect in a capital crime, and they were both known acquaintances. She hoped Erin had hidden reserves of her own. Marisa couldn't shake the feeling that they might very well need them.

Erin and Marisa hung back a bit when Sister Barbara led them outside; she went to confer with Sister Agnes at the hearse. "Marisa?" Erin looked over at her.

"I'd say that makes it unanimous." Marisa knew by the uneasy sound in Erin's voice what she was asking her. "If we're right, it may get bad."

"I know," Erin frowned. She glanced over to where Sister Barbara was speaking to Sister Agnes. Far off in the distance behind them she sensed, rather than saw, flashing red lights. "We protect Ziggie and the Prince, no matter what. Agreed?"

"No matter what." Marisa linked her arm through Erin and they started back inside.

"You are to hand this over, but only to His Highness, personally. I don't care if they are wearing a badge or a collar, only the Prince. Do you understand?" Sister Barbara handed the envelope to Sister Agnes, who nodded and tucked it into the side pocket of her habit.

"When his plane has taken off, call me on my cell. Let it ring three times then hang up. I'll send one of the Sisters to pick you up and bring you back here." She opened the front passenger door of the hearse and motioned Sister Agnes to get in, closed the door behind her. She took a step back and solemnly raised her hand in a blessing.

Marisa and Erin were half way back to the convent entrance when Sister Barbara rejoined them. "I think, right about now, we could all use a hot cup of tea, don't you?"

The powerful engine of the hearse could be heard behind them as it pulled away from the school. Sister Barbara knew no one could touch the hearse or its occupants under the cover of diplomatic immunity given by the Russian flag on its right front fender.

They reentered the convent to find a tray with tea service and cups waiting for them in the Parlor. "We have to somehow beg, borrow or steal at least thirty minutes from whomever comes in. It will take that long for the Prince's jet to get off the ground and into international airspace." Sister Barbara poured them each a cup of tea.

"It will most likely be someone from Homeland Security." Marisa warned. "If so, they will cite the Patriot Act as their authority to do whatever they want. Our only hope is to challenge their presence. It won't stop them, but we might be able to delay them long enough to gain the time needed for the Prince." She was looking forward to the battle of wills ahead.

"How will we know when the jet is in the air?" Erin asked. She took the offered cup of tea, sat back in her seat.

"I have set up a signal with Sister Agnes, who will let us know." Sister Barbara frowned. "I should probably send someone now to be there when she is ready to return. There may not be an opportunity to do this once the authorities arrive." She summoned one of the Sisters to give her instructions. "The only way I can think to alert you is to fake a cough or a sneeze."

"A sneeze." Marisa told her. "When we bless you, you'll know we understand. I doubt we will have to wait very long before company arrives." She looked over at Erin. "You realize there is a possibility we may end up being arrested because of our known connection to Ziggie. We would be separated and questioned. Should this happen, say nothing, not a single word should pass your lips. Don't believe anything they tell you about me or anyone else, understand?"

Erin nodded, sitting very still for a second or two with her cup part way to her lips. "They're here," she murmured, took a sip of tea.

"Bring it on," Sister Barbara calmly added a lump of sugar to her cup.

"You two need to get out more often," Marisa grimaced at their movie cliché phrases.

Four men in dark suits barged into the Parlor as though expecting trouble. What they got was three upper middle-aged women calmly drinking tea, laughing at something one of them had said.

Sister Superior Barbara rose to her feet and fixed them with a steely look. "Gentlemen, it is customary and common courtesy to knock and be given permission to enter a private residence. One could only hope you've been taught better manners than this." She could tell from the reactions to her stern reprimand, which of the four men had attended Catholic school in their youth. Their eyes involuntarily looked downward in embarrassment; their body language took on that of a boy being sent to the Principal's office. Unfortunately, their apparent leader had a look of disdain and self-importance about him that made it clear he followed his own set of rules.

"This is not a social call, Sister." He said the last as though spitting something nasty tasting from his mouth.

Marisa recognized his type from her years of dealing with numerous levels and power structures in law enforcement. He fell into her least favorite category; what she mentally referred to as "Bully with a Badge and a Gestapo mind-set". Sister Barbara was way out of her league here, whereas she had cut her teeth on people like him.

"If, as you have stated, this is not a social call, it would follow you are here on official business of some type." Marisa paused and expertly eyed their uninvited guests. "Judging by the fact that all of you are armed, I would submit that either you are members of a law enforcement agency who have failed to properly identify yourselves as such, or possibly private security agents, appropriately licensed to carry a concealed weapon. Could it be that you are seriously lost, and resentful that you've been forced to stop and ask for directions?" She smiled sweetly. "Would you care to enlighten us to which case this might be?"

"And just who might you be?" The lead agent practically snarled trying to intimidate her.

"She's my lawyer." Erin waved cheerfully from her seat.

"And you are?"

"My friend, and client," Marisa answered for her. She was beginning to enjoy aggravating him. "I would suggest you clarify who you are, what unit or Agency you represent and why you have illegally entered the premises or she will be calling 911 to report a home invasion in progress."

Erin smiled, held up her cell phone and waggled it around for all to see. "It's on speed dial."

"Don't play cute with me. I'm the only who gives orders around here, lady." He continued to bully Marisa, who merely shrugged her shoulders as if to say he had been warned, nodded at Erin to make the call.

"Now while we are waiting for the emergency dispatch operator to take down the address and dispatch the nearest patrol car, I should probably point out that this is not only a private residence, but a convent and the only person here authorized to give orders is the Sister Superior."

"Hang up that phone now!" The increasingly irritated agent ordered Erin. She held up a finger indicating she would be with him shortly, then calmly completed her call and hung up.

"Did you need to make a call?" She offered the phone to him.

"Enough!" he shouted belligerently. He looked back to Marisa, who in his mind was the obvious mastermind of their passive resistance. "You have no idea who you are dealing with, lady. The only thing this innocent act of yours will accomplish is to make it harder on you later on."

"I quite agree," Marisa smiled, nodded, "in that you have yet to tell us exactly who it is we are dealing with."

The sound of movement behind them had the four men looking over their shoulders. Standing in the wide arched entrance to the Parlor were two rows of black-robed Brothers of St. Augustine with their arms crossed. They were the brothers who had acted as pall bearers at the Grand Duchess funeral, who had been in the kitchen having lunch after loading the casket and trunks into the hearse at Sister Barbara's request. None of them spoke or gave any indication that they were anything more than interested observers, yet their size and numbers held an implied warning of its own.

"Excuse me?" A woman's voice sounded behind them and a Sister passed through their ranks into the room. She ignored the four men and spoke to her Superior. "Sister, there are some gentlemen from the United States Secret Service at the door, who have asked to speak with you."

"Thank you, Sister. Would you please show them in?"

The nun turned and left the room. Her voice could be heard near the front door. "If you gentlemen would please follow me, Sister Superior will speak with you."

Two men garbed in custom tailored suits, who gave no hint they were armed, entered the Parlor behind their escort. Recognition flashed across the face of one of them as they approached Sister Barbara. "Jenkins," he acknowledged the man in charge of the first group.

"Lawson." The acknowledgement was grudgingly returned.

"Gentlemen:" Sister Barbara took control. "I was informed you wished to speak with me?"

"Yes, Sister. I'm Agent Paul Lawson of the United States Secret Service and this is my associate, Agent Collins." Each man presented his credentials to her for verification.

"This is the way it is supposed to be done." Marisa commented to the man who'd been referred to as Jenkins. "I hope you are taking notes?"

Jenkins audibly ground his teeth; Agent Lawson frowned with a confused look toward Sister Barbara.

"It would appear you know who this man is?" Sister Barbara eyed Jenkins coldly.

"Yes, Ma'am." Agent Lawson politely responded.

"I will admit to be curious as to why the United States Secret Service might need to speak with me, and I am more than willing to accommodate you in this regard. But, I must say Agent Lawson, learning that you know this man is quite disturbing to hear." Sister Barbara looked pained.

"Ma'am?"

"Your admission of knowing him would indicate that he is in some capacity a fellow agent. Yet, while you and Agent Collins have been most courteous and professional since your arrival, he barged into our midst without warning and has failed to identify himself or his companions; he has been rude, disrespectful, overbearing and threatening to my guests and me."

"Is that so, Ma'am?" Agent Lawson shook his head.

"Yes, and unless the Constitution and Bill of Rights have been completely abandoned, which I'm certain would have made the Evening News, I am at a loss for a reasonable explanation for all of this. Perhaps you might help me here?" She looked at him expectantly.

Agent Lawson looked decidedly uncomfortable. "I'm sorry, Ma'am. I doubt I can be of much assistance to you. All I can tell you is that he is Agent Maxwell Jenkins attached to the Department of Homeland Security. As to his purpose here or directives, I will admit to being as much at a loss as yourself."

Marisa's first reaction was to utter a four letter word, but she clamped her lips and remained silent. She could only imagine why the Secret Service was there, but at least they were compelled to adhere to certain statutes with regards to an individual's Civil Rights. Homeland Security had more power than the Gestapo in their finest days. Coupled to the Patriot Act, everyone in the room could kiss their Civil Rights good-bye.

She glanced out of the corner of her eye at Erin to see if she comprehended that things had just taken a nose dive from bad to worst. Erin did.

"Thank you, Agent Lawson." Sister Barbara smiled. On the outside, she appeared to receive Agent Lawson's news well, on the inside she was praying. "I appreciate your patience and understanding. Now shall we attend to why you requested to speak with me?"

Jenkins, who had been fuming silently this whole time, spoke out. "Yes, Agent Lawson, please do share with everyone your reason for being here."

Sister Barbara suddenly sneezed. This was followed by a chorus of God bless you from other Sisters, the Brothers, Marisa and Erin. The two women hid their feelings of relief at hearing the prearranged signal that Prince Nikolai was in the clear. Now they had only Ziggie to protect.

Agent Collins glared at Jenkins, his dislike for the man apparent. Lawson caught his eye, warning him with a look not to react. "We were told, Sister, that you might know of the whereabouts of two suspects wanted for violations of the National Stolen Property Act."

National Stolen Property Act? Two suspects? Marisa was momentarily confused. *They're not looking for Ziggie?* Then it dawned on her. *They are looking for Erin, and me! They know were the ones who found the Dowry. They believe we gave it to the Prince! Shit! If they knew Sister Barbara and the other nuns helped us, they could be arrested as Accessories!* She stole a quick glance at Erin, who pinched her lips tightly together as if saying, not a word.

"Oh my," Sister Barbara gasped. "Why would I know something like that?"

"They are both former students of your school and were seen at a funeral held here today in your chapel." Agent Lawson replied.

"Agent Lawson, I think you may have been misinformed. The funeral you refer to took place at eleven-thirty this morning and was for the oldest member of our Congregation, who recently passed away at the venerable age of one hundred and six. She was the principal here for many years. It may be that many of our current and former students came to pay their respects, but frankly, I had my hands full keeping track of, and providing for, a large number of Sisters from our congregation and other congregations in the region. There were numerous others in attendance as well, including members of her family. The chapel was quite over filled. It has been hours since then, and with the exception of the Sisters in our congregation, I couldn't possible tell you the whereabouts of the other attendees."

"Possibly if you were to tell the good Sister the names of these former students, it might refresh her memory?" Agent Jenkins interrupted. "Then again, if it were me, I'd haul everyone in and sort it out later."

"But, of course you would." Agent Collins had no use for the way Jenkins viewed everyone and anyone guilty, until proven innocent. In some cases that wasn't enough for him.

Lawson felt the same as Agent Collins, but handled it in his own way. He ignored him. "I quite understand, Sister." He reached in to his pocket and withdrew a card and handed it to her. "The students in question are a Marisa Mendoza and Erin Sabine. Perhaps you might have a word with the other Sisters? Possibly one of them may have noticed them, and you could relay this to me at this number."

"Certainly, I will have a word with them and contact you." Sister Barbara accepted his card.

Marisa was more than thankful that she and Erin had left their purses, with their IDs, locked in the back of Erin's truck. There was nothing in the room that would identify them as the suspects Agents Lawson and Collins were looking for.

"Are you quite finished, Agent Lawson?" Jenkins had an oily smile on his face that seriously worried Marisa.

"For now," Agent Lawson nodded.

Jenkins turned to his men, snapping his fingers. "Haul them all in."

"What!" Sister Barbara gasped as she saw the men with Jenkins immediately turn to the Brothers of St. Augustine to begin to cuff their hands together with thick plastic zip ties.

"What are you doing, Jenkins?" Agent Lawson demanded.

"Marisa Mendoza and Erin Sabine are wanted by Homeland Security for acts of terrorism, as members of the terrorist cell that plotted the kidnap of a missing —and still unaccounted for— Jesuit, and the planned overthrow of the legitimate and democratic government of Russia."

"Planned overthrow of the Russian government?" Agent Collins muttered softly to himself in disbelief. Obviously, the two women they were seeking had seriously pissed off someone they shouldn't have.

"Why the mass arrests?" Agent Lawson glanced over at the black-robed brothers being led out of the building. Since he knew that Homeland Security didn't have to justify any of their actions, he was treading on thin ice by asking such a question. However, he was banking on the need of Jenkins power inflated ego to use this as an opportunity to voice his superiority by answering.

Jenkins followed Lawson's glance and smiled. "They all seem to be suffering from a mass case of amnesia where Mendoza and Sabine are concerned. A taste of our hospitality will eventually jog a few memories. Then someone will give them up."

"And if they don't?" Agent Lawson had to ask.

"Trust me. They always do." Jenkins turned to glare at one of his men, who was apologizing to stunned Sister Barbara as he placed the zip lock cuffs on her wrists. "Hurry it up there, Warfield! We haven't got all day."

The convent station wagon turned down the street leading to the school. "Slow down and turn at the next corner." Sister Agnes instructed the Sister driving. There were blue flashing lights atop unmarked cars and vans crowded in front of the school. Something terrible was happening.

Once they had turned, Sister Agnes had the Sister take a quick left at the next corner and pull up to the end of the street. She looked down toward the school. She couldn't believe what she was seeing: sisters and priests, with their hands wrapped in yellow zip lock cuffs, were being loaded into one of the waiting vans.

"Sister, what's happening?" The nun driving gasped.

"Turn right and park against the curb." Sister Agnes twisted in her seat and looked back through the rear window of the station wagon at the school. "Oh dear!" She saw Sister Barbara escorted from the convent along with Marisa and Erin.

"Why is this happening?" Her companion was near tears.

"I don't know, but I plan to find out. They watched a pair of well-dressed men exit the convent, who walked towards a car that was parked a short distance away from the other vehicles. She thought it odd that the man who'd opened the driver's side door paused and looked back at the scene they'd just left then began shaking his head before he climbed into the car.

Sister Agnes quickly reached for the back of her head beneath her veil. "Quickly, Sister take off your veil, wimple and bib!" The nuns hurried to divest themselves of their identifying garb, tossed it on the floor in front of Sister Agnes feet. "Now look over at me, fluff out your hair with your hand and laugh."

A few seconds later, the dark sedan containing the two men drove past a parked car holding two laughing women. Sister Agnes made a point to check out its license plate as it pulled down the road ahead of them. She frowned. What was a government vehicle doing at the convent?

It was a good ten minutes before the last car and van pulled away from the front of the school. Sister Agnes had watched carefully to see who was being loaded into the vans. Unless he had been taken away before they had arrived, Brother Ziggie wasn't among them.

"I think it is safe for us to go back now." Sister Agnes turned forward in her seat. "But, just in case, take us through the back way and pull all the way into the garage and close the door behind us."

The garage closed behind them, the nuns gathered their discarded clothing and hurried into the convent. "Check to see if anyone has been left behind." Sister Agnes called over her shoulder as she hurried towards the basement entrance and the catacombs below.

"Brother Ziggie! Brother Ziggie!" she called loudly as she neared his cell.

"What is it, Sister?" He moved into the passageway in front of her. Sister Agnes quickly explained everything she had seen as she led him back upstairs. By the time they had reached the main rooms of the convent, Ziggie knew what he had to do. "Lock all the doors and don't let anyone you don't recognize into the convent." He made his way to the nearest phone.

Sister Agnes nodded as she ran toward the front door. Three other nuns were coming down the stairs as she approached. "First things first." she told them. "Lock all the doors and close the drapes. Meet me back here when you're done. Nobody is allowed in without my say so, understand?"

"Yes, Sister."

Ziggie waited impatiently for someone to pick up at the other end of his call. A click sounded in his ear and an answering machine came on the line. "Damn!" He waited for the outgoing message to end.

"Carlos, this is Brother Zigfried. It is critical that you call me at this number as soon as you hear this message. Marisa needs you." He left the convent number and hung up. He could hear Sister Agnes talking with someone in the small parlor and went to see who it was.

One of the two nuns that had been able to hide while the others were being taken away was telling Sister Agnes everything that had happened: "The men from the Secret Service were here asking Sister Superior about Marisa and Erin. Sister avoided having to point them out, and the Secret Service agents were leaving when the horrid man from Homeland Security took over. He ordered his men to arrest everyone, even Sister Barbara and the Brothers of St. Augustine."

"Do you remember any of the agent's names?" Sister Agnes pressed. The other nun spoke up. "One of the Secret Service agents was named Lawson. He was the one who told Sister Barbara the other man's name was Maxwell Jenkins."

"Would that be his partner or the agent from Homeland Security?" Ziggie asked her.

"Homeland Security, Brother. Agent Jenkins said some horrible things about Marisa and Erin. He said they were part of a terrorist cell that had plotted and kidnapped you and planned the overthrow of the Russian Government."

"Good Lord, isn't it enough that You've taken Pablo from us?" Ziggie raised his eyes to the ceiling.

"Brother Ziggie, Pablo may be injured, but he isn't dead." Sister Agnes exclaimed. "I saw him myself, with Prince Nikolai at the airport."

"What is this? Not dead you say? But we were told a young man had been killed."

Sister Agnes nodded. "Sadly, a young man from the Russian Consulate died trying to protect Prince Nikolai. Pablo suffered a rather severe cut on his arm, but he is alive. The Prince stayed with him at the hospital while he was having his arm stitched up. After Pablo was released, he came to the airport with the Prince."

"Forget what I just said, Lord." Ziggie quickly looked up. He then wrapped Sister Agnes in a giant bear hug and whirled her around; his joy was so great at learning his friend was still alive. The phone in the other room began to ring, and one of the nuns hurried to answer it.

"Brother, there is a Carlos Mendoza on the phone, returning your call."

"Thank you, Sister, I'll be right there." He released his hold on Sister Agnes, his sudden joy tempered by the knowledge of the crisis still at hand. He hurried to speak with Carlos.

"Are you all right?" One of the others asked as Sister Agnes put her hand to her head to clear the dizziness she was feeling.

"Give me a minute, I'll be fine. I wasn't expecting him to react like that." She held her arms out to balance herself as her body readjusted.

"Sister Agnes, what can we do about all this?" The nuns all looked to her for an answer.

"For starters, you can pray. I need a few minutes to think." Fully recovered, Sister Agnes began pacing, trying to figure out what they could do next. She was on her third circuit of the small parlor when her gaze was caught by a stack of Alumnae Bios, left over from the recent Class Reunion held at the school. A slow smile creased her face. "Keep praying, Sisters. It's starting to work." She pulled the cell phone Sister Barbara had given her from her pocket, walked over to the stack of Bios. Lifting the top folder, she set it on the sideboard next to her, flipped it open toward the front and read what was on the page. She dialed a number. "Hello, Carol Ann? This is Sister Agnes. Yes, it's nice to hear your voice as well. Listen, Carol Ann, we have a slight problem here that you might be able to help us with."

In the Parlor, Ziggie had another receiver to his ear and was writing something on the pad next to the phone. "That's Flight 181 arriving from JFK at 11:00 a.m. Okay. Someone will be at the airport to meet you." He paused a second and added, "Don't be surprised if it's a nun. Okay, I'll be sure and tell her that. No, you won't be staying in the convent. I have a place you can stay. And Carlos, I'm sorry your trip has to be under such dire circumstances."

Agent Jenkins, convinced that Erin and Marisa were the ones he wanted, had released Sister Barbara and the others a few hours after arriving at the Homeland Security Building.

True to their pact, neither Erin nor Marisa had said one word through being fingerprinted, photographed, a rough and humiliating strip and cavity search and now found themselves in separate rooms being alternately interrogated by an ever-increasingly frustrated Agent Jenkins.

Jenkins popped a few more antacids in his mouth and swallowed them before he slammed his hand flat on the table in front of Erin. "You do realize that you've already been dismissed from your position at the University? They said something to the effect that they were appalled and ashamed that one of their faculty members could stoop to such perfidy. That's right. Your little friend told us that you were a professor at the Jesuit University, so we made a few calls to verify her story."

Erin refused to show any reaction. He'd touched a vulnerable spot when he'd told her what the University had said about her, but had blown it completely by adding that Marisa had been the one to tell them she worked there. Erin knew in her heart that her friend could out-stubborn a rock if she set her mind to it. There was absolutely no way she had said a single word to them. Jenkins was lying. He had been hammering at her for what felt like days, but more realistically was probably only hours.

The hard metal chair felt ice cold against her bare skin. None of her clothes had been returned to her after she had been subjected to the nightmare of a strip and body cavity search. Since that time, she had been forced to retain what little dignity she had left by keeping her arms crossed over her chest and her legs tightly together. Marisa had tried to warn her that it could get bad, but this went way beyond bad. She'd never been a prude or overly modest, but there was something quite barbarian about being the only naked person in a room where everyone else was clothed. She realized this was a psychological tool commonly used worldwide in the interrogation of prisoners. This knowledge did not frighten her, but rather made her feel not so alone.

Agent Jenkins straightened and began to walk in a circle around the table. "Did you know the coldest temperature recorded in Siberia was minus 90 degrees F? Believe it or not, this happened more than once and at two different places: Verkhoyansk and Oimehon, if I remember correctly." He paused before bending sharply until his face was barely an inch from hers, his voice a low growl. "I wonder what that feels like? There's a good chance you'll soon find out for yourself. We have an extradition treaty with Russia, which means you are facing a good twenty to thirty years to get used to the chill factor there. That is, if you live that long. I hear the death rate from exposure is fairly high."

"On the other hand," he offered, "it makes life imprisonment in a federal facility here sound like a prime vacation spot. All you have to do to earn yourself a reservation at this highly desired vacation destination is to give us the location where Zigfried Hoffman is being held. Otherwise, I can promise you less-than-budget accommodations in a perpetual freezer. It's all up to you." His hand came out of nowhere and grabbed her throat. His fingers slowly tightened, closing off her air supply. "I'll give you some time to think about this, while I go talk with your helpful friend in the other room." He released her and stalked from the room.

"Have those fingerprint verifications come in yet?" He demanded of the harried technician that met him outside the door.

"It may be sometime before that happens, Sir." He took a step back, knowing Jenkins didn't want to hear what else he had to say.

"It is a routine procedure!" Jenkins snapped. "I should have had those results hours ago!" Official confirmation that the fingerprints they had taken earlier were those of Marisa Mendoza and Erin Sabine were all that he lacked to slam the door on this case.

"Normally, that would be correct, Sir. But, there's a slight problem." The technician wished he hadn't drawn the short straw to be the one chosen to inform Agent Jenkins that their entire computer system had crashed. It could be hours, maybe even days before the system was back up and running.

"It what!" Jenkins balled up a fist and slammed it into the wall next to him. Ideally, he would much rather have used it on the idiot next to him, but physically attacking a co-worker was not the best of career moves. He grabbed a stack of papers nearby, used them to wipe the blood of his knuckles while he glared menacingly at the innocent wall. "Get someone to take the prints over to the FBI. Surely, their computers are still working."

"Yes, Sir. Right away, Sir." The technician practically ran to get as far away from Jenkins as he could.

"I keep telling you that temper of yours is going to get you in real trouble one of these days." A voice said from an open doorway across from Jenkins.

Jenkins looked over at the agent leaning against the door jam, shaking his head. "I didn't ask you for your opinion, Bates."

Agent Bates held both his hands up in front of him. "I'm not the enemy, Max. You've been grilling those two women for over twelve hours now, and neither one of them has said a single word. When are you going to realize you're not going to get anything out of them? Stick 'em in lockup and cut your losses. You still can't be sure you even have the right two women, for Chrissake."

"I have the right women, and believe me when I tell you that I **will** break them." Jenkins stubbornly insisted. "Back off and let me get back to my job." He walked ten feet to another doorway on his right, opened the door and went into the room beyond, closing the door behind him.

Marisa lifted her head and glared at Jenkins as he entered the room.

Chapter Seventeen

"Please notify me the minute we have reached International air space," Prince Nikolai ordered his pilot on the intercom phone next to his desk.

Sister Agnes had been waiting for him in the hearse upon his arrival at the airport. His Consulate had arranged for airport security to open the tarmac gates on the General Aviation side of San Diego International Airport, and he had sped straight through. Sister Agnes had given him the package of papers giving the provenance on every jewel and artifact he was carrying on the plane, just in case he were to have any problem anywhere en route. But en route to where? he thought, shaking his head.

He looked lovingly back at his aunt's casket, and addressed her in Russian. "Well, dear Aunt Maria, you have been mystifying the world for years. I suppose no one could possibly expect you to leave the world without a mysterious flair!" Noticing that the steward was most intrigued by his words, and relieved that the young man did not speak Russian, he said, "I'm sorry, Maurice, but I have been speaking so many languages the last few days that I suddenly forget which one you speak."

"I understood *aunt*, but I must admit that was all," the young man said, with a big smile, and he suddenly reminded the Prince of the young man from the Consulate who had taken the dagger for him, of Pablo, too, who had been cut badly. His entire body shook involuntarily.

"Are you well, Your Highness?" Maurice was sincerely concerned. He had been in the Prince's personal service for only three years since coming of age, but both of his parents had worked for the family since their youth. The Prince was not only his employer, but he and his wife were Maurice's Godparents.

"Yes, I'm fine, but what I was saying in Russian was that in honor of my dear Aunt, I believe we should toast to her eternal rest with a good cognac. Don't you agree?"

"Yes, of course, Your Highness."

Maurice served two large snifters in the galley, and returned to the main cabin with them. He sat across from Prince Nikolai and placed the Prince's snifter on the desk in front of him, and waited. The Prince raised his snifter, and Maurice raised his, as he had done on many occasions in private with the Prince, when he was not bound by the public formalities of Royalty. "To your eternal soul, dear Aunt Maria. May you finally be released from the sorrow of your memories!"

The two men clicked glasses, and sipped from their snifters.

"If I may dare to ask, Your Highness, why is the casket in shrink wrap?" Maurice stifled his desire to laugh.

Prince Nicholas didn't. He laughed aloud, shaking his head. "I can only surmise that the Sisters at the convent decided to wrap her casket just like they did the cargo trunks, but it did strike me as rather bizarre... as if they thought she might be opening it from within? Who knows!"

The Intercom rang, and Maurice answered it. "*Oui, mon Capitaine, que puis-je faire pour vous?*" There was a pause. "*Oui, mon Capitaine, tout suite.*"

"We are in International Air Space, Your Highness," he said as he hung up the intercom. He knew the ritual very well, as the Prince always waited until they were in International Air Space to place phone calls, with the exception of the European Community, where he tended to make satellite calls once the plane was barely lifting its wheels. "Would you like me to place any calls for you, Sir?

"Yes, Maurice, see if you can get the Russian Consul General in San Diego for me, would you?"

Maurice picked up the cordless satellite phone and took it to his tiny cubicle of an office, from where he would work during most of their flights around the world. Ordinarily, the Prince did not travel alone, so his tiny office served Maurice well to achieve a certain level of privacy while tending to the Prince's business.

Prince Nikolai Romanovich Romanov was a simple man who had never aspired to being the rightful heir of anything. He had never been particularly interested in the reinstatement of the Imperial Monarchy in Russia, nor had he ever been particularly motivated by tremendous wealth. He was a wealthy man in his own right, but only because of many years hard work and a good head for business. However, he lived simply. The only true luxury he allowed himself was his Gulfstream III executive jet, an addition to the Romanov Family Association that he had donated personally for the comfort of the more elderly members of the family, and of course, for his own use.

Maurice returned with the phone in hand, and gave it to Prince Nikolai. "Consul Petrovich is on the line, Your Highness," he said in a formal voice, and then whispered, "and he does not sound very happy."

The Prince put the phone to his ear, took a deep breath, and smiled. "Mr. Consul, how good of you to accept my call!"

The Consul was formal, but cold in his reply. "Certainly. What may I do for you, Sir?"

The tone was very different from the rather servile demeanor he had shown in San Diego, but the Prince forged ahead. "Mr. Consul, I understand that two acquaintances of mine, Marisa Mendoza and Erin Sabine, have been detained by the authorities due to a gross misunderstanding. Are you familiar with this situation?"

"Yes, Sir, I most certainly am." Consul Petrovich was offering nothing for the Prince to build on.

"Mr. Consul, I would be very appreciative if you would take a few minutes of your time to phone the authorities involved, to clear up this matter. I can assure you that these women are guilty of nothing, and any charges against them must be dropped. Anything less would be unacceptable."

"Sir, I assure you that I would like nothing more than to accommodate your wishes as our Ambassador has also requested, but there are a number of matters which are out of my control, such as the kidnapping of a Jesuit by these women."

Prince Nicholas interrupted. "I can assure you that the Jesuit was not kidnapped. He attended the Grand Duchess' funeral," he said dryly.

"Even if that were true, that doesn't change their terrorist involvement in a plot to overthrow the Russian government. I could not, in all good conscience, ask that they be released, nor would anyone pay the least attention to me if I did." Consul Petrovich cleared his throat. "And of course, there is still the matter of the Romanov treasure hoarded by the Grand Duchess, Saint Maria, which I assume is aboard your plane?"

Prince Nikolai was not prepared for the Consul's words. His mind raced wildly, but then he calmed himself. "Certainly, Mr. Consul. Where else would it be? According to the documentation I am also carrying, the provenance and rightful ownership is not in question. Not in the least. Why do you ask?"

The Consul knew his voice had become audibly shaky, showing the frustration and anger that he felt in the face of his professional failure to secure the valuables before the Prince's plane had taken off. That's what happened when one trusted the American authorities to cooperate in a Russian affair. The officials from Homeland Security had been so anxious to arrest the women, that they had completely ignored his request to find the treasure and confiscate it. Perhaps he had been too hasty in accusing the women of plotting to overthrow his government, but after all, wasn't that what they were doing? Albeit in a roundabout way?

"Shall I assume that the valuables will be deposited with the Russian authorities for display in the Hermitage upon your arrival in Saint Petersburg?"

"Why do you ask?" The Consul's words were bordering on blackmail, and Prince Nikolai didn't not like them one bit.

"Well, as soon as the valuables are safely in the hands of our government, I would not be surprised if our legal attaché was able to make, uh, arrangements for your women friends to be released?"

Nikolai shook his head sadly. Some things would never change in this world. Of that he had no doubt.

"I couldn't possibly ask you to do such a thing, Mr. Consul, but I greatly appreciate the offer," Nikolai said without a trace of sarcasm in his voice. "Now, you have a great evening, Sir, and again, please accept my most sincere thanks for your hospitality and assistance in San Diego. The Romanov family is honored by your kind attentions."

And he hung up. Maurice appeared out of nowhere, as usual, and the Prince handed him the phone.

"May I place another call for you, Your Highness?"

"Yes, Maurice. See if you can locate Jean Paul in Paris, and get him on the phone for me."

"Uh, but Your Highness, it's only four in the morning there."

"It doesn't matter. I need to speak to him about a matter of great importance."

He knew the pilot had filed his flight plan in San Diego, taking the Polar route to St. Petersburg. There was one technical stop on the Kamchatka Peninsula that the Prince was now quite sure they would not be making.

While Maurice was phoning his attorney, the Prince picked up the Intercom, and quickly explained to the Captain that any refueling would have to be done either in Northern Canada or in Greenland, depending on the Gulfstream's range, and that they would not, under any circumstances, be landing on Russian soil. He told the Captain not to change his flight plan with anyone, but rather to simply reprogram the flight computer from a previous flight to Europe via the Polar route from San Diego. Then he told the pilot that he would tell him where they would be landing, *tout suite*, right away.

Just as he had hung up the Intercom, Maurice returned with the satellite phone. "Your attorney is on the phone, Your Highness."

The Prince took the phone, and lifted it to his ear. "Jean Paul, I hate to be waking you at this ungodly hour, but I'm afraid I need some very quick advice. Otherwise, I may be flying around International Airspace for days with no idea where to land!"

"Nothing can be that bad, Nicky, but please... tell me what I can do for you. How did things go with your trip to San Diego and your Aunt's funeral?"

"Other than a fortunately failed attempt on my life, the death of a Jesuit seminarian and a Russian diplomat, an injury to a very kind young man who tried to protect me, not to mention the fact that I am carrying not only my Aunt's casket, but also a legacy left to me by her that is worth several billion dollars on my plane, and the Russian Government is blackmailing me by accusing two friends of kidnap and terrorism? I suppose you could say I had an absolutely lovely time!"

Jean Paul's voice sounded much more awake when he answered, "Very good, Nicky. I'm awake now, and you have my full attention." He laughed. "Seriously, what is really going on?"

"Exactly what I just told you," the Prince said insistently. "I'm not joking."

"Did you say billions of dollars? What are we talking about here, the Crown Jewels?"

"Among other things, yes." The Prince was becoming impatient. Although he had a great sense of humor, he would never joke about such a thing. "Look, Jean Paul, I need to find a place to take these things, including my aunt's casket, so I even need a temporary mausoleum worthy of an Imperial Grand Duchess. If I land on Russian soil, everything will be confiscated by the government. Should I take them home to Switzerland? Perhaps deposit the valuables in a bank vault there?"

"Dear God, no!" the attorney exclaimed. "In 2003, the Swiss Confederation amended their Federal Constitution in execution of the UNESCO Convention from 1970 on prohibiting and preventing the illicit import, export and transfer of ownership of cultural property. Any court of law would consider the booty you are carrying as cultural property, which means it could be confiscated the minute you landed in Switzerland."

Prince Nikolai took a long sip of his Cognac. "Does this mean that I will be flying around endlessly, stopping only long enough to refuel in friendly airports, never deplaning nor unloading?" He laughed. "Sounds pleasant enough, I suppose. I have always loved travel, but as comfortable as my plane is, I'm afraid it lacks certain comforts of home. A shower comes to mind, among other things."

"No, Nicky." His old friend laughed. "Actually, I do have a rather brilliant idea. How long has it been since you've seen your old friend, Queen Margrethe of Denmark?"

"Too long, I am quite sure."

"Just head for Greenland for refueling. It's in Danish territory. I'll set things up with Her Royal Majesty as soon as it's an appropriate hour to call, and then I'll call you back to confirm."

"Shouldn't I be the one to make that call?" Prince Nikolai always worried about propriety and protocol in matters regarding the contact with Royalty.

"No. Satellite communications are too easily traced." He had duly noted the concern in his old friend's voice. "Your Highness," he said almost mockingly, "I have known Her Royal Majesty since our very early youth. I assure you that I can set things up properly, respecting all protocols and proprieties." He made his voice sound as uppity as possible.

The Prince laughed. "I'll wait for your call."

But he didn't. He knew his old friend well, and knew that he would manage to arrange things properly. He picked up the Intercom and informed the pilot to refuel at the Narsarsuaq Airport in Greenland, and from there they would be continuing on to Copenhagen. The pilot asked if he should file a flight plan while in Greenland.

"If you are asked directly, then by all means," he said. "You would have to," he added. "But if no one asks, it would be to our advantage not to file anything."

At that moment, the satellite phone rang, and he answered it himself.

"Yes, Jean Paul."

"It's a done deal. I spoke with palace officials, who will speak with the Queen in the morning, but they were fully authorized on this level without waking her. There will be Palace vehicles and representatives waiting for you at the airport. All arrangements are being made as we speak. There will be a car at the airport in Copenhagen to take you to your hotel, then they are quite sure that Her Majesty will send a car for you to join the Royal Family for dinner. This will be confirmed by the Palace officials when they meet you at the airport."

"You're a good friend, Jean Paul. Thank you. Now, could you do me one more favor?"

"Of course. Just name it!"

"Do you still have any good contacts in the State Department back in the U.S.?"

"A couple, why?"

"Because two friends of mine have been detained by the authorities in San Diego, and I would like to see them released. They are guilty of nothing."

"What are they charged with?"

"As kidnappers of a Jesuit who was never kidnapped, and as terrorists plotting the overthrow of the Russian government." He could hear Jean Paul nearly choke on the smoke from the cigarette he knew he was smoking. "Jean Paul, when are you going to give up those things? I can smell the smoke from here."

Jean Paul forced an almost inaudible laugh. "Listen, I'll give it a try, but the terrorism charges would probably be lodged by Homeland Security, and my understanding is that they are impossible to deal with, and take orders from absolutely no one."

"I'd appreciate you at least looking into it, old friend. These women and their friends saved my life. Their names are Marisa Mendoza and Erin Sabine."

"I will do anything within my power to help them, but I fear my power is lacking here."

"I appreciate your trying, anyway."

"Just be safe, and call me when you're back in Switzerland."

"I will. Thanks again, Jean Paul."

Minutes after hanging up the phone, Maurice appeared to offer him a meal or snack, but the Prince was sound asleep.

Maurice returned silently to his little office, leaned back his adjustable seat, and slept also.

The ringing of the Intercom phone brought Prince Nikolai to a startled consciousness, and he jumped to answer it.

It was the captain, advising him that they would be landing in just a few minutes in the Narsarsuaq Airport in Greenland.

The Prince called out to Maurice, "Maurice, prepare for landing, please."

Maurice appeared immediately, and quickly collected the brandy snifters and anything else that could possibly turn into a dangerous projectile in case of a sudden altitude change. He glanced out one of the windows, and hastened his pace back to the galley to stow everything properly. Once the galley was battened down, he made his usual review, checking off every possible danger on his mental checklist.

Once assured that all was secured, Maurice took his seat and buckled his seat belt while stifling a yawn.

The Prince looked over and smiled at him. "Just another five or six hours and we'll be in Copenhagen, and you can rest until our flight tomorrow to Geneva."

"I'm fine, Your Highness. It's just taking me a little while to wake up."

"I understand completely. It took me over seventy years, and I still have a long way to go."

"Carlos," Sister Agnes insisted with her never ending smile, "Please trust me on this. I will have Marisa and Erin out very soon. Please, just go with Sister Rose, and I will be there just as soon as possible with your wife."

Carlos was still hesitant; beside himself with worry. This wasn't the first time that Marisa had gotten herself into a life-threatening mess, but if he had anything to say about it, it would be the last.

For some reason, Marisa's adventures always seemed to involve religious groups. The Franciscan monks had saved her life the last time, and now it was a bunch of nuns.

At least the last time hadn't cost Carlos his job. This time it had. Dean Lawfield had told him he couldn't take a leave of absence due to another of his wife's mishaps, under any circumstances. If there was one thing that Carlos had never lost from his heritage, it was a deep loyalty for family. That came first, and it always had. He had felt absolutely no hesitation in telling Dean Lawfield exactly what to do with his Spanish Department.

And to make matters worse, when Carlos had called Marisa's editor at the newspaper to explain the further delay in Marisa's return, Bill Kloss had informed him that it wouldn't be necessary for her to return. He had hired a replacement.

He hadn't even had time to fully assimilate the situation, but the couple's future was looking awfully bleak, assuming that they were even a couple anymore. In his last-ditch attempt to hold his marriage together, Carlos had practically given Marisa permission to have an affair. For all he knew, he might have become a fond memory to Marisa, and nothing more.

He didn't have the strength to argue with Sister Agnes, so he thanked her and followed Sister Rose from the airport.

Sister Agnes watched them walk out, and felt sad for her friend's husband. She hadn't meant to minimize the importance of his presence, but at the same time, he was too close to the situation to be objective.

She looked at her watch and then back toward the passenger exit, expecting Carol Ann to emerge at any minute.

She looked down at the jeans and sweatshirt she was wearing, hoping they were at least clean. She only wore them on the very few occasions when she worked in the garden, or on her occasional hikes into the hills around the convent.

Sister Rose had donned a similar outfit, in the interest of discretion. Their appearance had apparently passed muster, because they had walked boldly out of the convent without being recognized as nuns by the uniformed men posted at the main gates, and had walked right into the airport straight past two vehicles from Homeland Security with their flashing blue lights without being recognized, either.

She yawned, trying to remember the last time she had slept, but she was too tired to try to count the hours. Just as she had been making arrangements for Sister Rose to drive Father Zigfried to La Jolla, Pablo had arrived at the convent, managing to scale one of the back walls —even with his arm in a sling— to protect the stitches taken because of the deep cut he had received in the scrimmage at the Timkin.

He had come in geared up for battle, insisting on taking on Homeland Security, the Secret Service, and any other authority that got in his way in his zealous defense of his teacher and friend. Ziggie had calmed him, and then Sister Agnes had explained that there was a good plan in place which would take care of things.

She and Ziggie had finally convinced Pablo to return to his house in La Jolla with Ziggie, not only to wait for Marisa's husband to arrive, but to give Sister Agnes' plan enough time to work.

Suddenly she spotted Carol Ann, so the last leg of the plan could finally be executed.

"Carol Ann!" she called out, jumping above the other heads standing on both sides of the aisle cordoned off for passengers to get by. "Carol Ann, over here!"

Carol Ann finally spotted her old friend and waved with her free hand; carrying a very official looking briefcase in her other hand. A very attractive, tall and stately woman, she was wearing a three-piece power suit that would have made any man tremble with intimidation.

The women hugged. "You look like someone out of the movies!" Sister Agnes giggled, duly impressed.

"Sorry it took me so long to deplane," Carol Ann explained. "I had to check my gun inside a locked briefcase with the flight crew, then they had to stow it in a compartment that isn't accessible to the public, so I had to wait until all the civilian passengers had deplaned before they could return it to me."

"Oh, that's okay," Sister Agnes said, "but do you think you really need the gun?" Her eyes were as big as saucers.

"I certainly hope not!" Carol Ann replied with a smile. "I'm just required to be armed any time I am on duty."

They had reached the main terminal doors, and Carol Ann motioned to someone outside.

A young man ran in. "Yes, Ma'am?"

Carol Ann handed him a ticket. "This is for my bag. Did you bring two vehicles, as I requested?"

"Yes, Ma'am."

"Good. Thank you. Once you pick up my bag, please go to our offices in the Imperial Bank Tower, and wait in the van at the front entrance. Don't use the lights, but don't let anyone chase you away, either. If Jenkins comes out, he is not, and make no mistake here, definitely not to commandeer any vehicle. Understood?" The man nodded. "Please wait there until I personally order you otherwise."

"Yes, Ma'am. As you say, Ma'am."

Carol Ann and Sister Agnes exited the building, and Carol Ann pulled her to a white van with blue lights flashing. Another young man was waiting with the back door open for them. As he held out his hand to help them aboard, Sister Agnes noticed he was also armed.

"Thank you, Agent Marcus," Carol Ann said. "Hop in, and I'll bring you up to date."

Sister Agnes was grinning. She had never thought she would live such an exciting adventure!

Once in the van, Carol Ann told the driver to take them to the Imperial Bank Building, then explained to Sister Agnes that the fifth floor was Headquarters to Homeland Security in San Diego. Sister Agnes just grinned and nodded her head, inwardly a little disappointed that it was so close, but what she was hearing of Carol Ann's conversation with the agent sitting with them in back of the van quickly got her attention.

As Carol Ann was giving the last of her instructions to the agent, the van pulled up in front of the Tower. Agent Marcus opened the door immediately, and jumped from the van. Then he held his hand out for Carol Ann.

Carol Ann turned to Sister Agnes. "Agnes, maybe you should wait here? I don't expect any violence, but Jenkins is really a hard-core, Gestapo type, from everything I've heard, and after the two times I have had the displeasure of dealing with him, I wouldn't put anything past him. I don't want to risk putting you in danger."

Sister Agnes laughed. "Are you kidding? And miss out on the most exciting adventure I have ever had? Not on your life!" she said, and scurried out of the van.

"Okay, girlfriend, but it's not my life I'm worried about. It's yours."

Five minutes later, Carol Ann was in her office on the fifth floor. As West Coast Director of Homeland Security, she had executive offices and staffs in every major city in the Western United States. As soon as she had been informed that Jenkins was still interrogating the detainees, she had called all other personnel into her office for an emergency meeting, telling Reception to have any civilians vacate the fifth floor for at least one hour and to lock all the elevators from the floor except for one, which was to be open and emergency-stopped.

Sister Agnes was seated at the window, admiring the view of the San Diego Harbor beyond. She heard Carol Ann calling the meeting to order, and turned in her direction, smiling at her.

Carol Ann stood behind her desk and flashed all of her subordinates a sincere smile, but then she furrowed her brow deeply. "Thank you all for responding so quickly. I imagine you are all curious to know the purpose of my visit today." There were heads nodding. "A very disheartening situation has been brought to my attention, and it is something that must be dealt with. The Agent In Charge of this office, Maxwell Jenkins, will be relieved from his duties just as soon as this meeting is over."

There were gasps and murmurs among the agents and secretarial staff present, and Carol Ann lifted her hand, palm down, to quiet them. "There will be time for commentaries and discussion at a later date, but at this moment, I would prefer you were all quiet until I am finished." There was silence in the room. "I will be dismissing and disarming Jenkins personally, but I would appreciate your help with the other details involved. First, the secretarial staff should empty out all personal belongings from his office and pack it in boxes. Bates, you will be taking over as Interim Agent In Charge until either you are confirmed, or until another agent is appointed from Washington. You may move your things in immediately, if you wish. I have also authorized you at the highest levels, and your first duties will be to remove Jenkins from every list in the Department. He will have no security clearance to clean a toilet, from this moment on. Once I have read him the disciplinary order dismissing him, I will ask him to turn over all keys, computer security passwords, keypad codes, weapons, ammunition, etc. to you. By the day's end, which..." She glanced at her watch, "will give you about an hour and a half to make Jenkins disappear from absolutely everything having anything to do with Homeland Security."

Agent Bates was flabbergasted. "Yes, Ma'am," he stammered, and couldn't think of another word to say, so he shrugged his shoulders and muttered a simple, "thank you."

One of the secretaries spoke up. "Ma'am, the computer system has been acting up all day. We seem to be off-line."

Carol Ann smiled. "Not any more. Is that all?"

"Yes, Ma'am."

"Then I would say we are finished here. You may bring Jenkins to me, and Roberts..."

"Ma'am?" a young agent said.

"I'll need you to take the elevator that is stopped on this floor down to the lobby, and stay with it until the FBI arrives. Please have them come up and wait in my outer office for us to turn Jenkins over to them." She opened her briefcase, and extracted two documents, then looked up at two female agents.

"Diane and Nancy. Here," she said as she handed them the documents. "Make sure Marisa and Erin are given back whatever has been removed from their personal belongings, and then ask them to read these declarations and sign them before you bring them to my office, ok?" The women exchanged befuddled looks, and Carol Ann slammed her hand on the desk. "Have they been stripped?" She yelled, and the agents nodded their heads.

Every agent in the room cowered. The Director's temper was as legendary as her intolerance for anything even remotely resembling torture in any form. "Bring that son of a bitch to me. Right now!" she said to Bates in a calm but frighteningly serene tone of voice. "And ladies, please be sure that the detainees add a sentence in their own handwriting to that effect, before signing those documents."

She turned back to all the agents and secretarial staff and waved her arms toward them. "Go! Go! We all have work to do... oh, and folks?" They all turned. "I want a written report from everybody who works in this field office, from agents to drivers to secretaries to janitors, and I want it by the end of the day, before you go home. In the reports, you will outline not only what personal actions you took in participating in this infamy, and/or the extent of your constructive knowledge regarding this incident. Your future in the Department depends on this report, so I suggest that you be thorough and honest. Anything less and you will be joining Jenkins in a long sojourn in Club Fed." Her eyes slowly panned the room, meeting the eyes of every employee present. "And now," she said with an almost cheerful tone, "you may go about your business."

Bates hung behind a moment after the rest had left. "Agent Bailey, if I could just say that Jenkins obligates..."

Carol Ann cut him off. "I don't want to hear one more word about it, Agent Bates. We will review the reports together and I will interview every employee before making a decision," she said to the relief of Bates as he left her office, pulling the door behind him, "and then I will probably fire every single one of your asses," she said, finishing her sentence.

Sister Agnes cracked up.

Agent Jenkins was spitting mad when he walked into Carol Ann's office, but calmed himself slightly when he saw Sister Agnes, who had managed to control her fit of the giggles.

There's probably been another complaint lodged about Immigration, he thought, noticing the sweatshirt and jeans on the dark-haired woman sitting in the window seat. *They probably roughed up this woman's wetback kid*, he concluded.

"Carol Ann, how nice to see you!" he said effusively, and stepped forward with his hand out to shake hers.

"You just don't get it, do you Jenkins?" Carol Ann did not extend her hand. "Sit your sorry ass down, Jenkins."

Chapter Eighteen

"Gentlemen, I do believe we need to get matters into perspective," Ziggie said. He had understood enough of the words exchanged between Carlos and Pablo to realize that despite their calm demeanors, their emotions were getting the best of the conversation. He didn't need a full command of the Spanish language to understand that. "This has been a trying few days for all of us, but I can assure you both that it has been far more trying for Marisa than for either of you two."

The men both turned and stared at Ziggie.

"Now that I have your attention," he said with a grin, "I believe our host has just served us an exquisite taste of a very good Tequila, and I would like to offer a toast." The ambience reeked of testosterone as the feuding men regained their composure and lifted their shot glasses, not before sprinkling some salt on their hands between the index finger and thumb.

Ziggie noticed what they had done, and ceremoniously mimicked their actions. Lifting his shot glass again, he said, "To the magnificent women of Villa Vistamar! May they be an ever-present blessing in our lives! *¡Salud!*" he cheered in the one Spanish word he was sure he could pronounce properly.

The three men licked the salt, gulped the Tequila, then sucked the lime wedges Pablo had cut and placed on the tray in the middle of the coffee table.

Pablo was the first to dismount his raging stallion, by pouring another round of one of the finest Tequilas in his father's cache. Salting his hand again, he lifted his shot glass and waited for Carlos and Ziggie to do the same. "I would like to offer a toast to the man who has brought love, security and the deepest of friendship to a woman who might otherwise have been my mother." He noted Carlos' expression of bewilderment, and realized Marisa had probably not told her husband about his father, but it was too late now. He shrugged his shoulders, saying, "Now that I have met you, I can say with all honesty, that the best man won. To Carlos!"

He drank his second shot glass of Tequila, and immediately poured the next round as he avoided the bewildered gazes between Ziggie and Carlos.

As he started to pick up his shot glass, Ziggie reached out his hand and stopped him. "Now, wait one minute, my young friend. You cannot just drop a bomb that size and continue to guzzle Tequila. Would you care to explain that last toast?"

"Yes, by all means," Carlos agreed. "I can't wait to hear all about it," he said with a dry tone bordering on sarcasm.

Pablo thought about it a moment, then grabbed his shot glass and drank it in one gulp, not salting his palate before doing so. It burned, and he coughed, much to the amusement of the two older men.

"What the hell," he said, beginning to feel the effects of about six ounces of straight Tequila on an empty stomach. "But first, you two must have the next one on me, while I get us something to nibble on. Six ounces of 150 proof Tequila on an empty stomach is not a good idea."

He realized he was weaving a bit on the way to the kitchen, which was all the more reason to get something into all of their stomachs. He grabbed some crackers and dumped the box onto another tray, and then opened the cupboard. There was a good stash of caviar, so he grabbed one jar of red, and another of Beluga Black. Then he spotted a can of smoked oysters, so opened that into a small dish and placed it on the tray.

A quick trip to the refrigerator, and he had found a tub of whipped cream cheese, another block of Brie, and a good sharp Cheddar, all of which he put on the tray with some knives for spreading. That and a bottle of Chipotle pepper sauce and a jar of raspberry jam, and the meal was ready.

By the time he picked the tray up to take it to the living room again, he had eaten three or four of the crackers with a variety of cheeses, so he was weaving less now.

"Here we go, gentlemen," he said, placing the tray on the table.

He picked up another cracker; spread some cream cheese on it, then raspberry jam. He topped it off with a few drops of Chipotle pepper sauce, and popped it in his mouth.

"What!" he said looking at Carlos' disgusted expression. "Don't knock it until you have tried it, friend. Besides, it was your wife who introduced me to this particular delicacy. Try it!"

Carlos flashed a semi-smile, and fixed himself a cracker in the same manner. He ate it, but grimaced. "I think I'll stick to the caviar," he said. "But our discussion of hors d'ourves has not caused me to forget your promise. I'm still waiting to hear how my wife might have been your mother?" He laughed, and immediately realized that in some strange way, Pablo's recognizing Marisa as a possible mother figure had relieved his angst more than he was even willing to admit to himself. Now, it was slowly turning to anger.

Pablo served another round of Tequila, then sat back on the couch. Once both Ziggie and Carlos were gazing expectantly in his direction, he began his story.

"Well," he explained, "Marisa could tell the story better, of that I am certain, but I'm willing to give it a go," he said before gulping another shot of Tequila. "You see, my immediate attraction toward Marisa was simply a matter of genetics!" He grinned, but no one grinned back. "Don't you get it?" he grinned, but no one was getting it. He looked down at the empty shot glass, and stood up to serve them all some more Tequila, but suddenly felt the urge to remain seated.

He laughed. "Either you two are too drunk to get the joke, or I have forgotten the punch line," he said, and hiccupped. "Sorry!" He grinned again, and this time he definitely noticed a grin forming on Ziggie's lips.

But Carlos was serious; dead serious as a matter of fact, and that cracked him up. He laughed, but then he realized Carlos was getting angrier by the minute.

"Hey, chill, Bro! This is funny stuff. Well, maybe not all that funny, but hey... do you mean you honestly didn't know that Arturo Segovia was Marisa's first sweaty-handed little boyfriend? I mean, they went to her Senior Prom together!" He waited for a reaction, but there was none. "Hey, you don't believe me? Do you want to see their Prom portrait?"

Carlos was still deadly serious. "*Pablito*," he said the man's name in the Spanish diminutive form as if he were speaking to a child, "of course I know about Arturo. What does that have to do with anything?" He was offended by the young man's mention of his wife's past boyfriend. He couldn't understand why she would discuss her first love with this infant, and he was finding the entire conversation in bad taste.

"It has everything to do with everything!" Pablo exclaimed, and then framed his drunken head with his hands. "I am Pablo Segovia Santamaría, Arturo's son!" He broke up into guffaws. "Now, don't tell me that isn't funny stuff!" then he added, "And this very fine Tequila, if you want to get down to the nitty-gritty, has come to us with the compliments of my father. This is his home!"

Ziggie wasn't sure if Pablo was laughing hysterically out of humor or pain. "I had no idea," he said.

"Neither did Marisa, until the night you disappeared."

"But you did?" Ziggie was becoming very concerned about his young friend, and glanced over at Carlos, who was visibly uncomfortable with the revelation.

"I had figured it out earlier that day, when Papi make his monthly courtesy call from Paris," Pablo said, sobering quickly as he realized the effect his words had caused on both men.

He stood up, less wavering this time, and grabbed a cracker, spreading cream cheese on it before dropping a couple of oysters on top. Popping it in his mouth, he chewed slowly and deliberately, hoping for a word from Carlos.

There was none.

Pablo sat down again, and stared directly at Carlos. "You see, kind Sir, you have surmised my relationship with your beautiful wife entirely wrong. She is one of the more wonderful people I have ever met, and her interior beauty is only surpassed by her amazing loyalty to her family and friends." He could see Carlos' entire mood changing. "She honors you in her words and in her deeds, Carlos, and I can only pray that someday I find someone who is even half the woman that she is."

At that, he served another round of Tequila, but before drinking his, he turned to Ziggie, who was grinning widely, shaking his head.

"What?" he asked his friend and mentor.

"Either you are mending a broken heart after a closeted romance and what you just said is to convince yourself of your best intentions, or you have matured by leaps and bounds in the last week. I hardly know you. I like the new image, but it confuses me." He grinned again.

"I wouldn't be so quick to judge something as a closet romance, if I were you, Brother Zigfried." Pablo grinned right back at him. "No one is exactly blind to the looks that you and my Professor Erin seem to share more and more frequently."

He was immediately sorry for his words when he saw Ziggie's face twist into a pained expression that spoke volumes.

Ziggie picked up his shot glass and drank the Tequila down in a gulp, then he turned to Pablo. "Be careful where you step Pablo, because you are on the verge of falling into unchartered territory." He fixed himself a cracker with red caviar, and ate it slowly, never taking his eyes off Pablo. "And as of today, you may address me as Ziggie. I am no longer a member of the Society of Jesus and any exchange of words or feelings between Erin and me are absolutely none of your business. Don't overstep that boundary, Pablo. I beseech you to respect our privacy."

"What?" A voice was heard from the front hallway, and it was unmistakably Erin's. "Whose privacy would that be?" She walked into the living room with a Villa Vistamar Alumnae sweatshirt on, and a pair of black sweatpants. "Are we intruding on someone's privacy?"

Marisa was behind her, dressed the same, thanks to Sister Agnes' quick thinking before heading to the airport for Carlos, and then Carol Ann. "Yes, are we intruding?" she asked, grinning.

Carol Ann and Sister Agnes were behind them, bringing up the rear. "I hope not, because I need a good, stiff drink!" Carol Ann said, and Sister Agnes chimed in with, "and I could use, maybe, a nice glass of wine?"

Epilogue

Six months later…

Sister Barbara was at her desk, staring out the window toward the rose garden, when Sister Agnes entered the parlor. Her face had an ethereal glow to it, as if kissed by the hues of the winter's gentle sun. Although she was smiling, Sister Agnes could see that she had been weeping.

Agnes felt she must be intruding, and silently turned to leave Sister Superior to whatever private thoughts had brought her to this rare show of emotion. She glanced toward Ziggie, and he smiled, understanding perfectly.

"Sister Agnes… Brother Zigfried," Sister Barbara's soft voice followed her to the foyer, and Agnes turned back to see that Sister Barbara was standing next to her little desk, smiling at her. "Please come in. Sister Rose said you both wanted to see me?"

The afternoon sun shining through the window behind her seemed to frame her body in a golden glow reminiscent of a Renaissance painting of saints with their golden halos, and Agnes smiled. She started to speak, but was choked up with emotion.

"What is it, Agnes? Are you unwell?"

"No, Sister Superior, I'm wonderfully well." Sister Agnes said. "This is just one of those lovely days when I am reminded of why I entered the convent, and how blessed my life has been."

Sister Barbara understood the emotion, although she probably would have laughed dismissively if she had known what had inspired it.

"We've come to urge you to accompany us to the celebration of Pablo's doctorial reception this afternoon. It would mean so much to him, and to us all."

"I truly can't," Sister Barbara frowned. She waved her hand at the stacks of paperwork spread on her desk. "The next term begins in three weeks and I still have far too much to attend to here. There's next year's less than adequate budget to grapple with, applications to review, and correspondence to answer. It's quite impossible."

"Would it hurt that much for you to take one day off?" Brother Zigfried asked her. "Remember even the Father rested on the seventh day."

"He didn't have five lay teachers demanding salary and benefit increases, a century old building that needs to be tented and fumigated for termites, all on a budget that is already stretched paper thin." Sister Barbara shook her head. "If He had, I doubt that He would have rested at all."

"Excuse me, Sister. This just arrived." Sister Rose brought in a large Federal Express envelope.

"I wonder what it could be?" Sister Barbara frowned. "I wasn't expecting any deliveries. She glanced down at mailing label. "This is very strange indeed. It's from Paris." She opened it and emptied its contents onto her desk. Several items spilled out.

"Whatever it is, it looks very official." Agnes looked over at Ziggie, who shrugged his shoulders.

Sister Barbara lifted the thick document and began to read. "Why, it is a copy of the school endowment we received when Sister Thomas Marie came to us. I don't understand." She flipped through to the last pages. "How odd, something seems to have been added. But, I have no idea what it might be. It's in Russian."

"If you'd allow me, I could translate it for you, Sister." Ziggie offered.

"Please, if you would." She handed it to him.

Ziggie scanned the first paragraph and a huge smile appeared on his face. "It is very formally written and quite legal in tone. Would you like me to paraphrase it?"

"If it makes better sense, by all means."

"The original endowment agreement has been amended and expanded." Ziggie began, then paused. "Oh my…"

"Amended? Expanded?" The two Sisters were baffled.

"It says something about a receipt being enclosed. Is there by chance a blue envelope there?" Ziggie looked at the small pile in front of Sister Barbara.

Sister Agnes riffled through the pile. "Yes. Here it is." She held it up and handed it to her Superior. "Open it."

Sister Barbara opened it, read the amount on the check, and gasped. "This can't possibly be right. This says the amount of twenty million euros has been added to the Endowment Fund in loving memory of Sister Thomas Marie nee Grand Duchess Maria Nikolaevna Romanov!" She fell back in her chair in shock, pulled her Rosary from her pocket and crossed herself.

Agnes sat next to her. "Holy Sh… rine to Our Blessed Mother!" she exclaimed, and turned purple with embarrassment.

Sister Barbara dropped her Rosary and turned to Agnes. "My sentiments, exactly," she said, grinning. "I couldn't agree more!"

As he climbed the hill in the rented Mercedes, Arturo Segovia scowled at the speedometer, picked up his cell phone and dialed the agency. He impatiently waited as it rang.

Finally a male voice answered, but he didn't given the man a chance to pronounce the name of the agency. "When was the last time this infernal piece of crap was serviced?"

"To what piece of crap are you referring, Sir, and may I ask with whom I am delighted to be speaking?" Arturo could almost see him twisting his petulant little mouth into a snide sneer, and would have given anything for the pleasure of wiping it off his face.

"This is Mr. Segovia, and the piece of crap Mercedes you rented me is coughing on level land and can barely make it up the Muirlands road!" He shouted. "I expect someone to deliver one that works to my home within the hour!"

He hung up the phone and looked through the rear view mirror. Monique was following him in Pablo's graduation present, and he prayed beyond hope that she hadn't exaggerated when she'd said she knew how to drive a five-speed. The Lamborghini's motor wasn't broken in yet, and he was pretty sure he had heard a gear or two grinding as she had downshifted to begin the winding road up to the house.

He had let her drive it to Pablo's graduation party only because she had wanted to drive it so badly that he'd been afraid of having to sleep alone that night if he hadn't granted her that one little caprice. Actually, it had been many little caprices of late; alas, a small price for a fifty year old man to pay for the privilege of sleeping with a twenty five year old with a body any man —even one her age— would have killed for.

He pulled up beyond the driveway almost to the golf course, and motioned to Monique to go up the driveway. He'd wanted to park his son's new toy directly in front of the main entrance, but Pablo's truck was already there. Monique parked the Lamborghini directly behind the truck, and slid out of the driver's seat to the ground. He parked the Mercedes in a spot that the agency driver could reach easily, and got out of the car after throwing the keys onto the passenger seat.

Monique was waiting for him at the front entrance, so he climbed the steep driveway to meet her.

Just as he was pushing the key into the lock, the door swung open, and a tall, olive complexioned man about his age greeted him. "Come on in!" the man said. "Everybody is out on the terrace or in the hot tub."

Arturo shrugged his shoulders toward Monique, and stepped inside.

Carlos held out his hand. "I'm Carlos Mendoza, a friend of Pablo's."

Arturo shook his hand, and said, "Nice to meet you Carlos, I'm Pablo's father, Arturo."

He didn't introduce Monique, so Carlos held out his hand to her, and she took it in hers. "You must be Pablo's sister?" he asked, and immediately realized she was not Pablo's sister, by the enraged expression on Arturo's face. "No, of course you aren't," he said, hopelessly trying to fix the damage. "Pablo said he had no siblings. Anyway, it is very nice to meet you."

"Likewise, *Monsieur*," she said, smiling sensuously.

Carlos started to accompany them, but he stepped back realizing that it would be a superfluous act of servility in the man's own home.

Arturo made his way out onto the terrace, and helped himself to a glass of champagne from a nearby table, then turned to survey the scene.

"*Merci, Cherie,*" Monique relieved him of his glass and wandered towards the buffet table.

He shrugged and turned to replace his purloined champagne. A rich warm laugh cut through the air nearby causing him to briefly hesitate before claiming a new glass. *No. It is impossible. Your imagination is toying with you. It's only the house reminding you of old memories, nothing more.* His champagne secured, he turned back around just in time to see his son walk up to a petite brunette and sweep her off her feet whirling her around in a tight circle. The same rich warm laugh spilled from her throat as she wrapped her arms about Pablo's neck.

It is her! His stunned mind grappled to make sense of what he was seeing. "His" Marisa here at his home and in the arms of his son! Without conscious volition his body walked him over to them.

Pablo saw his father coming towards them, a blank look of amazement on his face. He set Marisa down leaving his arm curled around her back and kissed her on the cheek.

"Whatever was that for?" Marisa grinned up at him.

"Pay Back," Pablo whispered then turned allowing her to see Arturo's face as he came towards them.

"Is that?" She choked.

"In the flesh," Pablo turned on a big smile, his eyes dancing with glee.

He spotted Carlos near the patio door, grinning like the proverbial Cheshire Cat. Pablo discreetly winked at him, and Carlos nodded, laughing.

With his left arm still around Marisa, he reached out his right hand.

"Why Father, I had no idea you'd be here, but I can't even tell you how pleased I am!" he said.

Arturo took his son's hand in his, and couldn't find another word to say, managing only a half smile.

Pablo took full advantage of the moment. "And I believe you know my friend, Marisa?" Pablo said, never changing the expression on his face. He looked down lovingly at her and said, "Where are your manners, Marisa? Say hello to my father!"

Marisa looked up at Arturo, and realized that if she had run directly into him on the street, she wouldn't have recognized him. Not only was he almost completely bald and grossly overweight, but he had the swollen face and puffy eyes of a heavy drinker and smoker with poor eating habits who seldom exercised. "Nice to see you, Arturo. You never told me you had such a delightful son!" She grinned widely.

"Marisa?" he said, with an expression that Marisa found so comical she couldn't resist the temptation to laugh. She did, and was sorry as soon as she saw Arturo's brow furrow.

Monique wandered up, and gushed her greetings. "Ah, Arturo, so this is your handsome son," she said, and leaned over to kiss the air beside Pablo's cheek. "And you are Pablo's girlfriend, *oui*?" she said to Marisa, just as Carlos was approaching.

Marisa cracked up, and answered, mimicking Monique's accent. "No, *Cherie*, I am not Pablo's girlfriend," she said, giggling and accenting "friend" just as Monique had, "I am *this* handsome man's wife," she said, looping her free arm through Carlos' now that he was close enough. Then she turned back to Arturo. "Either this is the exact same woman I found you in bed with thirty years ago, or you married that one and this is your daughter?"

Arturo was numb and suddenly dumb. He couldn't think of a word to say.

Monique spoke for him. "No, *Cherie*. I am just his friend, not his daughter, and not his wife, at least not yet." She giggled.

She really doesn't get it! Marisa thought to herself. She discreetly winked at Pablo, and then looked at him with the most innocent of gazes she could muster. "Now, darling, since you and your father have similar tastes, this one is at least about the right age for you, and she is quite pretty... I mean, it might be the right thing to do, for the sake of my marriage. Don't you think?"

Carlos was thoroughly enjoying the entire scene, doing his best not to laugh out loud.

Pablo looked Monique over as she walked away furiously, as if he were observing a used car. After a long perusal, he said, "No thanks. I like them with brains." Then he grinned at his father.

The remark made Arturo lose whatever semblance of composure he had managed to maintain until then. "Now wait just one damned minute, young man. The doctoral diploma you just earned does not give you the right to.."

Carlos leaned forward and whispered, "Gotcha!"

Arturo had spent the previous five minutes with his fists clenched, and turned to face Carlos as if automated by a remote control.

He swung out and decked Carlos with a sucker punch right to the jaw; an obvious punch given his shorter height.

Obviously not ready for such violence, Carlos fell back, and landed directly into the hot tub behind them.

Marisa ran over to him and held out her hand to help him out. Carlos took her hand and pulled her into the tub, and kissed her. She was barely able to kiss him back. She was laughing too hard.

"My God, *Papá*, you'll never change." He smiled at his father. "Are you so naive that you can't see a setup?"

Arturo stepped back with a horrified expression on his face. "Oh, my God!" he huffed under his breath. "Did I just hit Marisa's husband?"

"Uh, yeah..."

"And you were all just..."

"Uh huh... setting you up. Geesh, *Papá*, can't you appreciate a good joke when you see one? This was good!"

Arturo suddenly felt very old, and very tired. He looped his arm in Pablo's. "How about a drink together in my, uh, your study, Son? I think we both need to get to know each other a little better. And besides, we need to talk about your future. I have a great job for you in the business, unless, of course, you still feel compelled and inspired by academia to earn but another useless degree."

Pablo acquiesced, and allowed himself to be led back to the house, although he would have much preferred joining the fun in the hot tub at that moment.

"Do you see what I see?" Sister Barbara asked as Erin pulled into one of the few blank spaces on the entire street and parked.

Erin had chosen to stay in the car while Ziggie and Agnes had gone into the convent to convince Sister Superior to go to Pablo's reception with them. She'd felt physically and emotionally exhausted, and her knees had felt like they simply wouldn't hold her up to walk the few steps from the parking circle to the parlor. It had been an exhausting six months of mentoring Pablo's doctoral thesis, but there had been no choice after Ziggie's renouncing his position at the Seminary and taking the one at UCSD where Carlos was teaching. She was, after all, the second mentor, and without her, he would have been in danger of having to start over. He had been too near and dear to them to abandon him. But today was her last: she had resigned five minutes after Pablo had been awarded his doctorate, with no idea whatsoever how she was going to earn a living.

Ziggie laughed from the back seat where he and Agnes were riding, their having insisted that Sister Superior occupy the front seat with Erin. "Oh, yes... who could miss it? That is one sweet vehicle, isn't it? I wonder whose it is?"

"No, not the car... the Federal Express truck!" Sister Barbara said, pointing to the truck parking almost in the middle of the street.

Sister Agnes giggled. "You don't suppose Prince Nikolai has sent a graduation present to Pablo, do you?" Her voice couldn't hide her excitement.

Ziggie shook his head. "I don't know, but it looks like a lot more than one envelope."

The four got out of the car and walked quickly to the front door. Erin's knees no longer hurt. Actually, they had felt much better from the moment Sister Barbara had offered her a teaching position at Villa Vistamar. In fact, with the increased endowment in Sister Thomas Marie's name, Sister had offered her the Theology Department, at a considerable raise in salary from what she had been earning at the Seminary, and of course, she had accepted gratefully.

They reached the door just as the Federal Express delivery man did. The door was slightly ajar, and Ziggie stepped forward to open it.

He turned to the messenger. "Are you looking for Pablo Santamaría? I'll find him for you, if you'd like." Erin and the Sisters had followed him in, and were waiting in the foyer. "Come on in," he added, and the messenger followed the rest into the house.

The messenger looked down at the envelopes. "There is one for a Pablo Segovia Santamaría, but there are packages for three other people, also, and I need signatures from each of them. Do you know a Marisa Mendoza, Erin Sabine and Zigfried Hoffman?"

"I knew it!" Sister Agnes was jumping up and down with delight, and Sister Barbara laughed. Sister Agnes' good humor was contagious.

"I am Zigfried Hoffman," Ziggie said with a trembling voice, and this is Erin Sabine," he said point at Erin. Then he turned to Agnes. "Sister, would you see if you can find Pablo and Marisa?"

Sister Agnes practically flew through the living room to the outside patio, yelling, "Marisa! Pablo! You have to come to the front door! Marisa! Pablo!"

Pablo heard Sister Agnes' shouting from his father's den, where Arturo was stating the facts of life as he had mapped them out for his son.

"So, Pablo, although I have already deeded this house to you as a graduation present, I would think it would be easier for you to run the business from our apartment in New York City, and if fact, you may even find the trip East rather pleasurable when you see what.."

"Excuse me, *Papá*, but I hear a good friend of mine calling me from the patio, and she sounds almost hysterical. I had better see what is wrong." He stood up grateful for the interruption, and started for the door. "I'll be right back, but New York? No thanks. I think I'll pass." Those were the most liberating words he had ever said. He had no idea what he was going to do with his life, but he definitely knew what he was not going to do with his life.

Just as he opened the door, he saw Sister Agnes pulling Marisa past him. Marisa was soaking wet, with a towel wrapped around her chest, as her wet blouse had become transparent. It had been plainly visible that she didn't use a bra.

"What's going on?" he asked.

Carlos was walking a few steps behind the women, and shrugged his shoulders. "Something about you and Marisa having to sign for some packages," he said.

Pablo shut the den door behind him and followed the group to the waiting messenger.

Both Erin and Ziggie were standing in the foyer with FedEx packages in their hands, Sister Barbara was next to them with the messenger's signature clipboard in her hand.

She handed it to Marisa, and said, "Here. Sign right here."

Marisa signed right between Ziggie's and Erin's signatures. There was another blank spot at before Ziggie's signature with Pablo's name beside it.

She handed the board to Pablo, and pointed at the blank. "You need to sign here."

As Pablo signed, Marisa leaned over and asked, "How is it going with *Papi*?"

Pablo grinned as he handed the board to the messenger, and hissed, "Swimmingly, thanks."

The messenger handed them their packages and excused himself. Sister Barbara started to open the door for him, but stopped and turned to Erin first. "As a lay teacher, you're not bound by the vow of poverty, Erin. Now be a nice lady and give this young man a good tip, will you?"

Erin laughed and quickly pulled a ten-dollar bill from her purse. Handing it to the messenger, she thanked him as Sister Barbara shooed him out.

The four looked at one another.

Sister Agnes jumped again. "I can't stand it! Open them!"

Ziggie turned to Pablo. "They're from an attorney in Paris. Sister Barbara just received a similar package at the convent, so I can safely say they are from Prince Nikolai. Open yours first, Pablo. You're the one who saved his life."

Pablo opened his package, and pulled out a large, square envelope. Opening it, he found a gold-embossed card with the Seal of the Imperial Family of Russia. Opening it, a smaller envelope fell out. He picked it up and then read the inside of the card aloud.

"You are cordially invited to the official interment of our Grand Duchess Maria Nikolaevna Romanov, daughter of and By the Grace of God, His Imperial Majesty, Nicholas II, Tsar, Emperor and All-Russian Autocrat and Her Imperial Majesty, Alexandra Fyodorovna, Tsarina of all the Russias. The interment will take place on the anniversary of her birth, June 14th in the Year of our Lord, Two Thousand and Six."

"It is the same invitation I received," Sister Barbara said. "We must travel together!"

"I wish!" Pablo said. "But I just turned down the only job offer I have had since they fired me from the restaurant!"

He opened the second, smaller envelope, and gasped. "On second thought, maybe we will be traveling together!"

In the envelope was a check for one hundred thousand dollars and another official looking card, describing a numbered bank account in Pablo's name at Volksbank AG, in Vaduz, Liechtenstein.

"Oh! MY! GOD!" The amount deposited read as Fifteen Million Euros. He handed the card to Ziggie. "How much is that?"

"I have no idea," Ziggie said, his opened envelope now on the floor and a banking card in his hand, "but I have the same invitation and a card from Volksbank in Vaduz, Liechtenstein," he said, "for the same amount, and another check for a hundred thousand. I am assuming I will be traveling with you?" He was obviously in a state of shock. "I also assume we are very wealthy?"

Erin and Marisa had ripped their envelopes open, and were staring blankly at the same amounts with their invitations.

Sister Barbara looked over at Erin. "I assume this means I have just hired and lost my Theology Director, all in one fine day?"

Erin started to speak, but Sister Superior laughed. "Hey, it's there if you want it, or if not, we can buy ourselves someone. Money is no object! The convent has an extra twenty million euros on hand!" she said nonchalantly. "But seriously, does anybody know how much fifteen million Euros is in dollars? Or twenty million?"

Arturo had heard the ruckus and was standing next to Carlos, to whom he had discreetly offered a heartfelt apology. "Yes, Sister. Fifteen million Euros would be approximately eighteen million dollars, give or take a couple hundred thousand, and twenty million would be around twenty four and a half million."

"Holy Mother of God!" Agnes said. "Now this deserves a flute of champagne if anything does!"

The End

About the Authors

Erica Fuentes

A successful attorney and author of several non-fiction books before bursting into the world of mainstream fiction, **Erica Fuentes** has delighted her readers with tales of intrigue, romance and international politics beginning in 2000 with her release of *Island Dreams*, followed by *Miguel's Cantina (First Love)*, *A Window To Paradise*, and *Hearts Ahoy* in 2002.

Fuentes' novel *Shakedown (Las Chicas de Palacio)*, released in June 2007, and currently being adapted into a screenplay, holds fast on the best seller list in Mexico. **Casablanca** just released its Second Edition.

All of Erica's novels have been published simultaneously in two versions: English and Spanish.

Erica's *The Hunt Club*, on which **Salve Regina, the Series** was inspired, will be published by **Casablanca** after the series' third book.

After many years abroad carrying out diplomatic and corporate assignments, Fuentes currently lives in her beach home somewhere…

Annemarie Stonewater

A Master of History, **Annemarie Stonewater** triumphed in the world of mainstream fiction in the United States and Great Britain with her series of successful historical novels: *Kindred Spirits*, *Montana Brides* and *Land of Gold* written under the pseudonyms of DeAnn Patrick and Mary Ann Hammond. After many active years spent in the world of Academia and Historical Research, Annemarie has returned to her first passion of writing, the results being a new collaboration with Erica Fuentes in a series of Ecclesiastical Intrigues.

Annemarie currently lives between her homes in Upstate New York and Mexico.

www.ingramcontent.com/pod-product-compliance
Lightning Source LLC
Chambersburg PA
CBHW031547240626
47153CB00002B/410